# My Fake Fiancé

# My Fake Fiancé

MAIRI LOUISE

First paperback edition May 2024

Book design by Mairi Louise

ISBN 979-8-9905370-2-6 (Hardcover)
ISBN 979-8-9905370-0-2 (Paperback)
ISBN 979-8-9905370-1-9 (eBook)

Published by Lakebound Love Publishing

*This debut is dedicated to my amazing family.*

*I love you all! Everyone has been such a great help and support with this project which is very near and dear to my heart.*

*Going into specifics, I have to say thank you to my parents; both for their support and my mom for having the same addiction to reading and willingness to edit this beast with me. And shout out to my nonreader sister who tried to read a heavily unedited version of this book.*

*I hope y'all enjoy the finished product!*

# My Fake Fiancé

# **Chapter 1**
## *Juliana*

"Hey! You get off soon, right?" My gorgeous best friend, Tatyana, struts into the store like she owns the whole world and greets me with a quick hug. then steps back to let me continue working.

"Hey, T! What brings you by?" I chuckle, shaking my head at her as I get back to work, ensuring all the dresses are hung correctly, in order of size, and with their price tags facing outward. "But yes, I'm just straightening up here, I'm off in a few minutes."

I shift to another rack and she follows alongside me, touching each dress along the way. I smack her hand away from the next dress, laughing. "Quit touching things. What's up?"

"Mike and I are going to this new club and want you to come with us." I hesitate and Tatyana keeps talking before I can say no. "You haven't been out since, like, the first night you moved in. And honestly, it is time to take a break from working so hard and have a little fun. You need to go out and get over that lousy ex of yours. It's been, what? At least five months. And it's been a month since you've moved in so who knows how long you were moping around at your parents' house."

"Fine, fine," I interrupt, mostly to get her to stop talking. "Okay, I will go out with you guys tonight. But nothing too crazy right?"

"I heard this new club is amazing and that can be our one and only stop for the evening. Just one simple outing. Just to check it out." Tatyana leans against a rack of clothes while I rehang and fix items.

"Okay, just the one club."

I quickly finish cleaning my section of the store, grab my things, and say goodbye to my manager. I run out the door with Tatyana by my side.

"We'll meet you guys there," Tatyana says to her boyfriend, Mike, and another one of their friends as we catch up with them near the exit of the mall. They both say a quick "hi" and "bye" to me and then leave the mall, as I give T a quizzical look.

"Why aren't we going with them?" I ask.

"Because Juli, you haven't been out in a long time and I think it's time for some new clothes." I laugh as she grabs my arm and pulls me back into the depths of the mall.

We hit every store we can think of, tossing aside most items because they are too expensive. And by 'tossing aside', I do mean that we respectfully rehung and folded each item. Tatyana was not too thrilled at how neat I wanted to leave everything, mostly because it took extra time but as a retail worker, I know how frustrating it is to come into the changing room or even out on the floor and see a huge mess.

Eventually, we find the right store and after a couple of failed outfits, I come out of the dressing room in a vintage, floral t-shirt, faded black jeans, and red velvet ankle booties. I stand in front of the long communal mirror, looking at myself in the outfit. Tatyana steps out of her dressing room. I see her in the mirror behind me and she is wearing the most ridiculous muumuu.

"What the heck are you wearing?" I turn to look at the outfit and Tatyana cackles. She lifts her arms to spread the outfit and shows me the whole crazy design on the fabric.

"What? You don't like it?" She gives me a spin then doubles over, laughing. "It was already in the stall when I went in. Someone must have decided they did not want this beautiful masterpiece."

"Yeah, I don't know why they wouldn't want that thing." I laugh with her then she turns serious and focuses on the outfit I am wearing.

"Perfect!" Tatyana announces and makes me spin for her. I oblige and laugh then pause to let her check the price tags. "Oh! And it's cheap! You're getting that!"

I quickly change back into my work clothes and bring my items to the checkout counter. Tatyana waits semi-patiently beside me while I check out then she tugs my arm, yanking me out the door and back to our apartment to get ready for the night.

"I'm going to take a shower!" I call out to Tatyana and make my way back to my room. Tatyana goes into the kitchen and makes a shot for herself. "Don't do too much pregaming!" I add as I hear her glass hit the counter again.

"Shhhh! Hurry up and shower, I think I need to rinse off too before we go." Tatyana calls from her perch on the counter and I look down the hallway at her.

"Yes, please," I tease then run into the bathroom before she can say anything or throw something at me. I can hear her laughing before I turn on the shower and fan. I try to shower quickly and when I get out I towel off my hair and add a bit of product.

"Hurry up!" Tatyana knocks on the door. I fling the door open making her stumble a bit.

"I'm done," I smile then scoot past her. "All yours."

"Thank you." Tatyana waves me off and shuts the door behind her.

# Chapter 2
## *Juliana*

Back in my room, I flop on my bed, already feeling tired and regretting that I agreed to go out. I lie on my bed coming up with different ways I can try to convince Tatyana to let me stay home, or that it's best if I stay home. When I hear the shower turn off, I immediately hop up and start getting dressed. She's been wanting me to go out for such a long time and since I actually agreed and we've gotten this far, she'd probably kill me if I backed out now.

"Hey, outfit check." Tatyana barges into my room, dressed in her robe with a towel wrapped around her hair, piled on her head. "Hmm, I thought you'd be further along in the dressing stage."

"Yeah…" I trail off, looking down at my half-dressed body.

"Oh no, please don't tell me you're backing out. Come on. It'll be fun! At any point in the night, if you want to leave, we can. Let's just try!" Tatyana whines at me, wiggling my door in her hand. Her dramatics convince me and I roll my eyes, going to pull out outfit options.

"You are such a drama queen. But fine, no I'm not backing out. Let's go out." I sigh as Tatyana squeals happily.

"Although, I don't appreciate the 'drama queen' comment. Okay!" She claps excitedly and then comes into my room, looking at the options I set out on my bed. "I don't hate all of these choices."

"Gee, thanks. We literally just got this outfit today, for tonight." I look down at the options laying on my bed next to her and put my hands on my hips. I point out the new outfit, trying to convince her. "And I like this one. It's a cute, simple, comfortable outfit for my first time going out in a long time. And the heels are stunning."

"Hm, true but I think we can live a little more dangerously than this. And yes I do realize we went shopping today and I like the outfit you bought but I've changed my mind. I have another idea. A better idea." Tatyana flings the new jeans off of the bed. I make a face but she pushes forward. She goes into my closet and when she comes out, she is holding a black leather mini-skirt that I am shocked I still have. "See, this is better. You can wear the new outfit some other night."

"Ugh, are you sure? I think I'd be more comfortable in the jeans." I start to reach for my new jeans but she smacks the skirt into my outstretched hands. "Right. Alright, fine."

I change into the skirt, making a face when it feels too tight. Tatyana nods approving it though so I press forward. She hands me the newly purchased top then hesitates and takes it back.

"Hmm, I think I'll wear this tonight." Tatyana holds onto it then grabs the other shirt off my bed and hands it to me. "This one will look better anyway."

"Did you make me buy that shirt just so you could wear it?" I roll my eyes as she yanks the tag off the new shirt.

"No, definitely not but I do love it and I will be borrowing it from time to time. And that includes tonight." Tatyana waves the shirt at me.

I look down at the shirt that she handed me. The shirt is an old, worn Metallica shirt. It looks familiar but I can't quite remember where it's from. I don't think it was originally mine. Tatyana notices me staring at the shirt.

"I think you stole that from my brother when we were younger." She lifts the material and looks at the tag before nodding. "Yup, see? Has his name on the tag. Very faded but you can still see."

"Okay," I nod. "Good." For a second there I was worried it was my ex's shirt. I like the shirt but it probably would have been a bad idea to wear it if it had belonged to my ex.

"Okay, I'm going to finish getting ready. Don't let me take more than an hour." Tatyana instructs me before darting out of my room.

I stay in my room to finish getting dressed then I go back to the bathroom to hang up my towels. To make sure everything is set for the night, I take both of our phones and plug them in. I set them on the table by the door so we won't forget them. I run back to my room and dig around my closet for some cute heels. I find a pair that would look cute with the shirt Tatyana took so I bring the shoes to her room and toss them on her bed.

"Ooo, perfect, thank you!" Tatyana says, darting her eyes, looking at the shoes before going back to focusing on her makeup.

"No problem! We're leaving in fifteen minutes!" I shout as I leave her room and go to sit down on the couch to wait for her.

"Perfect! Mike is expecting us in like half an hour so that should give us time to walk there. He's meeting us there with his friend and his girlfriend. I think her name is Savannah." Tatyana's voice carries down the hallway to where I'm sitting.

"Sounds good." I grab an apple out of the bowl on the coffee table and munch on it while I wait.

Tatyana appears eleven minutes later. She struts into the room and does a spin for me, showing off her outfit. She stops in front of me and gestures to her outfit.

"Amazing," I applaud her outfit then stand up and make my way to the kitchen. I toss the apple core in the trash and then retrieve our phones from the door.

"You know they'll have some food there right?" Tatyana comments as I hand Tatyana her phone and we both get our purses packed.

"Maybe but I am not feeling greasy bar food or nuts. No, thank you." We head out the door right at the fifteen-minute mark. The night air is warm but there is enough of a breeze that the half-mile walk to the club will be pleasant.

"No, seriously. I heard they hired this famous chef from a fancy restaurant in Chicago. Why he decided to come live here and take a job as a cook at a nightclub, I have no idea." She pauses her explanation as we continue walking to the club. "Okay, the story doesn't entirely make sense so it's quite possible that it isn't true. But still, the point is that they actually serve good, real food. Not just typical bar food."

"Right, sure." I make a face at her. "I want to see this 'real food' menu as soon as we get there."

"Alright, don't worry about it. I got you, girl." Tatyana links her arm through mine and she points out the club sign on the corner of the next street. The sign and entrance to the club look like an old-time movie theater. The places where the movie titles and times would go instead show different Happy Hour drinks and prices. "There it is!" Tatyana squeals as she picks up her pace.

"Ah, I forgot about this theater. Kind of sad it's gone." Tatyana tugs me along beside her, down the sidewalk, as I reminisce.

"Oh, yeah? Did you ever see a movie there? Mhm," She says when I don't respond right away. "That's what I thought."

"Okay, maybe I hadn't seen one here recently, obviously, since I didn't even know it was sold off and turned into a club but I used to go there when I was younger. Once a month maybe. More during the summer. Especially if it was raining." I continue talking, trying to get out all of my nervous energy before we enter the club.

"Okay, girl. Calm down. Hopefully, you'll enjoy it as a club as much as you enjoyed it as a movie theater." Tatyana pats my arm and smiles sympathetically at me. "Let's have some fun!"

# Chapter 3
## *Juliana*

We get to the front of the club right as Mike and his friends walk up as well. It turns out the friend's girlfriend's name is Susannah, and she is very sweet. We all say 'Hi' as we fall in line to enter the club. We don't have to wait too long since it is still early. Soon we are walking through the doors. The loud music immediately overwhelms my ears and I wince. It's going to take some time to get used to this noise level again.

This new club isn't too wild, but it is packed already and everyone looks like they're having a great time. I scan the room and watch everyone dancing and enjoying the food. After a couple of songs, I go to a table off to the side of the club and pick up one of the menus. A waitress comes over to my table to take my order. I'm surprised they have waitresses at a nightclub but I guess it's supposed to be a fancier one. Which is still strange for this part of town.

I order a Margherita pizza and it doesn't take too long to arrive. It looks delicious and I am about to enjoy it when

Tatyana and Mike slide up next to me. Tatyana slowly reaches for a piece and I narrow my eyes at her.

"That looks delicious," she says as her hand lands on a slice. I think about smacking it away but I let her take a piece.

"Mike, would you like a piece as well?" I turn to him and offer the pizza then look back at Tatyana and make another face in her direction. She smiles at me and happily munches on her piece.

"It does look good but I'm not a huge tomato guy. Thank you though." Mike wraps his arm around Tatyana's waist and we talk for a few minutes while we devour the pizza. Which doesn't take long. It was a decent size but the two of us were pretty hungry, I guess.

Once we finish eating, we hit the dance floor. I am starting to relax and enjoy myself when the DJ gives way to the live band and a familiar song starts playing. I turn to face the stage and my stomach turns upside down. It's him. It's my ex, Callum, and his band. I stop dancing and stand still, staring at the stage. Tatyana notices my distress and hooks her arm around mine, leaning in close so I can hear her.

"I didn't know they'd be playing here," she apologizes, scanning my face to see if I'm okay. I nod my head. I know she wouldn't have brought me here if she had known. "We can leave…" I hear her say. I wave her off and just try to enjoy the music. I've always thought they were pretty good. A few of their songs are still familiar to me and it seems like some people in the crowd know them too. Tatyana smiles and gestures for her boyfriend and friends to join us on the dance floor, to distract me as I try to relax.

A couple of songs go by and I'm having fun dancing with my friends. The band eventually takes a break and I decide to make my way over to the bar and ask for a Dr. Pepper. I pull myself up on the stool, facing away from the bar, and survey the room. Tatyana hops onto the seat next to me and leans into me again.

"Oh, hey, isn't that your church friend over there? Kurt, right?" She points through the crowd to a group of guys a few years older than us, standing around and talking. I smile and nod.

"That is him. I haven't seen him in a while. I wonder what he's been up to recently. He's a lawyer, you know." I know I'm rambling but I'm nervous again. Nerves from the whole evening return and new ones appear at the thought of Kurt being here as well. I haven't seen him since last Christmas when I went to visit my grandparents and of course, we went to church. After church, most of the families stayed around to sing Christmas carols. I smile at the memory.

"Oh is he? I did not know that." Tatyana gives me a look. She knows I overshare when nervous. "He's very cute. You should go say hi." She nudges me in the ribs a little too hard but I just laugh.

"Maybe in a bit. He looks busy," I say. I'm not a very social person and seeing him with all of his friends, I don't really feel comfortable going up to him and saying hi.

"Okay," Tatyana shrugs and orders another drink for herself and one for Mike. "I'm going to find Mike. You okay here on your own?" I nod and wave her off. She grabs the drinks and then wanders off to find Mike.

I'm sipping my drink when I feel a warm body slide onto the vacated stool next to me. I don't feel like talking to anyone so I stay facing away from the bar watching the crowd, hoping whoever it is will catch my hint and leave me alone.

"Hey, sexy," I hear a deep, scratchy, familiar voice. I sit up a little straighter but don't turn to face him. I haven't heard his voice in the 5 months since our breakup.

"Hello, Callum," I say and try to keep my voice from wavering. So far, so good. I take a sip of my Dr. Pepper to try and appear calm. I can feel him smirking and I don't try to pull away when a large hand rests on my thigh and turns me to face him. I've learned that any type of reaction just encourages him.

"Can't get enough of me, can you?" His thumb is rubbing my legs and right now, I wish I hadn't taken Tatyana's advice. I wish I had stuck with wearing jeans. I can feel his hot sticky hand on my bare leg and his hand is slowly making its way up my thigh. Why is his hand so sticky? This is gross all around. I put my hand on top of his to stop its progress and get a quick scowl before the smirk returns and he regains his composure.

"No. I didn't know your band would be playing here tonight." I explain while I try to remain civil and polite. "Congratulations on the gig. Very cool that a new club hired you guys."

"Yeah, well, you've heard us. We're the best in town. Soon we'll be famous. Right up there alongside Rolling Stones, Guns N' Roses, those awesome bands." Callum has never been one to be humble. I roll my eyes and take a sip from my soda, hoping the conversation will end and he'll walk away. "So, wanna get out of here?"

"What? No!" I am appalled at his question.

"Oh come on, Juli. You miss me, we both know that. Let's go back to my place." Callum's hand continues its movement up my leg and his other hand goes to the small of my back. He places his hand firmly, putting pressure on my back to try to make me get up to follow him. "You can show me just how much you missed me, love."

"No," I say firmly then knock his hand off my leg and push his arm away to get his hand off my back. His hand returns to my leg, firmly pressing into my thigh. It's almost painful.

"And why not? Why are you rejecting me, gorgeous?" Again his hand continues its pathway up my leg and I start to panic. Callum was always pushy but this is going too far.

Before I can stop myself, words come tumbling out of my mouth. "Actually, I am here with my fiancé."

His scowl immediately returns and he jerks his hand off my leg. "Oh, yeah? And who is this "fiancé" of yours?"

I can tell he doesn't believe me, hell, I don't believe me. But again, before I can think, I'm escalating the situation, my arm is raising and I am pointing across the room, directly at Kurt.

# Chapter 4
## *Juliana*

What in the hell did I just say? I yank my hand out of the air and bring it back to my side as fast as I can then twist my fingers nervously. I grab my drink, squeezing it tightly. A splash of Dr. Pepper falls over the edge and onto my hand and I realize that my hand is shaking so badly that I've spilled. I grab a little napkin and clean up the mess trying to keep myself busy and distracted.

All I can think right now is…I hope he didn't hear me. But I know he has because his expression goes from scowling to downright vicious. I shift in my seat a little bit and see his murderous glare shift from me to focus on Kurt across the room.

Callum stands up, his 6' 2" frame towering over my shorter, 5' 6", as I slide off of my stool quickly and step in front of him.

"What are you doing?!" I shriek over the loud music. He takes a step forward and practically growls. "Stop, please don't do this. Please," I practically beg him. I put my hands on his arms trying to hold him in his place.

"Juliana, move," Callum growls through his words at me, his deep voice sounds threatening but I brace myself.

I made a big mistake opening my mouth. Maybe there is some way I can get him to walk away. His arms flex under my hands and I know he's getting ready to shove past me. It will be easy for him too. I tightened my grip just to try to brace myself.

"Callum, come on. Stop, seriously. Let's go outside and talk about this." I offer, trying to bribe him into calming down. I don't want to cause a scene and I hope he wants to take me back to his place enough that he'll agree to go outside with me. Callum hesitates a bit, debating. I can see him thinking about how the night could end in taking me back to his place or end in a fight. He only ponders for a few seconds before the anger wins out and I know he's decided against taking me up on the offer.

"Get out of my way." His glare has yet to leave Kurt and in that moment, I realize I won't be able to stop Callum from confronting Kurt. So, I know what I have to do. I have to warn Kurt. I have to get to him before Callum does and I have to explain what I did and what is about to happen.

I quickly turn and duck between moving bodies to make my way through the crowd. I appear in front of Kurt knowing I only have seconds before Callum is right behind me.

Kurt seems to be a little confused at first and I blush embarrassed at this sudden reunion. I know I need to warn him but I can't get myself to speak, I'm terrible at confrontation. After a second, it seems to click where he knows me from. His face lights up with recognition.

"Juliana!" He says brightly and gestures around the room. "What are you doing here?"

Before I can answer, I hear people grunting and complaining and a "Hey, watch it man", and a few curses and rude comments and I know Callum is right behind me.

"I'm so sorry..." I realize my time is limited but I am only able to say those three words before Callum shoves his palm against Kurt's chest, catching him off guard and making him stumble a bit. When he regains his balance, he gives Callum an annoyed look.

"Watch where you're going, man," Kurt says, thinking it was an accident.

"Don't try to take my woman," Callum responds, shoving him again. This time, Kurt is braced and barely moves. Kurt looks at me confused and I am too embarrassed to look at him.

"Callum. stop," I beg and try to step between them but Callum shoves me aside causing me to fall to the ground.

Before I can get up, I hear a loud crack and see Callum on the floor next to me, gripping his jaw. Then a large hand reaches down for me and I grab onto it. Kurt picks me up looking concerned and I can't speak.

"Are you okay?" He asks, searching my eyes. All I can do is nod.

Kurt lets go of my hand and I instantly miss its warmth, comforting me. He runs his hand over his hair and looks over at Callum who is surrounded by his bandmates. One handing him a cold drink to hold to his jaw. Tatyana has spotted me at this point and quickly runs over.

"Are you okay? What happened? I am so sorry I brought you here!" She says talking quickly and I smile a little.

"I'm okay," I reassure her. "I have so much to tell you, but I'll have to explain everything later."

"You're bleeding!" She exclaims and grabs one of my hands. I look at it and see a little cut that I hadn't noticed before. I guess I must have cut myself on something when I fell.

"It's just a little cut. I'm okay." I pull my hand back from her and grab a napkin to press into my palm. I hiss through my teeth at the stinging. Tatyana digs through her purse to see if she has a band-aid but comes up empty-handed, a guilty expression on her face. She looks like she is about to apologize again but she doesn't get the chance to.

"I live about a block away from here and I have some first aid items. You should clean your hand off." I look up surprised to see Kurt inspecting my injured hand as I hold it with my other hand, keeping the cut face up so nothing touches it. The blood is seeping through the napkin so Kurt decides for me. "Yeah, we should get you cleaned up." Before I can protest, he turns to his friends and tells them he is leaving. I look at Tatyana and she just grins at me and I have to roll my eyes at her.

"Text me if you need me," she whispers in my ear as she hugs me to say goodbye. I tell her I'll text her when I am headed back to our apartment and she winks at me. I quickly turn away before she can make any suggestive comments.

Kurt waits to see if I'm ready then leads me out the door with his hand on the small of my back and I feel giddy. His hand isn't being forceful like Callum's was earlier tonight. This is more gentle and secure. No, you don't have feelings for him. Stop it. I tell myself, scolding myself slightly.

We are quiet most of the walk back to his apartment but it's a short walk so the silence doesn't feel awkward. When we reach the building, he says, "Are you okay? What happened back there? If you don't mind me asking."

I shake my head telling him no, I don't mind. "Callum is my ex-boyfriend," I state plainly and pause wondering if I should continue. I don't know him very well but I feel like I can tell him anything. I shouldn't though, it would scare him to know what I told Callum. Although, then again, I should definitely tell him. Especially since I involved him. Because of my lie and the fact that he had to step in physically too.

Kurt nods but stays quiet as we enter the building, waiting to see if I'll say more. In my small bag, I hear my phone buzzing and buzzing but I refuse to look at it. Kurt says hello to a man in the lobby of his building before directing me to the elevator and we stand in silence as it ascends.

Once we get off the elevator, I open my mouth to speak, "Thank you so much for doing this. I don't mean to cause any trouble. It isn't that bad of a cut." He smiles at my babbling and shakes his head.

"It's not a problem," he says as he opens the door to his apartment. "The bathroom is right over there," he points to the first door on the right down a short hallway, "you can wash your hands off in there. The first aid kit is in the kitchen, I'll go grab it while you're cleaning your hand." He waits to see if I am okay then he goes to the kitchen.

"Thank you," I say and turn in the opposite direction to find the bathroom. I know I've already thanked him but I find myself thanking him again before going to the bathroom and shutting myself in.

# Chapter 5
## *Juliana*

I lean against the sink and clean off my hand carefully. I let out a huge breath that I didn't realize I was holding. I try to count each breath but it only makes me start to hyperventilate so I close my eyes and try to just breathe normally. My breath returns to normal after a few seconds. I can hear my heart beating loudly in the silent bathroom.

"Calm down. There is no need to panic." I reassure myself, whispering so Kurt can't hear me if he's standing near the door. I stare at the crazy person in the mirror who is telling me there is a reason to panic.

I grab my phone and see that I have 6 missed calls, and two voicemails from my mother along with multiple texts from her and my dad as well. Two missed calls from Tatyana and three texts from her. I also have a lot of missed calls and unanswered texts from Callum. I have no intention of reading or responding to Callum's messages but all the other missed calls and texts have me confused and worried. I listen to my mother's voicemails first.  Once I hear her first message, I can't bear to hear anymore.

*Juliana, you better pick up your phone right this instant.* She says, clearly frustrated. *Callum just called me and told me the news. Why didn't you mention this to me before? I didn't realize you and Kurt were even dating. Call me right away.*

Shocked, I drop my phone and I can feel my stomach beginning to turn. I throw myself down to the floor and grab the toilet hurling violently into it. After a few moments, the nausea passes, and I rest my head on the cabinets next to the toilet.

I stay that way, trying to calm down. The tile of the bathroom feels cool under my legs and butt. I yank my skirt down trying to cover myself more. I hear a knocking on the door and groan, remembering where I am.

"Juliana? Are you okay? Do you need any water?" I hear Kurt's voice, sounding worried through the door. And I try my best to regain my composure. I stand up, grab my phone off the floor, and read a text from Tatyana.

**Tatyana: Are you okay? Your mom just called me. She said you're engaged????**

Shit. How many people have my lie spread to? I send Tatyana a quick text saying.

**Juliana: WTF is happening rn?**

I want to wait for a response but I know Kurt is waiting outside the bathroom for me. I check my phone one last time before slipping it into my pocket, flushing the toilet, and washing my hands. I look at myself in the mirror and I am a bit freaked out to see how disheveled I look. I splash water on my face and run my fingers through my hair. My fingers don't help tame my hair so I end up tying it up. I brace myself for the conversation I know has to happen then I open the door to a confused face and apologize profusely.

"I am so sorry for everything that has happened tonight." I need to tell him what happened before he hears it from somewhere else. I need to get on top of this situation. It really shouldn't have escalated the way it did but now I have to deal with the consequences.

Kurt leads me over to the table in his kitchen. I sit down and he pulls a chair for himself in front of me. Before he sits down, he turns on the light right above us so he can see my hand better. He has the first aid kit set out on the table. When he holds his hand out, I  place my hand in his, with my palm up. He lightly dabs up any remaining blood to start with.

"Yeah, about that. What exactly happened?" He asks and continues his work with my hand. Once he gets a large bandaid on my hand, he sits back and looks at me, waiting for my answer. I swallow nervously then before I clam up for good I let everything pour out of my mouth, fast.

"Callum is my ex-boyfriend. He was never great toward me and before long he started getting physical with me, pushing me around and asking for things that I wasn't comfortable with and wasn't ready for and I couldn't... He eventually broke it off and it didn't end well. I hadn't seen him in a couple of months until tonight and he started hitting on me, getting too touchy/feely... I couldn't take it and I thought that if I told him I was seeing someone else, he would leave me alone."

Halfway through my spiel, Kurt gets up and goes to his fridge. He grabs himself a beer and then pours a glass of water for me. When he returns to the table, he slides the glass of water to me and I take a sip before continuing.

"But that didn't happen…and now I've just made everything worse…" I trail off and look up at him, standing above me, and see him slowly taking everything in. He nods, understanding then his head tilts in confusion.

"So, he thinks that you're seeing me now?" He asks, trying to piece everything together. "That would explain why he told me not to 'take his woman'," Kurt chuckles a bit and I hope he can keep that same attitude for what I am about to say next.

"Well kind of," I say then stare at the ground, unable to make eye contact. "I told him you were my fiancé."

# Chapter 6
## *Kurt*

"I told him you were my fiancé."

Fiancé. Fiancé? Juliana's voice echoes in my head. What the hell is going on? I take a step back and drag my hand over my head, thinking.

"Why…Why would you do that?" I ask her, trying to remain calm. I look around my apartment, avoiding looking at Juliana. If I look at her I know I won't be as freaked out because she'll be looking at me with those sad, scared eyes and I will feel sorry for her. I deserve to feel freaked out, so I let my eyes wander around the room.

Suddenly, I remember Ashley, my ex-girlfriend, was planning to come over tonight. She may show up at any time. She can't show up in the middle of this, things are already rocky between us as we have been trying to make things work between us. What is Ashley going to say when she finds out? *If*, I correct myself, If she finds out. Of course, she's going to find out. She's probably on her way over here right now.

When I finally force myself to look at her, Juliana is looking up at me, her eyes filled with guilt and worry. Why is she worried? I realize that I haven't spoken in a while, but Juliana hasn't spoken either. She needs to say something. What is going on?

"I am so sorry. He wouldn't leave me alone..." She repeats herself, seeming flustered. I wave my hand gesturing for her to move past that and continue explaining, I know it might seem rude but I need an explanation. "I have no idea why I brought you into it. I am so sorry. I just saw you across the room and it was the first thing that popped into my head... I wasn't thinking... I am so sorry..." She keeps saying sorry and it's starting to hurt my head.

I grip my forehead in one hand and stand up, feeling the need to get up and move around. My head hurts and my legs feel restless. I start to pace the length of the kitchen, trying to work through what she's telling me. I pause in front of her, looking down at her then I begin to pace again. I learned this pacing technique from my mentor in law school. He taught me how to use my pace to run through my thoughts. Each time I turned to pace in the other direction, I had to begin a new argument or new defense. Different strides helped me work through different scenarios. I still use the technique while I prepare for court, although I tend to stay away from pacing in the actual courtroom.

"We haven't seen each other in a while. Why did you say my name? Why did you point to me in the crowd?" I question everything she's said while I continue to pace. My speed picks up but right now this pacing technique is not helping.

I feel a bubble of laughter forming in my stomach. I want to laugh at this whole situation because it is ridiculous but the look on Juliana's face tells me that laughing would not be an appropriate reaction right now.

"Kurt," Juliana says softly. "I'm sorry. My friend saw you earlier in the night and pointed you out because she knew that I knew you. I was going to come say hello but then everything happened so quickly. I said I was engaged and Callum asked who and I just saw you and I don't know, it all happened so fast." Juliana is beginning to repeat herself.

Juliana's worry and fear seem to make her even smaller than her 5' 6" height, especially since she is hunched over at my kitchen table. I feel like a monster standing over her at 6' 3". I try to relax a little and let out a deep breath. I force myself to sit back down. I keep my hands in my lap and try to choose my words carefully.

"Juliana," I start, calmly, "it's okay. I understand." She looks up at me surprised, her eyes widening.

"Wh..what? You do?" Her big blue eyes look up at me and they help me relax a little more. I nod and clear my throat.

"Yes, I understand. It was an impulsive decision but you did what you thought would be best." She didn't mean to cause any harm, she just needed a way to escape. I can understand that. "So, yes, for the most part, I understand why you did it."

"Oh, thank you so much!" She throws her arms around me making my chair move backward a bit. She releases me and blushes. "Sorry... I was so worried you would think I was crazy or something..."

This makes me laugh. "I never said I didn't think you were crazy." She lets out a little embarrassed gasp and I chuckle again. My chuckle makes her smile, a small smile but still a smile.

No, her thinking was, for the most part, logical. Juliana assumed her ex would leave her alone if he found out she was with someone new. That might have worked but in her case, it seems that it only angered her ex. Which resulted in him coming after me and threatening me. So no, I don't think she is crazy for saying it. She might be crazy for other reasons though but I'm not sure yet.

Suddenly, her face pales and she can't seem to look at me anymore.

"What's wrong?" I ask, suspicious.

After a few seconds of silence, I hear her take a deep breath and push all her words out in a rush. "My ex-boyfriend called my mother and told her that…that we are engaged. She called my best friend and she left me a voicemail and I have no idea who else she or Callum have told. I am so sorry, I really had no idea it would get this out of hand. Shit, my mother is going to ask around and she will probably tell my grandparents and they will talk to your parents. Honestly, my mom might even tell your parents. Geez, I am so sorry…" She finally stops and is breathing heavily at this point still unable to look at me as her eyes dart around the room.

As I am taking in all of this information, her eyes land on a photo of Ashley and myself. "Oh my gosh, you have a girlfriend? I didn't even think. Oh gosh, are you going to get in trouble? I didn't… Oh my gosh, I am so sorry. I'm so sorry…" She trails off mumbling her apologies.

All of a sudden, I'm not too worried about Ashley finding out anymore. "Wait, my parents know??" I say harshly and then wince at how violent the question came out. My words are so harsh that Juliana jerks her head up to look at me. My face must not be as harsh as my words because her scared expression changes back to guilt.

"No, well I don't know. I don't think they know yet. I don't think my mother would call them right now. It's pretty late and she wouldn't want to appear rude by waking them up."

I nod and check my phone to see if I have any missed calls or texts from either my parents or my sister. Nothing but there is a new text from Ashley saying she will be over in ten minutes. That doesn't give me a lot of time and I don't want to be rude and kick Juliana out.

"My…Ashley will be here in ten minutes." I tell her and she nods, biting her lip nervously. She knows I'm hinting that we need to wrap up this conversation and preferably get Juliana on her way back to her own apartment.

"I don't know what to do…" She says quietly. Her soft words feel like she's confiding in me. It's almost like she's coming to me for help, looking to me to save her like I did when she was younger and getting into trouble as a kid. I guess she is asking for help now, but she is the one who caused the problem in the first place. I sigh.

My protective side is fighting to take over. I need time to process all of this new information but seeing Juliana worried and unsure of how to proceed, I want to step up and help her. I don't have time to process my emotions. Ashley will be here soon. I know I'm not doing anything wrong having Juliana at my apartment but I do not want to try to explain this to Ashley.

"Okay," I say and she looks up at me confused. "Okay," I repeat, "let's do this." Her head tilts in confusion and I am taken aback because it is one of the cutest expressions I've seen in a while. That's not good. I cough to clear my throat and my thoughts.

"What? What do you mean?" Juliana looks across the table at me, her eyes widening. She grips her own hands in anticipation then winces when she squeezes her wounded hand.

"I'll go along with this… this fiancé idea. Just until we are sure that your ex is going to leave you alone, for good." I clarify and her eyes light up, and her mouth opens slightly a second before she speaks. I can tell she's searching for the right thing to say.

"What? Really? Oh. What about Ashley? I can't let you do this to her and your family…" Why is she so worried? It's my life, I realize the consequences that might develop. I wave my hand, erasing her worry, and nod.

"I understand the consequences of this but you need help." I can't believe I am agreeing to this. "We will have to put on a show for our families and friends but if it helps you get rid of this ex. Then, I'm in." She grins when I stop talking and again throws her arms around me and this time I don't stumble but I catch her and laugh.

"Oh! Thank you so much. You have no idea what this means to me! Gosh, this is going to mess up your life. Are you sure you're okay with this? I don't want to get you in trouble with your family or girlfriend." Again she looks worried and guilty.

"Juliana, it's fine. You don't have to worry about Ashley. Well, right now we might but for this plan, don't worry." I reassure her that I'm okay and she gives me another hug before backing away quickly, the worried look returning to her face. And it takes me a second to realize why but then I hear it too. My apartment door is being unlocked. Shit.

"Kurt?" Juliana looks up at me then her eyes dart over to the door. She freezes where she is, gripping her injured hand to her chest. She said her hand was fine but she is favoring that hand a lot. Hopefully, I was able to bandage her cut properly.

"It's okay…" I say in response to her question and to address the door opening. I don't need Juliana starting to panic again. I also want to set some ground rules and explain why I agreed but I stop talking when Ashley enters the apartment and tosses her keys on the table before turning to face into the apartment. Her eyes narrow when she sees Juliana standing a little too close to me.

"Who the hell is she?"

# Chapter 7
## *Juliana*

Ashley is beautiful, which is even more intimidating. Especially since she is currently glaring at me and Kurt. Looking back and forth between us. I gulp nervously and suddenly I realize how close we are standing. I take a step away from Kurt. He rubs his hand over his head again and looks at the floor as if searching for answers.

Kurt said I didn't have to worry about Ashley but right now I am definitely worried. Since Kurt hasn't spoken up, I realize it's on me to say something. Kurt must still be processing everything I said and it has become even more complicated with Ashley showing up in the middle of our conversation. I got him into this mess, I should be the one to speak but as I step forward to respond to her, Kurt holds his hand up stopping me.

"This is Juliana. Juliana," he gestures, "Ashley." I put on my most polite smile and walk towards her sticking my hand out when I reach her. "Juliana is a family friend, we ran into each other this evening."

"Hi, it is so nice to meet you," I say and my smile grows real as she looks at me, confused but she shakes my hand politely. "I was just on my way out. I had a little accident at the club and Kurt was kind enough to help." I smile at her and then turn to Kurt. "Well… thank you. For helping me." I stammer kind of awkwardly and he nods.

"I can drive you home. Do you mind waiting by the elevator so I can talk to Ashley really quickly?"

"Okay, thank you." I thank him remembering that I walked with Tatyana to the club and would need a way to get home from Kurt's house. It's late so I don't entirely feel comfortable walking back to my apartment nor do I feel too comfortable getting into a random Uber. I leave the apartment giving him a moment to talk to Ashley. I head to the elevator and a few seconds later he appears next to me.

"What did you tell her?" He gives me a pained look and I sigh. "I'm sorry. We will think of something. I really didn't mean to ruin your relationship," I say as we step into the elevator. He pushes the button for the lobby and shrugs. After a couple of seconds of silence, except for the whirring of the elevator, he speaks.

"We aren't exactly together at the moment." I stay quiet and he continues. "We are trying…but it hasn't been working out." I nod, understanding.

"Well, I'm still sorry for adding…all of this to your life." I gesture vaguely to the air around us and he sighs.

"It's all right. I've never liked bullies anyway." I smile, bully is a good choice of word for what Callum is. The elevator doors slide open again and we walk out into the lobby. I follow him to his car and he unlocks the door and opens mine for me.

"Thank you," I mumble, not used to having the door opened for me. He nods and goes to the passenger side. I tell him the address of my building and then we sit in silence for a few minutes. I try to relax but once the quiet takes over, all I can do is think about how terribly I screwed up and after struggling to keep my mouth shut for a few minutes, I finally can't hold back anymore.

"I know I keep apologizing but I really am sorry. I didn't even think when I said that to Callum. Well, I mean I kind of did but I did not know he was going to act on it and I am so sorry that it caused a fight." I am about to continue rambling but I hear him chuckle and I scowl at him. "This is not funny!"

He just turns and grins at me. I can't help but start to pout which in turn makes him laugh at me even more.

"Hey! Don't pout at me." He chuckles turning onto the street of my apartment, our short ride almost over. I continue pouting and turn to face the window. Suddenly, I feel something poking my arm and I growl slightly which makes him laugh again.

"Stop laughing at me!" I huff then turn to face him. "I'm trying to apologize for the mess I've gotten you into. My mother knows what I've said and she will not hesitate to tell everyone. She is probably so happy her disappointing little daughter has found an appropriate man."

His face turns somber and he stares out across the road. I sit quietly, as he pulls into the parking lot and parks in front of the door to my building. We both sit in silence and I am about to reach for the door handle when he says something quietly.

"Your mom does not think you are a disappointment." I roll my eyes automatically and scoff.

"Not a disappointment," I correct, "disappointing. And you would be the perfect son-in-law for her." I wait a second before speaking again. "In all honesty, maybe that's part of why I said it. That you were my fiancé. Specifically, you. Because well, I know you and everyone loves you and you're a good respectable man… Maybe I was trying to…" I pause for a second, trying to find the right words. "…to make her proud? Get her off my back? Her and everyone else. I don't know. But I am sorry…I'll get this cleared up, you don't have to worry about it. Well, I guess I should get out of your car now. Goodnight Kurt." I sigh and open the door of his car, getting out and walking to my building.

"I told you that I would go through with it. And I will." I turn around, shocked when I see him about a foot away from me. I tilt my head at him, confused. "Yes, I am a man of my word and it would not be okay of me to let your ex torture you like this. So, yes, I will be your fake fiancé."

I smile and roll my eyes laughing, my spirits suddenly feeling much higher. "Well…uhm… thank you. I really appreciate this." He holds open the apartment doors for me and gestures for me to go inside. As I walk inside, he follows me and raises his eyebrows at me when I look at him again confused.

"Yes, I am walking you to your door." He teases. "Wow, your ex must have been a real gentleman." I laugh and nod.

"Oh yes, such a sweetheart. Held doors open for me and carried my school books." I laugh and he laughs along with me as we walk up the stairs of my building. I'm kind of embarrassed because it is nowhere near as nice as his apartment is.

We walk down the hallway talking quietly, as it's late and I know loud noises from the hall can be heard in each apartment. When we reach my apartment, I stop when I notice that the door is unlocked and partially open. I know Tatyana isn't coming home tonight and I begin to get nervous. The door shouldn't be unlocked, much less opened. Kurt notices my reaction to the door being opened and he steps in front of me telling me to stay behind him as we enter the apartment.

# **Chapter 8**
## *Juliana*

I peer around Kurt's shoulders, taking in the room in front of me. Nothing looks to be out of order but the room is quite dark and I can't see much. I want to go check the small two bedrooms and our one bathroom but the darkness makes the apartment feel eerie. I can tell something is wrong but I really can't see anything with the lights off. I step out from behind Kurt and feel my way across the wall to where I know the light switch is, I flick on the light switch when my hand lands on it.

When the light turns on, it illuminates the small living room, showing a large figure sitting on the couch. Callum sits with his legs spread apart, leaning back on the couch, making himself at home. His face is sporting a nasty bruise just beginning to appear on his jaw. I freeze instantly, staring at him while he glares at me. Callum has yet to move, he remains seated, just staring at me.

I can't seem to get myself to move either but Kurt takes action almost immediately. He leaves the door open to make for an easy exit then he walks over to the couch and looks down at Callum.

"Get up," Kurt says, his voice firm and warning. He stands above Callum, still keeping himself between Callum and myself.

An amused smirk appears on Callum's face that turns even more sinister when he notices Kurt standing in front of me, protecting me. Callum turns his stare on Kurt. He stands up off the couch, slowly. Kurt stands up straighter and while Callum is a tall and large man, Kurt's athletic stature gives his extra inch a lot of intimidation. But I've seen Callum fight and he does not play by the rules, nor is he one to give up easily. The idea of the two fighting worries me but I push that aside and bring myself back to reality.

"Callum," I say cautiously and Kurt looks at me while Callum continues to stare at Kurt. I try to stay focused on getting Callum out of my apartment, I'm not even quite sure how he got in in the first place. "What are you doing here? How did you get in?"

"You didn't think I would let you get away that easily did you, love?" I can feel my body wanting to shrink back and hide from him but I force myself to stand still. I take a deep breath and then sigh.

"Callum, you broke up with me. You need to move on." I put my hands on my hips trying to appear more confident but it only makes Callum smirk more. Callum turns his attention to Kurt when he speaks next. Eyeing him and looking back between the two of us.

"Oh? Do I? Just like you have?" Callum takes a step closer to Kurt who looks a little uncomfortable with the confrontation. But I see his emotions start to shift more towards being annoyed. Honestly, I am getting pretty annoyed with Callum's behavior too. "I can't allow you to get away with disrespecting me like that." He practically snarls at Kurt, taking another step closer, wobbling a little, clearly drunk but he regains his balance quickly.

Kurt holds up his hands trying to make peace. "Hey, man, I meant no disrespect. I just did what anyone would do if they saw someone pushed to the ground." His words sound innocent but I see him stand taller as if egging Callum on.

"Stay away from what's mine. Juliana is my girl." Callum spits venom as he speaks and I know I need to step in before he tries to start a fight. Before I can speak though, Kurt says something that makes me stop in my tracks.

"She isn't your girl. You broke up with her months ago and now, she is my fiancé. So, you need to back off." He finishes his point by giving Callum a look then grabbing his arm and dragging him to the door.

I just stand there unable to react to everything that's going on around me. I thought I had more control over myself than this but after everything else tonight, I am just exhausted.

Callum is obviously wasted, enough so that he doesn't put up a fight even when Kurt grabs him so maybe he won't remember this whole incident by the time he gets over the hangover he's going to endure tomorrow morning.

"I'll be back!" Callum shouts as Kurt ushers him out. "You can't do this to me and expect to get away with it. I will ruin you!"

I hear Callum's words getting quieter as Kurt pushes or drags him down the hallway. I also hear a thud and a couple of muted curse words then the slam of the stairwell door followed by silence.

The silence takes over the small apartment and suddenly my head begins pounding. The silence is too much for me, the headache is overwhelming. I sink onto the floor in the middle of the room and begin to cry, cradling my head in my hands.

It's been such a long night.

# Chapter 9
## *Kurt*

After I ushered Callum out of the apartment, I forced him into a cab ignoring his half-assed, Bond villain, threats and easily dodging his swinging arms. He kept swearing incoherently and threatening to expose our fake relationship. This statement gives me pause, but I know his words mean nothing, just a drunken exclamation. Callum recovers his pride enough to tell the cab driver his address before slamming the door shut and staring off ahead of him, pouting like a small child. His new demeanor makes me smile and I wave as the cab drives off, then head back into the apartment building chuckling to myself.

I wait until the cab disappears, just to make sure he isn't going to try to come back tonight. When I'm sure he's gone, I go back up the stairs to Juliana's apartment. When I go down the hall to her apartment, I notice the door is still open and I see her sitting on the floor in the middle of the room. She is cradling her head in her hands.

"Juliana? Are you okay?" I kneel next to her and lift her face to look up at me. As I search her face for any signs of emotion, I notice that her eyes are red and she looks like she's barely holding back more tears.

When I came back to her apartment I watched as her face went blank and she hid all emotion from me. I wonder why she thinks she would need to hide her emotions from me.

She nods then pushes my hand away from her face but I grab onto her elbow to help her stand. She brushes imaginary lint off her legs when she stands up.

"Thank you," she says quietly, her voice devoid of emotion.

Why is she shutting me out? I think to myself. I guess we don't know each other very well. Hopefully, that changes over time. I know I did the right thing when I agreed to go along with this fake fiancé idea. Especially after everything I've seen so far from Callum's behavior and how Juliana reacts to him. She is starting to hold her own against him but when he left, she completely collapsed and shut down. I can see how emotionally draining her relationship with Callum was. Maybe our relationship can help brighten her spirit again. Even if it isn't quite real, I can still show her what a good relationship should be. Or at the very least, we can have fun as friends.

"It's not a problem," I say, brushing away her thanks. "I've got your back," I reassure her with a smile.

"Thanks for everything. I know this isn't exactly how you pictured this night to go. But I am grateful for your patience." She speaks formally and for some reason, I know I shouldn't push her. I nod, accepting her thanks this time, and take a step away from her.

"Well, then I guess I should be going. Are you okay to be here alone?"

"Yes," she says again, formally. She looks around the apartment gathering her purse off of the floor.

"Okay, well I should head home. Probably have a lot of explaining to do where Ashley is concerned. If she is even still there." She nods and I catch a hint of emotion flash across her face but it quickly disappears. I grab a pen and notepad near the door and jot down my cell number. I tap the notepad to get her attention, "I'll leave my number in case you need to call me." I pause, waiting for a response, she turns to face me and I continue, "We should probably get together tomorrow to discuss a few rules. I'll pick you up. For coffee or something. Is that okay?"

"I have work tomorrow but I get off at 2 p.m." She accepts my offer of coffee and I smile, feeling as if I've made some progress.

"I'll pick you up at 3 then, here."

"Okay. Thank you, again." I laugh because this may be the hundredth time she's said thank you in the last two hours. Wow, has it really only been two hours? It feels like it's been many more.

"I'll see you at 3," I say before shutting the door on my way out.

When I reach my car, I sit in the driver's seat for a few minutes. Then, for the first time since this whole fiasco began, I check my phone. I have multiple missed calls from my mother. One from my father and I also have a few missed calls from my sister and of course, Ashley has left a few messages. I sigh and put my phone away. If Ashley is still at my apartment I'll deal with her but everyone else can wait until tomorrow. I'm too tired tonight.

I pull into the parking lot of my apartment building and park my car in my spot, taking a deep breath when I see Ashley's car still in the guest spot. I get out of my car taking my time, thinking about how to explain. When I reach my apartment, I pause before entering, then open the door.

"Ashley?" I call out. "Are you still here?" I toss my keys in my bowl on the kitchen counter and flick on the light. I don't see her in the kitchen or in the living room but as I head down the hall, I notice my bedroom door is open slightly and a light is on. I push open the door further and am about to speak when I notice Ashley is fast asleep on my bed. I must have been gone longer than I realized. I cover her up with a blanket and head back into the living room. I sit down on the couch and listen to a couple of voicemails.

*Hi, honey, it's mom. How are you doing? Are you still coming to church this Sunday? We would all love to see you there. Anyway, I heard some news recently but just wanted to check in with you first. It's getting late so I am going to bed in a few minutes. Call me tomorrow. Goodnight. Love you.*

I laugh, my mother is so polite. She must know about what happened tonight. I wonder how she found out. I guess she will tell me tomorrow.

I lay down on the couch stretching out my legs. My couch is huge so I have plenty of room when I stretch. I prop a pillow under my head and drift off to sleep.

# Chapter 10
## *Juliana*

*Beep Beep Beep Beep!*

What the hell is that noise? I groan and shift in my bed, my hand searching for my alarm clock, more specifically, the snooze button. I can't reach it so I wiggle around in bed to get closer to my nightstand and I lose my balance and land on the floor with a loud thud.

"Ow," I grumble but the fall has woken me up a little. I hit the clock to make the noise stop then I head into my bathroom. I step into the shower, the cut on my hand stinging under the hot water, reminding me of last night's events. I try to take a quick shower knowing I have work in 2 hours. I always set my alarm for two hours before I'm supposed to be at work. I know it is early but I like having plenty of time to get ready and then relax before working. After a quick shower, I wrap a towel around my body and another around my hair then walk into the kitchen to get the coffee started, noticing Tatyana hasn't been back to the apartment yet. While waiting for the coffee, I find the first aid kit and put a new bandaid on the cut, biting my lip at the tenderness.

When I get back into my bedroom I lift my phone from my nightstand and turn it on. As I wait for it to turn on, I towel dry my hair in front of my mirror and I notice the screen of my phone light up in the background of my mirror. I toss my towel into the bathroom promising myself I'll pick it up later then I grab my phone and stare at the numerous missed calls and unanswered texts from last night.

"Crap," I say quietly then toss my phone on my bed and decide to toss myself onto my bed, sighing. My hand grabs my phone again and I look at the screen, breathing heavily. When I see an unknown number has texted me, I immediately call the number without reading the message, assuming it's Kurt.

"Hello? Juliana? Is everything okay?" I hear on the other end of the call and I take a deep breath.

"So, last night really did happen, huh?" I say in lieu of a response. I hear a chuckle over the phone then the call sounds muted but I can make out someone in the background saying congratulations to him.

"You still there?" He asks.

"Yeah… Why did someone congratulate you?"

"Oh, it seems our news has gotten around," Kurt explains. I gasp then turn over on my stomach and bury my face in my pillows.

"Juliana?" I hear and I force myself to sit up. "Are we still on for 3 p.m.?" I nod my head then realize he can't see me so I speak up.

"Yes, would you like to meet somewhere?"

"No, I'll come to you." He states firmly and my heart flutters a little bit but I notice the time on the clock and shake off the feeling blaming it on my need to have relaxation time before work.

"Okay," I say, not knowing what else to say.

"Okay," he repeats back to me and I sigh, ready to apologize again but he seems to sense my next words and he stops me. "You don't have to apologize. I'll see you at 3." Then he hangs up.

I stare at the phone a little taken aback by his abrupt end to the call but then my phone dings, telling me I've got a new text and I open it. It's from Kurt and it reads, **Sorry for ending the call so suddenly, boss eyeing me… see you at 3**.

I smile and toss my phone onto my bed then hop up and head into my closet to find an outfit for work. Once I'm dressed, I chug a cup of coffee, pack my bag, and head out the door.

When I arrive at work, the store is crowded so I quickly put my things away and then clock in, going over to a young couple and their daughter. I help them pick out outfits and accessories to go along with them. When nearly an hour passes, they have everything they need and I head over to the cash register to ring them out. They thank me for all my help and thank me for my patience. I smile and tell them it's no problem at all. And it really isn't. I've enjoyed working with them and it has kept me distracted from thinking about what happened last night.

Before I know it, my shift is nearing its end. I help one last customer then look around, noticing the store is pretty empty. Everyone that is in the store is already being helped so my manager tells me I can leave.

I clock out and say goodbye to everyone before heading to my car. I sit in my car with the windows rolled down, waiting for it to cool off and I decide to call my mother.

"Hello?" She answers, not looking at the caller ID.

"Hi, Mom," I say, then toss my phone onto the passenger seat and fiddle with the AC in my car while my mother talks so loudly that I can still hear her very clearly.

"Why haven't you called me sooner?!" She practically screeches through the phone, and I can't tell if she is mad or excited. "I called you a hundred times last night and this morning! You have a lot of explaining to do, young lady. I've already called Gram and discussed this situation with her!" My mother prattles on but I stop listening. Oh no, since my mother and grandmother, Gram, know then our whole church congregation must know too. This congregation includes Kurt's parents.

I grab my phone off of the seat and send Kurt a quick text, while my mother continues to talk. I sent the text after retyping numerous times trying to figure out what to say and eventually settling with:

Juliana: **Heard from your parents today?**

He responds with a simple:

Kurt: **Yep.**

I groan forgetting my mother is still on the phone and she hears me.

"Juliana, what are you doing right now??"

"Sorry, I'm listening." I sigh and wait for more yelling but I hear a muffled sound and my mother greeting someone. "Mom, who are you with?"

"I'll have to call you back, dear. I'm having lunch with Mrs. Michaels." I inhale deeply. Kurt's mom.

"Mom, no. Don't tell her anything… yet." I beg softly but that's probably why they're having lunch.

"Why shouldn't I tell her anything?" She asks, annoyed.

"Well…" I search for an answer. "We are trying to keep it on the down-low for a little while first! So, we can enjoy it before sharing it with everyone else." I marvel at my quick response then remind myself to get Kurt up to date on what is happening.

My mother sighs but she likes being the first to know a secret so I know she's happy. "Well, all right then but I expect to see you at our house for dinner tonight at 6:30 p.m., to discuss what's been going on since you've moved out." I can hear Mrs. Michaels coming back to the table and I agree to the dinner just to make sure my mother keeps her mouth shut. "See you at 6:30 p.m.," she says, then hangs up the phone and I lean back against my seat and close my eyes. I just sit in my silent car for a few seconds then peek at the clock. 2:30 p.m., already? Jeez, I need to get going.

I start my car and crank my music, opening my windows and sunroof, letting the music spill out into the streets. I lean back in my seat and drive to my apartment, I see Tatyana's car in the parking lot and know I have a lot to explain to her but my clock reads 2:43 p.m. and I know I need to get ready before Kurt comes to pick me up.

# **Chapter 11**

## *Juliana*

I park my car and make my way into the building, climbing the stairs, my mind going crazy. When I reach my floor, I exit the stairwell, go to the apartment door, and unlock it, letting myself in. I shut the door behind me and lock it, then put my keys on the counter. I begin to head toward my room before I see Tatyana pop up off the couch and run over to me.

"Hey!" She calls out, making me jump. "Where have you been?"

"Work…" I say, not elaborating, and continue walking to my room. Tatyana does not give up and she follows me, jumping onto my bed. I kick off my shoes and she sits patiently, waiting for me to continue. When I don't, she sighs.

"Sooooo, want to tell me what the hell happened last night? And start from the beginning!" She says and I laugh.

"Jeez, someone is a little bossy."

"Well, when your friend is suddenly engaged without anyone knowing, one has to be bossy." I shake my head, laughing then flop onto the bed next to her.

"All right, all right." I puff out a breath of air and tuck a pillow under my head, and I realize just how badly I need to talk to someone about this whole situation. "Kurt is coming to pick me up at 3 so I'll tell you some now and I'll keep you updated."

She nods eagerly and nudges me, grinning a little. "He's coming to get you? For what? Are you guys actually engaged? Dating? What's going on???" I laugh at her persistent questions and she nudges me again to get me to talk. "The last I heard was that Callum broke up with you, like five months ago and you've still been moping recently so I didn't think you'd started seeing anyone?"

"Well…" I begin. "Yes, I mean no. I hadn't started seeing anyone."

"'Hadn't'? Like you had not been but you are now?" Tatyana questions and I shush her so I can get the full story out, knowing I don't have too long until Kurt comes to pick me up.

"Last night, Callum found me at the bar and he was just so slimy and acting like he was some God's gift to women or something, you know how he is." I wave my hand and she nods, rolling her eyes. "Well, I don't really know what happened but I just kind of blurted out that I was over him and engaged. I don't know what's wrong with me but he was just being so creepy and I wanted him to leave me alone. Ugh!" I cry out and pull a blanket over my head, hiding, only to have it quickly ripped away.

"Juli!" She shouts and I wince, closing my eyes. "What else happened?? The last time I saw you, you were leaving with Kurt. So, something obviously happened. How's your hand?" She asks, releasing my grip on the blanket so she can inspect my hand.

"Oh, I had completely forgotten about that. I guess it's fine then. Didn't get cut too badly." After confirming that my hand is okay, she lets go of it and then props herself up on her elbows, narrowing her eyes at me. "Okay, okay," I say. "He took me back to his place," I pause and give her a look, "and no, nothing happened. So, he brought me back to his place, to clean up my hand. While I was in the bathroom cleaning up, I checked my phone and found multiple missed calls and texts, from you and from my mother and father."

"How did your mother find out so quickly?"

"Callum," I roll my eyes. "Lord knows why but he called up my mother and told her." Before she can curse him, I continue talking. "Once I saw those messages and listened to my mother's voicemail, I lost it. Literally. I vomited, right there in Kurt's toilet. It was so embarrassing! And he heard me! I didn't know what else to do so I just told him the whole thing. Everything that had happened. And you know me, I don't know when to shut up." She nods in agreement, smiling. "Okay anyway, for some reason he agreed to it."

"What?! Wait, what? Agreed to what?" Tatyana asks, completely shocked and confused.

I nod eagerly. "Yes! He agreed to be my fiancé! Well, fake fiancé. I have no idea why! Except, he did say it was to help get Callum to leave me alone."

"He probably likes you." Tatyana teases hopping off my bed and going to my closet.

"No, he definitely does not like me. He doesn't really even know me. What are you doing?" I sit up and watch her toss things out of my closet and onto my bed.

"Helping you pick out an outfit for your date, duh." She says like it should be completely obvious to me.

"What date?" Then I realize what she's talking about. "Oh no, this isn't a date. We are just meeting to go over this… situation I put him in." I try to find the right way to phrase it but I really can't think of anything better than 'situation'. I pull myself out of bed reluctantly and look at the pile of clothes on my bed, sifting through them.

"Okay," Tatyana says as she emerges from my closet holding a plain black dress with a cutout back and my one and only jean jacket. "These, with these…" She hands them to me and then pulls out my light blue booties and a simple necklace to tie in the booties.

I laugh. "It's only 3! This isn't a nighttime/clubbing event. This is just coffee."

She huffs, shoves the shoes at me, and then returns to my closet for a few seconds then returns.

"A plain white shirt, a pair of jeans, and the booties, of course." I admire the outfit and then change into it quickly.

"I like it," I say as I finish pulling on the heels and twisting my body to look in the mirror. Tatyana hands me my jean jacket and looks over my outfit.

"Too much jean material? No, perfect." She nods her head in approval and then busies herself with my purse while I go to grab my phone and respond to Kurt's message that he has arrived. I text him back that I'll be down shortly. I quickly go back to my room and grab my purse from Tatyana.

Tatyana smiles at me and relinquishes my purse. She takes a step back to admire her work. A team effort really. But I do admit she helps a lot with my styling. I have to add my own touch as well or tame down her ideas but we seem to work well together because I feel good in every outfit we create together.

"What did you put in here?" I think about it then wave away the question. "Never mind, I do not want to know." She laughs and her eyes twinkle mysteriously. I roll my eyes but laugh too and yell goodbye as I run out the door. I race down the stairs and then pause to catch my breath before exiting the stairwell. I mess with my hair a little bit then I straighten out my outfit and carefully walk out of the stairwell. My booties are new but I love wearing heels so I have gotten pretty good at walking in them and I know to be careful. I take a deep breath and make my way to the lobby of my building.

# Chapter 12
## *Kurt*

I've been talking to one of Juliana's neighbors when I see her exit the stairwell, I smile and wave at her. She has her head down and doesn't seem to see me, so I take the opportunity to watch her walking across the lobby. I catch myself noticing how her heels show off her incredibly long, elegant legs, while her tight jeans hug every curve. I shake my head, trying to rid my head of those thoughts and I focus on how she interacts with the guests in the lobby. She's shy but polite. She smiles and says hello to an older couple who are sitting in the lobby talking, they smile back at her and look at her fondly. When she makes her way over to where I am standing, she smiles at me.

"Sorry to keep you waiting and for not inviting you up to the apartment. Tatyana was in the apartment and I didn't want her to accost you with questions." She laughs but I can tell she is embarrassed.

I laugh with her, trying to help her relax. "It's okay. You're right on time. Besides," I say, teasingly, "I enjoyed talking to James, here. He has a lot of very interesting stories."

Juliana smiles and thanks James for keeping me company and entertaining me while I waited. She even mentions how much she adores his dog, telling me that seeing the two of them out and about is the highlight of her day.

"I hope you didn't tell him too many stories, James," Juliana nudges him and laughs. He just winks back at her but doesn't say anything. Juliana shakes her head and leads me towards the exit. James smiles at her and I can tell he likes her. Not in a romantic way but as a little sister. I nod at him as I hold open the door to the building and she walks out onto the sidewalk. As she makes her way onto the sidewalk, she looks around the street. I can see her eyes searching and as she finds what she is looking for, she walks over to my car and waits patiently for me to unlock it. I smile to myself, enjoying learning about her habits and the way she thinks.

"What are you smiling at? Have I got something on my face?" Her voice interrupts my thoughts, making me jolt a little. I scold myself for getting distracted and absorbed in looking at her and thinking about her.

"Oh, no sorry. Just thinking." I reply then get into the car, turning on the engine. "Did you have any place you wanted to go to get coffee?" I ask, trying to change the subject. I watch her face as she thinks. Scrunching her eyes up and tilting her head.

"Ummm," she says, pausing and I still wait silently. After a few seconds, she lets out a burst of air as if she was holding her breath. "Nope, I got nothing." This makes me laugh and she looks at me, confused.

"Sorry," I say, a bit breathless. "But you took so long thinking, I figured you'd come up with an answer but you said 'nope'." I start laughing again but this time she smiles and laughs too.

"I really was trying to think of a place but I don't really know any coffee places!" She defends herself as we both laugh. I put the car into drive and pull out of the parking lot. "I know there are a lot of coffee places near here but I'm not a huge coffee person nor a breakfast person, so I really haven't been to too many. I mean Tatyana has dragged me to a few and most of them make the pastries fresh so they're usually pretty good. Although most of the breakfast places that would have coffee and treats are probably closed by now. I think some close at 3 or before."

Juliana prattles on and I hesitate to suggest another type of food or drink for our meeting but we've already agreed on going to a coffee house. Plus at this point, if I said we could change and go elsewhere, it might take a while to decide on a place. It's easier to stick with what we agreed upon.

"I think I might know a place," I say but add nothing more and she doesn't question me. She reaches for the radio, turning the dial until she finds a country station playing a song. She turns up the radio and sits back in her seat.

We ride in silence for a few minutes before I hear her sigh and I turn my head slightly to look at her. Her mouth is opened partially like she is about to say something. I turn back to focus on the road.

"Yes?" I ask. "Are you going to say something?"

I can tell she wants to ask how I knew she was going to talk but I don't want to admit to watching her, so I am relieved when she doesn't ask.

"I'm just really sorry about all of this. It was so stupid of me. Honestly, I don't know what I was thinking." She seems so guilty that I almost feel bad but I know I have to mention that my mother found out.

"Juliana," I start.

"Please, call me Juli. All of my friends do." She cuts me off with a wave of her hand as if I am being too formal by addressing her as Juliana.

"Juli," I start over, "I understand that you're sorry. But I've told you that I also understand why you said what you did and that I am here to help. And after your…Callum?" I ask, trying to remember his name, and she nods so I continue. "After Callum showed up at your apartment, I think you did the right thing and I stand by my decision to help you." I pause, taking a deep breath before telling her, "My mother knows."

"Your mother knows what?" She asks absently as if she is lost in thought. Then she shoots up, sitting tall in her seat. "WAIT! She knows? About what I said? About us? How did that happen? How could she know?" She keeps asking questions but her voice gets quieter, like she's talking to herself.

"Hey," I say to get her attention back on me. "It's all right."

She cuts me off again with a gasp. "Shit!" She curses and I laugh at her sailor's mouth. "Sorry, but I forgot! My mother had lunch with your mother today! Oh no. I practically begged her not to say anything. And I thought she wouldn't but I guess she did. Who knows why? Ugh." Then she goes on to say, multiple times, what seems to be her favorite four-letter word, shit.

I glance at my phone sitting in the cup holder and tap on it to check if I have any messages while she continues to talk. "I told my mother not to say anything but I did text you while on the phone with my mother so your mother must have already known but of course it would have been because of my mother anyway. Well, who knows if my mother actually told your mother but my mother definitely told my grandmother who was probably thrilled and told everyone at her church, which your parents attend, and a lot of other people they are all friends with so of course the news probably traveled around quickly..." She says, seeming to talk all with one breath, without stopping and I can't help but be somewhat impressed.

By the time she finishes, I am pulling into the parking lot and she doesn't seem to notice as I step out of the car to return my mother's call.

"Hi, honey. How are you doing?" She answers the phone politely and I can imagine her smiling.

"Hi Mom, I'm doing alright. How are you?" We always start our conversations with what people think are just formalities but she genuinely wants to know how I'm doing.

"I'm just great." She waits patiently for me to tell her the big news but I can tell she already knows. She's holding back.

"So, I guess you've heard."

"Heard what? Oh, yes well, I have heard something but I was waiting to hear from you." My mother is never one to push, she has patience with me and knows that when I am ready I will usually tell her anything.

"Well," I pause, taking a deep breath before blowing it all out and continuing, "it's all true. Juliana, Juli," I correct myself, "and I are engaged. To be married." I clarify, then hold my breath and wait for my mother's reaction. I don't think she will be upset, she has always liked Juliana and thought she was a great girl.

"Oh, Kurt! That is wonderful." She gushes, sounding so happy. I find myself grinning. "I had heard the news but I wanted to hear it from you directly. I had lunch with Juliana's mother and I could tell there was something she wanted to tell me and she sort of let some little hints slip but I am so glad to officially hear it from you!" I listen to my mother talking about how wonderful Juliana is and how we need to have a party to celebrate. While I'm listening, I look across the car and see Juli watching me. She looks nervous so I smile reassuringly and it seems to help because I see her let out a breath and she smiles back at me a little bit.

"Mom, I am actually with Juliana right now so I can't stay on the phone too long." I look down at the ground and kick a pebble while my mother talks.

"Oh, no sorry. I won't keep you long but don't you think it would be a fun idea to celebrate or at least have dinner with our families? I think we should all get together. Your sister," my mom begins and I groan.

"Even my sister knows? So I guess pretty much everyone knows at this point." I let out a sigh and look up at Juliana.

"Kurt," I can tell she is about to scold me but she refrains. "Kurt, we are all very happy for you two. I will text you later to arrange a dinner or a party." She sounds like she is leaning towards the party but I'm sure it would be better if we kept everything small. "Or you can call me later to discuss the details."

"Okay, Mom."

# Chapter 13
## *Juliana*

I gesture to Kurt that I am going to go inside and he nods in acknowledgment. As I walk inside, I can picture his grin when he told his mother about our engagement. It makes me smile and my stomach gets tight. I try to rush away the thought. He doesn't like me. He can't, he's just doing it to help me. I don't like him like that either. It's just pretend. It isn't real.

I have to keep repeating that to myself. It isn't real. It isn't real. It isn't real. I go to stand in line to order a drink for myself and I feel bad because I have no idea what Kurt would want so I just decide to order for myself so I don't accidentally get him something he does not like. When I reach the counter, my stomach growls, reminding me that I haven't eaten in a while so I order a blended frappe and an orange scone. I go to find a table and once I am seated, I nibble on my scone while waiting for my drink to be ready. I look up and try to see if I can see Kurt outside but I can't so I just go back to enjoying my scone.

A few seconds pass and someone slides into the booth opposite me. I look up smiling, assuming it was Kurt. But the smile on my face freezes when I see it isn't Kurt, it's Callum.

"Hello, love."

"Wh-what are you doing here? How did you find me?" I look around the shop, trying to find a way to safely exit. Callum senses my need to escape and suddenly a boot lands on the edge of the booth next to me, effectively trapping me. I look at him and try to look bored but he can tell I'm scared and he smirks at me.

"Where's your little fiancé to protect you now?" He asks, leaning across the table, sneering at me. When I don't answer he reaches across the table and grabs a piece of my scone and tosses it into his mouth. I sit patiently and try not to do anything to provoke him.

"What do you want, Callum?" I ask timidly. I clear my throat to try again, trying to sound stronger "You were the one who broke up with me. A while ago." I remind him.

He takes his time finishing the rest of my scone and I hear my name called. My drink is ready. I internally sigh in relief and I look at Callum. "That's my drink. If I don't go get it, someone will come over here." I say it as a threat, but my tone remains polite, so he doesn't suspect anything. He grabs my arm firmly, but not tight enough to leave a mark, he's smarter than that. He leans forward as if he is about to say something but my name is called again and he lets go and removes his boot, freeing me. I scurry out of the booth and up to the counter. By the time I grab my drink and sneak a peek at the booth, he's gone. I notice a napkin on the table though and I slowly walk back. On the napkin it says,

**I know you're hiding something, and I will find out whatever it is and expose you.**

I let out a big breath I was holding. Wow, that was interesting. Not the best written threat. So, he knows I'm hiding something but he doesn't know what. With all of his hostility towards me, maybe he thinks I cheated on him? No, I don't think that could be it. But he does know something's up. I sigh and sit down in the booth again, shoving the note into my purse. I take a sip of my drink and then feel a presence sliding into the seat across from me. I don't look up this time.

"Sorry, I took so long. My mom was very happy for us." Kurt chuckles. "She also insisted that we come to her golf club so she can host an engagement party for us. You remember the golf club that used to host us as kids for different church events. Or not even church events, I guess, really just church friends and family hanging out after services."

I nod, remembering different times I'd been to the golf club. I think back to when I was younger. Wow, I definitely had a crush on Kurt back then. Wait, he just said his mother wants to host an engagement party for us. I look up, confused and slightly horrified.

"Yeah, I tried to dissuade her from the idea but she already has her heart set on it, so what am I to do?" He looks at me and takes in my slumped form and my suddenly tired demeanor. "Are you okay? I can just take you home if you'd like? It looks like you've had a long day."

I let out a laugh and decide to tease him to avoid the subject, "That's not a very nice thing to say to a woman, let alone your fiancé." He laughs too and starts to apologize but I wave it away. "No, you're right. Everything just hit me but I'll be all right shortly. Did you want a coffee or something to eat?"

He nods. "Yeah, I come here often so they already started on my order when they saw me outside." He laughs and rubs his hand over his head, embarrassed. I laugh with him and sit up a little straighter, my mood lightening.

"So," I start awkwardly, "I guess we should get down to business. I know I've apologized a lot but I need to say it again. I am really sorry for this. I feel so bad. It was so dumb of me…" I trail off when I realize he is smiling at me. "What? Is there something on my face?" I wipe at my face with a napkin and he laughs.

"No, sorry. I didn't mean to stare. You just apologize a lot." I nod about to apologize for apologizing a lot then I think better of it. "I told you that I want to do this. We are not going to discuss this anymore. Now, what we do have to discuss is what we are going to tell our parents." I sigh and lean back against the booth, thinking. "Obviously, they both have already heard the news but how should we go about this to make sure neither party gets hurt when things…end." He pauses, looking at me and I smile weakly because there really isn't any other way to say it. This will have to end, and I wouldn't want to ruin any other relationships, with the ending of Kurt's and my "engagement".

"Shit," I cuss then blush when he gives me a look. "Sorry, I never said I was ladylike." He laughs and nods, agreeing. I lightly kick his shin under the table. "Hey! You don't have to agree with me!" I laugh with him as he rubs his shin, pouting, and pretending to be hurt. Or at least, I hope he's pretending.

"So, you want to go along with this party idea? Do you think we can pretend in front of all our family and friends? I don't know if I can do that. I don't think I want to…" I stop and think about my encounter with Callum just a few minutes earlier, this makes me sit up and nod. "You know what, let's do it. What better way to prove this is real? This will convince Callum we are serious and he will leave me alone," I say with confidence but inside I am questioning it. I don't know if Callum will stop after just one party. He knows me better than that. There is no telling how far he will go to find the truth.

I look up and see Kurt watching me. Confused by my quick change of heart. After a few seconds of silence, he speaks, "Okay. If you're sure? I'll call my mother back in a few minutes and let her know. We need to figure out a story. How we got together, how I proposed. Those things. The important details." He sits back and taps his fingers on the table, thinking.

"Good idea…"

# Chapter 14

## *Kurt*

Hanging out with Juliana this afternoon was more fun than I had thought it would be. I can look back now and see that I've always had fun when hanging out with her. The past few years we haven't spent much time together because we've all been busy but I have good memories from when we were younger.

After I've dropped Juliana back at her apartment, my phone starts buzzing in my pocket before I pull out of the parking lot.

"Hello?" I answer without looking at who is calling.

"Hi, sweetheart. I'm sorry to be calling you again so soon." It's my mom again. Her tone sounds a bit excited.

"It's okay. Sorry, I haven't called you back yet. I just dropped Juliana back off at her apartment."

"Oh, you spent a long time with her today." My mom sounds like she is smiling. "How is she doing?"

"She's well, mom. Are you calling about something in particular?" I finally pull out of the parking lot and set my phone in a cup holder messing with the buttons on my steering wheel to get the call through my car speakers.

"Oh right, well I was thinking if we wanted to do something more intimate for the engagement party, your dad and I could host the party at our lake house." My mom's voice comes over loud on the car speakers and I turn them down a bit. "You know I love the golf club but maybe we can save that for the wedding reception or even the venue of the ceremony." She takes a breath and I chuckle.

"Wow, you've really been thinking about this a lot, haven't you?" I keep my eyes on the road and switch lanes finding my exit. "Uhm, yeah, I'll let Juliana know. Did you have a date in mind for the party?"

"I was hoping to have it, not this coming Saturday but the following. So that gives us about two weeks to prepare for everything. Would that work for you and Juliana?"

"I will have to check with her but I think that should be okay. Far enough out that I shouldn't have anything scheduled. I do have to be in court on Monday morning but it isn't such a challenging case. I'll only need Sunday to look over everything one final time." I stop at a stoplight a couple of lights away from my apartment, and check the time. It's getting late, I should stop for dinner or groceries and actually make myself something for dinner.

"Okay! Great! I will start planning and confirm the time with you later! Please let me know if something comes up and the day doesn't work for either of you." Mom sounds excited and eager to get off the phone to begin planning.

"Alright, will do. Love you, Mom."

"Love you lots Kurt! Send Juliana my love as well." We say a final goodbye and then hang up.

The parking garage is mostly full when I reach my apartment and I pull into my spot. Walking into the building and to my apartment I pull my phone out again and send Juliana a text, updating her on my mother's plans for an engagement party. She doesn't respond right away so I figure she is busy but I follow up with a text asking when she wants to meet up again.

Once I get settled in my apartment, I find some food in my fridge and decide I can make a meal for myself. It doesn't take me long to whip something up. I've just sat down at the table to eat when I hear keys in the door. I look up right as Ashley enters the apartment.

"Uhm, hello?" I stand up and meet her in the entryway. She shuts the door behind her and tosses her keys on the counter. Well they aren't her keys, just my spare set of keys. I really should have asked for them back, when we first broke up.

"Hey cutie," Ashley smiles at me, her eyes a little glossy. She staggers a bit as she walks over to me. I grip her arms to steady her and she seems to enjoy the physical touch so I release her as soon as she's steady.

"What are you doing here, Ashley?" I turn away from her and towards the counter. Messing with her keyring, I slip off my spare set and pocket them before she notices anything.

"You've never been opposed to me showing up at your apartment." Ashley points out and while that is generally true, I seem to remember telling her she couldn't do it anymore.

"Ashley, I told you, we aren't together anymore. This isn't like our breakups before. This one is final." I turn to speak to her face to face. As I am speaking, I realize that I'm not just saying this because I'm going along with the fake fiancé idea but I am saying this because I am finally done with Ashley and our on-again/off again, love/hate relationship.

Ashley is silent as she takes in my facial expression and body language. She seems to get it and her demeanor shifts. "But.." she stammers, then closes her mouth.

"Here, let me walk you down and get an Uber for you." I hand her back her keychain and gently take her elbow, turning her back to the door and leading her out of my apartment.

"I don't think this will be the end," Ashley states and works her arm away from my guiding hand and then she links her arm through mine. I let her stay that way as we ride the elevator down to the lobby. "I'm sure we'll be back together in no time. Even if you do like that little girl I caught in your apartment, there is no way you can stay away from me. She'll probably break your heart anyway."

Ashley's words are cruel and hopefully untrue. I can tell she's been drinking so I try to ignore her words for the most part. Ashley has always been a jealous or competitive person. I don't think she even likes me that much but once she has her hooks in someone, she thinks they are hers forever. Or at least until she gets tired of them.

"Okay, Ashley. Stay safe." I stay by her side until a car pulls up in front of us. I check to make sure they're here to pick her up then confirm the address before helping her get in the car and shutting the door before she can say anything else.

With a sigh, I go back to my apartment to finish my now cold meal. I look up at the microwave to check the time and see that it isn't very late but I am already exhausted. Eating the last bite of my dinner, I bring my plate to the sink. Once the kitchen is cleaned, I make my way to my office and grab a couple of folders then come back out to the living room and spread my things on the coffee table. I sit on the edge of the couch and then slide down onto the floor, spreading my legs out in front of me. I pull the coffee table over my legs to bring my work closer to me.

My phone buzzes a couple of times on the table and falls off into my lap. I pick it up and see that Juliana has responded to my texts. I wonder if I should tell her about Ashley stopping by tonight. I decided against it and then read her texts.

**Juliana: Yikes. I  guess that's fine. I am free then, I'll mark it in my calendar now.**

**Juliana: Want to meet up Wednesday? I get off work at 5. We can go to another coffee shop if you want.**

I check my calendar for work to see if I have anything that might run long on Wednesday. Looks like I have a meeting from 2-4, it might run long so to play it safe I should see if she can meet around 7.

**Kurt: I can make it Wednesday but would 7 work for you? We can grab dinner.**

I text her back then set my phone aside to get to work. I just have some paperwork to finish up but I'd rather get it done now so I can shift my focus to other open cases. A few minutes later my phone buzzes again and I lift it to see Juliana's response.

**Juliana: 7 and dinner sounds good. Nothing too fancy tho, please :)**

I chuckle out loud and then try to go back to focusing on my paperwork. Only a half hour has passed before I get distracted and start thinking about ideas for dinner on Wednesday.

'Nothing too fancy', hmm. There are a lot of restaurants between our apartments, a lot of them are fancy though. I'll have to text her in a couple of days to see if she has any choices she'd prefer. And it would give me an excuse to talk to her again before the dinner. Not that I need to talk to her but I find myself wanting to talk to her again. I really enjoyed spending time with her today. She is so different from Ashley, in the best way. I haven't spent time with a girl like her in a while.

# Chapter 15
## *Juliana*

The next few days drag by slowly but finally, it's Wednesday morning. My alarm goes off and I am grateful I set it for two hours earlier than needed. It gives me time to take a long shower and get everything done that I need to, that way I will only have to rinse off after work before meeting Kurt for dinner.

Butterflies twirl in my stomach as I rub moisturizer on my face after my shower. I am excited to see Kurt again. We only talked briefly this week about the restaurant of choice for this evening. We decided on a cute little cafe that Kurt had been to. He offered to pick me up again and I accepted. I could just meet him there but he offered since I haven't been to the cafe so it'd be easier for him to just pick me up.

"Juliana!" Tatyana flings open the bathroom door. Luckily, I have a towel wrapped around me. I turn to look at her while I continue to lotion, moving to my arms.

"Yes? Can I help you?" I ask. She reaches her hand out and I squeeze some lotion out onto her hand.

"Just wanted to check in to see how everything is going. With Kurt specifically."

"Well, we are going to dinner at 7 p.m. this evening. After work, I will head back here and then shower. If you're around, maybe you'd like to help me get ready?"

"Oh duh! I would like to. I like Kurt. He seems great." Tatyana steps back to allow me to exit the bathroom then she follows me back to my room.

"Don't get too attached. This isn't really a long-term thing, I don't think." I rummage through my dresser to find clothes for work while we talk.

"Ooo, you don't think? But you kind of want it to be a long-term thing don't you?" Tatyana teases me. She flops onto my bed and flips through a magazine I just noticed she had in her hand.

"No, I mean that would be so weird. This is a fake relationship to begin with, so if I did want it to be a long-term thing in the end, it would be so strange to jump automatically to being engaged. Like, what? We actually go through with a wedding? We get married first and then we start dating and start having a real relationship? That's crazy." I ramble on, carefully getting dressed so my towel doesn't fall off even though I know Tatyana is too busy with the magazine to see me.

"Wow, have you been thinking about this a lot?" I sigh but she continues talking. "Oh! It would be sort of like The Proposal! With Sandra Bullock and Ryan Reynolds. You know the line he says towards the end. 'Marry me because I'd like to date you.' That line. That would be exactly your situation. Well, not that either of y'all are getting deported but still, similar idea right?"

Tatyana and I look at each other for a quiet second before we both burst out laughing. I sit down on the bed next to her and our laughs fill the room for a few minutes before we finally calm down.

"That is always the thing that annoyed me the most about The Bachelor and Bachelorette franchise. Literally none of them used that line to propose. So frustrating. I mean they literally have to get engaged to continue dating soooo why not use such an iconic line?" I go on a bit of a rant and Tatyana laughs.

"Trade marked maybe? Although you'd think they'd be able to afford it if one of the contestants wanted to use that for their proposal." Tatyana frowns and then rolls her eyes at the situation.

"Well, anyway, it's stupid," I say, standing up off my bed. "Okay, I have to go to work now. Will you be here when I get back? I'm off at 5 p.m. today."

"Hm, I don't get off until 6 p.m. What time is Kurt coming to get you? Also, I love the fact that he picks you up to take you out. Very sweet but also gives us a little extra time to get you ready."

"I know, it's very nice and helpful. Haha." I towel dry my hair, scrunching it a bit to get more water out of it and shape my curls more. "Dinner is at 7 p.m. but I'm not sure if that means he'll be here at 7 p.m. or we need to be at the cafe at 7 p.m. I don't think the cafe takes reservations so I think he'll be here at 7 p.m."

"Okay, I should be home by 6:15 p.m. but that only gives us 45 minutes to get you all cute and prepped for your date." Tatyana winks at me and I don't bother to correct her. It does feel like it's a date.

"That should work. Thanks, darlin'! Okay, I've got to get to work, I'll see you this evening. Have fun at work." I leave Tatyana lying on my bed flipping through her magazine. She gives a wave and says she'll see me tonight.

# Chapter 16
## *Juliana*

When I get to work, my boss has me in the backroom unpacking boxes and sorting things. I spend a few hours in the back then I make my way out front, rolling out a cart packed with new items to put out.

"Oh, perfect timing!" My boss comes over to me and plucks an item off the cart. "I was just telling a customer about these new earrings we just got in. Her daughter just got her ears pierced a couple of weeks ago and is ready to put new earrings in. I think these will be perfect for her!"

My boss loves her job and is genuinely excited about helping each customer. I always love working with her because she makes the day go quickly, smoothly, and actually fun. I watch her head off back to the customer and I turn back to the cart and begin dragging it around the store, restocking items and placing the new items in their designated spots.

Near the end of my shift, the cart begins to empty, and as I put out the last items my boss comes over to me.

"Once you're done with this, you can clock out. Katherine should be here soon. She's always a few minutes late but I can hold down the fort until she arrives."

"Okay, I'll put the cart away then grab my things before clocking out."

"Have a good evening, Juliana." My boss smiles goodbye and then goes off to greet a customer who has just entered the store.

I bring the cart into the back to put it away and make sure I've cleaned up all the trash that came with the unboxing of products. Once the space is clean, I take the now full trash bag out to the back hall to be taken out at the closing of the store. Then I grab my stuff and clock out. I walk through the store, give a quick wave to my boss, and say hello to Katherine on her way in.

When I reach my car, I check the time and see that it's just after 5 p.m. It shouldn't take me too long to get home which should leave me enough time to rinse off and chill for a little until Tatyana gets home to help me pick an outfit for dinner with Kurt.

Speaking of Kurt, my phone goes off as soon as I step into my apartment and a quick check shows a new text from Kurt.

**Kurt: Still expecting me at 7?**

I smile and shut my apartment door behind me then set my bag down on the counter before responding to him.

**Juliana: Yes sir, I'll be ready.**

He responds right away.

**Kurt: I just stepped out of a meeting but it shouldn't be too much longer. I will text you when I'm headed your way.**

**Juliana: Sounds good :)**

I set my phone on the counter next to my bag then head down the hall to my bedroom to strip and grab my towel. The shower is hot and steaming up the bathroom. I grab my hair cap, not needing to wash my hair since I did this morning. I start relaxing before I even step into the shower. The steamy room relaxes my muscles then I step into the stream letting the hot water pour over my shoulders.

I took a little bit longer in the shower than I originally planned but I needed to relax after work. Tatyana should be getting off work now, I check the time again and see that it is after 6 so Tatyana might be headed home already. That would be great because I am starting to freak out. This is my first evening date with Kurt. And yes, I have officially given in to thinking this is a date. Because technically it would be a date if this relationship was real. So I should just think of it as a date, just in case anyone runs into us out together.

"Juliana!" Tatyana shouts then I hear the apartment door slam shut. "I rushed home so we could have enough time to get ready."

"Yikes, I hope you didn't speed too badly."

Tatyana waves her hand dismissing the idea. "I'm here now, aren't I? Okay so any ideas for your outfit?"

We set out outfits on my bed and change our minds multiple times before finding the best one. I'm pulling on my jeans when my phone notifies me of a new text.

"Will you check that for me? I think it's probably Kurt."

"Got you," Tatyana responds and grabs my phone while I finish dressing. "Yep. It is Kurt, he says he's on his way."

"Okay, text back that I'll meet him in the lobby when he gets here."

"You don't want him to come up? Trying to keep me away from him? Hmm, I see you."

I laugh and give her a look. "Okay fine, he usually likes to walk me back here afterwards so tonight I will let him. I'll invite him in and then you can talk to him. But be easy on him"

"Hey, he's a lawyer. He should be able to handle it." Tatyana puts my phone away in my bag and hands it to me.

"Okay, I'll see you later."

"Sounds good. I will be waiting up. No matter how late you are." Tatyana says, narrowing her eyes, looking at me threatening a bit.

"We won't be too late. I wouldn't think so anyway. I should head down." I leave our apartment and head down the stairs.

# Chapter 17
## *Juliana*

When I reach the lobby, I see Kurt standing near the front desk area and talking to James once again. This time, his little doggy, Roger, is with him.

"Hi, James," I greet him first then stoop to greet Roger, earning myself full body wiggles and lots of kisses from the sweet dog.

James chuckles at his dog's reaction. "Good evening, Juliana."

"And hello, my fiancé." I smile cheerily at Kurt. When I come closer to him, I throw my arms around him. I am genuinely excited to see him but I'm also playing up the part a little. Kurt laughs and catches me in his arms.

"Hey, honey," Kurt says back to me before releasing me and leading me out of my building to his car. "How have you been?"

"Great! And I am so hungry right now."

"Good. The restaurant is about 15 minutes away, hope that isn't too far?" Kurt teases me and I love how easily we slide into this pattern of playful teasing.

"Hm, maybe. But as long as the food is good, I think I can forgive you." I smile at him as we get in the car.

Kurt gets us to the restaurant in under 15 minutes since most of the traffic has died down. We chat smoothly during the whole ride and before I know it we are pulling into the cafe parking lot. I admire the cafe on the walk to the front door and take in the crowd of people inside. There aren't too many people but it seems like a popular place for a Wednesday night.

I'm surprised I haven't been here before. Though I suppose I do have my favorite restaurants that I tend to stick to. But this place looks cute so I am excited to try it out.

Once we are seated at a table along the front window, we place our order, and our waitress brings us a basket of bread. I munch on the bread and Kurt pulls out his phone, opens his calendar and scrolls through it, getting right down to business.

"Okay, so the engagement party is now at my parent's lake house. In a week and a half basically. I have no way of knowing how many people will be there but I am going to assume; family, church friends, anyone else we're close to." Kurt seems like he's going to continue talking but I interrupt him.

"Hey, do you remember that summer when your family had all of us church kids spend like a week at the lake house? That was crazy. I think I ate like five s'mores the first night but they were delicious." Kurt leans back in his seat, remembering that week.

"Oh yeah. Those s'mores were good. I can't believe you tried to skateboard for the very first time while eating one. That was not the brightest idea." The waitress returns with our food and I dig in, my stomach growling a bit at the amazing smell.

"Hey! They were so good, why would I put it down to roll down a hill. Although it was not fun getting chocolate and marshmallow rubbed into my cuts."

"That was not fun to clean up," Kurt comments before he takes another bite of his meal. "Well, it wasn't horrible. But you were not happy at all. Understandably so since you were a bit hurt."

"What? Oh my gosh. Yeah, you were the one who helped clean me up." I  smile up at Kurt and remember how he took care of me during that time. I'm sure I had tears running down my face and dirt all over me from the fall but I remember Kurt helping me remain calm while he cleaned all the dirt and s'mores off of me. "Also 'a bit hurt'? I had multiple injuries."

"Well, you were mostly covered in dirt and s'mores, you barely had any injuries. Just a few bumps and bruises. And yes I was the one who helped you. I was one of the oldest kids there and since it was my family's house I knew where the safety supplies were. Plus you really would not calm down for anyone else. I guess you had a soft spot for me even back then." Kurt teases me and I blush.

"No? Really? That is so embarrassing." I duck my head and busy myself with eating my delicious meal.

"Yeah, honestly, a couple of other people tried to calm you down and help you out but you were not interested. I stepped in and got you to calm down and we finally got your leg cleaned off." Kurt sits back and watches me and I can see he is amused by my embarrassment.

"Okay, okay, I remember that. No need to embarrass me further. Maybe you were just really good at getting crying girls to calm down... Hmm, that didn't sound right." Kurt belts out with laughter. "You know what I mean."

"Oh no, please elaborate. I would love to know what you meant by that." Kurt sets his silverware down, finished with his meal, and is intent on giving me his full attention.

"Ugh, fine. Fine, yes, you were definitely the best at calming me down. Everyone else was just sort of grabby and trying to make me stop crying whereas you let me cry and just talked to me through the pain and the embarrassment I felt." I set my fork down and look up at Kurt as the waitress comes over to collect our plates.

"Yeah, I did notice you were not a fan of people hanging over you and dwelling on what happened," Kurt speaks again when we're alone.

"Exactly, like I said, it was embarrassing. So I was grateful that you just helped me out physically and talked to me normally. Anyway, that was a long time ago." Refills for our drinks arrive at the table and although neither of us wants the dessert that's offered, we stay at the table longer, chatting with each other.

When the waitress returns with the check, she sets it closer to Kurt, who automatically picks it up.

"Oh, here let me pay. You paid for our coffee date the other day, let me get this one." I offer, reaching into my bag to find my wallet and credit card but Kurt waves me off.

"What kind of fiancée would I be if I didn't treat my 'future wife' to a dinner here and there?" Kurt smiles and hands his card and the check to the waitress, who I can see looks a little disappointed to hear Kurt call me his fiancée. I smile a bit.

"Well, thank you. Next meal is on me."

"I might just take you up on that offer." Kurt gets his card back, signs the check then we both stand up to leave.

"Are you free on Friday? I have dinner with my parents but I might need a pep talk beforehand if you're available to hang out earlier in the evening?"

We reach Kurt's car and he holds the door open for me. Before he shuts the door for me he responds. "Yeah, I just have a lunch meeting on Friday then a pretty light day, so I can take off early if you want to meet around 4?"

"Sure, that sounds good. I have the day off Friday so I'm free any time." Kurt nods and closes the door for me then walks around to the driver's side, getting in as well. "I really liked that coffee house you took me to last time, can we go there again?"

"Sure, I can come pick you up. I'm glad you liked the coffee place. It's one of my favorites." Kurt drives now 25 minutes back to my apartment. Traffic has picked up in the later hours of the evening for some reason. A lot of people are going out on Wednesday, I guess.

"Thanks for dinner and driving me back." Kurt pulls up to the front of my building and I hop out before he can exit the car, I lean back down and talk to him through the door. "I'll see you Friday."

"I'll text you if anything comes up to change the time."

"Sounds good. Bye." I shut the door and give a wave then turn to head into my building. I look back when I reach the door and Kurt is still idling, I pull open the door and wave once more. He waves back and then pulls out of the parking lot.

When I get the apartment door open, Tatyana is waiting for me inside the door. I jump a little when I see her right in front of me. My heart beats fast.

"Oh my gosh, T! You scared me." I move past her and into the kitchen to set down my purse.

"Sorry, I'm just so excited. Where's Kurt? I thought he was coming up. Oh, never mind! Tell me everything." Tatyana bounces alongside me.

"This isn't the first time we've hung out together, why are you so excited for this one?" I haul myself up on the counter and Tatyana hops up on the counter facing me.

"This is your first dinner date! Not just a coffee get-together but a long dinner-involved date. Don't get me wrong, I  am always excited to hear about your coffee dates but a dinner date? And that cute cafe? Wow. Tell me, did he pay?" Tatyana swings her legs, her heels hitting the cabinets.

"He did but," I say before she can interrupt. "I offered and I said the next meal is on me."

"Smart, show him you are his equal."

I groan and lean my head on the cabinets behind me. "I am definitely not his equal."

"True but don't let him know that." I lift my head and narrow my eyes at Tatyana. She grins at me. I shake my head and she just laughs. "Hey, I am teasing."

"I know I know, but let's be real, he is so much better than me. He's a great guy. We are going back to that coffee house on Friday."

"Don't you have dinner with your parents on Friday?" Tatyana stalls her kicking of the cabinets. She eyes me.

"Yes, Kurt and I are going to hang out earlier in the day. I told him I might need a pep talk before seeing my parents." A yawn escapes my mouth and I blink, starting to get sleepy.

"Ooo, getting a pep talk from your man now? I guess you've replaced me." Tatyana smiles and wiggles her eyebrows at me. Then she switches up her expression and puts her hand on her heart, making a sad face as well. "I am so offended."

"Oh shush, but you know, now I need you for pep talks when going to hang out with Kurt," I reassure her and hop off the counter and pat her leg.

"Even better. Boy talk is still stressful but much more fun." Tatyana hops off the counter after me and we both head down the hallway to our bedrooms. We disappear into our own rooms for a few minutes then reemerge and enter the bathroom together to get washed up for bed.

"So how is the fake fiancé bit going for you two?" Tatyana asks while brushing her teeth.

"I told you about his parents planning our engagement party, right? Crazy. But it's going to be at his parent's lake house and we got to talking about the lake house this evening." I lean my hip against the counter, brushing my own teeth and keeping out of Tatyana's way. We take turns spitting then go back to brushing. "We actually have a couple of memories. Good memories. Well mostly good. I did hurt myself at his parent's lake house but our interaction was good." I chuckle and Tatyana gives me a weird look. "What? It was just good to reminisce about old memories. We completely forgot to discuss our current situation." I blush at the thought, mostly embarrassed we forgot the goal of the dinner.

"Mhm, see? It was a real date." I ignore her and finish getting washed up for bed. Tatyana finished close behind me. We both head back to our rooms. Tatyana stops before she shuts her door, she leans out into the hallway. "Goodnight future Mrs. Michaels."

I can't keep myself from smiling but I roll my eyes letting her know she is ridiculous.

"Goodnight, T."

# Chapter 18
## *Juliana*

When Friday rolls around Kurt sends a text later in the day asking if I am okay to meet him at the coffee house as he is running late from work. I sent him back a quick text letting him know that it was fine and asking what he wanted from the coffee place.

It's a nice day out and the coffee house we've been frequenting is only a couple blocks away so I decide to take my time and enjoy walking today. I get to the coffee house pretty quickly and order for myself and read Kurt's text to order him the correct items.

Kurt arrives shortly after I order and I meet him at the counter as my name is called to pick up our things. "Hey there," Kurt says as he slides up to the counter and grabs our pastry items while I take our drinks.

"Hi, Kurt," I smile in greeting. We find a table and set our things down.

"Thank you for this." Kurt lifts his cup to me before taking a long sip.

"Of course, no problem. Not technically the same level as Wednesday's dinner so start looking forward to another dinner date, on me this time. Any update on the engagement party?" I ask quickly, trying to gloss over my mentioning a date. Kurt sighs, leaning back and stretching his back out on the chair. "Oh sorry, did you have a long day?"

"Technically no, it was a very short day." I sit quietly in case he wants to say more, he does. "The case I'm working on took a turn and new information came to light today actually."

"Oh, I'm sorry. We could have rescheduled, Kurt. I would have understood, do you need to leave now, go back to work?" I start overthinking.

Kurt sits up straight and takes another drink from his coffee then starts on his pastry. I narrow my eyes at him, annoyed that he chose to eat first rather than respond to me. I cross my arms and he looks up at me laughing at my displeased expression.

"Sorry, no. It's fine. Nothing is going to change today. There is nothing I can do at the moment. This actually helps take my mind off work. So again, thank you." Kurt lifts his coffee again but he cheers me this time.

"Glad I could help." I lift my cup in return and take a sip when he does.

"So I realized that we hadn't figured out our story for how we started dating." Kurt settles in and starts eating his pastry.

"Oh, yes! Wednesday night wasn't very productive in that regard." I shift in my seat, sitting up straighter, intrigued. "Do you have a story in mind?"

"Well, I think we should keep the story simple." Kurt sets his fork down to lay out the story for me. "We just tell people that we went out to lunch after church one day, spent hours talking, decided to meet up again, and it just kind of progressed from there."

I nod in agreement, taking in the story. "Simple, but plausible. Wait but how do we explain getting engaged so quickly? I mean, I was just in a relationship not even six months ago and you were with Ashley until very recently."

"Right," Kurt says, pondering the question. "Ok, so we just decided we knew what we wanted. We'd both been in relationships that weren't going anywhere. We grew closer, as friends, and one day realized it was more than a friendship. And at that point, we both confessed our love and I proposed."

"Are people actually going to believe this?" Sighing, I sit back, lift my cup, and swirl it, giving myself something to do with my hands.

"I think so. But to be safe, don't offer any information unless directly asked."

"Smart. Such a lawyer thing to say." I chuckle and Kurt shakes his head with a smile. I sip my drink. "Okay, great! We have our story down. Oh no wait, people are going to ask how you proposed."

"We'll just say that when we made our confessions of love, I proposed in the spur of the moment. Nothing too extravagant but it felt right. Does that sound okay?" Kurt studies my face and I smile at him. He smiles back at me and we both end up laughing. Creating our fake relationship is so silly.

"Yes," I say after we stop laughing and I've caught my breath. "That sounds good. Should be easy to remember and hard to mess up. But we'll see."

After a couple of hours of discussing how to address our new relationship or engagement with others, we decide to meet up again another night just to hang out, and spend some time together. I really enjoy spending time with him. I check my phone and see by the time that I am cutting it close to dinner with my family.

"Kurt, I should head back to my apartment. I have to get ready for family dinner." I chuckle and Kurt nods.

"Let me give you a ride," He stands up and waits for me to get up as well before we head back to his car. I don't bother arguing with him and instead accept his offer of a ride.

When I am settled in his car, I lean my head back on the headrest and close my eyes. I am exhausted but I know I need my energy for this evening.

"You okay?" Kurt asks, turning down the radio so we can hear each other speak. I don't open my eyes but I can feel him casting glances my way. I let a yawn escape my mouth and Kurt chuckles. "Long day?" He pokes fun at my earlier comment. Even though he's turned back to look at the road and can't see it, I roll my eyes but also let a small smile appear on my lips.

"Oh, not really. But yes, I am okay." I keep my eyes closed until I feel the familiar bump when entering the parking lot of my apartment. I slowly open my eyes and rub at them a little, trying to chase away the sleepiness. "Thanks for driving me home."

"Hey, no problem, it's what any good man would do when taking his fiancé out." Kurt smiles at me, his eyes sparkling. I shake my head but smile as well. We might as well have fun with the situation that we are in.

"And what a great fiancé you are, my dear," I respond, then hop out of the car before he can get out, I wave him off. "I've got to go, no need to walk me inside tonight. Text me when you want to meet up again."

"Sounds good, have a good time with your parents tonight." Kurt leans over the passenger seat so he can still see me while he talks.

"Oh, I will," I say with a little laugh then give a quick wave and run into my apartment building. I look back when the door shuts and see Kurt just pulling away. If he doesn't walk me to the door, then he at least waits for me to get inside the building. It's very sweet of him.

The apartment is empty when I arrive. Tatyana must still be at work or out with Mike. I change into a plain white t-shirt and throw on a cute, knee-length denim skirt. I freshen up quickly as well then head back down to the parking lot to get into my car. I plug my phone in to play music and to charge it because it didn't get a lot of charge while I was changing. Then I back out of my spot and head out onto the road towards my parents' house.

# Chapter 19
## *Juliana*

When I pull up to my parent's house, I idle in the driveway, looking up at the house. I can see my mother inside preparing the table and my dad sitting on the edge of his seat, probably watching some sports game. I smile and get out of the car, turning it off then locking it and walking up to the front door. I have a key but I open the screen door and knock on the front door to be polite. I know my mother will be busy so she'll ask my dad to answer it. He does.

"Juli!" He says, happy to see me.

"Hi, Daddy," I say and forward to embrace my dad. He hugs me back tightly and then lets me into the house, shutting and locking the door behind me.

"How are you?" He asks as we make our way into the living room. He sits back in his chair, the TV on mute but I can see him check the scores before he turns back to me. I smile at him, I love him very much. He's always been the quieter one in my family. Supporting me through everything.

Although I may have done some things he did not like, he has always been there for me.

I sit back on the couch and sigh. "I'm okay. How have you been?" I ask, redirecting the conversation to him. "How has work been?" My dad works as the Director of Technology at a large company. With many team members under him, his job keeps him busy.

"I had a busy day today. A lot of meetings. I had to give two presentations today and we were the only group who used PowerPoint to present." I laugh, finding it funny that the tech group was the only group to use technology while presenting. The other presentations must have been very boring, I think to myself, but I guess it's good the tech group knew what they were doing.

We talk for a little while longer then he pauses and pats my arm. "You should go talk to your mother." I chuckle and nod then stand up and make my way into the kitchen, surprised she hadn't sought me out to talk about Kurt. She must be trying to restrain herself.

"Hello, Mother," I say, guarding myself and standing at the edge of the kitchen. She has her back to me but I know she heard me.

"Juliana," she says, formally, keeping up my awkward interaction. "It's good to see you. I've almost finished dinner. Would you please cut up the celery and tomatoes?" She asks but it's more of a request. I set down my things at the breakfast table then wash my hands before grabbing a smaller knife and cutting the celery first then slicing the tomato after I wash the knife.

My mother is quiet for a few minutes but I want to get this over with so I bring it up first. "Mom," I say. "about Kurt..." I begin then pause and wait for her to react.

"Yes, I was waiting for you to mention that. How come you didn't tell me sooner?" She turns on me and comes at me asking a million questions and not giving me any time to answer a single one. I continue slicing the tomato while she asks questions to her heart's content. Once I finish slicing the tomato, I wash off the knife and put it in the dishwasher. I then dump the tomatoes into the salad bowl and cut the celery in the bowl with the chicken. All while my mother is still asking questions. I try to hide my smile of amusement.

Finally, when she stops for a moment to breathe, I take my chance and answer a few of her many questions. "Yes, Kurt and I are engaged. I hadn't had the chance to tell you yet and wanted to tell you in person but then you kept calling before I could come see you and Daddy and so I am sorry you heard about it over the phone. Well, you heard it from Callum first, which, Mother, is completely disturbing. He had no right to contact you." I stop and calm myself before I explode. I begin mixing the celery into the chicken and mayonnaise to give myself something to do. "Kurt's mother has arranged for us to have an engagement party tomorrow night at their lake house. You and Daddy are, of course, invited."

She brightens at all of the news and is suddenly happy once again. "Well, I am just so excited for the two of you. I was very hurt to hear it from your ex, which I agree was weird. I have since blocked his number," she tells me and I nod and smile in appreciation. "But I have always adored

Kurt. He is so polite. His family is quite proper, you know. You'll have to shape up if you expect them to accept you into their family."

"Gee Mom, thanks so much for that." I roll my eyes and brush the insult away. Mom reaches over and squeezes my arm, giving me a loving smile and a laugh. I shake my head but smile and grab the salad bowl and the bowl of chicken salad and make my way to the table. My mother follows behind me with potato salad and fruit salad. I smile thinking about our 'Salads Nights'. We try to make every salad imaginable. Well, the ones we will eat. Which includes; chicken salad, potato salad, fruit salad, and actual salad with iceberg lettuce. Tonight does not include my Mom's delicious taco salad though. That dish has its own night.

We set the food on the table then I go into the living room. "Dad? Dinner's ready." He nods and gets up, his eyes still on the game then he mutes it again, and pulls his eyes away, following me into the dining room.

Once we sit down and fill our plates, my dad begins the conversation. "Oh hey, your mother told me about you and Kurt, congratulations. Are you happy?" He looks at me, searching my face to find my real emotions. I smile.

"Yeah, I am. He's a great guy." I say and start to eat so I don't have to say much else. My dad watches me for a second but then starts eating and to keep the conversation civil, he tells us more about his presentation.

Halfway through dinner, my mother brought up the party tomorrow and suddenly, I am nervous again. Luckily, I make it through dinner without too many more questions and I leave my parents' house in one piece. As I drive back to my apartment, I realize how exhausted I am and know I am going to sleep like a rock when my head hits the pillow.

# Chapter 20
## *Juliana*

On the day of our engagement party, I am stressed beyond belief. I pick up my phone and call Kurt for the third time. He answers after the first ring and he doesn't waste time with formalities.

"Stop worrying." He says automatically and I sigh, feeling better just hearing his voice. "It will be fine. And no, it isn't a dressy evening. I'm coming over now. I'll be there in about ten minutes. Okay?" He always seems to know what to say so I nod, then realize he can't see me.

"Yes, okay. You can come up when you get here." He responds again telling me not to worry and that he'll see me soon then he hangs up. I sit back on my bed and let out a breath.

After very little convincing, Tatyana agreed to come to the party for moral support. She and Mike had plans before the party so Tatyana is already out of the apartment, leaving me alone to freak out. Before she left though, she gave me a little "pep talk". This "pep talk" mostly included her telling me that

Kurt was cute and I should have a little fun. It wasn't very helpful but her teasing made me feel a little more relaxed. But now, I was alone, sitting on my bed, my hair dripping wet from my shower and nothing on but a shower towel. And I was back to freaking out.

I get up off my bed and start pacing the room. After about two laps around the room, I remember how stupid this is. I don't even like pacing, it has never helped me solve anything. Sighing, I go out to the living room, I go to the door and unlock it so Kurt can get in easily then I throw myself onto the couch. I grunt when I land then I reach for the remote, turning the TV on and trying to distract myself.

I'm flipping through channels when I hear a knock on my door. "Come in!" I yell and I hear the door open but I'm too lazy to look up. I should not have unlocked the door because the next thing I know, there are fingertips lightly trailing down my leg. I jerk away from them and jump up off the couch, knowing Kurt would not be that forward with me.

"Callum! What are you doing here? How did you get in?" I ask then realize how stupid I am. "Why are you here?" I step away from him, very aware of the fact that I am not wearing anything except my shower towel. I was so stressed and nervous for tonight that I decided not to get dressed before lounging, waiting for Kurt to help me decide what to wear.

"Just checking in on you, love." He says, trying to sound innocent but he smirks as he rakes his eyes up and down my body. I take another step back and grab a blanket off the couch, wrapping it around myself.

"You need to leave," I state firmly, my voice not wavering for a second. Hey, maybe I am getting stronger.

Callum just takes a step closer. "Why? You're my girl. No one else would want you." I'm more than a little offended by that comment and am about to respond when I hear another voice.

"Actually, that isn't true. I want her. I asked her to marry me. And she said yes. So, she is no longer yours. And I agree with her when she says, you need to leave. Now," Kurt says as he comes to stand by my side, wrapping his arm around me and pulling me against him. I'm surprised by his gutsy behavior but also very grateful for his timing.

Callum doesn't say a word but he glares at both of us and at Kurt's arm around my waist, then he turns around and stalks out of the apartment. Once the door slams shut behind him, I let out a breath of relief and sag against Kurt. His arm tightens around me.

"Are you okay? How long had he been here?" I laugh a little because he has picked up my habit of asking multiple questions without pausing to hear the answers or even breathe. "Why are you laughing? This is getting serious. This is the second time he has come into your apartment. Did he hurt you?" I can tell he is going to continue asking questions so I cut him off by pulling away from him.

"No, I'm fine. You got here just a minute or so after he did." I refold the blanket and set it over the back of the couch. I look up and see Kurt staring at me. "What?"

"Sorry, you're…you're not dressed."

"Oh, yes, sorry. I didn't know what to wear and you said you were coming over so I decided to wait so you could help me." I laugh, realizing how silly that sounds. "Sorry," I apologize again. "I'll go get ready." I step back and look at his outfit choice. Dark jeans, a light blue, collared shirt, and of course, his cowboy boots. Cute. I have the perfect outfit to make us look like the perfect couple. I think about it again and decide against it. I don't want to make it look like we are trying too hard.

# Chapter 21
## *Juliana*

We arrive at the lake house owned by the Michaels and there are a lot of cars outside lining the edge of the driveway. I nervously tug at the flowy dress that I found in the back of my closet with the tags still on. It's white with a colorful pattern over my chest, with long sleeves and a short skirt. I too decided to wear my cowboy boots but mostly because they look amazing with my dress.

Kurt comes around to my door and opens it for me. "You ready?" He asks. And I nod, finding it hard to speak as I get out of the car. He smiles then slips his hand into mine and gives it a quick squeeze. Then he tries to tug me along to enter the party but I stop short.

"Are you sure we can't just ditch?" I ask desperately, sounding like a child, which makes him laugh. He tugs me along and I come with him reluctantly. "Fine," I grumble. He hushes me which makes me laugh then the door flies open and Tatyana appears in the doorway.

"About damn time you showed up." She grabs my hand and gives me a miserable look. She tugs me inside and I lose Kurt in the crowd. "I've been here for hours. Where the hell have you been? I'm only here for moral support. Mike is actually loving this. I have no idea why." She stops to breathe then lets out an, "Ugh."

"The party just started like ten minutes ago. You have not been here for 'hours'." She gives me another look and I shut up but smile. "Thank you for coming." I lean in to talk quieter and make sure she is the only one who hears. "I don't know how I can do this. Everyone is so happy and excited for us. I just feel like a giant liar and it sucks." Tatyana nods along and loops her arm through mine. She offers me a glass of champagne but I shake my head and she drinks the whole thing easily then reaches for another one.

"You're fine. He agreed to this, didn't he?" I nod and she continues. "So, he knows the consequences, okay? Now man up, there are a lot of people here who want to talk to you. To congratulate you." I groan but she keeps me walking and soon she lets go of my arm and I lose her in the crowd.

"Juliana? Is that you, dear?" I turn around and see Mrs. Michaels coming toward me. I smile, genuinely happy to see her and she pulls me into a hug.

"Hi, Mrs. Michaels. How are you?" I hug her back and she squeezes me.

"I'm so happy for you two, dear." I smile at the way she always calls me dear. She is very motherly to everyone. Speaking of mothers, I spot mine making her way toward us with a pleasant yet strained smile plastered on her face.

I give her a look and she nods at me, telling me that she plans to keep her promise from last night. I sigh in relief then turn back to Mrs. Michaels. "I am so sorry we didn't tell you sooner." I'm about to continue apologizing but she smiles and waves it away.

"Oh, no. It's fine. I understand, you two just wanted a little time to enjoy it before all of this." She waves around at the party and chuckles. I nod, accepting her reasoning. She holds onto my hands squeezing them in her hands. My mother and Mrs. Michaels continue to talk for a few minutes and I start to feel at ease.

After about half an hour of mingling, Mrs. Michaels announces that we should all make our way out onto the deck. I walk outside and look around for someone I know. I don't see anyone other than church acquaintances so I go and pick up a slice of watermelon and eat it while I look around. Eventually, my eyes land on Kurt and I smile and start to make my way over to him but I stop when I see him talking to Ashley. What is she doing here? I slowly make my way over to them, staying hidden behind clusters of people, trying to get close enough to hear them. What am I doing? Their conversation is none of my business. I straighten up and look around for Tatyana.

Before I can find her, Mrs. Michaels steps in front of everybody and begins talking. "Hello, everyone. Thank you all so much for coming out tonight. We asked you all here so two people very close to us can share their special announcement." She turns to me and smiles warmly, then she smiles at the person to my right and I turn to find Kurt next to me. He smiles down at me and takes my hand leading me to stand next to his mother.

Kurt pulls me against his side and whispers in my ear. "Don't act too surprised." I look up at him in confusion. He just grins at me then turns to face the eager crowd.

"Hi, everyone. Thank you for coming out this evening. Juliana and I wanted to share our special announcement with everyone. Juli and I," he pauses for dramatic effect, "are engaged, to be married." He smiles out at everyone as they cheer and holler. He waits for them to quiet down and then he continues. "When I proposed, neither of us had really expected it to happen right then but I knew in that moment that I wanted to spend the rest of my life with her." He smiles down at me and I blush a little but hold eye contact with him, trying to act like I'm in on the story. "When I proposed, I was not well prepared. So, in front of all our friends and family," he says as he gets down on one knee in front of me, taking my hands in his. "Juliana Louisa Johnson," I wince at my full name and this makes him laugh, smiling more as he lets go of one of my hands and pulls a small box out of his pocket. I tilt my head in confusion, my eyes growing wide as I look at the box and then look at him. His eyes twinkle, he's enjoying this too much. "Will you officially accept my proposal of marriage?" He squints his eyes, thinking about the odd phrasing of his question and it makes me laugh.

"Of course!" I say enthusiastically and let him slip the ring onto my finger then I throw my arms around him as he stands up. He lifts me in a hug while everyone cheers. I flick his neck and he laughs at my annoyance. "Where the hell did that come from?" I whisper to him. He just smiles and sets me down then holds up my hand for everyone to see. I take the time to look at the ring and am shocked about how big it is. "Damn," I say to myself quietly but apparently not quiet enough and Kurt gives me an amused look. I blush, "Sorry, it's…it's very big." He laughs at my surprise and then we are surrounded by family and friends congratulating us and wanting to see the ring.

Eventually, I make my way back into the house, excusing myself and locking myself in the bathroom. I splash water on my face and lean against the counter, looking in the mirror. "Okay, pull yourself together. The party is almost over." I pause, lift my hand, and stare at the ring. "Damn," I say again. This thing was freaking huge. I hear a knock on the door and I call out, "Just a minute!"

"It's me. Open the door." I sigh and relax a little when I hear Tatyana's voice. I open the door and let her in. She shuts the door behind her and crosses her arms giving me a look.

"What?" I ask, going over to sit on the edge of the bathtub. She rolls her eyes and comes over, flipping the lid of the toilet down and sitting on it, leaning back.

"He likes you." She states, staring at me.

"No," I say, "he doesn't. He was just doing that for show." I pause and she's silent, still watching me. "I saw him talking to Ashley." Her expression changes because I had told her about Ashley and Kurt. "Yeah, I didn't know what to do. I was going to try to listen in on their conversation but then I thought, I'm not that crazy. Yet." I sigh and shift then slip and fall into the tub. Tatyana jumps up to help me but I start laughing so she laughs too and grabs my arm and pulls me out but we both slip and she falls into the tub next to me. We both start laughing and someone knocks on the door.

"Are you okay in there?" We both try to stifle our laughs and I shush her while I try to respond.

"Yes, I'm okay. I'll be out in a minute." I laugh quietly and we both lay in the tub breathing heavily from laughing so hard. "Wow, this situation is so strange." She nods and leans her head back, letting out a sigh.

"Wanna ditch?"

"Yes," I answer immediately and we both wiggle around to get out of the bathtub. Tatyana grabs my wrist when we get out of the tub and she looks at the huge ring on my finger. She holds it up to the light to get a better look, making a dramatic show of it. I laugh and yank my hand away. "Yes, it's real. Trust me, I checked."

"Damn." She says and I laugh.

"Yeah, that's exactly what I said. Twice." I blow out a breath and brush a strand of hair out of my face. I look in the mirror again then over at Tatyana. "How do we get out of here without anyone seeing us?"

"I might have an idea. This is going to be fun."

# Chapter 22
## Juliana

"Go, go, go." I hear Tatyana and see her gesture dramatically, and I try not to laugh as I sneak my way out of the bathroom and down the hallway, popping into rooms when Tatyana gestures or talks loudly to draw attention to her and not to myself. I feel my phone vibrate and see a text from Tatyana.

Tatyana: **Go now!**

I smile and dash out into the hallway before I see Tatyana making wild gestures and I quickly duck into another room, bumping into somebody.

"Shoot, I am so sorry. I didn't see you there." I back up and hear a chuckle.

"It's okay. Where are you running off to?" I look up and see Kurt watching me with an amused smile.

I cross my arms over my chest giving him a look, trying to hide my embarrassment by acting annoyed. I don't answer his question and instead walk further into the room, looking around. "Is this your room?" I look at the twin bed in the corner and the shelves overflowing with books. It looks like a teen boy's room, a smart boy though, an intelligent and book-loving one.

He laughs nervously, "Yeah. Don't judge. My mom hasn't changed a thing since I moved out for college." He gestures around the room. "This is all from my teen years. More specifically, high school years."

I give him a look, smirking a little. "Cute," I comment and he laughs. I feel my phone vibrate again and I pull it out of my little purse.

Tatyana: **Coast is clear all the way to the door! Get out now!**

I look up from my phone and Kurt is watching me. I lift my phone and wave it a bit. "Escape plan."

"Ah," he nods. "Got room for one more?" He grins at me. I grin back and open the door peeking outside and Tatyana sees me and gestures for me to go now. I pop my head back into the room and gesture for Kurt to come closer. He stands next to me and I grab his hand.

"Ready?" I look at him and he nods. "Let's go." I open the door quietly and pull him out into the hallway then we race down the hall and out the front door. He follows me and we crouch behind Tatyana's car. The car unlocks and I open the door and climb in, sliding across the back seat to make room for Kurt.

"Keep your head down," I say quietly. Soon, I hear footsteps on the gravel road, approaching the car, and the front doors both open. I see Tatyana and Mike get in but they don't turn around.

"Are you in here?" She says, pretending to talk to Mike.

"Yes, and we have a stowaway," I say, mentioning Kurt.

"I owe you guys," he says. "That was fun." We all laugh and Tatyana pulls out of their long driveway. "You guys can come up now. I think we made it." Tatyana says as she finally pulls out of the driveway and Kurt and I sit up normally. I give a sigh of relief and look around.

"No offense to your parents and everyone there, but that was way too much." He laughs at my statement and nods, agreeing with me. "Oh no, what about your car?"

"I'll pick it up tomorrow." He says waving the thought away. I lean back feeling a bit guilty. I try to brush it away and I look out the window watching the trees go by and then watching the buildings when they start to appear.

"So…" Kurt says, hesitating.

"Oh, no. I've heard a 'so' like that before." Tatyana says from the front seat and I turn to face Kurt.

"What is it?" I ask, skeptically, narrowing my eyes at him.

"Somehow, my parents… well, they think or rather expect us, to… move in together." He finishes quickly and I hear a snort from the front seat. I groan and fall against the door, banging my head on the window. I rub my head and look out the window, taking a deep breath before allowing myself to talk.

"Why would they think that?" I ask calmly and I hear Tatyana's intake  of air and I know that she knows my calmness is not good. Kurt hears her intake of air and looks at her curiously but when she gives nothing in return he turns back to me.

"I honestly don't remember how they landed on that idea but they think cohabitating would be a great idea since we are moving so quickly, it would give us more time to see if we work… So, you should probably move in with me, soon." He says, casually. I snort.

"Oh, yeah, okay. Sounds good." My sarcastic response is met with silence. "Really? No one is backing me up on this? This is a stupid idea." I look at Tatyana and I catch her and Mike sharing a look. "What? Tatyana? What is it?"

"Well…he does have a point," Tatyana says, cautiously, looking in the rearview mirror at me. "You guys are engaged. Most people in your position would probably be living together at this point…" I roll my eyes. Really? "But then again, many couples wait until after they're married," Tatyana adds, seeing my displeasure.

"You don't have to totally move in. We could just move some of your stuff into my apartment and just make it look like you live there." He offers but it's not convincing me.

"No, absolutely not. No, I cannot move in with you. Not even falsely. That's too far." I complain and give Tatyana a look when she starts to object, so she keeps her mouth shut.

"Juli, you asked me for help. I think this is the best idea. It'll convince everyone that we are together." He emphasizes the word 'everyone' indicating Callum and I nod reluctantly.

"Fine. Fine. They think we are already living together?" I ask and he nods looking a bit embarrassed. "You have neighbors, right? Wouldn't they be a bit confused if suddenly you have a fiancé living with you? Who supposedly has been living with you for a while?"

"Yeah, I guess so. But they know Ashley has been in the building," I flinch internally at his mention of Ashley and I scold myself. "They don't know her, or her name really so maybe I can convince them that she was really you…" He trails off. "But we should invite them over and maybe my co-workers, to introduce you to them?" He says as a question.

"Okay," I agree. "If we are going to do this, that sounds okay." I look up at the quiet pair in the front seats. "This is crazy, isn't it?" Tatyana and Mike laugh.

"Yes, it definitely is," Mike responds and Tatyana reaches over and whacks him playfully.

"Don't listen to him. He is crazy, well, then he would know crazy when he sees it." She laughs and he grabs her hand, holding it on her leg and I smile at them. They are cute together and a little part of me envies their relationship. I look over at Kurt and see him too, smiling at their hands intertwined together.

"Okay, so we should have a get-together?" I ask to make sure that was the end plan. Everyone in the car agrees.

So, like that, we decided to host a housewarming party. We planned for the party for another hour before Kurt drove me home and over the next few days we got together and planned the party between work and sleep. Kurt has a steady job but often works longer hours if his caseload requires more time, so sometimes we can't get together until later in the evening.

After much discussion, we decided that for it to be more authentic and to plan the house party, I should stay at his apartment for a short period of time. I felt bad that I would be moving into his home for a while and that is why I started looking for a second job but Kurt is kind and tells me I didn't need to worry about paying for anything. I still feel guilty for putting him in this situation so I decide take on extra hours at work while searching for a new job and give my money wherever I can to help.

# Chapter 23
## *Juliana*

Move-in day finally arrives and I am a bundle of nerves. I was able to rope Tatyana and Mike into helping me pack up a few of my things to make it look like I had actually been living there for a little while. Kurt was at work while I moved in so I had time to make it look like our place.

"You don't think he'll be mad?" I ask and Tatyana laughs, Mike rolls his eyes.

"If I came home to this, I'd be mad," he responds and Tatyana grins happily.

"Yeah, but you would end up loving it. Just like Kurt will. It looks authentic. It's a little overwhelming but you two are still a newer couple so people will understand why he hasn't tried to tone you down yet." Tatyana laughs again and puts a floral pillow on the couch, arranging it with other similar colored pillows.

"He's going to be home soon." I look around the room nervously. "Are you sure he won't mind? I think it might be too much."

Mike shrugs. "Nah, it's fine." He turns to Tatyana. "You ready to go?"

She nods then pulls me into a hug. "The place looks great. Don't worry about it. Have fun."

"Wait, y'all are leaving me to deal with this all by myself?" They both laugh then Mike tugs her out the door and I pout as the door shuts behind them. I look around the room and twirl my fingers nervously. I make my way into the bedroom and put my suitcase in the back of the closet, folding a few of my smaller bags to fit inside the suitcase. While in the closet, I straighten out a few of my dresses and dress shirts. I hope I'm not taking up too much room.

I'm in the closet organizing my many shoes when I hear the door being unlocked. I stand up and make my way out of the closet and the bedroom, stopping to check my appearance in the mirror before walking into the living room. Kurt enters and he sees me and smiles.

"Hi honey, I'm home," Kurt says. I laugh, appreciating his sense of humor. He makes his way over to the kitchen, tosses his keys onto the counter, and puts his bag on a chair at the table. I watch as he goes and grabs a glass and makes himself some water. Then I wait as he looks around the room, taking everything in.

"Is it too much?" I ask nervously and I take in the room again. He takes a minute, studying the little changes. New couch pillows, a few decorations of mine on the walls, and some pictures placed here and there. "I put some of my things in the closet... I hope that's okay."

He nods, taking a sip from his glass before replying. "That's why I moved some of my things, to make room for yours. Just like an actual fiancé would have to do." He chuckles and I smile.

Suddenly, I get a little nervous and a bit embarrassed. "Oh gosh, I am so sorry. I should have had dinner made for when you got home or at least had it started. You've been at work all day, you must be starving. Well, I hope you ate lunch but still, that was a few hours ago so you're probably hungry again. Gosh, I'd really make a poor wife. Thank God you're not actually marrying me, right?" I laugh awkwardly, rambling to no end and he laughs alongside me and shakes his head.

"I figured we could just order a pizza and we can continue planning our party, keep your first night lowkey." I nod agreeing and go to get my computer to place an order. I sit on the couch to place the order, letting Kurt take the computer to add his toppings and any extras, and then I set my laptop aside and pull out a notebook. Kurt gives me a look. "Why do you have a notebook? You have your computer right next to you."

I shrug. "I like hand writing things when I can." He nods and I open my notebook and put the date on the top of the page. When I look up, Kurt is staring at me again. "Sorry, force of habit." He smiles and laughs at me which makes me roll my eyes. "Shut up. It's helpful sometimes." I huff and tuck my legs under me before leaning forward over my notebook. "Okay, so we already have the date for the party. You said you've got the band taken care of?" I tilt my head back to peer up at him. He nods.

"One of my friends made a suggestion so I booked them. Is that okay?" He asks, suddenly looking a little worried, but it makes me smile knowing he discussed me with his friends.

"Of course. I don't really know any bands. I probably would have just played music off of my phone and I don't really have any music so that would have been very lame." I laugh then quickly talk so he doesn't make fun of me. "Okay so, band? Check. Food? Actually, when I was moving my stuff in I saw a cute little deli down the street. I was thinking about asking them to make a platter or something. Like little sandwiches?"

"Yeah, that sounds good. My neighbors like to drink a lot, which you will notice soon, but I can get a few different bottles for the party. Any suggestions?" He opens the notes app on his phone and creates a new note as a reminder to get drinks, then he looks at me for my suggestions.

"Uhm, no, whatever you want should be fine," I answer politely because I have never had anything to drink so I wouldn't know what to suggest. "Okay, so food and drinks are covered too. This really isn't the type of party to decorate for so I guess we're good there. Did you reserve the community room?"

"Yes, the room is reserved for 3 hours and the sliding doors will be opened for guests to use the pool as well," Kurt tells me and I start to get excited.

"Ooo!" I clap. "A pool party? Tatyana is going to be so bummed she missed out." Kurt chuckles. Tatyana is taking a couple of days of vacation to join Mike on his work trip, so they won't be able to make the party.

"I added the deli to my notes as well. Should we get a variety of sandwiches?" Kurts asks as he scrolls through their website on his phone. "Also, I'll have them drop it off the day of the party so we don't have to worry about it."

"That sounds good, thanks. And yes, a variety of sandwiches is probably the best idea." I wait for him to finish and then he sets his phone down to give me his full attention. "Okay, we should go over our story again. Just to refresh." I clear my throat and sit back on the couch pulling a pillow into my lap.

"Okay," he says and he leans back in his chair. "We haven't been together for very long. But when you know, you know." He says and I laugh.

"I've heard that too much recently. Okay, so we knew. We were friends first and just fell in love. It was more of a spur-of-the-moment thing which is why you did a more official proposal at your parent's house." I take my pillow and give his chest a light whack. "That was incredibly embarrassing. I had no idea you were going to do that!" He leans back laughing, clearly amused that he surprised me.

"You looked terrified!" He continues to laugh so I whack him again but then I start laughing too.

"You're horrible!" I cry out laughing and I fall back onto the couch then I remember something I need to confirm and I shoot up from my relaxed position. "Oh my god! Is this ring real?" I thrust my hand out to show him the ring. Then I pull my hand back to look at the ring myself. I'm so busy staring at it that I almost don't hear when he starts talking.

"It's real." He says but doesn't say anything else. I stare at him and wait for an explanation but nothing comes. He smiles mysteriously then gets up to refill his water. I lean back and groan.

"Come on. Tell meeeee!" I whine, feeling comfortable around him. My whining makes him laugh but he just shakes his head.

"All I will say is that it is real. And that's it." He raises his glass to me and I roll my eyes.

"When we get divorced, I'm totally keeping this." I wiggle my fingers which makes him laugh more.

"I want a prenup." He threatens, teasingly.

"Nope!" I shout happily then we both start laughing.

# Chapter 24

*Kurt*

Our first night together at my apartment is going smoothly so far. We are chatting and laughing so much that I almost miss the call on my cell telling me the pizza guy is here and needs to be let up. I type in the code to let him up then go back to my conversation with Juliana.

"That was the pizza guy, he's on his way up now." I sit on the arm of the couch, not getting comfortable again since I know I'll have to get up soon to receive the pizza. "Thanks again for buying the pizza for dinner."

"Not a problem, it's the least I can do to say thank you for letting me move in and going through this whole fake fiancé thing with me. Also, as your fake fiancé, I should have had dinner waiting for you when you got home. Especially because I get off so early and I also like cooking. Sorry, dropped the ball there." Juliana rambles on and blushes once more, feeling embarrassed about the dinner again.

"Don't worry about it," I reassure her. "I assume you were too busy unpacking and making yourself at home." I loosely gesture around to all the new items she has added to my apartment. Juliana blushes again but I begin laughing and she looks up at me and notices that I am just teasing her. She smiles and laughs too.

"Hey, at least I didn't overrun your apartment with all of my pink, frilly things. And trust me, I have a lot of those." Juliana joins in on the joking.

"Oh, I believe you," I tell her as there is a knock on the door. "I'll get it." I get up off the arm of the couch and make my way to the door.

"Delivery for Juliana?" The pizza man asks when I open the door. It's strange hearing it but I nod and accept the boxes. "Have a good evening."

"Thanks, you too." I shut the door when he turns to walk away then bring the boxes into the kitchen. "How many things did you order?" I call out to Juliana. She leaves her perch on the couch and comes into the kitchen, looking at all the boxes.

"Hm," I watch her spread out the three boxes then I hand her a plate. She accepts and flips open the lids of each box. All three boxes are the same size. Smalls for all three items. "Well, we didn't agree on a pizza to share so I just ordered us our own pizza then I got dessert too!" Juliana smiles and flips open the third and final box. Inside is a delicious helping of cookie brownies. I reach in and grab one of those first.

"Mmm," I take a bite and let out my appreciation for the still-warm treat. "That's really good. I don't think I've had this before."

"I know, right? Glad I can introduce you to something so good. Although, I should be smacking your hand away and telling you to eat your dinner first, but it's been a stressful week so I think we deserve a little dessert first. And I'm not your momma." Juliana smiles at me and reaches for a smaller piece of the dessert. She takes a bite and savors it but she doesn't finish the whole piece. She sets it aside for later.

I laugh at the 'not your momma' comment then finish my piece of the cookie brownie before loading up my plate with a few pieces of the individual pizza she ordered for me."I guess next time I should just get a large pizza and we can do half your gross pizza and half my delicious pizza," Juliana comments dramatically.

"'Gross pizza'? Wooow." I grab my plate and some napkins and go to sit at the kitchen table.

"Oh yeah. Who even likes pineapple on pizza?" Juliana makes a face as she comes to sit with me at the table. I pick up a slice of pineapple off my pizza and pop it into my mouth.

"Delicious." I chew the pineapple before biting into my pizza.

"Ew." Juliana makes another face then starts in on her veggie pizza. "I really don't think pineapples are supposed to be warm. Room temperature I guess would be slightly acceptable. But who has ever heard of a hot fruit? That's just wrong." I laugh and continue eating my pizza.

"You make an excellent point about hot fruit but somehow pineapple on pizza just works." I smile at Juliana and she rolls her eyes and makes another grossed-out face but she doesn't comment on it again. "Also pie is full of hot fruit, most pies are fruit-related."

Juliana scrunches up her face, trying to think of an argument but then she sighs and her facial features relax. "Fine, I can accept warm fruits, but only in desserts. And definitely not with cheese."

I nod, relenting. "You know what, that's fair. I can understand that." I devour my piece of pizza and move on to the next one.

"Sooo, we should talk about sleeping arrangements." I look up from my next bite and raise my eyebrows at her. I pause before my next piece of pizza and sit back to listen. "I'm more than happy to sleep on the couch obviously since this is your apartment and I've put you in this position and now I am taking over your whole life basically."

"You don't think we can sleep in the same bed? I mean, it's a pretty big bed." I raise my eyebrows at her, joking.

"Well," she hesitates and sets down the slice of pizza she was eating. "I didn't want to assume that you were going to share the bed with me. Or would even be comfortable sharing with me."

"You are my fiancé after all, I would never let you sleep on the couch when the bed is perfectly big enough for the both of us." I take another bite of my pizza and wink at her playfully. Juliana blushes a bit but I see a smile at the edge of her mouth.

"Thank you, how very kind," she says bashfully.

***

~Juliana~

We sat around chatting and watching TV for an hour after dinner before Kurt told me he needs to work a little bit longer so I grab a book and sit beside him on the couch and read quietly while he works. As it grows later, I start to get nervous. I have had sleepovers before but not with Kurt and whenever I went over to Callum's apartment, I never stayed the night because I didn't want to get pressured into doing anything I wasn't ready for. I know I shouldn't be nervous because Kurt is nothing like Callum but that thought doesn't help calm my nerves.

"Hey, Kurt," I say quietly to get his attention but not bother him too much.

"Hm?" Kurt hums and drags his eyes away from his work in time to see me yawning. "Oh, you tired?"

"Yeah, I think I am going to get ready for bed," I tell him and he nods.

"I shouldn't be much longer but I will wait for you to get ready first," Kurt informs me, looking back at his work. He shuffles through some paperwork and I think he's finished talking so I set my book down and get up. I'm starting to walk away when he looks up again. "We can build a pillow wall between us if that would make you more comfortable."

The offer makes me chuckle. "A pillow wall?"

"Yeah, you know, a wall made of pillows," Kurt explains, looking a little embarrassed.

I nod and laugh some more. "Yeah, I know what it is." I clear my throat, trying to kill my laughter but Kurt's cheeks are red from embarrassment and it's making me giggle even more. "I'm sorry," I say between giggles. "We can definitely do that if that would be best for you."

"Well, no. I just thought it might make you feel better," Kurt offers, trying to cover up for himself. When I only giggle more he rolls his eyes and stands up, going into the bedroom. I follow along behind him to see what he's going to do. "Just for all the laughing, I am going to make the wall long and tall."

This sets me off in even more giggles, especially watching him pull back the covers and line up the pillows. I start handing him pillows to help him build it.

"See, aren't you glad I brought all these extra pillows when I moved in?" I tease and Kurt shakes his head at me but there is a smile on his face.

"Yeah, yeah, sure," Kurt grumbles as he finishes the wall.

"Beautiful," I comment when he stands back to admire his work.

"I agree. Now, go get ready for bed," Kurt tells me and I narrow my eyes at him.

"Wow, someone is bossy," I point out and put my hands on my hips, feeling my stubbornness kick in. "I don't think I knew that before we got engaged."

"Yeah, well, there is a lot we didn't learn about each other before getting engaged," Kurt says and I feel the tension in the room thickening. I was trying to make a joke but I realize it was distasteful. I know we hardly know anything about each other.

"Yeah, you're right." I look down at my feet. Kurt clears his throat and I look back up. "I should go shower," I say after a few seconds.

"Okay, I am going to finish up some work." Kurt gestures back to the living room and I nod then we go our separate ways.

When I am alone in the bathroom, I take a deep breath. This doesn't feel real. Everything is happening so fast but also feels so slow and I feel like I am starting to lose it. This whole situation is messed up and it is all my fault. I can't believe he would go along with everything to this degree. I can't see how this will end well for either of us. Kurt is just too good of a guy and I am ruining his life.

I turn to let the shower water hit my face, trying to clear my head a little but I start to get nervous again as I finish washing up in the shower. I finish showering and wrap my hair in a towel and then grab a robe to put on. I step into the bedroom and see the light still on in the living room so I quickly go to the closet to change into my pajamas. When I come out of the closet, Kurt is entering the room. He looks tired and stressed and I want to help him out but I know that I am probably the main cause of his stress, although I know his job has been rough lately too.

"Bathroom is all yours," I tell him and he nods but doesn't speak.

He disappears into the bathroom and I hesitantly climb into bed. I can tell which side is Kurt's by the nightstands so I climb into the opposite side and pull the covers up to my chin. I can't decide if I want to keep reading or pretend that I am already asleep to avoid any more awkward interactions. I'm tired, so I decide to turn off my light and turn over to have my back facing the wall of pillows.

Kurt comes back into the room a few minutes later and tries to be quiet as he goes about the room. He bangs into something and mumbles quietly. I turn over and see him hopping around a bit, his face pinched with pain. I giggle and he looks over at me, narrowing his eyes.

"Don't laugh. I stubbed my toe," Kurt explains and I gasp a little. "Yeah, ouch."

"You can turn on a light," I tell him but he just shrugs and drops onto the bed. He shuffles around in the bed a bit before getting comfortable.

"So, do you think we're ready for this housewarming party?" Kurt asks when it is clear neither of us can fall asleep.

"I think so," I say hesitantly. "We've discussed everything and just need to finalize the plans and make sure we can order from the deli for the sandwiches to arrive on time."

"It shouldn't be a problem," Kurt says and we fall back into a comfortable yet tension-filled silence. We both have work tomorrow so we need to sleep but the nervous energy is keeping me awake.

"Are you asleep?" I ask after a few minutes.

"Yeah," Kurt responds. When I don't say anything else, he chuckles. "Was there a point to that?"

"No, just checking."

"Goodnight, Juliana." Kurt shifts in the bed and I can feel him turning as the bed moves.

"Goodnight, Kurt," I say softly as I stare up at the ceiling, willing sleep to come.

# Chapter 25
## *Juliana*

Our party planning is quickly finalized and the party will begin at 3 p.m. on Saturday in two weeks. I hope it wasn't too late of notice but both Kurt and I agree that the sooner we have the party, the better. It still gives us enough time to settle into a working system for living together.

I offer to go door to door with Kurt to deliver each invitation to his neighbors but instead, Kurt said his doorman to hand out when he sees his neighbors or he will leave them in their mailboxes.

So, after sending out the invitations we just wait for the day to arrive. Over the next few days, we get a couple of notes left at the door accepting the invitations and we each are stopped by neighbors who accept the invitation in person. It is great for me because Kurt's neighbors stop me to introduce themselves and accept. It helps me get to know some of them before the party.

One of his neighbors, a nice woman named Evelyn, invites me over for tea. When she hears of my love for dogs, she is even more excited and tells me to come over whenever I want to see them.

While we wait for the day to arrive, it is easier and easier to live together. Over the week, it grows natural. By the second week, we have found a routine and I quite like having him as my roommate. I miss Tatyana of course but living with Kurt is a little different. Well, quite different actually.

With my job, I tend to be home before Kurt and I'm getting in the habit of making dinner for us each night. If Kurt finds he's getting off early, he calls me midday and to see if I want to eat out for dinner. I always take him up on the offer. I do enjoy cooking but it's always nice going out to eat. We explore different restaurants each time we go out. Some places give me new ideas for dinners, especially when I notice meals that Kurt really liked.

One night we have leftovers after dinner so Kurt and I went down the hall to visit Evelyn and her dogs. Evelyn is so grateful. She shoos Kurt out of the apartment to take her dogs for a short walk because she wants to spend some time talking to me. She asks questions about Kurt and myself so I'm able to put our story to the test again. She seems thrilled by the story and I highly enjoy telling her. The story feels more and more real these days. I do feel like Kurt and I are getting a closer and stronger friendship. But I have to keep myself from feeling more than that.

When Kurt came back from walking the dogs, Evelyn and I were giggling uncontrollably and Kurt walked in with a smile. The two big golden retrievers ran over to Evelyn and me. I happily received kisses from them then stood up to go.

"Thank you so much for bringing this over," Evelyn gestures to the containers of food sitting on the counter.

"Not a problem, Evelyn. I hope you like it." I smile and walk over to Kurt. He slides his arm around my waist and I lean against his side.

"It was delicious, so I'm sure you'll enjoy it." Kurt smiles down at me then smiles at Evelyn as well.

"I'm sure I will. Thank you for walking my boys, Kurt, and thank you for bringing Juliana to our community." I blush and give another smile. Evelyn winks at me. "She's much better than that last girl you had over."

"Evelyn!" I scold her in a teasing manner, then let out a laugh. Kurt looks embarrassed. I put my hand on his chest and give him a pat. I look up at him "Not that I disagree with you. Though it seems our boy's taste has gotten much better."

"Thanks for that, you two." Kurt rolls his eyes then starts to make his way towards the door. "And on that note, it's getting late so we should head back down the hall."

"Alright. So nice seeing you, Evelyn." I reach out and hug her. She gives me a tight squeeze before stepping back and hugging Kurt as well.

"I'll bring back the tupperware when I'm finished." Evelyn waves us off and shuts her apartment door behind us.

We walk back to the apartment with Kurt's arm still around my waist. We awkwardly bump hips as we walk and end up tripping over one another right as we reach the door. Our laughs echo down the hallway and we quickly shut the door behind us so we don't bother anyone with the noise.

# Chapter 26
## *Juliana*

After dinner most nights, we chill on the couch together. Some nights we chat while the TV is on but with the volume turned down low. Only a couple of times has Kurt brought work home and spread it out on the coffee table, tonight is one of those nights.

"You sure this is okay with you? I thought I could finish up at work but some information came in later in the day and I need to make sure this case goes well." Kurt explains as he sorts through the files on the coffee table. He stops and looks up at me to focus on me when I respond.

"Yeah, of course, it's fine. Why haven't you brought home your work more often? I thought that was something that happened more." I lean back on the couch and kick my legs up, spreading out since Kurt positioned himself on the floor.

"It kind of feels rude bringing work home while you're here. Like being on your phone while you have company. That sort of thing."

"Ah. Well, no, it is totally fine." I sit quietly behind him on the couch reading a book.

I like watching him work so I look at him every so often and a few times I catch him looking back at me. We smile each time we catch the other looking. I hope I don't distract him too much. I try to keep my eyes focused on my book but I can tell Kurt is starting to get stressed.

Kurt leans his head back, his hair brushing against my legs. He sighs softly, closing his eyes. I keep reading but automatically reach my free hand out and start rubbing his head, almost absentmindedly. He keeps his eyes closed for a few minutes and when I go to turn the page in my book, he sits up and gets back to work.

Once I've turned the page, I reach back out and start massaging his neck. He tilts his head forward a bit exposing more of his neck for me to reach. We sit together silently, me rubbing his neck, occasionally turning the pages while I read and Kurt sitting on the floor in front of me, preparing his argument for court.

After a while, my hand begins to cramp up so I roll my wrist a few times then go back to reading quietly beside him. I hear him clacking at his keyboard.

"Oh crap," Kurt says, turning back to face me. "Juliana?"

"Mm?" I look up from my book and give him a small smile then a yawn escapes my mouth.

"Yeah, exactly." Kurt laughs and gestures to my yawning. "It's late. We need to get to bed." Kurt shuts his laptop and stands up, stretching.

"What time is it?" I look around the apartment and realize we have a lot of lights on which is probably why neither of us noticed that it was getting late.

"Almost 2:30 in the morning." Kurt checks his watch to confirm then nods his head. "Come on, let's get some sleep."

Kurt lets me use the bathroom first to wash up and get ready for bed while he puts away his work and clears off the coffee table.

When he comes back into the bedroom, I've just exited the bathroom wearing a long t-shirt and my pajama shorts. I squeeze his arm as I offer the bathroom to him. I climb into his comfy bed and snuggle in.

"Hey, don't forget that the party is tomorrow," Kurt calls from the bathroom. I grunt and turn over to look at him standing in the light of the doorway, taking a minute to admire his physique.

"How could I forget?" I ask which makes him chuckle. "You ready for your neighbors, coworkers, and whoever else shows up to completely invade our private lives? Probably snoop around the apartment." I giggle.

"I fully expect some snooping," Kurt admits with a mouth full of toothpaste. "That's why you moved in, isn't it? But thankfully, most of the party will be out in the community room and pool."

I shrug and snuggle into the bed. I have come to love this mattress and the whole sheets set in general. Whenever I have to leave, I might take a set home with me.

I'm almost asleep, even though I left the light on for Kurt when he comes back into the room and gets into bed next to me. I shift over, away from him because I know I've kicked him in my sleep before, even breaking through the wall of pillow between us. He hasn't said anything but I am aware of my flying body parts.

"Juliana? Are you still awake?" Kurt asks softly a few seconds after turning the light off.

I turn over to face him and can see him through a gap in the pillows, the moonlight lighting up his face as it streams in through the top of the curtains. "Yes?" I answer quietly.

"Thanks for tonight." Kurt looks over at me and our eyes meet in the gap of the pillows. I can see something in his eyes but I'm tired and I don't want to try to figure it out tonight.

"What do you mean?" I yawn and close my eyes so I don't have to see the way he's looking at me. I feel him moving as he talks, his voice growing clearer.

"Just for being with me while I worked, and helping me when I got stressed. And for not being upset that I brought my work home with me." Opening my eyes, I see Kurt watching me, the pillow wall no longer between us. I smile and then narrow my eyes because he probably threw them all on the floor.

"Of course, not a problem. I enjoyed tonight. Now, shh. Bedtime. Night night." I speak in short sentences, tired and not wanting to address the absence of the pillows and what that means. I blink sleepily before giving up and letting my eyelids close.

"Goodnight Juli."

# Chapter 27
## *Juliana*

It's 2:30 p.m., the party begins at 3 and I am extremely nervous. We've prepared as best as we can but I'm still so scared. Kurt invited some of his work colleagues and a few of his neighbors. The neighbors worry me because I haven't been to Kurt's place many times before I moved in and even though they have seen me and talked to me in the hallway since then, I don't actually know what they think of me or our engagement. And I don't know for sure what he has told them about Ashley since she was here quite soon before I moved in.

"Are you okay?" A hand touches my shoulder and I flinch before I can stop myself. He removes his hand but continues watching me. I smile apologetically and look up at him nodding. "We can do this. Everyone loves parties, you don't have anything to worry about." He smiles down at me and I can see the worry in his eyes as well.

I let out a breath I didn't realize I was holding then I speak up. "Okay," I say, then tug my hair and look around the community room. "It looks good." He nods in agreement and

I hold my breath again as I hear the first buzz of the intercom. I watch as he walks over to the door and presses the intercom button but I shut off and continue to look around the community room as he talks to the guests through the intercom and props open the door for their arrival.

"You ready?" I nod my head and tug my hair again then let go as he reaches for my hands just as our first guests arrive. He squeezes my hand and then leads me over to introduce me.

The band is running a little late and my heart drops when I see them walk in. I must have made a noise of horror because a lot of people have turned to look at me. I see the lead singer smirking at me and I look over at Kurt and catch his eye, he gives me a confused look when he sees the color drain from my face but he hasn't seen Callum yet. I cough a little and apologize, "I'm so sorry, just a little sore throat." Then I excuse myself to get some water from the kitchen area of the community room. After I distance myself from the band and all the guests, I lean against the counter trying to breathe.

"What happened?" I hear and turn to face Kurt. His face shows a hint of annoyance written across it and I don't blame him. I can tell there is also some worry in his eyes but I'm not sure if it is just an act so we don't make even more of a scene. I was rude in front of his neighbors and coworkers. I should apologize again later but right now I just needed space to breathe.

I stand up straight and finish my water then fill my cup again. "You can have some wine, you know. Even the hostess is allowed to drink," Kurt teases me. I shake my head and sip from my cup again.

"I don't drink..." I say quietly because I have not told him that about me. I haven't told him a lot but then again, he hasn't shared all that much about himself either. He looks a little shocked but also impressed and it makes me smile a bit.

He nods his head, accepting this fact. "Should we go back out? There are a few more people I should probably introduce you to." He runs his hand over his head, a gesture I've noticed before. It seems to be an old habit from when he had longer hair. I try to think back to see if I can remember him with long hair but I can't and he doesn't have any pictures around his apartment that show him with long hair. I brush the idea away and pick up my half-empty cup of water. He offers me his hand, I take it and let him lead me over to other guests and after he introduces us, I apologize for my startled noise early, making excuses of a dry or sore throat. They laugh it off and keep chatting with me. The party seems to be going well and even a few guests have made their way to the pool.

After an hour or so, I am just starting to relax and enjoy myself when I hear the band strike up a new song. I've heard most of their songs before but this one is new. I continue talking to the assistant at Kurt's office but begin to hear the words of the song.

"He doesn't knoooow.." croons Callum, his voice filling the community room. "He doesn't knoooow... What he's getting into. She's a .. she's a .. PRUDE!!"

I gasp but cover my mouth in time and the loud music helps drown out my reaction. I get distracted from my conversation and pay attention to the lyrics. The band breaks into song again after a long guitar solo and Callum belts out the next verse, "Never could get her into bed. What's wrong with her head? She's such a tease because she will never please…. YOOOOU or anyone else for that matter!"

The horrid lyrics go on, talking about a girl who won't let her boyfriend do anything with her and how the one time he got her to give in to something, she wasn't very good at it and the rest of the song talks about how big of a disappointment she was and how no one will ever want someone who is such a prude.

About halfway through the song, I can't stand it anymore. I don't remember when I started crying but I hear a sob escape from my lips and I quickly stand up apologizing before pushing my way out of the community room and heading back to Kurt's apartment quickly. I make it to the far side of the bedroom before I collapse against the wall, slide to the floor, and hug my knees to my chest sobbing violently.

How could Callum do this to me? He knew I wasn't ready to go further in our relationship, I let him do all that I was comfortable with... I sob harder thinking back and remembering the night he broke up with me. It had been about a month of him trying to get me to have sex but I wasn't ready. One night he was angry and tried to convince me I should, then tried to force me but I put up a fight and eventually, he gave up. He called me many nasty words and told me no one would want someone who is such a prude and that I should be lucky he even tried. Then he left.

I bury my head further between my legs trying to cry silently. Wishing that this horrible day would end.

# Chapter 28
## *Kurt*

I've been talking with my neighbor for a couple of minutes and the band I hired is playing an inappropriate song about a girl that I can only assume he used to date. I feel so bad for his ex because this song is horrible. I look around the room and notice Juli is missing. I excuse myself and go over to my assistant, Cathleen, whom Juliana was last talking to, and ask where she went.

"I think I saw her heading toward your apartment. She just started crying and got up, excused herself, and ran off. I don't know why she started crying. We weren't talking about anything that would be upsetting..." Cathleen prattles on but I stop listening. I look up to see the lead singer smirking at me and he looks very familiar.

"Callum," I instantly curse myself. Why hadn't I been paying attention? She told me he was in a band. A friend of mine had recommended this band so I hadn't realized her ex was in it. I would have noticed he was here if I wasn't so busy talking to the neighbors and my coworkers. I hadn't really been listening to the song but it was something offensive and hurtful enough that it caused Juliana to run off crying. I excuse myself from Cathleen and she smiles telling me how much she likes Juliana and how happy she is for us. I smile back at her to be polite and say a quick thank you before hurrying off to my apartment.

I knock on the closed bedroom door and hear a muffled sobbing. "Juliana? Are you in there?" I know she is but if she chooses not to answer, I will know to leave her alone. Almost instantly, I hear a sad voice frantically apologizing.

"I'm so sorry," the sad little voice says between sobs and hiccups, "it was so rude of me to run off. I didn't mean to be so dramatic. I hope I didn't ruin the party..." She trails off and I open the door stepping inside and closing it behind me. My room isn't very large so I reach her in three strides and kneel beside her. I put one hand under her chin and tilt her head to look up at me. When she looks at me I see the sadness and pain filling her body. The pain I feel in my heart startles me and I debate letting go of her but seeing her this way makes me want to protect her.

"You didn't ruin anything," I say softly and I cradle her head in my hands. I brush her tears away before speaking again. "What's wrong?" I ask cautiously. I've pieced together some of the story but I need to hear it from her. I need to know why she is hurting so badly.

She sniffles a little and I let go of her face to grab her a tissue box then I sit down next to her. I sit quietly, letting her clean up and breathe a bit before I press further.

"That's Callum's band…" I nod encouraging her to continue, feeling like a complete idiot for not remembering it was his band. "That song… that song is about me. I have never had sex. I'm a virgin. I never felt comfortable doing a lot with him. The one sexual act that he talks about in the song, he guilted me into doing it. I didn't want to. So of course, I wasn't good at it. And then… and then he dumped me when I wouldn't do more with him." She seems to say this all in one breath and is breathing heavily as she stares at the wall across from us.

"Juli…" I say then stop, unsure of what needs to be said. It shocks me, her confession to me about being a virgin. I don't know why but I had just assumed she wasn't. I stay silent for a little while, still looking at her.

She turns to face me and quietly whispers, "Say something…" I can see the pain and worry in her eyes. The worry confuses me. What is she worried about? There are so many things running through my mind and I can still hear the band playing songs and our guests talking. I need to get rid of them. I stand up and see her eyes widen, scared. I squat down in front of her and rub my thumb over her cheek.

"Stay here," I say and my voice comes out sounding rough and strange. I wait for her to respond and when she nods, I stand up and exit the room.

# Chapter 29
## Kurt

I try to tamp down my fury as I walk back to the community room, but I grow angrier with each step. I walk up to Callum and grab him by the collar of his shirt. I lean in close to him and practically growl, "Get off this property, right now. Or I will not hesitate to call the police." He genuinely looks frightened for a second then he smirks.

"You invited me." His smirk grows, as he throws my own stupidity back in my face. "What? You didn't like the music?" With this last question, I lose it before I can stop myself, I step up and shove him. He stumbles backward, losing his balance, and falling directly into the pool. The room full of people gasps as some rush to see Callum climbing out of the pool, drenched. I take a step back, taking a few seconds to calm myself then I turn to face everyone.

"Thank you all for coming. I am so glad you all were able to finally meet Juliana, but I believe the party is over. You are all more than welcome to stay and enjoy the pool but I must excuse myself now. Thank you all for coming out," I add for good measure and my co-worker and friend Dave, nods at me and begins to usher people out of the community room. He leads the group by jumping into the pool fully clothed. This seems to lighten the mood and everyone gets back to having fun.

While Dave handles everyone else, I turn back to Callum who is being checked over by one of his bandmates, the same one who helped him the last time I hit him. Besides a bruised ego, he seems to be fine, but I notice he still has a bruise on his jaw from where I hit him last time. I smile a bit and admire my handy work for a second and am grateful none of the band equipment fell in the pool. That would have been messy and possibly a lawsuit.

"Get out. If I ever see you near my building again, I will tell my doorman to call the police officers, immediately." I threaten as I walk over to them, feeling my need to protect Juliana takeover. Callum sneers at me but his bandmates seem to think wiser of it and they scurry to pack up and leave the building. Callum and I stand about a foot from each other, glaring.

"You're not fooling me." I narrow my eyes even more at him when he opens his smug mouth, daring me to hit him again. "I know this isn't real. And I don't plan on keeping it to myself much longer." He threatens and I just roll my eyes.

"Good luck trying to prove your ridiculous idea," I say then my doorman, Marvin, appears, one of my neighbors having called him about the disturbance, and he escorts Callum out of the building.

"You alright, man?" Dave asks, looking at me from the community room kitchen where he has begun the cleanup. He's still dripping from the pool but has a towel around his waist.

"Yeah..." I stop a moment to calm down then join him, taking the trash bag away from him. "Thank you for your help, I've got it from here."

"Okay, let me know if you need anything. Hell of a party." He grins at me before making a swift exit. It gets a chuckle out of me then I sigh a breath of relief. Most of the guests are out at the pool so I finish cleaning up the community room and say a few goodbyes before heading back to my apartment, realizing that I'd left Juliana alone for quite a while.

When I make my way back to the bedroom, where I last saw Juliana, I find her packing up her things.

"Where are you going?" I ask and she jumps, not having heard me enter the apartment. I walk over to the bed where her suitcase is laying, half full.

She stops folding her things and looks at me, her eyes puffy from all her crying. "I can't stay. We can't keep doing this. I heard what happened out there. Your neighbors and co-workers probably think I'm a horrible influence on you, bringing such drama into your life..." She trails off, looking sadly out the window before she continues folding her things.

"Juliana, it's okay. They will understand. Everyone has had a crazy ex before. Besides, they're all out enjoying the pool right now, so it's not as if anyone's night has been ruined." I laugh airily, trying to lighten the mood and she smiles, grateful for the attempt. "You don't have to give up. If anything, tonight's disaster has made me realize that you were right for telling him we were engaged. He isn't going to leave you alone easily and I want to make sure when he does, he leaves for good." I stand up and put my hand over hers to make her stop her folding. "I know this has been hard for you, trust me, it isn't all that easy for me either," I say then instantly regret it when her eyes fill with tears again. "No, no don't cry. I didn't mean it like that. It certainly hasn't been easy but it's been fun. Hasn't it?"

She shrugs her shoulders. I sit on the bed and watch as she continues to fold her things. We remain in silence, the only noise being the ceiling fan and her bracelet jingling as she folds. I don't stop her at first then when she goes back to her dresser to get more clothing, I get up and take things out of her suitcase and go to put them away. She turns around and sees me and I think I see a small smile on her face.

"What are you doing?" I smile at her.

"Helping you unpack."

"Why? I shouldn't stay here anymore. Today was a disaster," she trails off but I've gotten her attention and she sits down on the bed, clutching a shirt in her hand. She looks so vulnerable right now. I walk over towards her and kneel down in front of her, lifting her chin to make her look at me.

"Juliana, look at me." I see a spark in her eyes and I hold back a smile knowing she is about to sass me.

"Well, I kind of have to look at you when you're grabbing my chin, don't I?" She blurts out without even thinking which makes me chuckle. She bites her lip blushing. "Sorry."

"Don't be. It's good to see you've still got some fight left in you. Even if it was directed at me." I let go of her chin and she smiles up at me but just slightly. "I don't entirely know what happened just now but I'm here if you want to talk about it... I don't like seeing you cry."

"I'm not a fan of crying, especially in front of other people." She stands up, calmer now, and wipes her face with the back of her hand. "Okay, I'm okay." She says, more to convince herself than me but I nod and take the shirt she has in her grasp. She releases it reluctantly then turns to grab more clothes out of her bag and replace them into the drawers.

It only takes a few minutes to unpack everything. Once we are finished, I take her bag, look her in the eyes, and place the bag on the very top shelf of the closet where she very much cannot reach it. She watches, her mouth hanging open a little and the edges curling up into a smile. She shakes her head in disbelief and rolls her eyes.

"Wow, that's cool. Sure, okay, okay. Mhm." She rambles on and I can tell she's enjoying herself and that she appreciates the gesture. I smile and shut the closet door.

"Do you want to go out and grab something to eat? I couldn't help noticing that you didn't eat anything at the party?" Once I mention food, her stomach makes a soft growling sound, she lets out a huff like she is upset at her stomach for betraying her. I know she was looking forward to the deli sandwiches but she never had a chance to grab one.

"Yes, I guess I am hungry. Can't deny that."

"I've heard worse," I joke, winking at her before grabbing my wallet off of my dresser. "I'll leave the room in case you need to do anything to get ready. I'll meet you out front?" I ask. She nods and smiles as a thank you so I exit and shut the door behind me, going out front to give her some space.

"Did you clean up already? I didn't think I took that long." Juliana says as she finds me near the community room. Looking over my shoulder, I take in the outfit change, a bright yellow T-shirt and flared jeans that look like something my mom would wear. Oddly, the look on her brings a smile to my face.

"Ah, no," I say, bringing myself back to looking at the community room. "Our guests were pretty clean. Dave, from my work, also helped clean up a little before he left."

"Oh, well that's nice of him."

"Yeah, he's a good guy." I offer my hand and Juliana takes it and we head out to my car.

# Chapter 30
## *Kurt*

"I was thinking," I start as I lock the car after we get out. "Dave mentioned that his wife had talked about us coming over for dinner at their house. We don't have to if that would make you uncomfortable, but it might be nice to make friends as a couple."

"Couple of friends," she smiles. I roll my eyes, trying to pretend I thought her comment was funny. Instead, I watch as she tugs at the hem of her shirt as it rides up exposing her lower belly as she walks and I feel something stirring in my stomach. I shouldn't be looking at her like that. She shifts a bit when I don't respond to her play on words. "Sure, that sounds fun."

"Great, I'll let him know we are available whenever they want." She nods and then stumbles as we make our way down the street. The parking isn't so great around here so I had to park a couple of blocks away. I grab her elbow and keep her standing, then slide my hand down her arm and our hands find their way to each other, intertwining our fingers. It seems natural and she doesn't seem to mind. "Where do you want to eat?" I ask, even though I already have a place in mind.

"Oh," she pauses, stopping in the middle of the sidewalk. "I hadn't actually thought about that. I want chicken strips," she says, absolutely sure of her decision.

"I agree, that sounds good. I know just the place. And don't judge it by how it looks on the outside, well, and the inside. But they do have great chicken strips. And fries." She laughs and I see that twinkle in her eyes again.

"Oh, baby, you should know by now that I never judge anyone by their outward appearance," she pats her hand on my chest and smirks a little then skips off ahead of me.

"Hey! What is that supposed to mean?" I laugh as I jog to catch up with her. She slows down to wait for me and I drop my arm over her shoulder causing us to jostle together before we figure out how to walk side by side.

"Nothing," Juliana teases. I roll my eyes but let us fall into a quiet walk. It isn't awkward, it's just peaceful.

Juliana trusts me to lead her in the right direction and allows me to steer her over a few blocks and across a couple of streets. We are nearing the more run down part of town but I stop on the outskirts and lead her towards an old bar with the sign barely hanging from a few rusted old nails. I sense her hesitation as I hold the door open for her.

"What happened to not judging outward appearances?" I tease, then gesture for her to keep walking. And she does. She steps into the bar and I follow close behind, putting my hand on the small of her back and ushering her to a booth near the back. The bartender, Benny, catches my eye as he helps a very drunk older gentleman onto a bench in view of the bar so Benny can keep an eye on him. He gives me a nod and grins before gesturing to let me know he'll be right over.

"So, when and how did you find this place?" Juliana asks as Benny makes his way over to our booth. He delivers a slap on my back making me wince and Juliana smiles up at him.

"Benny and I went to law school together." Juliana's eyebrows draw together in confusion.

"I bet you're wondering why a man who went to law school ended up as a bartender in this dump?" Juliana looks like she is about to protest but Benny's laugh stops her. "Don't worry sweetheart, no offense taken."

"Benny only went to law school because he got bored sitting around in his mom and dad's mansion playing video games. Or rather inventing new ones and selling them off for millions of dollars." I boast about Benny's accomplishments and enjoy teasing my friend while also watching the look of amusement in Juliana's eyes.

"Oh, so you own this place?" She guesses correctly, and I can tell she is impressed but also confused as to why he would choose to own this bar.

"Yes, ma'am. Owner, chef, bartender, lawyer, you name it, I can do it."

"Speaking of, we would like two baskets of your famous chicken strips and fries combo. And yes, I am ordering two because neither of us will want to share, I can promise you that." I give Juliana a look and she nods, licking her lips hungrily and I can tell she is excited.

"Alright, two chicken strip baskets coming up. Any drinks I can get you before I get started?" Benny asks as he slowly backs away from the table, his fingers twitching and ready to get back to the kitchen.

"Did I mention he also has a passion for cooking?" I look across the table at Juliana and her smile brightens the room. "No, go have fun in the kitchen, I'll help ourselves to some water." I confer with Juliana and she gives a nod of approval so I slide out of the booth and make my way to the side of the bar where Benny keeps a full pitcher of cold water and clean glasses.

"This is kind of a family-style bar, you just help yourself to whatever you need. There are, of course, limitations to that, because of the health code, like not going in the kitchen. We try to make sure the bar wouldn't be shut down but of course, Benny and I, and other friends from law school would be all willing to fight for this place." The glasses make a *clank* on the table as I set them down, Juliana takes the pitcher and fills both cups. She nods while I talk and she watches me closely.

I sit back and take a breath realizing that I am the one now rambling. Normally, I am not one to ramble. I've always been able to speak clearly and concisely but ever since Juliana came into my life as my fake fiancée, I have been stumbling over myself trying to figure everything out; I need to find my eloquence again.

Once I pause, Juliana's eyes dart around the room, taking everything in. She notices every little detail and her eyes stop on a photo of our group of friends that was taken right after we passed the bar.

"That's you," she gets up and makes her way over to the photo. I follow behind her to look at it as well.

"Yep, that's us. That group right there is the only reason I made it out of law school and passed the damn bar." I let out a puff of breath remembering all the late nights and tough exams before the big one.

"That's cool," she says, admiring the picture a little longer before drifting down the wall to look at more of the pictures and posters, some new from Benny and some older from the previous owners.

I hover back a few steps but follow her and point out funny sayings or explain posters to her on the way. By the time we make it around the whole bar and back to our seats, Benny is headed our way carrying two baskets overflowing with fries.

"Dinner is served," Benny announces and slides our steaming baskets onto the table, pulling a ketchup and ranch bottle out of his apron pockets and plopping them on the table. "Enjoy," he says and takes a bow, winking at Juliana before he walks off to talk to a group that just entered the bar.

"Wow, this looks delicious." Juliana reaches for her chicken strip splitting one open and watches as steam comes billowing out, she blows on them gently before greedily taking a big bite. I wait for her reaction and smile as she closes her eyes. "Wow, and it tastes as good as it looks."

"Homemade too," I comment before beginning to devour mine as well. We fade into silence as we both realize how hungry we are.

# Chapter 31

## *Kurt*

After our dinner in silence we find ourselves seated at the bar making friends with every customer that comes in. Juliana was shy at first but this atmosphere is too inviting and getting food in her has really opened her up. Benny has been steadily supplying me with beer but Juliana doesn't seem to notice. I find myself leaning into her with each beer and my hand rests on her thigh. She flinched when I first touched her but I didn't back down and she eventually relaxed and her hand is now perched on top of mine, her thumb gently rubbing my hand while she chatters aimlessly to her new companions. The gesture seems almost absentminded and I don't mind.

At one point in the evening, I lean over and plant a kiss on her cheek, which quickly turns a shade of pink while the women in the group give a collective sigh. I turn back to make further conversation with the gentleman to my right but overhear the women telling Juliana how cute we are together. I smile, we are cute.

"Kurt," I feel Juliana tug on my hand gently and I turn to face her again. I look into her eyes and notice how tired she is. "It's getting late." I look at my watch and see it has gotten late. It's almost midnight.

"Wow, how did that happen? We've been here almost four hours." I stand up, staggering a little and Juliana gives me a look that I can't quite read. But the look passes quickly and she wraps her arm around my waist, I toss my arm over her shoulder enjoying the feel of her up against my side.

"Leaving so soon?" Benny teases, I nod and put my card down on the bar sliding it to him but he just shakes his head and pushes it back to me. "This one's on me. But not for you," he stops me before I can protest or even thank him. "For Juliana, you're one lucky guy." He winks at Juliana and grins at me. I pocket my card and give him a nod.

"Thanks, man. I am pretty lucky." I turn and plant a kiss on Juliana's forehead and pull her close to me. She puts her hand on my abdomen to keep me from wobbling and I am grateful because I definitely should not have had that final beer. The warmth of her hand stays on me as we walk down the street.

"I texted Dave to let him know we were up for that dinner invitation." I let her know and she smiles looking at the ground, watching where her feet are going. "He said his wife is excited to meet you. I made sure to let them know that they shouldn't judge a book by its cover." I tease and she lets out a loud laugh that echoes across the empty street.

"Thanks for that." She bumps her hip against mine, making both of us stumble. We laugh together as I regain my footing and straighten her out too.

"Hey, careful, if I go down, I'm taking you down with me." I eye her evilly and this earns me another laugh. She pats my stomach, leaving her hand there again until we make it to the car. Juliana holds her hand out for the keys, and I hand them over willingly. She helps me get in the passenger seat and then she drives us back to our apartment. Her warm hands return to my body and I let her help me to the apartment. She fumbles with the lock but I know I would do a worse job so I wait patiently, leaning up against the wall.

"Juliana.." I start and she looks up at me just as she gets the door unlocked, she holds it open for me and I try my best to walk like I am not as drunk as I happened to be. She follows behind me and locks up the apartment, I sit on the couch and she busies herself cleaning up the leftover food and drinks that Marvin must have brought up. I left him a note to do so if my guests left a mess, even though I had planned to go back to clean up.

Once Juliana is finished putting everything away in the kitchen, I hear the sound of ice being scooped into cups and then the sound of running water. Juliana comes back into the living room and hands me a glass which I gratefully accept, downing most of the water quickly as she drops onto the couch letting out a sigh.

"That was fun," she smiles, her eyes shining while her eyelids begin to droop from exhaustion. "Benny is really funny. He was telling me some stories of your law school days. They were quite interesting." She teases me but I like it.

Feeling bold from the alcohol intake, I reach over and pull her onto my lap. She doesn't protest and straddles me, sitting back so we can look at each other. "Hi."

I chuckle. "Hey," I say back. I keep my hands resting on her thighs, a sensation beginning to form in my abdomen but I can control myself, for now.

"Thanks for talking me down today, I don't normally run out of a room crying. I mean, yes, it's happened before but I try not to make a habit of it. Oh, I mean me bursting into tears, I'm not sure I've run out of a room before but it's possible, my mom likes to remind me how dramatic I was as a child. And thanks for taking me to Benny's bar. It was delicious and everyone was so nice and welcoming. We should definitely go there again. I want to try more of that menu. Well, I also want more chicken strips but I'll try new things too." She pauses. "Sorry, rambling." She waves her hand as if dismissing her ramblings but I've started to enjoy them.

"Juliana..." I start but hesitate when she looks at me with her tired yet excited eyes. Without realizing what I'm doing, I lean into her, wrapping my hand behind her neck and pulling her down to press our lips firmly together.

She hesitates at first but soon she is kissing me back. Her lips are soft and I lean into her while pulling her thighs down closer to me so she's sitting perfectly in my lap. Her hands slide across my chest touching me softly and then they slip down and begin to tug at my shirt, I oblige and lift it over my head.

I lift her up and stand up, letting out an embarrassingly primal growl as she wraps her legs around me and I feel her mouth open to deepen the kiss. I feel her tongue brush over my bottom lip as I bring us into the bedroom. I set her down on the bed keeping her legs around my waist as I lean down with her.

I pull away from our kiss and look down at her. We are both breathing heavily. I look down at her and I feel guilty for some reason but the animalistic lust inside me pushes me to continue. I hold her face gently in my hands and kiss her breathless. Her hand slides over my chest and down. But something inside me makes me grab it before it hits its mark.

"Juli..." I groan, my voice heavy with lust and longing but something else is there too, regret?

# Chapter 32
## *Juliana*

"Juli..." I hear him say and lean back breathing heavily. His voice sounded regretful. My cheeks flush with embarrassment and I can't look at him. He is the one who kissed me first, why is he pushing me away now?

"I'm sorry. God, I want to. I really do." He mumbles, then lets go of my hand. I move back on the bed getting out from under him and look everywhere but at him, pulling my legs to my chest.

"This is awkward." I chuckle nervously, trying to lighten the mood but I don't feel like laughing. I want to crawl under the covers and hide, from him and from everyone else. Instead of facing the awkward situation in front of me, I stare at the wall across from the bed and try to pretend it isn't happening.

I hear him laugh to humor me, but his laugh has no joy in it and it does nothing to erase my embarrassment.

"Juli," he says my name again before he pauses. When he doesn't continue right away, I peek at him and he is staring at me.

"I'm sorry," I say and he smiles sadly which makes me frown. Why is he sad? Wait, he said he wanted to, didn't he? Wanted to what? Keep going? I shake my head trying to brush away the thoughts and he gives me a strange look. I must look insane arguing with myself in my head.

"Juli," he begins again and the way he keeps saying my name makes me want to scream. "I... I like you. I like you." He repeats and I'm about to tell him I like him too but he holds up his hand to stop me. "No, let me finish." He waits until I nod then he continues. "I like you. I have always liked you. First, as friends when we grew up together. Well, you're a bit younger so I guess I grew up then I watched you grow up." I give him a disapproving look and he winces. "Yeah, okay that didn't come out right. I'm not good at this. Okay, so yes, I like you. It started just as friends but I've realized that now it's developed into a type of like that goes beyond friendship. I'm not to the point of fiancée liking yet but who knows." He pauses to take a breath and I jump in quickly.

"Kurt," I say as I put my hand over his. "We don't have to do this tonight. It's been a really stressful day." Kurt chuckles and nods. I smile at him, noticing his eyelids starting to flutter as he gets tired. "Also you're definitely a little drunk. So I am going to apologize for almost taking advantage of you."

Kurt's burst of laughter makes me laugh as well. I squeeze his hand and get off the bed. I grab his arm and haul him off the bed too. He stumbles a bit but I am able to catch him and he leans against me.

"Where are we going?" Kurt asks. I lead him to the bathroom and set him on the edge of the bathtub, making sure he's steady before releasing him and going to the stand-alone shower. I turn it on then grab his fresh towel out of the cabinet and hang it beside the shower. "Do I smell that bad?" Kurt teases me when he realizes what I'm doing.

"Honestly? Yes, it's not horrible but you smell like Benny's bar, and no offense to him but it's time for a deep clean." I stick my hand in the shower and feel that the temperature is decently warm. I dry my hand off. "Okay, I will go grab your pajamas for you. Are you okay to shower?"

"Yes," Kurt stands up. He wobbles a little bit and I make a move to go to his side but he puts his hand up to stop me. "I'm fine. I've got this."

"Okay, I'll just stay in the bedroom. Holler if you need anything." I turn to leave but Kurt reaches out and touches me gently. I turn back to face him. "Yes?'

"Thank you," Kurt says, then drops his arm to his side. I nod and give a small smile in acknowledgment. "And I'm sorry. For tonight, it kind of got out of hand."

"Don't worry about it." I offer another smile. "I was right there with you. Anyway, go shower. I'll be right outside." I say then exit the bathroom, shutting the door behind me. I hear him stumbling around for a minute then hear the shower door open and close. I turn on the TV to at least pretend like I'm doing something other than dwelling on this whole day then I sit down on the bed and send a text to Tatyana.

**Juliana: We just made out...**

Tatyana responds almost immediately.

**Tatyana: What?!?!?!?**

**Tatyana: Tell me everything**

I grin down at my phone. Part of me feels giddy from what happened and what Kurt confessed but another part of me is dwelling on the fact that he pulled away. I chew on my lip thinking about how to respond to Tatyana.

**Juliana: Long story short - we had our housewarming party, Kurt unknowingly hired Callum's band, Callum sang a really inappropriate song about me, and I fell apart**

**Juliana: Kurt fixed everything, took me out, he got a little drunk when we got back he pulled me in into his lap, we kissed, made our way to the bed**

**Juliana: But right before it could go any further, he stopped it**

Tatyana responds before I can tell her the rest of the story.

**Tatyana: WHAT?!!?**

I hear the shower shut off and can hear movement in the bathroom. Whoops, I forgot to put his pajamas in the bathroom. I set my phone on the bed and go to the closet. Kurt's typical nightwear, I've learned, is an old t-shirt and boxers. I open his dresser and grab one of each out of the top drawer then set them on the edge of the bed, not wanting to go into the bathroom and disturb him.

When I go back to my side of the bed, I scoop up my phone and see Tatyana has texted me a few more times, impatient as ever.

**Tatyana: We will talk about Callum later but KURT why did he stop???**

**Tatyana: ?**

**Tatyana: ????**

I quickly text back, listening to the noise in the bathroom and hearing the sink on while he brushes his teeth. I know he'll be done soon so I skip to the good part.

**Juliana: He said he likes me!**

**Tatyana: I knew it!**

**Tatyana: Oooh I sooo knew it!**

**Tatyana: I told you!**

**Tatyana: Did you tell him you like him too????**

I sigh and look up at the bathroom door again. Maybe I should tell him. Kurt opens the door and comes into the room. He only has a towel around his waist. I quickly look away, but not after his glistening chest stirs something in me.

"I put your pajamas on the bed." I gesture to the end of the bed, where the clothes lay. I keep my eyes on my phone and my head down even though I very badly want to look up.

"Thank you," Kurt grabs his things and then goes back to the bathroom. He doesn't shut the door all the way but I again keep myself from looking. Instead, I focus on responding to Tatyana.

**Juliana: I did not... Maybe he doesn't even like me for real, you know?**

**Juliana: I've forced him into this crazy situation, we've been spending a lot of time together, and then with what went down at the housewarming party...**

**Juliana: He's probably just feeling protective of a friend and confusing it with feelings of more than that...**

My fingers fly across my phone typing as fast as I can without any typos. I really need to see Tatyana in person soon so we can discuss everything. Texting is just not doing it for me.

**Tatyana: Juliana! Don't second guess everything, you both like each other.**

**Tatyana: Ugh we need to have a girl's night soon!**

I smile at my phone, grateful she feels the same. I send her a quick text back agreeing and telling her that I want to hear all about her trip with Mike then I put my phone away as Kurt enters the room again. He's dressed in his pajamas this time. Kurt slides under the covers and looks over at me, his eyelids drooping. I wait for him to say something but when he doesn't, I look over at him. He's just silently watching me.

"What?" I ask and he smiles sleepily up at me but he still doesn't speak. "Okay then." I laugh then get up off the bed. "I'm going to shower now."

"Hey," Kurt finally says before I get to the bathroom. I look back at him and wait. He reaches out his hand and waves me toward him. I take a few steps closer and put my hand in his outstretched one. Before I know what's happening, he gives my hand a tug and I topple over the bed, half on him. I try to right myself to a standing position but his hand goes behind my neck and he keeps me down on him. He shifts himself and then pulls me gently until our lips meet. I'm surprised, our second kiss, in one evening too.

I press my lips firmly against him, tasting his minty fresh breath, and leaning into him which loosens his grip on me. It loosens enough for me to pull away. I push myself off the bed and stand up beside him. He looks up at me and smiles.

"Enjoy your shower."

I bite my lip and then roll my eyes at him.  I get to the bathroom and shut the door behind me. I hear him chuckle, his laugh deeper than normal, filled with sleep.

The bathroom is still steamy from Kurt's shower and the water heats up quickly for me. When I get in, I spend a few minutes just standing under the hot stream, trying to relax after a long stressful day. I try not to think about everything that happened but of course, I can't stop myself. My thoughts go to Kurt and how he handled Callum's immature behavior and my tears. It reminds me of when we were younger at his parent's lake house when he comforted me through the tears and pain. We were just talking about that recently and again he proved that he is great at comforting me through the tears.

Close to the end of my shower routine, I'm brushing my hair and thinking about Kurt. I want to talk to him before bed. I need to hurry up. I finish washing my face and then turn off the shower. I dry off, put my hair up in a towel, and wrap my shower towel around me. I take my time brushing my teeth then peek back into the bedroom. Kurt is facing away from the door and I can't tell if he is awake or not. The TV is still on, with the volume off but that's how I left it.

The closet is a short distance away from the bathroom and I'm able to grab a t-shirt, underwear, and pajama shorts. I head back to the bathroom and change quickly, hoping Kurt is still awake. When I go back to the bedroom, I take a closer look at Kurt, his eyes are closed while he breathes deeply.

Darn, I guess I'll just have to talk to him tomorrow. I sigh quietly before turning off the TV and making my way to my side of the bed in the dark. I slide beneath the covers and turn to face Kurt. He is facing me as well, deeply asleep. I smile.

"Goodnight, Kurt."

# Chapter 33
## *Kurt*

Waking up, I grip my throbbing head. I look over at my alarm clock and it shows that it's barely past 7 a.m. Turning back over, I see Juliana sound asleep next to me. Flashes of last night come back to me and I remember us kissing. I remember more than just a normal kiss, it meant something to both of us.

Before I can think about it too much, my phone starts ringing. I forgot to turn the ringer off last night so the blaring noise is startling. I quickly turn off the sound and take a peek at Juliana, seeing her stirring from the noise but she only turns over and does not wake up. Answering the call, I hear my mom on the other end.

"Good morning, Kurt." My mother's cheery voice comes through the phone loud and clear. I get out of bed and move away from Juliana so I don't wake her.

"Hey, Momma," I say, shutting the bedroom door behind me, going to sit on the couch. I prop my feet up on the coffee table and yawn. I start to ask her about her weekend but she continues talking after my initial greeting.

"Are you and Juliana coming to church today?" I can sense she has an ulterior motive when asking this question.

"Uhm, I'm not sure. Juliana is still asleep and honestly, I'm still pretty tired too.' I rub my eyes and hold back another yawn while I talk. When I finish my sentence though, the yawn escapes.

"I know everyone would love to see you two again. And your father, sister, and I were hoping to take the two of you out to lunch after church." Ah, there is the ulterior motive. I close my eyes and lean my head back on the couch. "Of course, we want to invite Juliana's family too. We didn't really get to spend time with our two families at the engagement party. I talked to Juliana's mom and she agreed with me. Obviously, if you two have plans today then we can all get together another time but I figured since we will all be at one place today, for church, then we can go out after."

"Uh, yeah, sure. Church starts at 10 a.m., right?" I look over at the clock and it's 7:30 a.m. now. I'm still exhausted but I guess I can try to sneak in at least one more hour of sleep.

"Yes, 10 am sharp. Well, not sharp, they usually run a few minutes behind." My mother pauses. She sounds excited. "Okay well, I will let you go back to sleep but don't forget about church and lunch today!"

Her excitement elicits a chuckle from me. "Okay, mom. I'll let Juliana know so she can prepare herself." This gets a laugh from my mom.

"Okay, honey. See you in a few hours. Love you."

"Love you too, mom." I hang up and debate getting up to go back to the bedroom but a headache has come on strong and I just want to go back to sleep now. I quickly set an alarm on my phone to make sure I actually wake up in time to attend church and also give myself some padded time so I can tell Juliana so she'll have time to get ready as well. I give myself only one hour to sleep, setting the alarm for 8:30 a.m. before tossing it next to me on the couch and falling back asleep.

# Chapter 34
## *Kurt*

Waking with a start, I see Juliana standing in front of me. Her hands are on my arm and I can tell she's just been trying to shake me awake. I sit up and run my fingers over my head, looking around the room.

"Hey, your alarm is going off." Juliana moves away from me when she sees that I'm awake. I reach over and grab my phone, shutting off the alarm.

I watch Juliana walk around the kitchen and soon the smell of scrambled eggs makes its way to where I sit on the couch. I catch myself from gagging but it does not smell good. Then she starts using the blender. Oh no, why is she doing this to me? Is she doing this on purpose? Did I annoy her or make her angry because of my actions last night? Maybe I don't want to know the answers to those questions.

I haul myself off the couch and join her in the kitchen. I lean against the counter as Juliana makes breakfast for us. She has two plates set out and two glasses. She blends one more time and I wince. She doesn't seem to notice though. When she stops blending, she pours equal amounts into each glass and then hands one of the glasses to me.

"Thank you," I say before taking a sip. She nods and takes a drink from her own glass. I take another small sip then take a bigger one. "Wow, this is really good." I finish the smoothie quickly and my head is already starting to feel better, even the eggs start to smell alright. I go over to Juliana, peering over her shoulder and wrapping one arm around her waist.

"Eggs?" Juliana offers as she leans back against me, scraping the bottom of the pan and mixing the eggs so they cook evenly. She sprinkles on some cheese, salt, and pepper. Then while she waits for them to finish, she grabs the salsa from the fridge, unraveling herself from my grip.

"Sure, thanks." Juliana turns off the stove, puts some eggs on each of our plates, and then scoops out some fruit from a bowl that I didn't even notice we had. We bring our plates to the kitchen table and sit silently eating breakfast together. After a few minutes of silence, I remember that I haven't told Juliana about church and lunch with our families. "Oh hey, my mom called this morning and wants us to attend church, that's why I set my alarm. And then apparently, she is setting up a lunch with our families afterward."

"Oh, okay, sure. What time do we need to leave?" Juliana keeps eating her breakfast but shoots a glance at the clock.

"Church starts at 10 so we probably need to leave about 9:40." I polish off my eggs and get up to get a second helping. There isn't that much left so I lift up the pan to offer more to Juliana, she shakes her head no so I dump the rest onto my plate.

"Okay. We have almost an hour then." She pauses to finish her breakfast then she brings her plate to the kitchen where I've stopped to eat the rest of the eggs at the counter. They ended up being delicious as well. "What are you going to wear?"

"Excuse me?" I look over at her and she smiles, tilting her head at me.

"What are you going to wear to church? It's not a hard question." Juliana laughs a little at my perplexed expression. "You've never been asked that question before?"

"Not about church, no. I don't think I've been asked that since…" I tail off thinking, I don't remember Ashley ever asking. "I don't know, since college? And that was for dances where every couple wanted to match."

Juliana laughs as she washes her dishes and puts her glass and plate into the dishwasher. "No, no, we don't need to match. I'm just trying to see if we're dressing up; cute, fancy, cozy, casual?" She smiles when I still have a funny look on my face. "Right, well since it's church and lunch after, with both of our families, I would say leaning towards fancy. Not *fancy* fancy but church fancy."

"Wow, I have a lot to learn." Juliana laughs at me as she reaches for the pan on the stove but I wave her off. "Don't worry about it, I will clean up since you made breakfast. You can go get dressed in your 'church fancy' outfit that way I can see what that means and dress accordingly."

"Sounds good," Juliana says and smiles at me. She looks like she wants to say something but she doesn't. Before she can turn and walk back to the bedroom, I pull her toward me and plant another soft kiss on her surprised lips. When I pull away, her surprise morphs into a smile. I smile back and then release her to go get ready.

I finish cleaning the kitchen and then head back to the bedroom to get dressed. I knock on the door to make sure I don't walk in on her. She opens the door and is wearing a pretty pink and blue floral church dress. She steps back to let me into the room then she turns her back to me.

"Can you zip me please?" Juliana gathers her hair and moves it over her shoulder so I can access the zipper. I reach out and take hold of the zipper, my fingers accidentally brushing her skin. She shivers slightly, but I can't tell if she likes my touch as much as I like touching her. And I have found myself wanting to touch her more and more.

"Gorgeous," I say quietly and she looks over her shoulder at me. Again there seem to be words left unspoken between us. But it seems like neither of us wants to be the first one to bring it up. She turns back to face in front of her, red spreading across her cheeks. I make quick work with the zipper, pulling it up when I'd rather be pulling it down. No, I cannot think like that.

"Thank you," Juliana says then she goes back to the closet to grab a pair of shoes. She pulls out a pair of short heels that have a similar blue as the dress. She really knows how to pull an outfit together. I've always noticed and liked that about her.

"So that is what 'church fancy' means? I like it." Juliana smiles at my comment and does a quick spin for me then sits back on the bed laughing. "Absolutely stunning."

"Do you want me to help you pick out something to wear?" Juliana offers, sighing in playful annoyance. She smiles up at me, looking excited, it makes me happy.

"Of course, I'm sure you have some great ideas." I go over to the closet and open the doors. Juliana gets off the bed and comes to stand next to me.

"I do." She begins going through all my button-up, hanging shirts. She slows down when she reaches the right color blues. She pushes a couple aside then pulls one hanger off the rack and hands it to me. "I've seen you wear this one before. It looks nice on you and I think it's the same blue as the blue in my dress. Unless you think it's too matchy with me?"

"No, I like it. Nothing wrong with matching." I smile at her and take the shirt off the hanger. I put it on and begin buttoning it up while Juliana grabs a pair of the khakis I tend to reserve for church. "Thanks," I say when she hands them to me as well.

"Sure. I'll leave you to get changed." Juliana exits the bedroom, shutting the door behind her.

Getting ready doesn't take long but I do take the time to freshen up in the bathroom. When I'm done, I sit on the bed to put my socks and shoes on and then I check my phone and see that it is 9:35 am. We should probably head out soon.

"Juliana?" I call as I exit the bedroom. Juliana looks up from her perch on the couch. "Oh hey. You ready to go?"

"Yep." Juliana hops off the couch and grabs her purse off the cushion beside her. I hold the door open for her and she waits outside the door while I lock up.

The car ride to church is relatively quiet. I look over at Juliana occasionally and I can tell she is nervous. Although we had our engagement party with everyone there, going to church is a little more intimidating. There are fewer people so there will be more chances for one-on-one conversations. I reach over and take her hand. The gesture might be too intimate and I debate pulling back but Juliana looks up and smiles at me. She squeezes my hand gently, and I bring her hand up to my lips, kissing it softly.

"Are you nervous too? Or am I just being silly?" Juliana asks to recover from the blush my kiss caused. I smile at her reaction. Her hand feels good in mine and I have to remind myself to focus on the road and to focus on what she's saying to me.

"Uhm, no," I say, then remember she asked two questions. I clarify. "No, you're not being silly. And I guess I am kind of nervous. This is our family. Our church. A small community.." I trail off and glance over at Juliana. She's looking at me with a guilty expression. "What?"

"I'm sorry, I feel so bad. Should we bail before church? We can leave a voicemail for our parents and tell them we got into a fight or something." Juliana rambles and I know she can go on longer if I don't stop her.

"Hey," I interrupt and squeeze her hand. "It'll be okay. It's just church then lunch. We can survive that. And I don't think anyone would believe that we would ever fight," I add, which thankfully makes her laugh.

We pull into the church parking lot as I finish my sentence, so no backing out of this now. There are a lot of cars today so we have to park further away. The parking lot is mostly void of people. I check the clock in the car and see we made it with one minute to spare. Getting out of the car, I walk around to Juliana's side and help her out. I take her hand in mine and smile down at her, trying to reassure her.

"We've got this. Right?" Juliana hesitates, looking up at me. She squeezes my hand in a nervous gesture.

"We've got this." I hold onto her hand and we make our way into the church. Luckily, church has already started so we only have to offer a few smiles to those who turned to see us enter before slipping into the last pew, settling in for the service.

# Chapter 35
## *Juliana*

Church ends sooner than I want it to. I enjoyed the service and it helped me relax but towards the end, I grew nervous again. Throughout the service, people kept glancing back at us. Most of them send us small smiles. I try to keep my head ducked down as the organ music plays and everyone stands up to mingle before going about their day, the knots in my stomach return.

"Here comes your grandmother," Kurt says quietly to me before he stands up to greet her. I stand up beside him. "Hi, how are you?" Kurt gives her a hug and then steps aside so she can get to me.

"Hi, Gram." I lean in and give her a hug.

"How are you two doing? Can't say I was surprised by the news. I always thought the two of you would find your way to each other. You two were such great friends when you were little." Gram clutches my hand in hers and reaches for one of Kurt's hands as well. She smiles up at the both of us. "I'm so excited for lunch today." Gram beams up at us, looking back and forth at us and landing on me, smiling bigger.

"We're excited too, Grams." I smile back at her, a little suspicious. I look up at Kurt and he shrugs. I want to ask what's going on but then Mrs. and Mr. Michaels come over to us.

"Hi!" Mrs. Michaels greets us all, pulling each of us into a hug. "How are you doing? Y'all ready for lunch?" Mrs. Michaels hooks her arm through mine and pulls me away from Kurt. I look back at him and he's watching me while talking to his dad. Gram matches our steps and my mom falls in line behind us. "Juliana, I am so excited y'all are able to join us for lunch today. I know the engagement party was a bit much so we are grateful to have this time to sit down with just our families to celebrate and enjoy this beautiful day."

"Thank you for the invitation to lunch," I say then offer a compliment because it was great. "And thank you for throwing the engagement party for us. It was incredible."

"Oh, it was no problem, sweetie. I love any reason to throw a party and this was a pretty special reason." Mrs. Michaels squeezes my shoulders and gives me a big smile then she looks over at Gram and my mother. "Should the girls all drive over together?"

"Oh! That sounds like fun!" Gram claps her hands excitedly then excuses herself to go find my grandad.

"Sure, that sounds good." My mom agrees then she turns to go off to talk to my dad and let him know as well.

"Kurt!" Mrs. Michaels calls out and I turn to see Kurt walking with his dad and my dad. My mother stays beside Mrs. Michaels and me while the three men walk over to us.

"Hi, Daddy." I wrap my arms around my dad and give him a big hug.

"Hey, Juli, how are you?" My dad keeps his arm around me while we stand in a group talking.

"The girls have decided that we will all ride over to the restaurant together." My mother tells my dad and he nods his head.

"You all have fun, don't bombard Juliana with too many questions. I'll see you guys in a few minutes." My dad smiles at me and then gives my mom a kiss before going to their car.

Kurt pulls me aside when his mom starts informing his dad of the plans. I guess Kurt's dad is riding with Kurt and Mrs. Michaels will be driving the girls in their car.

"Hey, are you going to be alright?" Kurt smiles at me, a sort of teasing smile. I bite my tongue to keep from saying something sassy but I give him a look that makes him laugh. "Yeah, you'll be fine. We're going to Flanagins. It's only a few minutes away."

"I'll be fine." I nod my head. I haven't been to Flanagins in a while and I am starting to get hungry thinking about it.

"I'd better grab my dad and head over. Enjoy your ride with all the women." Kurt laughs and winks at me. I smile and laugh a little too. I've really been enjoying spending time with him, my feelings for him have been growing stronger. They shouldn't be, even though I know I shouldn't act on my feelings, I often let them take control. Before he can walk away, I grab Kurt's hand and pull him to me, giving him a hug and a gentle kiss on his cheek.

"Aw, isn't that so sweet?" Mrs. Michaels comes over to us and slides her arm through mine. I blush a little and look up at Kurt, he's watching me with a mixed reaction on his face.

"Sorry," I say automatically to Kurt, feeling bad that I did that. Especially in front of everyone.

"What are you sorry about, dear?" Mrs. Michaels asks and I freeze.

"Oh, uhm. Public displays of affection you know? Not always appropriate." I make up my explanation on the fly and smile apologetically. Kurt is still watching me, a small smile growing on his face.

"Oh, don't worry about it, sweetheart. Young love is beautiful." Mrs. Michaels grins at both of us and waves her hand, dismissing my apology.

"You ready to go, son?" Mr. Michaels steps in and gains Kurt's attention. He looks over at his dad and then back at me. He squeezes my hand and I smile. I didn't even realize I was still holding his hand.

"Yeah, let's go." Kurt pulls his keys out of his pocket. He hesitates then takes a step towards me, still holding my hand. He leans down and kisses me. He kisses me on the lips, in front of his parents and my mom and grandma. When he pulls back, he smiles down at me and I bite my lip to keep from grinning up at him. "See you at the restaurant."

After Kurt and his dad walk to his car and get in, Mrs. Michaels waves to them and then turns to face the three of us girls.

"Should we head out?" Mrs. Michaels asks.

"Yes, we should head over. My husband just left, I don't want to keep him waiting too long," my mother comments. She and Gram head over to Mrs. Michaels' car. Mrs. Michaels and I follow behind them and I offer to sit in the back with my mother so my grandmother can sit up front.

"Juliana," Mrs. Michaels calls from the driver's seat. "I hope you don't have any plans for the rest of the day because we have a surprise for you after lunch. I don't know if it will take the whole day but you never know." I look over at my mom sitting beside me. She smiles politely and usually, I can count on her to share any secret but she stays silent. "So, are you free for the rest of the day?"

"Oh, uhm, yes I think so. I'll have to check in with Kurt though to see if he's available." I know Kurt usually uses Sunday evenings to relax or get ready for the work week.

"Oh no, honey, Kurt isn't invited today." Ms. Michaels looks at me in the rearview mirror and smiles mischievously.

"Oh, okay." I'm very nervous now. "Well, I still want to check in with him anyway. Sometimes we have plans on Sundays," I add just in case I can use it as an excuse in the future.

We pull into the Flanagins' parking lot and I see that all of the men's cars are already here. We are the last to arrive but the men are all waiting outside for us. We park the car and walk over to them together. I make my way to Kurt and stand by him when he holds the door open for everyone.

"How was the ride?" He asks when the last of the group walks inside. He holds the door open for me too then follows me inside.

"It was fine, short. They didn't have time to question me too much. But your mom has plans for me after lunch. I think my mom and grandmother are coming too." I tell him what his mom said in the car. Kurt looks over at his mom, narrowing his eyes.

"I wonder what she's got planned for you. Oh no." Kurt stops when the front door opens. I turn towards the door and in walks his sister.

"Hi!" His sister goes around giving hugs to everyone. She gives me a long hug and a big smile. Before she can say anything besides a greeting, Kurt chimes in.

"Hey, Merrin. What are you doing here?" Kurt gives her a hug then we all move forward in the line to order.

"Sorry, I'm a bit late," Merrin apologizes to their mom then turns back to address Kurt. "Mom invited me along to lunch and for the girls' plans after lunch. And I couldn't resist." Merrin smiles at both of us. I am so curious as to what the plan is. I shoot a glance at Kurt and he just shrugs.

"Come on y'all, the line is moving. Don't hold anyone up behind you." Mrs. Michaels interrupts to keep us from asking any more questions. She waves us to move forward and we step up to the next available register. Kurt and I order together, I order second so I am able to pay before Kurt can offer.

"Thanks," Kurt grabs our number to bring to the table then he stands beside me waiting while I sign the receipt.

"Of course," I smile over my shoulder at him. "I did tell you I'd pay one of these days. Not just for a coffee date." Kurt laughs and nods his head.

"That you did, my dear."

We make our way to the table where the rest of our group is already seated. Conversations have already begun and Kurt and I are quickly dragged into them while we all wait for our food.

# Chapter 36
## *Kurt*

When our food arrives at the table, the conversations don't die down completely but everybody is hungry and the food smells great. I dig into my burger, making comments between bites whenever someone addresses me directly. My mom has separated the men from the women so we can have our own conversations. Although, I don't know why since my mom has a whole girls' day planned after lunch.

Partway through lunch, I need a refill on my drink. I ask if anyone else needs anything and there are requests to bring back more napkins. I get up to get my refill and some napkins for the group. While I'm at the refill station, I look around the restaurant and see the old arcade still standing in the corner. A few games are gone or replaced by new ones but it still reminds me of after church lunches when we were younger.

Merrin and I used to play the games together and try to beat one another. One Sunday, one of the older couples at church invited all of us kids to come eat and gave us unlimited quarters. Merrin and I were once again competing when

Juliana walked over and wanted to play with us. Merrin, being a lot more competitive than me even as a child, didn't want Juliana to distract her so she for the most part dismissed her. I, on the other hand, was a lot nicer, and even back then I had a fondness for Juliana so I let her watch while I played. I also explained to her how to play and took a few hits while showing her how to work the controls. Eventually, I lost the game, Merrin was triumphant and rubbed it in my face. Juliana felt bad and guilty for my loss. I almost had to console her but I could see her tighten her face then she held out her hand and offered me the quarters she was holding. I told her no at first, I wanted her to save them for herself but she insisted and said she wasn't any good but she liked watching me play. So, I eventually gave in and took the quarters from her. Juliana pulled up a stool beside me and watched while I played. We sat like that, barely talking, for ten or so minutes until everyone else was ready to leave.

"Hey, are you done?" A voice jolts me out of the memory and I look behind me at the gentleman waiting to get a refill. I look down at my drink and see that it is full, luckily it hadn't overflowed onto my hand.

"Yeah, sorry, all yours." I take my drink and pull a handful of napkins out of the dispenser next to the drink machine before walking back to the table. I toss the napkins on the table then sit down and go back to eating my lunch. The conversation continues around me and I only half pay attention until I hear my mom bring up something in particular.

"So, have you guys discussed what date the wedding will be?" My mom looks at Juliana then myself. "Not that I'm trying to rush y'all I was just wondering if you'd discussed it yet. It's never too soon to start discussing it."

"Uhm," Juliana stutters a bit, not knowing what to say. Looking over at Juliana, she looks a little flustered with everybody watching her so I decide to step in and answer the question.

"No, we haven't discussed it yet. We are just enjoying spending time together. We've only been living together for a few weeks,  so we've been learning how our schedules work and different aspects of cohabitating." I try to add a lot of details so there won't be any follow-up questions. Hopefully, the answer I've given will satisfy everyone for now. Juliana looks over at me and gives me a grateful smile.

I can tell she's still a little uncomfortable so I finish my fries, wipe my hands clean then stand up. Everyone looks up at me but I make my way over to Juliana and squat beside her.

"Hey, you wanna go play one of the games in the arcade? Like the good old days?" I ask and she looks at me with a smile growing on her face which is now also filled with relief.

"The good old days?" Juliana smiles up at me and I nod. I dig in my pocket and pull out a few quarters. I hold them out as an offer to her. I can tell everyone is watching and I'll never get used to that. "Okay, but I might be a bit rusty." Juliana wipes her hands on her napkin and then accepts the coins from my open palm. I stand up and step back for her to get up too.

"If everyone will excuse us, we are going to go play some games." I offer my hand to Juliana and she takes it, smiling happily. Merrin laughs.

"Good luck, Kurt. You're so bad, you'll need it." Merrin teases me.

"Hey, I was pretty good at these games," I respond to her jab.

"Oh sure," Merrin laughs and rolls her eyes. "Juliana, you come get me if you need some help kicking his butt." Merrin winks at Juliana.

"We'll come get you two when we're ready to leave," my mother tells us, giving us her approval to leave the table. I squeeze her shoulder and then gesture toward the arcade area. Juliana leads the way, still holding my hand in one of hers and the quarters in the other.

"You ready to get your butt kicked?" Juliana quips, hopping on a stool near one of the games and sliding quarters into the slot. I take my place beside her.

"Are you sure you can beat me without help?" I raise my eyebrows at her and settle into my seat as the game loads. Juliana leans over and smacks me but she's laughing. Her laughing causes her to miss her first chance to score points, I take advantage of it and come out a few points ahead from the get-go.

"Hey! No fair, you distracted me!" Juliana complains, whining a bit. I laugh at her distress and she shoots me a pouting glare before getting into the game.

The game goes on for a few more minutes, Juliana keeps up pretty closely to my score but with a minute remaining I pull ahead with a big lead.

"Oh yeah! You're not going to be able to catch up now!" I laugh and am about to win but my thumb starts cramping. "Nooo, ow, ow ow. Cramp!!" I cry out, trying to power through the pain but my thumb starts twitching, throwing off my game.

"Yes!" Juliana hunches over, getting more into the game, catching up to me. My thumb keeps cramping as Juliana's score grows, minimizing my lead. "Ooo, this is gunna hurt you so badly when I make a huge comeback and win!" Juliana taunts me, showing no sympathy for my cramping thumb.

"Oh no! I'm still ahead by a few points. Don't start celebrating yet." I look at the countdown in the corner of the screen and see only a few seconds left. I am still ahead of Juliana but she's gaining quickly. I haven't scored any points since the cramp began. I throw around the idea of calling out for Merrin to take over but with ten seconds left, I power through. "Come on, come on…"

"Yes! I did it! I won!" Juliana pulls ahead with two seconds remaining and there is nothing my cramped thumb can do to beat her. She jumps off the stool and throws her arms in the air cheering. I laugh and notice Juliana is drawing the attention of some people in the restaurant. They're all smiling at us though, no one seems bothered by her cheering. She cheers again and I hear a couple of people clapping for her. I roll my eyes, smiling.

"Alright, alright. Fine, I concede. You won, I'll admit it." I raise my hands in surrender right as Merrin and my mom walk over to us, followed by the rest of the group.

"You lost?" Merrin asks and I nod. Merrin holds her hand out to Juliana and she gives her a high five. "Not too surprising but still pretty impressive, Juliana."

"Thanks," Juliana says and smiles proudly. She looks so happy and it is cute, I can't help but reach over and pull her to me. She looks up at me surprised right before I kiss her. It's just a quick kiss but I know I shouldn't have done it. We can't get too attached, even though I want to, and each kiss brings us closer and closer together.

Juliana leans back in my arms and looks up at me. I don't know what to say and she doesn't seem to know what to say either.

"Alright, ladies!" My mother's voice interrupts us and Juliana looks away from me. "Time to get going, we do have an appointment to get to."

Juliana looks back at me, raising her eyebrows. I shrug, I still don't know what's going on. I release her from my arms and Merrin links her arm through Juliana's, pulling her away from me.

"Don't worry, we'll have her back before dinner." Merrin starts to pull Juliana away and all the women follow

"Maybe!" My mom calls out and hustles all the women out to the car. Juliana looks back at me and she looks a little scared. I laugh and wave to her. She waves back and then is whisked out the door. I look over at my dad who is still standing around talking to Juliana's dad and grandfather. I walk over to them and Juliana's dad pats me on the back.

"Does anyone know what they're doing?" I ask the group of men and I am mostly met with shrugs and 'no's. "Great. Anyone want to come to our apartment for Sunday football?"

"Yes," my dad agrees readily.

"Sure," Juliana's grandad replies, looking over at his son, Juliana's dad.

"Okay, sounds good. I was just going to watch the games at home anyway." Juliana's dad shrugs. "I need to go home and change out of the church clothes first."

"Good idea." His dad responds, taking his car keys out of his pocket.

"Okay, Dad, I'll swing by and pick you up, okay?" Juliana's dad turns to talk to his father who nods, agreeing. They both nod at my dad and I then head out of the restaurant to their cars.

"You want me to swing by your house first for a change of clothes?" I ask my dad as we head out to the parking lot. My dad looks down at his polo shirt and jeans then back up at me. "Right, well some people actually dress up for church." I tease him.

"Hey! This is my good polo." My dad laughs and takes my making fun of him on the chin. "Looks like Juliana dressed you for church today." He pokes fun at me now, I'm a bit embarrassed because she did in fact dress me but I don't mind being dressed up for church.

"Actually, she did." My dad gives me a look then we both start laughing.

"Well, you look good." Dad gives me an approving nod as we get into the car. We chat more on the way back to mine and Juliana's apartment, the whole time I am wondering what my mother dragged Juliana into doing for the day.

# Chapter 37

## *Juliana*

"Juliana, are you excited?" Merrin nudges my side with her elbow. I am wedged between Merrin and my mother while Mrs. Michaels drives us with my grandmother in the passenger seat.

"Well, I still don't know what we're doing... Sooo..." I trail off and hope one of them will fill me in on what the appointment is. No one finishes my sentence so we ride the rest of the way to the appointment with Mrs. Michaels leading the conversation. I answer politely whenever directly addressed but for the most part, I stay quiet.

Merrin and my mother block most of the windows so I can't see where we're going. Eventually, we pull up to a curb, Mrs. Michaels parallel parks effortlessly and we all pile out of the car.

"Ta-da!" Mrs. Michaels gestures excitedly and grandly at the store in front of us. I look up and see white lace dresses lining the windows. My eyes dart up to the name above the door. *Beautiful Bride*. A bridal shop. My heart starts beating faster. Before I can say anything the door to the shop flies open and Tatyana bursts out onto the sidewalk in front of us.

"Oh, thank god," I say under my breath and move forward to greet her. I shoot her a look as she grabs me in a hug.

"What the hell is going on?" Tatyana whispers.

"I was just about to ask you that!" I whisper back, she pulls back and gives me a similar look I gave her a few seconds earlier.

"We booked a wedding dress appointment!" Mrs. Michaels cheers and looks so excited, that I feel guilt creeping up inside of me.

"Wasn't that nice of Mrs. Michaels?" My mother asks, pushing me to speak so I don't come off as rude for not responding right away.

"Yes, thank you. That was very thoughtful of you."

"I know it's pretty soon and I asked your mother who else to invite but we figured to keep the group small, just family and your best friend, Tatyana." Mrs. Michaels gestures to Tatyana, her smile growing as she beams with pride at her idea.

"No, of course, this is great. Thank you." I step forward and give her a big hug. "Thank you," I say again, softly and offer her a smile.

"Of course! Anything for my future daughter-in-law!" Mrs. Michaels says those words and I have to keep myself from physically reacting. I look over at Tatyana and she senses my need to be rescued before someone notices my restrained reaction.

"Should we get inside? I'm sure they have other appointments after us, we wouldn't want to keep them waiting." Tatyana speaks up and opens the door to the shop for us while gesturing for the group to move inside. All of the ladies file in with Tatyana and I bringing up the rear.

"Thank you," I whisper to her as I enter the shop. "I don't know how I would have survived this without you here."

"We don't know if you'll survive it even with me here." Tatyana comments as we follow the rest of the group further into the shop. "Who knows if I'll survive either!"

"Wow, thank you for the support." I narrow my eyes at Tatyana, not amused with her response, even if I agree with her.

"I don't know how much help I'll be. I guess we should just try to enjoy it." Tatyana gives me a look and I know she feels almost as guilty as I do for this whole situation. "Just maybe don't fall in love with any of the dresses. Oh! I will help you pick out the worst dresses and hopefully, your mom and Kurt's mom and everyone won't like them either, and then if we are lucky we can escape this appointment without choosing a dress." I nod in agreement. It's not a terrible idea but hopefully, our ideas for the worst dresses are the same as theirs.

We make our way to join the rest of the group and I can feel my nerves getting worse. I wasn't expecting them to take it this far, especially so soon. I should call Kurt and tell him. I need to talk to him, I have no idea what to do here. I am about to excuse myself to use the restroom and call Kurt but Merrin reaches her hand out before I can speak.

"Okay, hand over the cell phones, ladies," Merrin says and wiggles her fingers at me. I look at her hand then over at Tatyana and around at the group. Everyone else begins digging through their purses or pockets to retrieve their cell phones. "Come on, bride. Hand it over. We can't have anyone interrupting or giving away the surprise if we find the dress or dresses."

"Dresses?" I ask as I reluctantly hand over my phone. Tatyana groans and puts up a bit of a fight but Merrin is persistent and eventually, Tatyana hands it over.

"Yes, dresses. Of course, we are here to find your wedding dress, Juliana but they also sell bridesmaid dresses here. I thought it would be fun to look at those as well!" Merrin beams happily at me then her smile drops and she looks a bit embarrassed. " Oh wow, sorry it's not that I'm assuming I will be a bridesmaid, I just thought with Tatyana here we could have her try on dresses and I can too if you want, and then you can see different styles on different people and how they would look together." Merrin grows quiet and the room is quiet too. I realize everyone is watching me and waiting for my reaction but I've hardly had time to process what is currently happening so it takes me a few minutes to understand what Merrin just said to me.

"Oh!" I say when my brain finally catches up. "Oh no, it's okay. Of course, I want you to be a bridesmaid, Merrin. You are Kurt's only sister but you've also always been sweet to me. That sounds great and I'm sure Tatyana would love to try on a dress as well." I look over at Tatyana and give her a smile, kind of an evil smile. She narrows her eyes at me but puts on a smile for the group.

"Sounds awesome," Tatyana mutters through her teeth and the group smiles happily. Mrs. Michaels gives me another hug and then hugs Merrin and Tatyana. I can tell she is very excited.

"This is so great! Thank you so much for having me as a bridesmaid!" Merrin pulls me into a big hug and squeezes me a bit before pulling back. "Okay! Let's look at bridal gowns first!"

"Of course!" Mrs. Michaels grabs the attention of one of the ladies working and they come over to greet us and tell us we are free to wander around for a few minutes to see if anything catches our eyes, seeing as how I don't have a particular style in mind. Everyone spreads out in the store and I stick close to Tatyana.

"See any that look hideous?" I whisper to Tatyana and we both giggle.

"You girls having fun?" Mrs. Micheals calls out to us, hearing us giggle.

"Yes, so much," Tatyana responds and pulls me to the back of the store where there are racks of dresses on sale. Some from brides who returned the dresses including custom-made dresses that were returned as well. Tatyana and I shift through them and we come across a very puffy, off-white ballgown-style bridal dress with sparkles throughout the entirety of it.

"Oh no," I say with a grimace on my face.

"Oh yes." Tatyana pulls the hanger off the rack. "Oh, but we must. We have to." Tatyana smiles at the dress and brings it over to the slowly growing wall of dresses everyone wants me to try on. I groan but keep looking through the sales rack.

"Should we find nonwhite dresses? Or is that too much?" I trail my fingers over a mermaid-style dress that happens to be gray. I don't think I'd look good in a mermaid-style dress and both of our families are pretty traditional so gray might be a deal-breaker for everyone.

"Oooh, yes! That is horrible! And you hate mermaid style." Tatyana comes over to admire my pick and nods her head in approval.

"I think my mom does too so hopefully she'll express her opinions on this. She's been rather quiet about this whole thing recently which is definitely not like her." I add the gray dress to the rack.

"Yeah, I've noticed that too. Maybe she's growing up." Tatyana comments and I chuckle a little. We go back to searching the sales rack and the racks nearby. We only find one more dress before Gram comes back to join us.

"Hey, Gram," I say as we shift through the racks.

"Hi, girls," Gram smiles at us then focuses her attention on me. "Are you ready to start trying on dresses? I think we may have picked out way too many so we should probably get started."

"Oh, okay yeah." I look over at Tatyana but let Gram lead me back to the part of the shop that has a changing room and big mirrors. The rest of the group has already taken their seats in the little half-circle in front of the changing room. Tatyana takes a seat next to Merrin and gives me a thumbs-up. The shop worker, or stylist, comes over to me with the first dress and leads me into the dressing room so she can help me put it on.

The first dress is not one of the ones Tatyana or I picked out but it's also not my style so I'm not worried about it. The stylist helps me get into it and she ties up the corset-like back then she waits for my nod before pulling open the curtain of the dressing room. I step out of the dressing room and take the stylist's hand to step up onto the little platform in front of the mirrors. I look at myself in the mirror and wait for reactions. It doesn't look horrible but not great either.

"Well," Mrs. Michaels starts, "you look beautiful, of course, but I don't think that's the one." A few people across the couch agree and I see Tatyana in the mirror smirking. I shoot her a glance and she bites her lip.

"I think we can all agree this one is a miss. Should we move on to the next dress?" Gram looks among the group and everyone nods. The stylist ushers me back into the dressing room and helps me get out of this one and holds out the gray dress Tatyana and I picked out.

Once we've got the gray dress situated, the stylist once again leads me out to the platform in front of everyone, I step up and look at myself in the mirror. Oh goodness, this is horrendous.

"Oh my," Mrs. Michaels comments.

"Oh, well... uhm.." Merrin stutters, trying to find something nice to say. I was right about mermaid style not working with my body and the gray makes it even worse. Gray does not go well with my skin tone.

"I don't mind it," Tatyana says and I can see her stifling a laugh. Even the stylist is trying her best not to make a disapproving face.

"Are you wanting a dress that isn't white?" Merrin finally finishes her sentence. "I'm not a huge fan of the gray but maybe an off-white or a light pink or light purple? Pastel colors maybe? I don't know."

"Pastel colors? I think that is a great idea," my mom comments and I can see her barely holding back further comments. She knows I like pastels but I think she can also tell something is going on with me.

"Yeah, just a lighter color. I mean I guess the gray is pastel, ish. But I think pink or purple or even blue would be better than gray." Merrin explains and her mom nods.

"Normally I would like to see you in a white dress but whatever you prefer, sweetie." Mrs. Michaels smiles at me sweetly, encouragingly.

"Well, you should at least try on some of the white dresses too, don't you think?" Gram asks, hopeful that one of the white dresses will sway me.

Truthfully, I would prefer to wear a white dress for my wedding but seeing as how I won't actually be wearing any of these dresses because this isn't a real wedding, I am having fun weighing the pros and cons of wearing a nonwhite dress for this fake wedding.

"We only have one more dress that isn't white, if you'd like to try that one on next?" The stylist makes the suggestion and then she adds, "To get it out of the way before we move onto the more traditional bridal dresses."

"Maybe we should," my mom says and gives me a look that I can tell means she is onto me. I see her glance at Tatyana who quickly puts her hand over her mouth to hide her smile.

"It's not any other color," I defend the dress. "It's just an off-white." Mrs. Michaels nods and Gram waves her hand, smiling. The stylist helps me off the platform and back into the dressing room. She grabs the off-white sparkly number that Tatyana found on the rack.

"You sure you want to try this on? I know I work here but even the lady who bought this dress and returned it said she had made a huge mistake." The stylist smiles and I laugh a little. I run my fingers down the puffy dress where it hangs inside the dressing room. My fingers come away covered in sparkles. Pink sparkles to be particular. I may have forgotten to mention that even though the dress itself is only slightly off-white, the sparkles are pink. They are pastel pink sparkles but still, pink. Which is perfect for Merrin and my mom's pastel idea.

"Oh yeah, we need to show them this." The stylist chuckles then she helps me step into the dress. The dress is a typical ball gown style but it looks more fairy princess rather than a bride. I let out a breath. "Alright, bring me to the village people. I feel like I need a wand to go with this outfit."

The stylist laughs but quiets herself as she leads me out to the platform once again. I avoid looking at everyone's faces but I can hear a few murmurs and gasps. I sneak a peek at the corner of the mirror where I can see Tatyana and I see her biting her lip to keep from grinning and probably laughing. I turn to face everyone with a smile on my face.

"So? What does everyone think?" I smile politely at everyone and take a look at their reactions.

"I love it," Tatyana says and lets the grin take over her face. I shoot her a look then roll my eyes and focus on everyone else.

"I know you like pink and we just talked about the idea of pastels… but you look like a fairy, not a bride," my mother says, much to my surprise. I try to stifle my laughter because she's not wrong but I can't believe she would make that comment in front of Mrs. Michaels. Merrin snorts at the comment and Tatyana lets out a laugh and nods in agreement.

"Shall we move on to the white dresses now?" Mrs. Micheals asks, not saying anything about the dress I am currently wearing. I let out a quiet sigh and let the stylist bring me back to the dressing room.

The stylist helps me into two more white dresses that have the group agreeing unanimously that they were not the ones for me. The next dress has my heart fluttering.

Oh no, I can't get excited about a dress for a fake wedding.

The dress is a beautiful A-line gown with detailed lace on the bodice and the skirt. The straps match beautifully with the bodice and when the stylist helps me with the dress, it fits perfectly. It hugs all of my curves but not in a bad way. Not in the usual way where I want to get a size up or wear a sweatshirt or sweater to cover myself. This dress makes me look gorgeous.

"Are you ready to show everybody?" The stylist asks, smiling at me.

# Chapter 38
## *Kurt*

I check my phone for the fifth time. Why isn't she answering me? I've texted her a few times but I haven't heard back yet. I don't want to come off as the annoying guy who needs to know where their girl is at all times, but I am stressing out thinking about Juliana alone with my mom and her mom and my sister and Juliana's grandmother. That is a lot of people who want this wedding to be real and who think it is real. I hope they aren't scaring her or pressuring her.

"Kurt, the second half is starting soon, you coming?" My dad calls from the living room. I make my way back into the room and drop onto the couch next to him.

"Any update on what the ladies are doing?" Juliana's dad asks. He looks over at me from where he sits in the matching chair across from his dad. Everyone looks over at me but I shake my head.

"I haven't heard anything," I check my phone again as I say it.

"Your sister probably confiscated everyone's phones." My dad says and I look at him, confused and he nods and shrugs his shoulders.

"She's gotten into this new thing where she wants everyone to be fully involved and off their phones when there is a planned event. I mean, I get it. You want someone's full attention when you're hanging out. It is a little dramatic to actually take away everyone's phone." My dad leans forward to grab some chips off the coffee table.

"Oh, I was wondering why Juliana wasn't texting me back. That would explain it." I set my phone down on the arm of the couch. Now I am very curious. "So no one was informed about where they are right now?"

"Nope," Juliana's dad says and his dad agrees. His wife, Juliana's grandmother, didn't say anything either.

"I'm sure wherever they are, they are having fun. I just hope your mom doesn't scare Juliana off. Hopefully, there will still be a wedding after today." My dad makes the comment and chuckles as he takes another chip. The comment should be funny and not too worrisome but it makes me feel guilty.

Sometimes, I feel fine with our situation but other times, when comments are made or happy feelings are expressed by those around us, I start to feel guilty. Guilty that we are getting everyone's hopes up and making everyone happy when Juliana and I both know this isn't going to have a happy ending. Then again, maybe one day it will. It obviously won't be as soon as everyone is expecting but my feelings are real and growing stronger the more I get to know Juliana.

My dad looks over at me and I guess I didn't hide my reaction as well as I should have because he leans forward and says quietly to me, "Hey, you okay? I didn't mean anything by that."

"No, no," I shake my head. "It's fine. I know Mom can be a bit overwhelming." I smile and emphasize *a bit* and my dad smiles and nods his head, sitting back on the couch. He glances over at me, still concerned but I keep my attention on the TV.

They've only been gone a couple of hours, but anything could have happened in that time. I contemplate for a minute then decide to send a text to Mom to see if she has her phone.

**Kurt: Are y'all still out for your girls' day?**

I send the text and set my phone on my knee so I can feel it vibrate if she responds to my text. A few minutes pass and I still don't have a response from Mom. Normally she has her phone on her and responds quickly so I guess Merrin must have taken her phone away too.

"Relax," I hear Juliana's dad's voice and I look up at him. He looks at me and gives a supportive smile. "Juliana is a strong young woman. She can handle a few hours of a girls' day. I also heard her mother on the phone with Tatyana, so she will at least have one person in her corner."

I sit back and give a quiet sigh of relief. Okay, she has Tatyana with her. Together they can handle the other four women, I hope.

The rest of the game isn't bad but it doesn't distract me from thinking about Juliana. The more time passes, the more I think about her. I catch myself glancing at my phone every so often and even though there are other people in the apartment with me, I feel lonely. The apartment just feels more like home with Juliana here.

"So, have you and Juliana started planning anything or even brainstorming ideas for the wedding yet?" Juliana's grandfather asks me when the game goes to a commercial. My dad looks over at me for my answer but when I hesitate he gets up and goes to the kitchen.

"Uh," I stutter a bit, trying to think of what to say. I clear my throat and try again. "Well, I know my mom wants us to have the wedding at the country club. Juliana and I both have agreed that we like that idea. It is something we are considering. We have good memories from when we were younger and hung out there so I think we are leaning towards that. Honestly, right now we both just have a lot going on so we haven't discussed the wedding that much. I have a lot on my plate at work, with a few different open cases that I have coming to court soon. Juliana also has been quite busy. She has a lot of hours at work because she wanted to contribute to the bills around the apartment, which I told her she didn't need to do but, of course, she insisted. She is quite stubborn, well, I don't have to tell you that."

I realize I've just gone on a long-winded rant and I pause to take a deep breath. I was trying to explain or rather make excuses for why we haven't really discussed the wedding but I probably came off a little stressed. After spending so much time with Juliana, I've begun taking on more of her mannerisms. One of those being her constant ramblings. It's a habit that I need to knock fast. It's cute when Juliana does it but no one needs a rambling attorney in court.

"Well, there's no rush. Some people stay engaged for a few months, they have a short engagement and then some couples stay engaged for a few years. It's really up to you and Juliana. Don't let anyone else's opinions or preferences influence you one way or the other. If you two are both busy for the foreseeable future, just enjoy being engaged and spending time together." Juliana's grandfather smiles at me while offering his advice and I feel myself relaxing a bit. Even if this wedding isn't real, I am just grateful that we have some support.

"Thank you," I smile gratefully at him and he nods.

My dad comes back to the couch and sits down with us. He cracks open another soda and takes a drink before he speaks.

"So, how do you feel about your daughter being engaged to Kurt?" My dad asks and I let out a chuckle. Juliana's dad laughs too then clears his throat and sits up a little straighter.

"Very disappointed in her choice. I mean Kurt? Really? She couldn't do better than him?" Juliana's dad chuckles and pokes fun of me. He gives me a big smile to show he's being sarcastic. I roll my eyes but smile as well.

"Thanks for that," I say in response and my dad laughs and slaps my back.

"No, but seriously, you're a great guy Kurt. Of course, I'm happy for both of you. I was a little surprised at first, I think a lot of us were." He takes a breath and I jump in.

"I know, we were a little surprised too. But, and I'm sure you've all heard the story before, we were friends and grew closer and fell in love. The engagement was pretty quick since we were really just friends before I proposed but when you know, you know. And I think we both knew." I say the common phrase that I've heard so many times.

"Hey, I can believe it," Juliana's dad raises his hands in defense. "I know y'all both had crushes on each other when you were kids but that was years ago. It's funny to see that it came back stronger than just a crush."

"She had a crush on me?" I ask, smirking a little. "That's cute."

"Don't start feeling all good about yourself because you definitely had a crush on her as well." I start to deny it but my dad shakes his head and laughs. He continues talking, "Oh, don't deny it. You did, we all knew it. Your mother thought it was adorable."

"Okay, fine," I relent a little. "Maybe when I was younger I had a bit of a crush on her too. Just a small one."

"Just a small one?" My dad laughs and shakes his head at me. "A small one that led to y'all being engaged many years later? I think it may have been a bigger crush than either of y'all would care to admit. But hey, that crush led you both to the place you are now and you both genuinely seem quite happy. So that is all that matters."

Juliana's dad nods, agreeing with everything my dad has said. The game comes back on but we keep the volume low while we continue talking. I start to relax more and only glance at my phone a few more times, but not as nervously as I had been doing earlier.

"Do you remember that time the Sunday School kids went out to y'all's place and you took care of her after she got hurt? She didn't stop talking about that for a whole month. And every Sunday she wanted her mom to help her pick out her cutest outfit and she would talk about you all morning then when we were getting close to Church in the car, she grew quiet and got so nervous. I doubt she even looked at you let alone talked to you then." Juliana's dad confesses and laughs at the memory. I can't help but smile. Juliana and I talked about that day recently and it was fun to hear the aftermath from her dad.

"You're right, I do not remember her approaching me after that event." I laugh and her dad laughs with me. "I think I made sure to check in with her the Sunday after that weekend at the lake house but it was just a quick check-in to see if her cut was healing alright. I remember she showed it to me then she ran away." I let out another laugh recalling the memory. Looking back on it now I can see how her actions showed how nervous she was because she had a crush on me.

# Chapter 39
## Juliana

When the stylist asks if I am ready to show everyone, I have mixed reactions. I know that she can tell I love this dress. I nod reluctantly. That's why we came here. That's why Ms. Michaels set all of this up. To see all the options for a wedding dress. I shouldn't show them this dress. I know I shouldn't. Maybe they won't like it as much as I do. But then again maybe they'll see how much I like it and that will make them like it more. There are too many thoughts going through my head. Before I know it, the stylist has me up on the platform and I hear gasps and murmurs again. This time, they sound like good reactions. After they admire the back of the dress and take peeks of my front in the mirror, the stylist helps me turn around to face them.

Looking around the group I see three out of the five have tears in their eyes. Merrin and Tatyana are the ones without tears but Merrin is grinning. Tatyana looks like she wants to love it but she knows our situation and she gives me a sad look. I realize I have a smile on my face but as soon as I see

Tatyana's reaction, the smile fades. I look down at the floor, seeing the beautiful train of the dress twisted around the platform.

"So, what does everyone think?" The stylist asks everyone and reaches down to straighten out the train of the dress. The train is delicate lace and extends maybe three feet longer than the end of the dress, which is kind of a dramatic length but it looks incredible with this dress.

"I love it!" Mrs. Michaels chokes out, dabbing tears from her face. She reaches over and squeezes my mother's hand. My mother has tears in her eyes as well. She smiles over at Mrs. Michaels then gets up to stand beside me in front of the mirror. My mom takes my hand and turns me to face the mirror again, she smiles at me in the mirror.

"You look beautiful," my mom says softly. Everyone gets up off the couch to join us and get a closer look at the dress.

"Wow, Juliana, this is the one." Merrin touches the bodice of the dress, mesmerized by it. Everyone takes their turn touching different parts of the dress, admiring it. "This is the one."

"Yeah, I think this is the one." Tatyana agrees with her and I shoot her a look, she shrugs and mouths 'sorry'.

"Oh, Juliana," Gram comes to stand beside me as well. "This dress is amazing and you look incredible. I agree, this is the one."

I sigh and look at myself in the mirror. Obviously, I can't buy this dress. I can't spend real money on a real wedding dress for a wedding that isn't going to happen.

"I don't know…" I see everyone's faces in the mirror. Everyone is staring at me and they are all smiling. Everyone looks happy. I don't want to let anyone down but I know if I bought the dress it would just make everything worse. "I do like it. I love it. I just don't have the money to purchase it at the moment. Especially since we don't even have a date set for the wedding." I turn around to face away from the mirror as everyone goes back to their seats.

"That's true," Tatyana pipes up. "You shouldn't get the dress too soon because you never know how long the engagement will be. Could be short but also could be a year or so. You two should really have that conversation." Tatyana gives me a pointed look as she plops back into her chair. She crosses her arms and leans back in the chair.

"Thank you, Tatyana." I smile a tight smile at her and she laughs. I turn to address the stylist. "Thank you, it's beautiful but for now I think it will just be a dream for the future." The stylist nods and helps me back to the dressing room to change out of the dress and back into my normal clothes.

When I come out of the dressing room Mrs. Michaels and Gram are admiring the dress where it hangs, on a hook outside the dressing room. They look up as I exit and they both smile at me.

"I'm sorry that we sprung this little trip on you." Mrs. Michaels tosses her arm around my shoulder and pulls me into a side hug. I smile and lean into her for the hug. "I hope it wasn't too much for you."

"Oh no, of course not. It was very nice of you to set this up for me and everyone. I had a lot of fun. I'm sorry it didn't exactly end up with a happy ending."

"Oh dear, don't worry about it." Mrs. Michaels waves her hand, dismissing my apology. "I should have realized it was too soon to go dress shopping, I guess I got a little excited."

"Can we still try on bridesmaid dresses?" Merrin pops up next to us, smiling and lifting the mood. We look over at the stylist who smiles at us.

"You do have a five-hour appointment. And it's only been about three." She checks her watch to confirm and gives a nod then looks up at me for approval. I turn to look at Tatyana and see her face looking a little terrified. I smile and nod my head in approval.

"Oh, yes. I think we should. Can we go around the shop again and look at the dresses for the bridesmaids?" I look back at the stylist and she points out all the racks for bridesmaid dresses. I excitedly make my way over to Tatyana and drag her off the couch. She groans but lets me lead her to a rack of bridesmaid dresses. Merrin joins us and soon we are all crowded around the different racks.

"So, is there a theme that we want to stick to when looking for bridesmaid dresses?" Mrs. Michaels asks. I've noticed she's done most of the talking today. My mom usually talks a lot as well but I guess she is trying to be on her best behavior in front of Mrs. Michaels, her future in-law. Well, not really but she thinks so, everyone thinks so. This is so hard.

"I like pastels." I offer up, not really sure what theme I want but drawing from their earlier discussion. Mostly because there isn't a real wedding to have a theme for. Of course, I have thought about my wedding a few times, more than a few times but that does not mean I thought specifically about this wedding right now.

"See! I knew it. I mentioned pastel earlier, didn't I? I totally did." Merrin claps her hands excitedly and starts shifting through dresses to find pastel-colored ones.

"That you did," My mom says and gives me a look. I shrug. "I thought you always wanted your wedding to be pink and sparkly, with tons of flowers?" My mom smiles as she teases me. She seems be having fun and enjoying herself today. I smile and laugh at the comment.

"I still like pink, certain shades. And flowers. But sparkly? Not so much." I laugh again remembering that I did in fact want a pink, sparkly, and floral wedding when I was younger.

"And I don't mean pastel pink, I am talking about bright pink, hot pink." My mom teases me more and we both are laughing. "Hm, that would be a fun idea for the bridesmaid dresses?" She looks at me and raises her eyebrows, smirking a bit then looks over at Tatyana. Tatyana's face drains of color and she looks horrified.

"Oh lord, please don't make me wear hot pink." Tatyana groans again showing her disgust at the idea.

"Yeah, normally I would say yes to whatever you, the bride, would pick but honey no. Please no hot pink." Even Merrin looks a little worried which makes my mom and I laugh even harder. Mrs. Michaels starts snickering a bit too and Gram follows soon and we all start laughing. Tatyana still looks a little scared but I reach out and squeeze her arm.

"Don't worry, I won't force you two to wear hot pink. I think I grew away from that a few years back. We should probably stick with pastels for now. Oh! Here's a cute one!" I pull a delicate blue dress off of the rack and hold it out for everyone to see.

"Ooo, yes. That is beautiful." Merrin reaches out and I hand the dress to her.

"There are more dresses similar to that dress, if you'd like to see?" The stylist comes over to us. "It is part of a collection. We have the same dress in multiple colors and then we also have the same color dress but in different styles, if either of those ideas is of interest to you."

"Uhm, can we see the same dress but in different colors first?" I make the decision and the stylist nods and goes to pull more colors in the same style.

The stylist brings them back over and hangs them all for display on a rack facing our group. There are four different colors including the blue one. The other three are; green, pink, and gray. All the colors are light pastels and would fit the theme I have in mind if the wedding was real. This is probably going too far at this point but I don't know how to stop it, I don't know how to get out of this day. Hopefully, there aren't more days like this in the future. I have enjoyed hanging out with everyone but dress shopping for a wedding that isn't going to happen is such a stressful situation. Especially spending five hours on it.

Tatyana reaches for the gray dress but I'm quicker, I smack her hand away and hand her the pink dress. She groans audibly but accepts the dress. I turn to Merrin and think for a second then hand her the green dress. She smiles and accepts it, excited by the choice.

"Okay!" The stylist claps her hands and then gestures to the dressing rooms. Tatyana and Merrin each go into one of the other rooms and the stylist moves to help Merrin while I offer to help Tatyana. The stylist thanks me and shows me the back of the dress and how to fashion it once the dress is on. I nod my head while watching and confirm that I understand. Once I'm in the dressing room with Tatyana, she whispers to me.

"I can't believe you're actually letting them pick out bridesmaid dresses and your own bridal dress!" She whispers harshly and I shush her. "And worst of all, you're making me try on the pink dress!"

"You're lucky they didn't have a yellow option for this dress," I whisper back while I lace up the back of her dress and fix the fabric to get it right; the way the stylist showed me.

"Uh!" Tatyana gasps looking at me in the mirror. "You wouldn't!" I chuckle and give her a look with my eyebrows raised. My expression says, 'Test me, I dare you'.

"Oh, come on. You look great in yellow." I tease her but honestly, she does look good in yellow. She hates it but also knows she looks good in yellow.

"You ladies ready to come out?" The stylist calls to us and I hear her push back the curtain of Merrin's dressing room.

"Yup, all set here," I say then push our curtain back and step out then I take Tatyana's seat to see the show of bridesmaid dresses.

Merrin and Tatyana step out pretty much at the same time and the stylist helps both of them up onto the platform in front of us and the giant mirrors. There are a few initial reactions that show everyone is relatively pleased with the dresses.

"So what do you all think of the dresses?" The stylist asks, looking around at the group.

"I like the dress, I do. I'm not sure which color. Can we see the blue dress on someone?" Mrs. Michaels asks the stylist and she nods looking over at Tatyana and Merrin. Tatyana looks pretty bored but I know she'll want to get out of the pink dress.

"Actually, we have both of their sizes in the blue if you are interested in seeing them wear the same style and color bridesmaid dress?" The stylist looks at me for approval.

"Oh, sure. I'm open to anything at this point." I shrug and Tatyana looks annoyed again but accepts the dress when the stylist hands it to her. I get up to help again but Mrs. Michaels waves me off.

"No dear, you shouldn't have to help. Just sit back and relax. I'll help her with this one." Mrs. Michaels smiles at me and goes over to help Tatyana. Tatyana gives me a look over Mrs. Michaels' shoulder, which thankfully she doesn't notice. I shrug and sit back down.

"Are you having a nice day?" My mother comes to sit beside me. I straighten my back, sitting up, ready to be evasive if she asks about the wedding or the relationship.

"Yes, thank you. It was very sweet of Mrs. Michaels to set all of this up. Even though Kurt and I just got engaged." I add, trying not to press the matter but still a little confused why we needed to jump into dress shopping so quickly.

"She's just excited," my mom says, keeping her eyes on the dressing rooms. "We all are. It was all a little sudden so we were also surprised but this is exciting news. Kurt is a great man."

"Thanks, I know," I respond and smile at her. The more I spend time with Kurt the more I get to know how great he is. "And yes it was sudden which is why we've discussed taking our time with the engagement. We don't want to rush to the altar, we want to enjoy living together and getting to know each other better for a bit first. So I hope no one expects us to have a wedding right away." I say it as politely as I can but try to speak firmly.  I really should be saying this with Mrs. Michaels around but I think my mom will also tell her what I said.

"What are you ladies discussing?" Gram comes over to sit with us. She puts her arm around me to give me a hug, I lean into her.

"Juliana was just saying how she and Kurt are probably going to have a long engagement," my mother responds for us and I clear my throat.

"Kind of. I was explaining that since we just moved in together and we got engaged pretty fast, we aren't going to rush the wedding." I offer the half-baked explanation but I'm already tired of lying to everyone. The guilt is starting to eat at me and shopping for dresses has escalated the whole situation. Gram nods in understanding and pats my back.

"Alright, here are the two blue dresses in the same style." The stylist says as she steps out from the dressing room, pulling back the curtain. Mrs. Michaels pulls her curtain back a second later and she steps out of the way to let Tatyana out. Tatyana and Merrin both exit their respective dressing rooms and come to stand on the platform in front of us once again.

"I need to step outside for a minute," I say, suddenly feeling overwhelmed by everything. I stand up quickly and everyone looks concerned. Tatyana looks at me, questioning if I want her to come with me but I shake my head. "I just need some air." I excuse myself and walk outside, leaving Tatyana to cover for me, bringing everyone's attention back to the dresses. The door closes behind me before I let myself lean against the wall and take a deep breath.

"Did you just come out of that bridal boutique?" A deep voice asks, shocked.

Oh no, seriously? Why do I always have to run into him at the worst time?

# Chapter 40
## *Juliana*

"Juliana?" The voice repeats and I force myself to look up and away from the concrete sidewalk.

"What?" I look up and paste on a polite smile. "Oh, hi Callum."

"Did you just come out of that bridal shop?" Callum repeats, his voice still confused and shocked. I sigh and tug my hair a bit, a headache is starting to grow and quickly at that.

"Yes," I say but offer no further information. Callum nods and looks down at me.

"So I guess you guys are moving along with this wedding?" Callum rolls his eyes, clearly not amused by the development. When I don't say anything, and he clocks the glare on my face, Callum smirks. "What? You don't look happy to see me."

"Callum, after your childish display at our house party, I would be happy to never see you again." I stare up at him with a cold look, as hard as I can manage when my head starts pounding.

"Juliana," Callum starts and I see his hand reaching for me but I take a step back, pressing my back against the wall. I decide I don't want to be trapped, my back literally against the wall so I sidestep around him and feel freer out in the open. "Look, I wrote that song about you when I was mad at you. And it's not like I lied about any of it." Callum looks kind of smug, looking down at me with a smirk on his face.

"That's not fair, and you know it," I say, tears threatening to spill from my eyes. "I wasn't ready."

"Oh, you weren't? But you are now?" Callum steps closer to me, his eyebrows raising and his smirk growing. A pit opens up in my stomach and I feel sick, my head is throbbing even more now.

"No. Please stop." I put my hand up to keep him from advancing but he just leans into my hand until my hand is sandwiched between our chests. He leans down until his face is near mine. I turn my head away from him and stumble back a little because of his weight.

Callum maneuvers me again and my efforts to remain untrapped are rendered useless. He backs me up against the wall of the dress shop and I'm fighting back tears now. I know Callum has a temper and I don't want to cause a scene by trying to push him off.

When I don't make any moves, Callum huffs a little. "So, you are ready now but not with me? Hmm, I guess that new guy of yours is better than me, right? Of course, he is. Because I am always the bad guy."

"Well, if the shoe fits," I say. My voice wavers a little bit and the phrase is a bit cheesy but at least I was able to speak up for myself. I gesture to his intimidating posture with my free hand.

Callum laughs a little, but there is no humor in it. He stands up straight and takes a step back. He doesn't move too far away but at least there is some distance between us now.

I am about to say something else when the door to the bridal shop opens and Tatyana comes hurdling out of it. Before either Callum or I can react, Tatyana, still dressed in a bridesmaid dress, launches herself at Callum with her knee up in front of her and nails him right in the sweet spot. Callum doubles over and then falls to the sidewalk, groaning and grabbing himself.

"What the hell are you doing here, you -" Tatyana starts to go on a long rant filled with curse words but I jump in and grab onto her arm as I see her launch towards him again.

"Heyyy, hey there. As much as I appreciate this, you probably shouldn't do that with the company inside." I make a face and Tatyana makes a 'whoops' expression.

"Stay away from her," Tatyana says, then loops her arm through mine and we go back into the shop leaving Callum on the sidewalk groaning in pain. Once we are inside, Tatyana smiles at me. "See I refrained from calling him anything that last time."

"Yes." I laugh and smile appreciatively. "I am so proud of you. Thanks for coming out there and defending my honor." I chuckle and squeeze her arm.

"Anytime." Tatyana hip-bumps me and leads me back to the rest of the group. I look back for a second and see Callum getting off the ground and limping away. I smile, I have the most amazing best friend.

"Everything alright over here, ladies?" Mrs. Michaels walks over to us and I quickly step away from the window to meet her so she doesn't see Callum disappearing down the street.

"Yes, I just needed some fresh air. I'm not used to all this attention and trying on so many gowns," I trail off with a small smile. "Whew, a lot of them were quite warm."

Mrs. Michaels laughs a joyous laugh and links her arm through mine, pulling me back toward the group. "That is completely understandable. Take as many breaks as you need."

"Thank you," I say but look back at Tatyana as Mrs. Michaels drags me away. "*Help*," I mouth. Tatyana shakes her head but reluctantly follows behind us.

We settle back on the couch and watch as Merrin tries on a few more dress options. Instead of joining her, Tatyana taps out and after changing back into her own clothes, she comes to sit beside me. She has a glass of champagne in her hand as she leans into me.

"Are you okay?" She whispered, trying to keep her voice low.

I look around to make sure no one can see us before I respond to her. "I don't know how I keep running into him. I don't know why he won't leave me alone."

"I'm sorry, kid. We'll figure it out." Tatyana rubs my arm to comfort me.

When we are finally finished with the appointment at the shop, I've almost forgotten that this whole thing wasn't real. Mrs. Michaels and Merrin made me feel so welcome and having my mom and grandmother with me had only brought all of us closer. Tatyana even looked like she was having fun.

"Thank you so much for such a wonderful day," I say to Mrs. Michaels as we all head back to the cars. The others walk ahead of us while Tatyana trails behind.

"Oh, of course, dear. I am so glad we were able to spend some time together. Hopefully, we can get together soon," Mrs. Michaels says and pulls me closer to her to give me a side hug.

"I would like that," I admit and she nods then gives a little wave as she gets in her car with the rest of the group. Thankfully, I don't have to travel back with them now that Tatyana is here.

I say a quick goodbye to everybody else before finding peace and quiet in Tatyana's car. I close my eyes but I can feel her staring at me. I grunt and point to the road. She starts the car with a chuckle.

"Drinks?" Tatyana asks as she pulls out of the parking lot. When I don't say anything, she looks over at me and I peek at her from under my eyelashes. "You just want to go home?"

"I'm sorry," I say with a nod but Tatyana just waves the worry away.

"You've had a long day. Hey, since it's basically dinner time, do you want to stop somewhere? We can just get things to go and you can bring something back for Kurt," Tatyana suggests and I nod, realizing I am very hungry.

"Thanks for coming out today," I finally speak.

"Of course, I love helping my best friend in all her schemes." Tatyana is only teasing me but I groan. I feel bad. "Hey, do you think Kurt knew about this outing today?"

"I'm not sure, I doubt it. Oh, speaking of," I say as I pull out my phone. I have a few missed calls and unopened messages from Kurt. It makes me smile seeing him reach out to me so much. I text him back saying I am on the way home and picking up dinner for both of us. He responds pretty quickly and gives me his order for the restaurant.

Tatyana and I chit-chat a bit while we wait in the drive-through. I make Tatyana let me pay for her dinner as a thank you for coming dress shopping today. She puts up a bit of a fight before she eventually gives in and hands over my credit card to the woman in the window.

When we get back to Kurt's apartment, I hug Tatyana and thank her again. "Thank you so much for coming out and putting up with everything. I know you aren't a huge fan of dress shopping but I am so glad you were there, especially when Callum showed up. You are literally a lifesaver. You are the best best friend I could ever ask for."

"Oh, I know," Tatyana comments, making both of us burst into giggles. After such a stressful day, it feels so good to laugh. "Okay, go bring dinner home for your man."

"Thank you!" I blow her a kiss as I jump out of the car. She laughs and rolls her eyes at me but waits until I get inside the building before she drives off.

I greet the doorman, Marvin, and make my way up to the apartment. Knocking on the door as I push it open, I call out into the apartment.

"Hi, honey! I'm home!"

"Hey! There you are. What have you been up to?" Kurt smiles at me from the kitchen. He's washing dishes and it looks like he had a few guests over. I come into the kitchen, kiss his cheek without hesitation, and then go set my purse down before setting the bag of food on the counter. I grab a few dishes and help him finish up, standing side by side as we work.

"Whew," I breathe out. "That was a long day. Your mother surprised me with a girls' trip to a dress shop. A wedding dress shop," I add in case he didn't see the big deal.

"Oh. Oh, wow." Kurt hands me dishes to stack in the dishwasher when he finishes rinsing them. We work together as a team and finish in a few minutes.

"I know! It was quite shocking," I admit when our focus shifts to the food I brought home for dinner. I pull out plates for us and set our food on the plates. Kurt watches me with a smile and waits patiently until I hand him his plate. "Although we spent most of the time on the bridesmaid dresses which Tatyana hated, Merrin loved."

I chuckle but Kurt still hasn't said anything as we bring our plates to the kitchen table to sit and eat together. I take a few bites and look at him nervously.

"Don't worry, though. I know it isn't real. We didn't actually purchase anything. It was just fun going out with everyone and playing dress up," I say with a giggle and Kurt offers another warm smile. "So, what did you get up to while we were all there?"

"Ah, football. Both of our dads and your grandpa came over to watch the game. That's why I had so many dishes to wash," Kurt explains and I nod. "It was a good day."

"It was," I agree with him.

We chat while we eat our food, mostly talking about our days. I tell him about dress shopping but I hesitate to tell him about the interaction with Callum. When I pause, Kurt narrows his eyes at me.

"What are you not telling me?"

"Well," I start. Kurt raises his eyebrows at me and gestures for me to continue. I sigh. "Okay, so don't freak out."

"Why would I freak out?" Kurt asks, trying to hide the fact that he is starting to freak out.

"See, I can tell you're starting to get worked up and worried about what I am about to say. But before you do, I will just let you know that I was fine. I handled the situation and then Tatyana pummeled the situation." I look at him to see his reaction and now his eyes are narrowed at me.

"What does that mean, exactly?" Kurt tries to remain calm and arranges the features on his face to appear neutral. I stare at him for a few seconds, a touch weirded out about it but I can see how he would be an excellent lawyer, remaining calm under pressure in court.

"Okay, so… The dress situation was a bit stressful so I stepped outside," I tell him and his eyebrows knit in concern but that isn't even the part of the day I am worried about telling him. "And I ran into Callum. He was a little aggressive and kind of trapped me and I don't think he would have done anything but he didn't get a chance to because Tatyana came out and basically kicked his ass and saved me. So, yeah, that is all that happened. I'm sorry that I didn't tell you sooner."

I rush through the story, trying to tell it quickly and make it not as dramatic as possible without lying about what happened. Kurt sits back and looks at me for a few seconds, I wait patiently for him to say something.

"Wow," Kurt finally says. "Are you okay?"

"Yeah, yeah. I'm okay. You know, I am used to him and his antics," I admit and Kurt's forehead pinches in frustration and further concern.

"That's not good, Juliana. You shouldn't be used to that. He shouldn't be acting like that, around you or anyone else," Kurt says but I think he can tell that I am not in the place for a lecture so he stops short. "I'm glad Tatyana was there when you needed her," Kurt says, changing his concerns into appreciation.

"Yeah, me too. She is an amazing friend."

Our conversation trails off and I ask him about the football game. I can tell he wants to say something more about the interaction with Callum but instead, he lets me change the subject and acts like a willing participant.

We finish the night by cuddling on the couch and watching TV. Well, we're not exactly cuddling but we sit close to each other and Kurt has his arm over the back of the couch. I keep sneaking glances at him but he's staring straight ahead at the TV.

I reach up and touch his chin lightly. Only then does he turn to look at me. "What's going on in your head?" I ask quietly, worried he's freaked out about the dress shopping.

Kurt stares down at me and I try to read his expression and the look in his eyes but I can't tell what he is thinking. "Are you sure you're okay?" Kurt answers my question with a question of his own.

I nod, snuggling into his side, pleased that he is worried about my safety and not freaked out. His arm drops from the couch to settle onto my back. We're still looking at each other and I don't want the connection to stop. I tilt my head back, opening up to him. His eyes flash as his emotions shift. A small smile appears on his face, indicating that he understood the implication of my movement.

"Are you sure?" Kurt asks as he slowly leans down, getting closer to my lips.

"I'm sure," I whisper, almost breathless with anticipation.

Kurt's lips touch mine lightly, barely brushing against mine. He's waiting for me to let him know I'm okay. As a response, I slide my hand behind his head and push gently while pressing my lips firmer against his. Our mouths crash together and the kissing turns fervent. Kurt pulls me into his lap and I feel him against my thigh. I feel my cheeks heating up, turning red, and I am glad Kurt cannot see the innocent nerves.

# Chapter 41
## *Juliana*

Kurt's hands grip my ass, pulling me closer to him. My legs fit on either side of him and I settle in, fitting against him perfectly. I moan against his mouth and he grunts in response, opening his mouth to taste my moans. I'm a little embarrassed thinking about if my breath is okay or not but when one of his hands moves around to my front and slips under my dress, I lose all thought. All I can think about is his hand touching my bare thighs. He pushes the skirt up, exposing more of my thighs and he rubs his hand over my leg, keeping one hand firm on my ass.

His hand slides up my thigh and around to grip my hip. I start to memorize the way he touches me, the way he squeezes my hip and moves his hand to my abdomen, spreading his fingers across my belly. Every place his fingers touch leaves a little spark on my skin. His touch elicits a feeling deep inside that I haven't felt before.

The feeling makes me adventurous and I slide my hands down Kurt's chest until I reach the bottom of his skirt. Kurt leans back, opening a space between us so I can also get my hands under his shirt. Our mouths stay locked together as we explore one another.

When my fingers find their way under his shirt, Kurt lets out a sharp hiss, pulling back from the kiss.

"I'm so sorry, are you okay?" I ask, breathing hard.

"Yes, yes, sorry. Your hands are cold. It's okay, baby. Please don't," Kurt says when I remove my hands. He is breathing heavily too, and his eyelids are low. "I want you to touch me." Kurt's words spark my heart even more and I practically pounce on him.

My mouth captures his again and we fall into another deep kiss. I put my hands back on his stomach, and he stiffens but after a few seconds, he relaxes under my touch, my hands warming from his heat. I raise my hands up his chest, lightly dragging my nails back down. The action makes him groan against my mouth and I kiss him hungrily.

Kurt's hands are both on my ass now, gripping once again before they move up my back. He shifts his hands, sliding them around my side until his thumb rubs against the wire in my bra. My breath catches in my throat which makes his fingers stop moving. To encourage him, I shift in his lap, pressing myself down onto him. His jeans press against my panties and I'm sure he can feel the heat between my legs. His hands continue on their path until his palms spread out just below my breasts. When I don't stop him, his hands cup upwards, grabbing me in his large hands.

I gasp a little, crying out softly. We break apart once again but he doesn't release me. "Are you sure you're okay?" Kurt's voice is husky and the sound makes my heart beat faster. I look at him with flushed cheeks and he smiles back at me, his thumbs rubbing over the material of my bra. I wore a lacy bra with no padding today so I can feel every touch. I nod and bite my lip, trying to stifle another moan.

Kurt's hands grip and grope me, kneading me through my bra. His hands are warm and strong against me but he's being so gentle as well. We part to breathe and he moves his mouth to my neck, planting little kisses across my shoulder, nipping and sucking at my skin. I remove one of my hands from his shirt and tangle my fingers in his hair, holding him close to me. I push my hips forward, shifting on his lap which makes him groan against my neck.

"You need to stop moving," Kurt says in a deep, gruff voice.

"Why?" I whisper. I sit back a little, angling my hips forward again, and giggle when he groans once again. His eyes close as he leans back on the couch. "Is this bothering you?" I tease, moving my hips forward and backward, pressing down on his lap.

"Juli..." Kurt's voice is strained and when he opens his eyes to look at me, I stop moving from the intensity in them. Before I can do anything else, Kurt wraps his arms behind me and flips me onto my back on the couch. I look up at him, breathless and shocked by the seductive action. He chuckles at my reaction, making me blush. He holds himself above me, half sitting on the couch, my legs draped over his thighs. My thighs are spread wide to fit him between my legs, the skirt of my dress pooling around my midsection and I am very aware that my panties are peeking out but Kurt doesn't take his eyes off my face.

Kurt runs his fingers lightly down my face, my neck, between my breasts, and then down to my lower stomach. His hand rests on my stomach and I can feel its heat through the material of my dress. "You are so beautiful," he whispers, letting his eyes wander down my body and the little smile on his face grows. I can feel my cheeks heating up but I feel excited that he likes what he sees, even if I am not yet naked.

I reach between us and Kurt looks up, surprised. I tug at his pants a little, needing my second hand as well to undo the button. Kurt watches for a few seconds before he grabs my wrist gently. My hands still and he removes them, placing them by my sides.

"What's wrong?" I ask, fighting back the emotions of being rejected.

"Shh, don't be upset," Kurt reassures me, his hands returning to my hips. His hands start moving and I realize he is lifting my dress higher, exposing more of my panties. "I wasn't rejecting you, I'm not rejecting you. I just want to make sure that you are comfortable and happy. I can wait. This makes me happy." Kurt's words are soothing and make my stomach tingle.

"I've never…" I start and Kurt looks up at me, waiting for me to continue. "I mean, Callum never…" I still can't finish the sentence but instead gesture down to my bottom half which makes Kurt chuckle. I furrow my brow and stick out my bottom lip pouting, but that just makes him laugh even more.

"I promise, I am not laughing at your lack of experience. I am laughing at your gesturing, which is very cute, so don't be embarrassed," Kurt says, squeezing my hips in reassurance. "I would like to though, if you're okay with that and want me to," he tells me, making my heart beat faster with anticipation and appreciation for him checking in with me.

I nod which makes him smile but instead of going down, he leans up toward my face and kisses me softly.

"Juli," Kurt says to get my attention when he pulls away from the kiss. He has my full attention already. "I need you to talk to me, tell me what you want."

"I want…" I trail off when his mouth finds a sensitive spot on my neck. I gasp a little and feel shivers all over my body as his mouth moves down my chest until he hits the fabric of my dress then he pauses and looks up at me. He pushes up the skirt of my dress until it is bunched just below my breasts, and he drags his thumbs over my rib cage.

"What do you want, Juliana?" Kurt asks me again, his hands moving lower until he hooks his fingers in the waistband of my panties.

"I want your mouth," I admit, my voice shaky as he plants a kiss on my thigh. He smiles at me and kisses down my inner thigh, getting closer and closer to where I want him to be. "Please," I say softly, almost ashamed of how much I want him.

"It's sexy when you beg for me," Kurt says, a smirk on his face. I bite my lip, narrowing my eyes at him. "No, don't stop now," Kurt teases.

His fingers grip the waistband of my panties and he pulls on them gently. "Lift your hips, please," Kurt instructs and I lift them willingly. He pulls my panties off quickly and smoothly. I drop my hips quickly and he lifts my legs to get rid of my panties entirely.

Kurt doesn't take his eyes off of me, his eyelids lowered with lust. I can see his pants throbbing. I pull my skirt down over myself, suddenly feeling self-conscious. Kurt narrows his eyes and looks up at me before lifting my skirt again.

"Don't cover up for me. I think you are beautiful, so incredibly stunning," Kurt marvels.

I want to beg him to devour me but I don't know how far either of us is willing to go. And I'm not sure if I am ready for everything. I like him, I want him and I want to be with him but I'm not sure if I can give everything to this if the relationship is doomed from the start. I never thought this would happen after calling him my fiancé to scare off Callum. I hadn't realized all of these emotions and feelings would develop between us.

Kurt's mouth finding my sensitive spot effectively pulls me out of my head. All thoughts disappear, and all worries evaporate as my back arches and fireworks fill my mind. I squirm under Kurt but he doesn't let me go. He holds my hands and looks up at me from between my legs. I watch him and bite my lip to keep from being too loud, my reactions only seem to encourage Kurt and he works even harder to make me feel so good. It isn't long before a wave of pleasure is crashing over me.

# Chapter 42
## *Kurt*

Juliana tastes delicious and I can't get enough. Her squirming is making it hard to do my best but she doesn't seem to notice. She closes her eyes and I watch her face conforming, twisting with all of the emotions taking over. Her moans are soft and timid and I vow to get her to feel comfortable enough to lose control. Her hands squeeze mine, and she holds on tight. When she finishes, she releases my hands, breathing heavily. Instead of stopping, I slide one hand up her stomach to grip her breast and bring the other hand down to meet my mouth, pushing into her wetness.

Juliana gasps and I can feel her legs quivering on either side of my face. She does not last nearly as long this time and is soon grabbing my hair, crying out.

Finally, I stop, letting her lie back and relax. I sit up, still between her legs, wiping my mouth off. I look down at her and she looks so content with a little smile on her face. I reach down and touch her cheek softly. Her eyes flutter open and she looks up at me.

"Are you okay?" I ask.

"Yes," Juliana speaks, breathless. "That was...wow."

Juliana can't seem to find words but her response makes me smile. The ego boost is not needed but I am happy that I made her feel good. She starts to sit up, her skirt falling back down to cover her as she reaches for my pants once again.

I really want to let her but I can see that she is getting sleepy and I don't want her to think that she has to reciprocate. "Juliana, you don't have to," I tell her. She looks up at me with a little frown. "I'm not saying I don't want you to, believe me, I do. But I know today has been such a long day. We have time," I say to her and she looks relieved. I can tell she wants to please me as well but she is still holding back for another reason, so I don't want her to feel pressured to do anything else tonight. I am more than content with just pleasing her.

"Are you sure?" Juliana asks and I nod. "I'm sorry."

"No, Juliana. You have no reason to be sorry," I tell her, trying to reassure her.

"But..." Juliana trails off as her eyes go to my bulging crotch. I chuckle a little and sit back on the couch, pulling Juliana into my lap.

"It's fine. It will go away soon," I say and then I think better of it and slide her off my lap, she frowns. "Probably better to keep you off of me." Juliana blushes at my explanation but nods, understanding.

"Uhm, I think I should go shower and get ready for bed," Juliana says, standing up, her skirt falling back into place. Her chest is heaving as she breathes heavily, trying to calm down.

I can't take my eyes off her chest, her nipples poking through her top. I look away because it does nothing to help my situation.

"Okay, yeah. I think I am going to finish this episode then I need to take a cold shower," I say with a chuckle.

"Alright, I will try not to take too long," Juliana says, backing away from me.

"Take your time," I tell her as she leaves the living room. I watch her go, admiring her ass as she walks away. I drag my eyes back to the TV and let out a breath. I was not expecting that to happen tonight but I was more than pleasantly surprised. I want to go further but I don't want Juliana to feel uncomfortable or rushed. I am willing to wait for her.

The thought shocks me but I realize that I really like her. I want her to feel comfortable and safe with me. I want to explore with her and help her open up.

I hear the shower turn on and immediately start to picture her. I want to join her but I don't think that would be appropriate yet. Instead, I sit on the couch, trying and failing to pay attention to the TV show. The minutes pass by agonizingly slow and eventually Juliana comes out of the bathroom with a towel wrapped around her.

"The bathroom is all yours," Juliana tells me and I look over at her. Her body is still glistening with beads of water and her cheeks are still flushed from the evening's activities.

"Okay, thank you." I wait a few more minutes before turning off the TV and getting up to go shower. The bathroom smells like Juliana, and I breathe her in. The smell of her shampoo almost makes me hard again. I quickly turn on the shower, stripping down to take a cold shower.

When I finish in the bathroom, nothing in my mind has been cleared up and when I see Juliana reading in bed, my heart beats faster. I smile at her but she doesn't look up, too engrossed in her book. I set all my things on my bedside table and climb into bed. Juliana looks over at me and she smiles sweetly. I move closer to her, draping my arm over her thighs, as I lay on my stomach. She sets her book on my arm and I chuckle.

"You comfortable?" Juliana asks, looking down at me snuggling into her side.

"Yes, very," I admit, closing my eyes and yawning.

"Do you want me to turn off the light for you to go to sleep?"

"No, it's okay. Read as long as you like. I do have work tomorrow so my alarm will probably wake you up," I remind her.

"Oh, it's okay. I have work too. I should probably go to bed," Juliana agrees. She sets her book on her nightstand and then she turns off the light. I let go of her while she wiggles down to get comfortable then put my arm back out, this time across her stomach.

We lay in the dark in silence for a few minutes but I can tell she is still awake.

"Should we talk about what happened tonight?" I ask, my voice a shock in the quiet.

"What do you mean? Did I do something wrong?" Juliana asks, worried.

"No, no. Everything that happened tonight was natural and normal," I tell her and she lets out a breath of relief. "I just mean, if you want to talk about how our relationship is escalating."

"Our relationship?" Juliana asks. I chuckle.

"Well, we live together because of our fake relationship but I feel like we are developing a real one. Especially after tonight and lately, we have been getting closer," I explain. "So, I thought we should probably talk about what this means."

"Oh, okay," Juliana says, her pulse picking up. She looks over at me and we are almost nose to nose, lying next to each other. "So, is this where I'm supposed to ask 'what are we'?" Juliana says with a giggle. I roll my eyes but don't mind the joke.

"Basically," I admit.

"Okay, so… what are we?" Juliana asks with a little smirk on her face.

"Well, I'm not sure," I admit honestly. "I know that we are not fiancés, obviously." Juliana nods and waits patiently with a little smile on her face. "But I also know that we are definitely more than friends."

Juliana moves closer to me and we both turn our bodies to face each other. I pull her leg over my hip and hold onto the back of her thigh. We stare into each other's eyes, each trying to read the other's thoughts.

"Definitely more than friends," Juliana repeats back to me. "So, what does that mean?"

"I don't know." The response bums both of us out but I don't think either of us knows how to define this budding relationship. I don't know that we could or should put a label on it when we are already pretending to be fiancés.

"Maybe we will think of the answer after a good night's sleep," Juliana suggests.

"Yeah, maybe."

Juliana leans in and kisses me softly. I press my lips firmly against her and she parts her mouth for me. We spend another hour or so kissing and just touching each other. Her hands are nervous at first but grow more confident over time as she explores my body. We kiss until we grow tired and fall asleep in each other's arms.

# **Chapter 43**
## *Kurt*

I wake up before my alarm goes off and find Juliana wrapped around me. Her hair is spread out over my chest and her arm is wrapped around my stomach while her legs are intertwined with mine. The connection makes my heart beat faster. She looks so beautiful right now. The light is streaming in from the side of the curtain and it's casting a line over her back. We are both fully clothed and the heat between us is making me sweat.

I reach over to try to grab my phone off my nightstand to turn off my alarm before it goes off. While reaching for it, Juliana stirs. She yawns and opens her eyes slowly.

"Good morning," I say and she looks up at me from her perch on my chest. She yawns again and then sits up, stretching a little as she untangles herself from me.

"Good morning," Juliana says through a yawn. "How did you sleep?" She asks and I can tell she is already thinking about our conversation last night. I wonder if she found any clarity while sleeping, I know that I did not.

"I slept alright, how about you?" I sit up beside her, resting my hand on her thigh.

"Me too." Juliana nods. "So, did you find an answer?" She asks, looking nervous.

"No, I gotta admit, I was pretty tired. I don't think I thought about anything," I tell her and she nods, smiling a little.

"Okay, good because me too. I passed out and there was nothing going on in here," Juliana says, poking the side of her head with a laugh. "Glad we are on the same page, then."

"Exactly," I say then I lean over and kiss her gently, still thrilled I get to do that now without worrying what she might think. "Should I not do that until we figure this out?" I ask when I pull back, hoping she will disagree. Juliana's eyes are still closed from the kiss but she opens them slowly.

"Oh no, I think kissing is okay." Juliana smiles and bites her lip. She is extra playful this morning. Her hand rests on my chest, her fingers rubbing gently.

"Good." I lean in and kiss her again, moving over her to deepen the kiss. She slides back down until we are lying together but then my alarm goes off and I curse myself for forgetting about it when she woke up. "Shit, I guess we have to get up now."

"Mmm," Juliana moans against my lips. "Five more minutes. Just hit snooze or something."

I chuckle but let her pull me back down to kiss some more while my alarm continues to go off. After a few seconds, the alarm gets louder and Juliana groans, letting go of me.

"Never mind, shut that off, please."

I reluctantly get off of her, turning off the alarm and lying on my back for a few seconds. I close my eyes and feel Juliana shifting beside me. I feel her weight climbing on top of me as she straddles me. I open my eyes to see such a pleasant sight of her perched on top of me. I put my hands on her hips and smile up at her.

"I'm not stopping here," Juliana says with a big smile, leaning down to kiss me. "I just wanted to tease you as I got out of bed." With that, she continues over me and climbs out of bed. Now, it is my turn to groan. Juliana laughs at my agony as she skips off to the bathroom.

I join her in the bathroom a few minutes later and we stand side by side brushing our teeth together. I finish first and leave her to get ready alone. When she finally comes out, she goes immediately to the closet and gets changed. She leaves the door open so I take it as an invitation to take a couple of peeks. She changes with her back toward me so the only view I can admire is her backside and her panties cover the best part, but it's still an amazing view.

When she comes out of the closet, she winks at me, clearly knowing what she has done to me. I shake my head at her and she giggles.

"Hey, do you need a ride to work? I mean, do you want me to drive you?" I ask as we head to the kitchen for breakfast.

"Okay, that would be great. Thanks," Juliana says, smiling at me.

Juliana whips up a quick breakfast of eggs and cuts some fruit for us both. We eat at the kitchen table and Juliana chatters away, telling me all about her upcoming job interview she got called back for. I want to tell her to drop it because I can easily take care of her but I understand her need to contribute and she seems excited about the job, so I keep my mouth shut and just ask questions here and there.

When we are both finished, we walk hand in hand down to my car and I rest my hand on her thigh while I drive her to work. Juliana seems happier today, more relaxed than she has been in a while. I can only hope both of our good moods continue for a while.

# Chapter 44

## *Juliana*

When I come home from work, there is a weird quietness in the apartment. The past week has been normal, with nothing eventful happening, thankfully. Kurt and I are learning to adjust to each other's schedules but we still find time to hang out with each other even when we aren't pretending to be engaged. We haven't done anything more than some heavy make-out sessions lately but most days we are both tired. Kurt is busy working on an important case, and I am exhausted from working extra hours and job hunting.

Callum hasn't messed with us since I ran into him outside of the dress shop and I'm starting to calm down, just enjoying my time with Kurt. Unfortunately, we have yet to talk about the growing relationship between us. I haven't wanted to say anything yet because I've been too busy enjoying whatever it is that is happening. But when I open the door to the apartment, I can feel something has shifted.

"Juliana," I hear Kurt's voice and I follow it into the bedroom. I see him standing by the closet where a big bag is hanging.

"Hi, what's that?" I greet him, smiling. My smile disappears when I see the look on his face. "What's wrong?"

"This was delivered today while you were out." Kurt steps away from the bag as I approach and reach for the zipper. There is no label on the bag but I can tell it's for some type of garment. When I unzip the bag about halfway, I gasp.

"Oh my god!" I step back from the bag letting go of the zipper. I look over at Kurt and he kind of looks scared.

"Look, Juliana, I like you, I really do but this isn't real. This wedding that you're planning, it's not actually happening. You shouldn't be purchasing a dress, or well, I guess my mom purchased it for you." Kurt tries to explain and I can tell he is trying to be nice or polite but he isn't phrasing it well and I interrupt him.

"Kurt," I say and put my hand over his. I decide against sharing my own feelings and instead, explain. "I am so sorry, you were not supposed to see that. Hell, I didn't even know it had been purchased, let alone already on its way here…"

"We already had this conversation and I thought we were on the same page. I know I  mentioned maybe some time in the future thinking about marriage but I didn't mean, like, a week in the future. I meant a couple of years, at minimum." Kurt runs his fingers through his hair and he starts to pace, a pattern I've grown familiar with.

"No, no we are on the same page, Kurt. I told you, that day after church, that's what your mother had planned for a girls' day. I didn't tell you but there was a dress that everyone fell in love with. I mean, I did too but I knew it wasn't for me, for obvious reasons. I told them that I couldn't afford the dress at the moment so I thought that was the end of the conversation. I had no idea she would buy it for me." I try to explain but Kurt still looks sort of panicked.

"I think this has all been too much. Everything we've done. Every party we've been to, everyone we've deceived. Maybe we started to believe the lies too.." Kurt trails off. "We went too far this time. I think we should stop. I think that we should end this. I'll tell everyone we broke off the engagement... don't worry about anything. I'll fix this..." He watches me with wild eyes and then he stands, clearing his throat.

"It's okay," I say when I finally find my voice. I'm choking back tears but I hold my head high. "I got you into this situation, I will figure out how to deal with the consequences of the fake engagement coming to an end. But what about the real relationship we've developed?" I hate that I have to ask, especially when he is so upset, but I need to know if this means everything is over. I don't want to lose him.

"What relationship?" Kurt practically scoffs in my face. "So we've made out a few times and I went down on you once, that does not put us in a relationship."

His words sting and my heart throbs, I feel like I've been punched in the stomach. I am completely caught off guard. I know he is upset but I didn't think he would hurt me like that.

I blink a few times, trying to keep the tears from spilling out. "Okay, you're right." I try to remain calm but I can feel my strength wavering.

He hesitates and I can see him searching my eyes, almost as if he feels guilty for what he said, but I refuse to give him anything. He doesn't seem completely satisfied with this conversation but he gives a curt nod. "I'll give you some space to pack your things."

I thank him and then watch as he leaves. I wait until he has left the apartment before I let the tears fall. I lie on the bed and curse myself, I curse Callum and the stupid things I did. I try not to think about the "what ifs". Everything had just started to get better, to get real, and now it is all coming to an end.

After crying for what seems like hours, which was probably only twenty minutes, I get up and begin to pack my things. I shouldn't have let myself get so comfortable here.

It's all too much for me and I feel as if I'm going to have a breakdown any moment when suddenly, the door of the apartment flies open and I see Tatyana come in carrying a huge grocery bag and a box I can only recognize as the one filled with my favorite movies. I smile, feeling the meltdown slowly fading, and then I think of what she is doing here and know Kurt must have called her. Instantly, I start crying and my heart aches. He is so kind. Even when he is hurting, he puts others first.

"Honey, I'm hooooome!" Tatyana shouts and I hear her dumping stuff on the kitchen counter. I come out of the bedroom and sniffle a bit, wiping my eyes. I walk into the kitchen.

"Hi," is all I say and she turns to face me.

"Oh honey. You doing okay?" She asks before pulling me into a big hug. She rubs my back a few times then pulls away looking me over. And by this time, I'd started crying again. She wipes at my tears and then leads me over to the tall stools at the counter. I sit down and she starts pulling things out of her grocery bag.

"Kurt called," she says but doesn't pause to wait for my reaction, "We've got the place to ourselves this evening and it is a girls' night. And you know what that means. Well, actually you probably don't but I'll tell you. So, movies, junk food, soda, and lots of popcorn. And I'm not talking about those sob-fest movies. Got it? I'm talking Fast and Furious, our favorites only. Jason Bourne, again, favorites only." She digs through my movie box and pulls out all of the Jason Bourne movies, including the one with Jeremey Renner and she holds them victoriously in the air. "No, we have all of them, we will watch all of them!"

I lean back in my chair and watch as she bounces around the kitchen pulling out bowls for our junk food. At one point, she tosses me her phone and tells me that I am the DJ while she preps our food. I scroll through her songs and really want to listen to sad songs to sob my heart out too but I know that tonight is not the night for sobbing so I find her pump-up playlist and hit shuffle. The first song is My House by Flo Rida and Tatyana instantly begins singing. I love this song and about a minute into it, I join in and hop down off of the stool to help her pour various candies into different bowls.

Maybe I'll be alright after all.

# Chapter 45
## *Juliana*

"Okay so Tokyo Drift is over. Now what? Jason Bourne? Psych? Covert Affairs?" Tatyana lists off movies and TV shows. "But the thing with TV shows is, how much do we watch? Do we watch the whole thing? Like for Psych, that's 8 seasons and a couple of movies too! That seems like a lot," she rattles on and I get up to make more popcorn. While in the kitchen, I open another bag of mini M&M's and dump them into our almost empty bowl.

"Psych. Definitely, Psych." I contribute. "I need a little laughter right now. And as funny as Vin's accent is, I think I need some Shawn and Gus right now." Tatyana cheers and I pour the popcorn into a large bowl and bring over both bowls while she sets up the TV. "Season 3 is my comfort zone, it's the season I've owned the longest." Tatyana nods and pops in the third season for us.

We've been at this all night until the wee hours of the night. Sometimes I catch myself wondering what Kurt is doing or wondering when he will be back and I have to force myself to stop thinking about him. I can't pretend what we had was real. It wasn't. It was just a game.

"So," I say to distract myself. "How was your trip with Mike? We never have had time to talk about that."

"Oh, it was amazing! Mike was in meetings most of the day and had to attend a few dinners as well, so I was on my own for the most part, but I had tons of fun!" Tatyana tells me. "My boss kept emailing me things to do so I did spend some time working in the hotel. But thankfully, it was easy things like charts and updating info. Easy stuff I could finish before noon and then spend a few hours at the pool."

"Ooo, I thought you looked tanner!" I compliment her and she holds her arms to show me. "Amazing, dang girl." I hold my arms up by hers to compare and we both burst into giggles. She was already tanner than me before but now it's even more drastic.

"Yes, thank you. But anyway, Mike's conference was very successful. He's a great salesman," Tatyana chuckles. "That's how he got me." We both laugh but she's not wrong. I've seen him in action and he is quite good.

Tatyana talks a little more about her trip and her job, mostly complaining about her boss, Shelby, and her inability to do anything on her own, aside from looking up stocks, ones she is fond of. When Tatyana trails off, distracted by the TV show, I sit back into the arm of the couch and sigh. Tatyana looks at me. "Are you thinking about him?" She asks softly. I nod and she gives me a sad smile. "Juli, he likes you. Okay? He really does. I've told you this from the beginning. Who knows, maybe he has liked you for a while now." She is about to continue talking but I cut her off.

"No," I say and dismiss her words with a wave of my hand. "He doesn't. It was all fake." I pause and I can feel her watching me. I sigh and pull the blanket up to my chin. "I just feel so stupid, you know? I mean you don't know because you have your boyfriend and he's awesome and real and loves you." I ramble on, forming sentences that aren't really sentences. "But Kurt, Kurt wasn't real. Everything we did wasn't real. And I made it even worse with that stupid, beautiful dress."

"Wait, what did you guys do?" Tatyana sits up a little bit, interested. She leans in closer and a smile threatens to spread across her lips. I blush and hide behind my hands but then quickly respond so she doesn't get the wrong impression.

"No, nothing! I mean, okay, I maybe tried to do stuff..." I trail off blushing even more and she pushes my shoulder laughing.

"What did you do?! I knew you guys liked each other." She nods her head, proud of her detective skills. It makes me smile. I feel like a schoolgirl talking about her crush on an older man. (Not too much older but you know in middle school when you had crushes on like a high school senior or something? Something like that).

"I don't know. I was acting all emotional and I kissed him and then kind of pulled him on me and I was trying to uhm undo his pants." I say blushing a bit from embarrassment. She grins at me. "Yeah okay, but he stopped me. He was the one who stopped." I sigh and shrug my shoulders. "Then a few days after that, the day we went dress shopping, I came home and we just…came together. We made out for a while and just touched each other and then he…" I trail off again and Tatyana jumps up, sitting forward, enthralled in the story.

"What? What did he do?" She looks so eager to know that I chuckle a little.

"He, well, he went down on me," I admit and she squeals. Her squeal is so high-pitched that I cover my ears with my hands. When the noise stops, I drop my hands again and continue. "I was going to return the favor, you know, but he said he was happy to do it and he didn't want me to rush into anything and all of that."

"So he was basically the perfect gentleman," Tatyana says and I nod. "Wait, did he get you to finish?"

"Mhm," I respond and bite down on my lip. Tatyana raises her eyebrows and her smile grows. "Twice," I add and she squeals again, pounding her fist on the couch in excitement.

"Yessss, OMG. I am so happy for you," Tatyana cheers excitedly.

"Me too. Or I was. I don't know. I guess I was just caught up in the whole performance. I was having fun and forgot that it had to end at some point." Again I sigh. "I'm probably just repeating myself now but that's really all I can say. Well, besides the fact that I definitely like him."

"I knew it!" Tatyana tosses popcorn at me. "Also, duh. Everyone believed you guys were a couple. And you're terrible at acting." I roll my eyes but she is right. I'm really bad at it. "Maybe he stopped you from going further because he wants to try a real relationship. Start where normal couples start." She offers and I have to shrug again. I honestly don't know. I don't think he wants a relationship though. I sigh and lean my head back against the couch.

"I doubt that. If that were the case, he would have been a lot more understanding about the whole wedding dress thing. I clearly did not mean for that to happen, I had no idea," I say and Tatyana shrugs. "Plus, he laughed when I asked about it," I tell her and she gasps.

"No, he did not?!" Tatyana asks, horrified. I just nod. She shakes her head, clearly upset and disappointed. "Wow, that's a little cruel. I mean, I can understand that he's feeling a lot of emotions, but to laugh about it? That's not cool."

"Yeah," I mutter. "It stung more than I care to admit," I tell her and she nods in understanding.

"Did you confront him?" Tatyana asks, moving to the edge of her seat as she gets worked up from the interaction.

"No," I say, barely above a whisper.

"What?!" Tatyana smacks her hand loudly against her thigh. "Juli! Does that mean that you still haven't told him how you feel?" Tatyana's question makes me feel a pit in my stomach.

"I know I should have but he deserves better than me." Before Tatyana can interrupt to protest, I continue. "I have been the cause of the chaos in his life and he deserves better. It will be easier for him to move on if he thinks his feelings are not reciprocated," I add and Tatyana stares at me for a few seconds.

"You deserve to be happy, you know?" Tatyana says as she pulls me into a hug. I hold onto her for a few seconds before releasing her.

"Thank you," I say and then quickly change the subject. "We should probably start moving my stuff out of here…" I say quietly, looking around the apartment.

Tatyana shakes her head, "Nope, sorry. You can't come back. I won't allow it." I stare at her, open-mouthed, in confusion. She nods. "I have just decided that you cannot come back to live with me unless you actually try to work this out and it just doesn't work. Then and only then can you come back to live with me." She says and pats my arm affectionately. I roll my eyes.

"Okay, so what do I do now?" I pull a blanket up to my nose, hiding from the future.

# Chapter 46
## *Juliana*

I check my phone constantly, checking the time, waiting for him to get home. I know I should just walk away. I shouldn't keep putting him through this but I need to know. I need to know if he feels the same way. This is a messed-up way to start a relationship. I know that. And who says we will even have a relationship? Especially after everything that's happened.

I look around the apartment. My things have been cleared out, and Tatyana agreed to let me come back. She put up a fight but in the end, she agreed to let me stay with her again. But she made me promise that I would give this a try. She convinced me to stick around to have a conversation with Kurt. Although, I really don't know what I'm trying to do anymore. I check my phone again. Where is he?

Just as I ask the question, I hear a key fumbling to be put in the lock. I give it a few seconds then I start to make my way over to the door to help him get in.

"Let me help," a breathy, female voice says and I hear a wrestle for the keys. I freeze, my hand hovering over the lock.

"I got it," a familiar voice grumbles and I take a step back. I hear a bump on the door and the sound of kissing. My heart falls into my stomach and I wrap my arms around myself, willing the tears to stay away. The struggle to open the door continues shortly and I hear more heavy breathing. Thinking quickly, I look around the apartment and run into the kitchen. I hope they don't see me but I figure they will head straight to the bedroom and I should stay close to the door so I can make a quick escape.

The door finally opens and I duck down behind a counter, hugging my knees to my chest and pressing my face against my knees, squeezing my eyes shut tightly as if the back of my eyelids could protect me from the scene going on right on the other side of the counter. I hear the rustle of clothing and I whimper silently. The kissing noise becomes fainter and I pray they've gone to the bedroom so I can escape this apartment that now feels like a prison cell.

Slowly, I crouch in a squatting position. I peek around the edge of the counter and the sight in front of me makes me gasp. I quickly slap a hand over my mouth to keep them from hearing my heart leave my chest.

Looking out into the living room I see the back of Kurt's head, sitting on the couch. With Ashley straddling his lap and working on leaving an impression on his neck. I squeeze my eyes shut tightly for a few seconds before looking over at the door and am grateful they were too distracted to lock it behind them. I look back and forth between them and the door. When

I look back at them, Ashley is staring right at me. When I make eye contact with her, an evil smirk stretches across her face. She makes sure I am watching before she tilts her head back purring.

"Oh, Kurt. That feels sooo good." She moans softly and I feel a tear slip down my cheek silently. I quickly wipe it away then jump up from my hiding place and make a dash for the door. I quickly open the door and run out without looking back.

Before I leave I hear Kurt ask, "What was that?" But I don't stick around to hear Ashley's answer.

Running down the hallway, I have no patience for the elevator and I burst into the stairwell. I run down the stairs and on the last flight, I trip and stumble down ten steps. When I reach the bottom, I land on my hip and cry out, the pain sharp. I sit on the floor for a few seconds and let the pain of the fall and the pain of seeing Kurt with Ashley take over my body and the sobs I emit, shake my body.

I sit in pain, letting my tears subside and letting my breathing return to normal. Once I've calmed down, I exit the stairwell, limping slightly. I make my way to the restrooms in the lobby and I quickly splash water on my face. Gazing at myself in the mirror I notice my sad eyes. I take a paper towel and dab at the moisture beneath them then I bat my eyelashes, blinking to clear away the tears appearing in my eyes again.

"It's okay," I tell myself. "You are fine. Maybe a little bruised, physically and mentally but you are completely fine." I stop talking quickly when I hear a toilet flush. I smile politely at Evelyn, who exits the stall. She smiles back at me and makes no mention of having heard me talking to myself.

"Are you okay, dear?" Evelyn asks, handing me a tissue from her purse to wipe my tears. I accept the tissue, grateful for something softer than the paper towels.

"I'm okay," I try to say without my voice wavering. "Thank you, Evelyn."

"Okay, dear. You have a good night." Evelyn squeezes my arm.

"You too."

As she goes to leave, she turns back to me and says, "I am so glad you and Kurt are together. I've never seen him so happy." I smile politely but am shocked. She exits the bathroom leaving me to process what she said. I don't recall seeing him extremely happy. We did laugh a few times but I don't know. She probably just heard what I was saying and felt bad for me so she said something sweet. I try to brush it off, not wanting to overanalyze it.

I dab my face dry before I leave the bathroom. I quickly leave the building and make my way to the nearest coffee shop. Thankfully, the coffee shop is open late so I pull open the doors, breathing in the coffee aroma that now reminds me of Kurt. Once inside, I order a drink I know I have no appetite to drink and then I pull out my phone.

"Tatyana?" I say, grateful that she is still awake to answer my call.

"Hey, that was pretty quick. How did it go?" She asks quickly, wanting to know all the details then she goes quiet, waiting for me to respond.

I barely get a word out before I burst into tears. I speak to her with broken sentences, "It…it di-didn't go-o well…" I get out, barely audible, my voice catching at the end. I tilt my head down, pulling my hair to cover my face like a curtain. I feel ashamed for crying in public, for crying at all really.

"Oh sweetie," she says, her voice calm and steady. It helps me calm down.

"I wa-wa-waited for hi-him. You know? A-and and he came in with Ashley!" I hold out until the end of the sentence then I burst into tears, again. I sob, trying to keep my cries quiet but I notice people giving me looks. Some are sympathetic, others are glances of annoyance. I take a napkin and dab at my eyes, I need to stop crying over him. I sniffle a bit and try to calm down enough to listen to Tatyana.

I hear her gasp and she says one word, "Dick." I nod but instantly feel bad. He really isn't a dick. I messed up his and Ashley's relationship. It's my fault. If I hadn't come around and opened my big mouth, they would probably still be together. What happened tonight was probably a normal occurrence. I sigh into the phone. "Okay, Juli, come home. I'll wait up for you." I nod eagerly, forgetting that she can't see me.

"Thank you," I whisper, barely able to speak. My tears have turned into hiccups but I'm starting to feel better. Tatyana tells me that she isn't at the apartment but the key is still hidden where it always is. I thank her and apologize for being so weepy. She promises everything will be okay and tells me we are going to fix things when she gets home. I accept her proposition then we say our goodbyes and hang up.

I look around the coffee shop and everyone has gone back to their conversations and meals, officially blocking me out of their lives. I stand up and throw away my completely full cup of coffee before making my way to the front door. I exit the shop and let the cool breeze of the early morning air, brush away my tears.

# Chapter 47

## *Kurt*

I groan, stretching in the bed. My hand brushes against soft hair and I jump up, looking over at the figure sound asleep next to me. The naked figure at that. Unable to see her face, I scan the room, looking for clues to who she is. I can't remember much of last night. After Juliana left, everything went to shit. I couldn't help myself, all I wanted to do was forget Juliana and how upset I had made her.

I lean my head back on the headboard and groan, remembering how upset Juliana was and how I just left her when she was vulnerable. Part of me still hoped the figure in my bed was Juliana but I just don't think after what happened that we would end up in bed together. Anyway, I wouldn't want our first time together to be something I couldn't remember.

"Good morning, baby," a familiar voice says, startling me and taking me away from the thoughts in my head. I look at the girl who looks up at me with triumph in her eyes. Crap, why is Ashley in my bed? Why does she look so happy? I think to myself. My face must look horrified, this makes Ashley chuckle. "Don't worry baby, you told me you and that other girl," she practically snarls, "aren't together anymore." She grins happily and sort of evilly and I get up out of the bed quickly.

"You need to leave," I tell her and quickly put on my boxers then I begin to gather her clothing. She just laughs and rolls over stretching, making the sheets fall away from her body, exposing herself. "Ashley, now," I say and busy myself by putting on more clothing. Once I finish, I gather all of her clothes and set them on the bed for her. "I'll leave the room while you get dressed," I tell her and then before she can protest, I leave the room, escaping to the living room and shutting the door behind me before I freak out in front of her.

Once alone in the living room, I spin around. I look around at the room, now void of anything that had belonged to Juliana. What the hell happened last night? I rake my hand over my head, an old habit I still haven't shaken. I hear Ashley grumbling as she gets dressed and I look around for any more of her things so she doesn't have to stay any longer. I go into the kitchen and notice something on the floor. I bend down to pick it up and look at the little Eiffel Tower keychain. "How did this get in here?" I ask out loud, standing up.

"What is it?" I look up startled and see a dressed Ashley standing above me. I hold the keychain out for her.

"Here you dropped this." She squints at it and then crinkles her nose.

"That's not mine," she says then the edges of her mouth turn up in a little smile before she turns and prances away. I look at it more closely and notice that one of the legs on it is twisted, not fully broken off though. I pocket the item and push aside the emotions that begin to arise when I realize who it must belong to, Juliana. I make my way back into the living room and see Ashley sitting on the couch putting her shoes on. I sigh.

Walking over to her, I hand her purse to her and the jacket she brought. She looks a little put out but I can't have her in my apartment any longer. I feel so guilty. I know Juliana left and I know it was never real but I still can't help but feel guilty.

Ashley leans in and gives me a long kiss on the lips, catching me off guard. I push her away gently and give her a stern look. "I'm sorry for whatever happened last night. It was a mistake. And I really need you to leave." I tell her firmly and an emotion of rejection flashes across her face before she plasters a fake smile on it.

She keeps the fake smile on for a few seconds then she sighs and rolls her eyes. "Nothing actually happened." She chuckles. "But Juliana thinks something did." She opens the door with that last sentence and then waves happily. "Bye! Good luck with everything!" Then she laughs and slams the door behind her.

"Wait, what the hell," I say to no one in particular. "Nothing happened? Juliana was here? Crap." I look around the room again panicking and take the Eiffel Tower out of my pocket, rubbing it between my fingers as if a Genie will pop out and grant my wish. I toss it onto the couch and then let my legs give out, allowing me to collapse on the couch as well. "What can I do?" I need to do something.

What can I do? I messed up. I didn't listen to Juliana and then I went to Ashley to try to forget about her. If Juliana was here to talk about it and she saw Ashley and I together, she probably felt betrayed.

I shouldn't have walked away during our argument, I just saw the wedding dress and freaked out. I like her and I was enjoying spending time with her. I felt like our relationship was becoming real but then I saw the wedding dress and everything hit me. We were lying to everybody we loved, and they were so happy for us which made me feel even more guilty.

I argue in my head, taking on both sides of the debate about whether to go after Juliana or not, then I get my lazy ass off the couch and grab my keys. Rushing to the door, I grab a light jacket and then shut the door behind me.

# Chapter 48
## *Juliana*

I let myself into the apartment, carrying my remaining bags from Tatyana's car into the apartment. I make it as far as the living room before I give up and let my bags slide off my drooping shoulders, landing on the floor with a thud. I rub my shoulder that held the most weight and look down at my things. I'm too tired to unpack now. I sit down on the couch and prop my feet up on my bags. I lean my head back and stare at the ceiling until I feel dizzy. I let the blood rush to my head and begin to feel the pounding in my ears. I let the pain begin to numb me then I quickly sit up, getting a head rush. I groan and then reach for the remote.

I spend the next hour or so flipping channels, trying to kill time and take my mind off of everything that happened in the last 24 hours. I was still reeling from the break-up and the betrayal I felt from seeing Kurt bring Ashley home, the same day I left. I couldn't believe he had done something like that. The fact that it probably wasn't even a break-up doesn't help at all. This morning I came home and Tatyana had bundled me into the apartment and left all of my stuff in her car, too exhausted to deal with it. At the time, I went straight to bed and Tatyana didn't try to talk about any of it, thankfully. Now, I had finished unloading all of my things out of her car and reality was sinking in.

I curl up on the couch, feeling my body begging for some peace. I cry myself to sleep and only wake up when I feel someone shaking me.

"Kurt?" I mumble, opening my eyes, hopeful. Tatyana's face appears in front of me, blurry. I blink a few times and see her worried expression. Mike is standing a few feet away, looking worried but he doesn't say anything. The sight of him standing there looking so worried makes me feel even worse. I have caused such a chaotic situation and everyone is suffering because of it.

"No, honey, it's me," Tatyana says, rubbing my arm as I sit up. "You okay? You were pretty shocked last night."

"This whole thing is so messed up," I say, choking back a sob. Tatyana shoves me over and sits down next to me on the couch. She pulls a blanket over both of our laps and wraps her arms around me.

"I know. This sucks, hun." Tatyana comforts me. I lean against her shoulder and sob into her shirt. She holds me in silence for a few minutes. "Mike, why don't you let us have some girl time," Tatyana suggests and I look up with a sniffle.

"Oh no," I protest weakly. "I don't want to kick you out. I'm so sorry."

"No, no. It's fine. Mike has other things he can be doing right now. Isn't that right?" Tatyana addresses Mike, widening her eyes at him so he gets the point. I try not to laugh at her not-so-subtle attempt, Mike smiles at her and nods.

"She's right. I've got some things I need to do today, so I will leave you two to do whatever you need." Mike comes over and kisses Tatyana on the lips then smacks a loud kiss on my forehead. Tatyana laughs and I grumble, wiping off my forehead. "Have fun, be good! I'll send some food over for you two in an hour or so!" Mike calls as he leaves the apartment.

"He's a good guy," Tatyana practically swoons.

"The food was a nice touch," I agree.

Tatyana sits up, pushing me off of her. She claps her hands, ready to get down to business. "So, do you want to talk about everything or do you want to be distracted?"

"I want to be distracted," I whine.

"Wrong answer. I was only giving you the option because I thought you would pick the right one," Tatyana scolds me and I groan. "I told you that you weren't coming back here until you and Kurt worked it out. Obviously, with this new development, that is going to be a little more difficult than we were expecting but I still think that you need to talk to him. But I am not kicking you out. You are always welcome to come back here."

"Thanks," I pout. "I don't know what there is to talk about. I thought we were getting close but then he freaked out, kicked me out, and the same day, he brought his ex back home. That...that is just so messed up. And yes, I understand that our whole situation was messed up from the start but I actually thought we were developing a real relationship. I guess I should have known it wasn't real to him when he didn't want to put a label on it."

"Now, see, I can understand that. You two are already in this fake engagement so everyone around you sees you two as fiancés. So, I can understand why it would be weird or confusing to add a different label, even if it is a real one." I give her a look and she shrugs. "I'm your best friend, I am going to give you my honest opinion. And keep in mind that I have been supportive of this whole situation, from the start."

"Fine, that's true. Okay, I can kind of understand it but if we were starting to build a real relationship why would he kick me out without even listening to me? Why would he immediately get drunk and go running to Ashley," I choke on her name as another round of pain hits me, tears streaming down my face.

"Oh, baby." Tatyana grabs a tissue and wipes my cheeks, dabbing under my eyes. "You're right about that. That part is pretty messed up. I can't defend that," Tatyana admits.

"Okay, I have to stop crying over this man. I have to. I can't let this fake relationship ruin my life, even if I thought it was starting to be real. I just had one incredibly horrible relationship and fake dating Kurt was a great experience. Now I know what I want and how I deserve to be treated, and this ending is not it. I deserve better than that, no matter the circumstance," I try to toughen my resolve but I can feel my strength fading. This whole thing has been exhausting and part of me is relieved it is almost over even if losing Kurt would create a huge hole in my life and in my heart.

"You know, maybe this is good. You learned some very important lessons, you got Callum off your back." Tatyana makes a face. "We think. And you're raking in the dough from working so much. You're getting your life together and that is all that matters."

"I guess that's true. Can I wallow in it for a few more hours? I promise after that, I will pull on my big girl pants and get to work."

"That's fair. I will accept that," Tatyana relents and we sit back on the couch.

She starts playing Psych and a few minutes later she gets a notification that we have food on the way. We both praise Mike when some chicken wings and fries arrive at our door.

We spend the next few hours wallowing in my sadness. Tatyana indulges me to a limit and I promise myself I will knock it off as soon as we decide that it's enough. I hope she allows me at least another hour but I can tell she's starting to get tired and she keeps checking her phone, probably talking to Mike which makes me feel even worse because I know I keep cutting into their time together. I hope that I am not putting a strain on their relationship

*Knock, knock, knock.*

Tatyana looks over at me when we hear the knocking on the door. "You should get it. You haven't gotten up off this couch in a few hours." I laugh a bit and throw a pillow at her before getting up.

"Technically, you haven't you either." I point out as she ducks away from the pillow as it lands short. She picks it up off the ground and tucks it behind her head.

"This is mine now." She goes back to watching TV and I make my way to the door. "Hopefully, it's the pizza guy. We ordered like twenty minutes ago!" She complains and pats her stomach. My stomach growls a bit and I agree, I hope it's the pizza guy. Even though Mike sent us food right after he left, I wasted so much energy crying that I was now hungry again.

I open the door and my heart drops to my stomach, a feeling I am all too familiar with recently. "Kurt," I say, holding onto the door.

Tatyana peeks up, looking over the back of the couch to watch the scene unfold. "Wait, how did you get into the building?" She asks him, pretending it wasn't her who let him in.

I haven't looked away; my eyes are too busy staring at his face. He ignores her and stares only at me.

"Can we talk?

# Chapter 49
## *Juliana*

Seeing Kurt in front of me, asking to talk, is shocking. I hadn't expected to see him so soon. I look over at Tatyana and see her quickly getting up.

"I'll just get out of your way. I should probably go into the office today. I'll just go get lunch with Mike before." She grabs her bag and pauses at the door, she looks at both of us and then at me again. She pats my arm, giving me a look to ask, *are you going to be okay?* I nod my head and she smiles. "Okay, I'll see y'all around." She gives a quick wave and then heads out the door, leaving us alone.

I stand there awkwardly, not really knowing what to do. "Well, are you going to let me in?" He asks, teasing me a bit.

"Oh, yeah, sorry." I step back and let him into the apartment then I shut the door behind him. I follow him over to the couch and he sits down on one end, leaving enough room for me but I sit down in the single chair, further away from him. "So, you wanted to talk?" I push, not knowing what else to say.

I did not want to bring up what I saw happen last night and I couldn't figure out why he was here. Maybe he had gotten his fix so he was ready to spend more time with the virgin. I curse the words at myself and wrap my arms around my chest. I had thought that I was doing enough to keep him interested. I was doing everything I was comfortable with and I thought that we were both enjoying ourselves, but maybe it wasn't enough.

He sits forward on the couch, his hands folded, resting between his knees. "Yes," he says but then he just stares at the ground, not saying anything else. I wait patiently, not wanting to be the first to speak. He bounces his knees and I clear my throat. "Sorry," he says and stops bouncing then shifts in his seat. "You shouldn't have walked away." He starts.

"Okay, I didn't actually walk away. You left. I was in your apartment for hours, you knew where I was, you could have come back." I take a deep breath, trying to calm myself down and let him speak.

The images of Ashley on top of him keep flashing in my head. I close my eyes and rub my hands on my thighs. I gesture for him to continue talking.

"You're right," he says and I look up at him. He looks like he really means it like he just realized that what I said is true. "I shouldn't have started this conversation by saying that because I know it was more than that. I should have stayed or at least come back." I nod, agreeing with him. "We could have talked it out." He offers. "I'm sorry. I just freaked out. Everything was built up inside me, all of the guilt and stress, and then I saw that dress and I just couldn't deal with it anymore."

"I'm sorry," I tell him because I am. I understand this whole situation has been so complicated and I feel even guiltier dragging him and his family into this. "Look, Callum hasn't bothered me, since that run-in at the dress shop. So, I think you were right, we can stop this. This can be the end. We don't have to pretend anymore."

"I am so sorry that I said that, Juliana. I said some things that I didn't mean. I wasn't pretending. I mean at first I was, but then it became real and I wasn't pretending. Were you?" His words hurt me and I want to tell him I wasn't pretending either, that I had fallen for him but I can't. Not after what I saw last night.

"I was. I was pretending," I say without looking at him because if I look at him, I won't be able to do this to him. It might be a lie but it's what he needs to hear. I can't let him throw away his life because of me. "I might have overindulged and I apologize. Callum didn't treat me well and I guess I was just enjoying how well you treated me and how you made me feel." It isn't a complete lie, but the truth is so much more than that. I stare at the door and hear him shift in his seat, he clears his throat.

"Okay, then I should go." I can hear the hurt in his voice but he isn't fighting for me or us so I just nod, still unable to look at him. It's better if he thinks I was pretending, then he can go back to Ashley, and forget about me. I stand up and he follows suit. "Well, I'm glad this worked out for you. And I am glad that I was able to show you what a good relationship should look like. You deserve one, you deserve everything and I hope you get that."

He looks at me and I still can't look at him. He finally gives up and walks to the door. I follow him and open it for him. He looks at me one last time and I allow myself to look up at him. He looks sad and dejected. I quickly look away. "Well, goodbye. I'll see you around I guess." I nod and he starts to leave the apartment.

Before he can leave, I remember something, "Wait, Kurt..." He turns around, hope written on his face and I feel like I am about to vomit. It makes me sick to think of hurting him this much. I quickly slip the ring off my finger and hold it out to him. "Don't forget this..." He looks down at my hand and his face quickly falls again. He reaches for it and our fingers brush for a few seconds before I pull away, uncomfortable with the spark I get from his touch. "I'm sorry..." I say quietly, looking down at the ground.

He doesn't say anything but eventually, I see his feet turn and walk away. I close the door to the apartment and go back to the couch. I text Tatyana letting her know that he left and that he probably wouldn't be back any time soon. She texts me back saying that we are going to go out tonight, no more staying in. I agree, then put my phone aside. I go into the bathroom and take a long, hot shower.

I immediately regret my decision to shower because I spend too much time thinking about Kurt. I get out of the shower and realize I still have a few hours before any place fun opens for the night so, I decide to go for a walk. I put on leggings, a sports bra, and a T-shirt, and then I grab my headphones and head out the door.

Once outside the building, I decide to start jogging. I hate running, I really do but it hurts my body and I need a distraction from the pain inside my heart so I pick up my pace. I run around the corner and slam into a firm body, knocking me to the floor and the other person stumbling a bit.

"Shit, I am so sorry. Are you okay?" I hop up and immediately apologize to the person I ran into. I hear a chuckle.

"You're so small, love. You could never hurt me." I roll my eyes at the nickname I am no longer fond of.

# Chapter 50
## *Juliana*

"Hi, Callum. Sorry, I ran into you." I turn to start my run again even though I am quickly losing the desire to run but he steps in front of me.

"Wait." He doesn't touch me but I automatically move back, away from him. "I won't touch you, don't worry. So, how have you been, Juli?" He asks, tucking his hands in his pockets, looking genuinely interested in the answer. I eye him up and down.

"I'm alright," I say but don't elaborate, confused as to why he is being so civil when only a week ago he was harassing me.

"Cool. Cool. So, I was wondering. Would you want to grab a cup of coffee? Talk about some things? It doesn't have to be coffee. I know you're not a huge coffee drinker, but I just thought it would be good to sit down and talk." He finishes and waits for my response.

My jaw hangs open slightly, this is the politest I have ever seen him and I have never heard him ramble before. It catches me off guard and I nod my head automatically before I can fully process what he said. A smile grows on his face and he looks excited by my response.

"Sure," I say when my voice finally comes back to me.

"I'm free right now if you've got some time." I nod again, even though I probably look wrecked from trying to exercise.

Callum gestures for me to walk in step with him as we walk around the corner and stop at a little diner. He holds the door open for me and lets me walk in first. Again, I am shocked at his politeness. I thank him before making my way into the restaurant. A hostess leads us to an open booth and I slide in on one side and Callum slides in on the other.

The hostess sets our menus down and then tells us our waiter will be right with us. I thank her politely and then pick up my menu, feeling a bit hungry. I look over the menu, not really paying attention, my mind too distracted by Callum's sudden change in behavior.

Callum clears his throat. "So," he begins. I put my menu down and look up at him, bracing myself for more ridicule or taunting but he looks almost apologetic. "Juli, I am so sorry for how I have been acting recently. I was a complete dickhead. You know how jealous I can be. Seeing you with that guy just made me so angry." His hands curl into giant fists but he lets out a breath and uncurls his knuckle. "I overreacted. Badly too. I was a real jerk." I nod my head in agreement and he laughs a bit. "Hey, you don't have to agree. But okay, I really was. And I have been trying to get better at controlling my temper." He pauses and looks up at me, looking into my eyes. His eyes pleading with me. "I want to try to work on us. I miss you, Juli. I love you, you know that. And I am sorry for how I treated you. I really want to try to make this work."

I look at him, my jaw dropping once again, completely dumbfounded. "I…I don't know what to say," I tell him honestly. "I guess Tatyana knocking you on your ass really helped straighten you out."

Callum chuckles and runs his hand through his hair. "Yeah, you could say something like that." He reaches across the table and takes my hands in his. "Baby, I know I've been a lot of work in the past, but I've been taking a hard look at myself and I know I can be better for you. We were meant for each other." He squeezes my hands gently. My mouth is open but I can't seem to form any words yet. He looks at me, waiting then he notices our waiter coming over to the table and he squeezes my hands once more before letting go. "Just think about it for now okay? We can order our drinks and food then we'll talk more about it?" He says as a question and I nod, accepting.

The waiter approaches the table and introduces himself, we tell him we are ready to order and he writes down our cravings then tells us an approximate time for our food to be ready then he goes off to get our drinks ready. Once he leaves, silence falls over the table. I look across at Callum and he is watching me quietly.

"I don't know what you want me to say." I put my hands in my lap and play with my fingers nervously.

He nods, understanding. "I know, it's a lot to take in. And I know you're with Kurt right now," he laughs rudely and rolls his eyes. "I don't know what you see in that guy. But I respect that you're in a relationship but I am still here for you. I love you and I need you. And I am willing to fight for you."

I sit back in the booth to process. He was not respectful before. He was creepy and acted like a stalker. Maybe he really has changed, but it hasn't been that long since he was a jerk so I don't know if he could change that quickly.

I sit up and place my hands on the table. "So, what is your plan?" I ask, wanting to know his intentions.

"I want to be with you." He states plainly and I am about to speak but he cuts me off. "And I know you're still with Kurt but I don't think he's right for you." I huff, annoyed at being interrupted and annoyed that he is making assumptions.

"Look, Kurt and I aren't together anymore but you don't need to insult him." I scold myself for being so quick to defend him. I sit back, trying to relax. I gesture for him to continue.

"Oh, okay," he sits up a little taller. "Let me take you out." I laugh and look around the room. "No, no. This doesn't count. Like a real date. We used to go out on dates all the time and then I stopped taking you out. I stopped showing how much I care about you. I want to do this the right way. Okay?" He leans forward. "Come on, you know you want to. You're intrigued." I laugh again as he keeps pressing me.

"Fine, fine. Just shut up already." I smile, giving in too easily. Pushing aside the thoughts of doubt. I need to get my mind off Kurt and maybe Callum has changed. I really liked him, and I still have some sort of feelings for him. So, I allow myself to give in. "One date, we will see how that goes…" I trail off, not knowing how to finish the thought. He lifts his fists triumphantly, cheering. I quickly shush him, laughing. "Shhh! Everyone is staring!" I scoot down in the booth and cover my face, blushing a little.

He laughs happily and then thankfully he shuts up and our food arrives soon after. We eat our food mostly in silence, with a few generic conversations taking place. We catch up on a few things, he tells me about different gigs his band did while I sit quietly and listen. When he notices I'm not really talking, he tries to get me more involved in the conversation. I start to notice different ways he has changed, but one meal isn't enough to convince me. Once we both finish, he pays for our food before I can say anything.

"Thank you," I say when I notice he has paid.

"It's no problem." He waves away the thanks and puts his wallet back in his pocket. "So, I'll pick you up outside your apartment tomorrow at 7?" I smile and nod.

"That sounds good." We both get up and make our way to the door.

"Alright, well, I'll see you then." He leans in and kisses me on the cheek and I let him, leaning into him slightly.

I watch him walk away and he turns around and smiles giving me a little wave. I smile and wave back then he turns back around and continues down the street, rounding a corner before disappearing from my sight. I take a moment to process everything that just happened, and then I begin my walk back to the apartment, completely giving up on my run.

# Chapter 51

## *Kurt*

Driving back to my apartment is a sad and lonely journey. I turn on the radio to try to distract myself. My favorite song is on but it doesn't make me feel any better. I look down at the cup holder beside me and that stupid ring stares back at me, mocking me. I don't know what I was thinking, giving that to her. None of this was real so why did I think it was a good idea to give her a real ring? I'm so stupid.

My phone starts ringing and I feel my heart leap. Maybe it's her, maybe she's calling me to tell me that she made a mistake. I curse myself trying to get my thoughts under control. Damn, I really like this girl.

"Hello?" I pick up the phone without looking at the caller ID, not wanting to be let down right away.

"Hi, sweetie." It's my mom. I let out a breath, relaxing a little. I haven't heard from her in a while and I forget how she was able to calm me down.

"Hey, mom. How are you?"

"I'm well. How are you, honey?" I hear noise in the back of her call but she shushes whoever it is and exits the room. The background once again goes quiet.

I clear my throat, trying to keep the sigh from escaping my lips. If I sigh, she will know something is going on and it's too soon for me to talk about it, let alone talk to her about it. "I'm okay, Mom. Just tired. I had the day off today but I think I'm going to head into work later." I tell her the silly things that don't seem to matter anymore and she seems happy with my response.

"You had the day off? That's wonderful. Did you and Juliana do something special? How is Juliana? Is she there with you right now?" She sounds so happy and curious about Juliana, I know I can't tell her what happened. Not yet at least.

"No, Mom, she isn't here right now," I say and leave it at that hoping she won't push the conversation. I can hear her little sigh, annoyed that I won't give more details but she doesn't say anything more on the subject.

"Will you two be available to come to dinner tonight?" She asks, hopefully.

I rub my hand over my eyes and try to navigate through the traffic while navigating around my mother's questions. "I don't think Juliana will be able to make it. Maybe another time." I promise and instantly feel guilty for lying to my mother. "I'm free tonight if you'll have me." I tease her a bit trying to cheer both of us up.

She laughs and agrees. "Yes, do come. Your sister will be here too. We haven't had a family dinner in a while. It'll be fun!" She says cheerily. "Oh, I know just what to make! Or what I want your dad to make." She laughs and then goes on talking about the different dishes she wants my dad to make and I tune her out, focusing on the road in front of me. When I pull into the parking garage of my apartment building, she switches to the topic of what to serve at the wedding, and I feel my heart falling apart all over again.

"Kurt?...Kurt?... Are you there? Did you hear me?" I turn off my car and pick up my phone, putting it to my ear.

"Sorry, what did you say?" I pretend to have not heard her and keep the pain out of my voice. I'm not ready to talk about Juliana let alone the wedding that will never be and never was going to be.

"I asked what Juliana would like to serve at the reception. Have y'all talked about it yet? You should probably start looking for a caterer." She is about to continue rambling but I cut her off.

"Hey Mom, I just got back to my apartment, I have to go get ready for work."

"Oh, okay, honey. We will talk about it more tonight at dinner!" I stifle a groan.

"Okay, Mom. I'll see you tonight." I say and then am about to hang up when she speaks again.

"Be here at 6! Love you, honey. Bye." I tell her I love her too then we both hang up. I sit in my car and take a deep breath. This is not going to be fun.

Getting out of my car, I make my way into the building and up to my apartment to get ready for work. I know I'll have to deal with this pain tonight but for now I can at least distract myself with my work.

I get ready for work quickly, calling my boss to let him know I'll be coming in today and he seems grateful. We have a big case and they have been needing help on it. I smile, excited for the distraction then I get in my car and drive to work. When I get to work I toss my things onto my desk and go to the conference room to join the others. We sit at the table for hours working on the case, collecting information, and finding trails that lead to the defendant.

It's around 5:35 p.m. when we finally find a stopping place for the day. Our boss tells us we did a great job and jokes about bringing us some of his famous donuts the following day. We all laugh thinking of how disgusting those must be considering he is dairy and gluten-free. Then he laughs with us promising to buy some real ones from the store.

I'm packing my things, and checking my watch to make sure I don't arrive late. When I finish packing, it is 5:45 and I hustle out the door.

"Kurt!" Someone calls and I look over, seeing three of my coworkers headed my way. "Hey, we are all going out for a drink tonight, you should come!"

"Sorry, can't," I say, walking backward to my car. "Dinner at my parent's house. I'm a momma's boy. Can't disappoint. Maybe next time!" I wave as they 'boo' and tease me, laughing with me. I hop into my car and take off, driving at the speed limit, of course, trying to make it to my parent's house on time.

I turn on the radio to help distract me, but I can't keep my mind off of her. Every song that comes on reminds me of her. I have no idea why. I shut off the radio, giving up. Putting my arm on the ledge of the window, I stare at the road.

"What am I going to tell my parents?" I wonder aloud. "Mom is going to be so upset." I rub my forehead, a headache beginning to form.

Pulling into my parent's driveway, I see my mother sitting on the front porch talking to my sister. I pull up and park then get out. They stay in their chairs, chatting as I make my way to them. I lean down and hug my mom, kissing her cheek.

"Hi, Mom. Dad inside?" She nods, smiling and waving me inside. I give my sister a hug hello then walk inside leaving them to their conversation. The kitchen is bright with lights and music. Dad is listening to Latino music and dancing around the kitchen. I lean against the door jam and laugh before knocking my fist against the cabinet to gain his attention.

"Hey, Kurt." He says when he turns to face me, his hips and feet still moving to the beat. I smile and make my way over to the counter, reaching for the platter of sliders. Before I can get one, my hand is whacked with a wooden spoon. "Not yet. But if you help set the table I'll give you the biggest one." I laugh and roll my eyes.

"I'm not five anymore, Dad," I remind him but narrow my eyes. "Fine, the biggest one." He nods, smiling and then he hands me a couple of dishes to carry into the dining room. I set them down on the table and notice the table is set for five people. My mom probably expected Juliana to come, even though I told her she wouldn't be able to. I make my way back into the kitchen to grab more dishes. "Jeez, Dad, how many things did you make? And why do you always listen to Latin music when you're not making anything remotely Latin-related?"

He shrugs and keeps swiveling his hips, making it extra dramatic. I laugh at him. "Okay, okay. Slow down. You're going to break a hip.'

"How old do you think I am?" He asks, mock offended before going back to a little less dramatic version of his dancing.

"Hey, if you think I'm five then I am allowed to think you're about a hundred." He waves me out of the kitchen, as I laugh and bring the rest of the dishes to the table. Walking outside I go to get my mother and sister.

"Hey, guys. Dinner is ready." I put my hand on my mother's shoulder and squeeze gently. She smiles up at me.

"We will come in just a minute. Girl talk, sweetie." I groan slightly then remember I am a grown man.

"Don't talk for too long. Food is on the table and I am hungry." I say before making my way back inside to meet my dad as he comes into the dining room.

"They coming?" He asks.

"Girl talk," I say as an explanation and he nods.

"Ah." We sit down at the table and as promised, Dad slides the biggest slider onto my plate. I grab two more just in case the one isn't enough and my dad doesn't complain as he piles his plate with three as well. I shove the burgers towards a corner of my plate and put a scoop of creamy mashed potatoes onto my plate alongside a helping of fresh-cut green beans. My stomach growls and I glance eagerly towards the door before speaking to my father.

"Do you think they'll be much longer?" I look back down at my plate of food.

"They don't have to know we had three burgers on our plates, maybe I didn't make these extra two…" I grin at my dad and we cover our burgers in a blanket of ketchup before digging in. As soon as our mouths hit the buns, my mother and sister walk through the door, catching us in the act.

"Oh, I know y'all did not start without us." My mother tsks, shaking her finger at us. My dad and I look at each other and blush sheepishly. My mother just laughs and sits down at the table. "Oh, go ahead. I know you're still a growing boy." I am about to protest but given the go-ahead to eat, my stomach growls again reminding me of my priorities and I dig into the juicy burger once again.

Once I've dealt with the need to scarf everything down, I slow down and take my time to enjoy the home-cooked meal. The conversation is kept light. My mother and sister have gone back to gossiping and my dad and I are discussing a recent sports game. Or rather, the lack of any good recent games. My mother turns back to me and asks the one question I had been dreading and hoping she would not ask.

"So, Kurt, how is Juliana?" I cough a little, trying to buy some time. "Is she working late tonight? I hope she's doing alright. I haven't spoken to her in ages. She did send me a sweet text after she received the dress. I hope you weren't home for the delivery. It was supposed to be a surprise for both of you." My mother turns back to me, quiet and looking at me expectantly.

"Unfortunately, I was home," I say but don't elaborate. Instead, I address Juliana's absence. "She's doing alright. Something just came up last minute. I know she would have loved to be here." I say, trying to keep my response short but elaborating enough for her to not question further. She looks sad but doesn't press the issue. The conversation comes to a lull and I stand up, collecting dirty dishes.

After clearing the table, my sister comes into the kitchen to help me put everything away. I stand at the sink, concentrating on getting the burnt pieces of the mashed potatoes off the bowl. My sister comes over and hip-bumps me lightly. I hand her the bowl and she expertly cleans the stain. I lean against the counter trying to figure out how she does it so easily.

"Kurt," she begins cautiously, making me sigh with annoyance. I don't want to deal with any more questions about Juliana. "How's work?" She asks, surprising me. I push myself off the counter and begin to put what little extras we have into containers.

"It's great. I love my job. We are working on a new case. I was almost late for dinner because I got so caught up in the work. It was really fun." I love talking about my work and relax a little, grateful for the change in subject. "I went out for drinks with my coworkers the other night. They wanted me to come out again tonight but obviously, I declined."

"Did they tease you for being such a momma's boy?" I laugh at how well she knows me. I clip the lids onto the containers then stack them in my arms and swing open the fridge to put them away. I leave out one container, filled with a little bit of everything to take home for another meal for myself.

We poke fun at each other while we finish cleaning the kitchen. When we finish we make our way out to the porch where our parents are sitting. I lean against the porch railing, enjoying the cool breeze while my parents talk quietly. I check my watch and then stand up.

"I should get going. Thank you so much for dinner." I kiss my mother on the cheek and give my father a firm hug before throwing a fallen leaf at my sister and walking to my car. Maybe I am five years old. I get in my car and drive home, leaving the radio off so I can enjoy the silence.

# Chapter 52
## *Juliana*

Tatyana finally comes back home and finds me sitting on the couch once again. "What are you doing? What happened?" She launches herself onto the couch next to me.

"I don't really want to talk about it, but I think it's over for good," I admit. Tatyana pats my leg.

"Well, that's too bad. I liked him. Should we go out and find you another man?" She grins at me, trying to keep me from feeling gloomy again.

"Ugh, no," I groan, leaning back on the couch. "I cannot deal with men anymore. Plus…" I say and then trial off, looking over at Tatyana. She narrows her eyes at me.

"What?"

"I ran into Callum right after Kurt left," I tell her and her eyebrows shoot up.

"What? How? Was he in the building?" She jumps up and starts to ask more questions but I interrupt her.

"No, no. I went out for a run and I ran into him. As always," I say with a shrug and she once again narrows her eyes at me, suspicious.

"You went out for a run?" She judges me.

"I went out for a run, yes. I didn't end up doing much running though," I admit and she holds back her comments, waiting for me to continue. "I ran into him pretty early on and he was civil, caught me completely off guard. He invited me to catch up over coffee or something and I was hungry so we went to that diner around the block."

"Wait, wait, wait," Tatyana interrupts, waving her hands around to make me stop. "You went on a date with the ex that you made up a fake fiancé to try to avoid? Wow, you're an idiot."

"Yes, I know. And no, it wasn't a date. Although, at the end of the lunch, I did say yes to going out with him tomorrow night," I say quickly, trying to get it out as fast as I can because I know how horrible it sounds.

"Juliiiii," Tatyana groans, closing her eyes and rubbing her hands over her face. "Come on. That is such a bad idea. I know he was your first love and everything but he's awful. I'm sure one day he'll be able to turn his life around and be a decent human being but I don't think that has happened since the run-in at the dress shop. And you can't hide that interaction from me because I was there, and I kicked his ass. But I don't think I kicked it hard enough to give him a whole new personality."

"Yeah, you're right. And I am skeptical, but maybe this will bring me closure," I try to reason with her but she just shakes her head, pulling me off the couch to go get ready for a night out.

"I think the best closure for you two would be just straight up ignoring each other for the rest of your lives. Just forget about him," she adds and I nod. It makes sense but part of me is still holding onto him.

"I don't plan on starting a relationship with him again. I just want to hear him out. I think I owe him that, at least," I tell her as she drags me into her room.

"No," Tatyana stops in her tracks and faces me, pointing her finger at me and fixing me with a stern stare. "You literally owe him nothing. You have done way too much for that sad sack of a human being and there is no way that you owe him anything more in this life."

Tears prick the corners of my eyes and I want to look down but her stare is so direct that I can't look away. "You're right," I admit eventually. Tatyana nods and stares at me for a few more seconds before pulling me the rest of the way into her room to find outfits for tonight.

When we get to the club, Tatyana is able to finesse our way to the front of the line and we are let in without issue. I don't question her tactics and instead try to enjoy the night out. I want to listen to music and have fun with my friend and forget about the two men in my life for as long as I can.

The drinks start flowing, coming from men around us and I quietly trade a few of them for water or a Dr. Pepper, often sliding the other beverages to Tatyana. After only an hour we have to start rejecting drinks because she has had too much. We are both chugging glasses of water and have visited the sketchy bathroom once already. There were a lot of other girls that Tatyana spilled my situation to. Everyone was offering advice and sympathizing with the dilemma. A lot of them could relate to what happened. Well, not the fake fiancé part, but the not wanting to let go of a guy so suddenly.

We leave the bathroom with Tatyana giving me an 'I told you so' face. I roll my eyes at her and sidestep her when she tries to dance around me.

"Why aren't you dancing?" Tatyana yells over the music in the club. She leans against me to shout into my ear and I flinch away. She backs off a bit with a grimace. "Sorry, but you should be out dancing and enjoying yourself."

"You know this was never really my thing," I shout back at her and she shrugs then gestures for me to join her on the dance floor, wiggling her fingers at me while she shakes her hips. I laugh and shake my head at her but she keeps it up until I give in.

I finish the rest of my water, setting the glass on the nearby table before letting Tatyana lead me out onto the dance floor. There are not that many people dancing but that doesn't stop us from having fun. I let myself lose control and we dance wildly together. I know we are getting a few strange looks but most people are supportive and one of the girl groups that was in the bathroom comes and joins us on the floor. We dance until we are practically panting, my lungs screaming at me to take a break.

The bar calls my name and I get a fresh glass of water, chugging half the glass while I try to spot Tatyana on the dance floor. I thought she was right next to me but I guess we got separated when the other girls joined us. I finally spot her making friends and dash off to join her, bringing the water with me.

I thrust the glass into her hand when I reach her and she finishes the water, smiling gratefully at me. She introduces me to the group when she is done drinking the water. Her temple is beaded with sweat but she is still bouncing on the balls of her feet, always filled with energy.

"T." I tug on her arm to get her attention back. "I'm ready to go," I tell her when she turns to face me.

"Yeah, I think I'm getting there too. One more song?" Tatyana suggests right as a throwback song comes on. She grins at me and shimmies her shoulders to entice me. I laugh and shake my head at her but dance my way back out onto the floor while she cheers and follows me.

Before long, the song is over and we are headed back home, crashing into our apartment while trying to be quiet for our neighbors.

"I still can't believe you said yes," Tatyana says as we finally get the front door open. She kicks her shoes off and follows me into my room, flinging herself dramatically onto my bed.

"I thought we weren't going to talk about this anymore," I remind her once again since this is the fourth time she has brought it up this evening. She groans.

"I know but I still think it is a bad idea," Tatyana points out and it's my turn to groan.

"You said that already, like, a lot." I change into pajamas and then go to the bathroom to wash up for bed.

"Callum suuuuuucks," Tatyana calls from the bedroom. I chuckle and almost choke on my toothbrush. "But," she says, strolling into the bathroom, "Kurt is pretty cool."

"Kurt is amazing and my heart is broken," I tell her and her face falls. She frowns, looking sad for me. "It's fine. I don't think it is fully broken, you know? I was falling in love with him but I don't think I was all the way there. Seeing him with Ashley was so shocking. That's probably why I am so…distraught over it." My explanation makes sense to me but I can see that Tayana isn't fully buying it.

"Okay, I can understand that. It hurts when someone you trust does something to betray you. Even if it wasn't real," Tatyana says, and I know she is testing me.

I spit into the sink and wipe my mouth. "Right, it wasn't real."

I won't let her trip me up. If I want to get over this, I have to accept that it wasn't real. I can rationalize why Kurt and I bonded, we were forced to. We spent so much time together and specifically faking an engagement, that is pretty intimate, it is no wonder we both started to act like it was real. But it wasn't. I just have to keep reminding myself that.

"You've already admitted it was real to you, I don't appreciate you taking it back," Tatyana scolds me. "You are allowed to fall for your fake fiancé. You two bonded through the trauma of pretending but that doesn't mean the bond was fake. I really think you should have had an in-depth conversation with him and told him how you were actually feeling because I know you held back. He needed to hear the whole truth, even if some of it was ugly."

"Stop being so smart." I pout as I go back to my room and leave her to wash up by herself. "Also, how did you come up with all of that while completely trashed? That's very impressive." Tatyana cackles as I walk away.

Tatyana doesn't pester me for the rest of the night but I can't help but think that maybe she is right. I shouldn't let Callum back in my life and I shouldn't let Kurt get away so easily. Maybe neither is right for me but with the way I am feeling about Kurt, I at least owe it to myself to talk to him and be honest.

The history with Callum is what holds me back. I always thought he would be the man I ended up with. I always thought he could be a better man but I had yet to see it. I had an image of him in my head that was nothing more than a fantasy. I shouldn't let him drag me back under whatever spell he had on me.

I fall asleep thinking about both of the men in my life. Both situations broke my heart and made for a dreamless sleep.

# Chapter 53
## *Juliana*

I pace around my room, going back and forth between the closet and the mirror. "Why isn't this mirror closer to my clothes? I'm sweating up a storm!" I huff and make another trip back to my closet. I hear Tatyana laughing on my bed and I throw a hanger at her. "You could be helping me right now!" I say as I stomp back to the mirror to admire or rather judge my next choice in outfit.

"No," she says, sitting up and pointing her finger at me. "I refuse to help. I don't support you going on this date with Callum."

I twist my hips trying to see myself from different angles. The skirt sticks out and makes my hips look huge. I yank it off, tossing it onto the growing pile of discarded clothes. I hear the bed creak as Tatyana gets off it. She appears next to me in the mirror, looking over me, processing.

"Okay, I'll help. But not because I approve, only because you desperately need my help." She takes a step back and looks at me again then she turns her focus on the discarded pile of clothing. She begins to dig through them, tossing items every which way. "Where is he taking you?"

I bite my lip, thinking. "I don't actually know. He never said anything specific." I pull out my phone and debate texting him, wanting to know what attire I should wear.

"Put your phone down, I have the perfect outfit. It'll work for any date. I am so good at this." She hands me different articles of clothing, jumbled in a ball. I pull my light-toned, ripped jeans over my thick thighs, jumping and wiggling a bit to get myself into them. I breathe heavily when I get them buttoned.

"They are a little tighter than I remember." I frown and look at myself in the mirror. My hips are a little muffin top-looking but then Tatyana hands me a cute gray, long-sleeved but thin crop top with purple and green flowers on it. The crop top is longer than usual ones so it kisses the top of my jeans. I twist to uncomfortable angles to look at the outfit. "Okay, not bad. But what if it's chilly out?" She goes into my closet and digs through a drawer of scarves. She returns carrying a beautiful green one that matches the green of my shirt, a scarf that I did not know I owned. I wrap it around my neck and nod. "Okay, fine, that is cute and keeps my neck warm but what about my arms?" I turn to face her. She hands me a pair of gray booties and socks that won't be seen and I plop down on the bed to put them on.

"Honey, if he is trying to prove he's a gentleman, he will give you his jacket." She states firmly then leaves my room. I struggle to get off the bed with my tight pants on, then I follow behind her, grabbing my purse and sifting through it to make sure I have everything I might need. "Don't be out too late. And you better come right here afterward. I mean that. He isn't taking you back to his place, he isn't taking you to another location, none of that. You got it?"

"Yes, Mother." I roll my eyes and she throws a pillow at me as she dives onto the couch.

"I am going to wait up." She states, leaving no room to argue. "Text me if you need anything. I'm serious. If he's being a jackass, which is likely to happen, text me and I will come pick you up."

I nod then blow kisses at her which makes her roll her eyes but smile at me. I leave the apartment, shutting the door behind me and head to the stairs. I wish we had an elevator, I don't want to get sweaty. I take my time going down the stairs and then find myself at the door to the lobby. I check my reflection in the window near the door and tuck stray pieces of hair behind my ear.

Once in the lobby, I look around. The small lobby has a stand for the doorman and a chair next to it but little else, and we've never had a doorman either. I check my watch and see the time is 6:58 and I push open the doors of the building, the gust of wind making the door heavy before I am let out into the humid air. I guess I won't be needing his jacket. I look down each side of the sidewalk, seeing unfamiliar faces before my eyes land on a figure leaning up against the side of my building. When I see him, he looks up and grins at me. He walks over to me and offers his hand.

"Shall we?" I smile and accept his offer, sliding my hand into his. And it doesn't fit. His hands are warm and clammy. I think about how perfectly my hand fits into Kurt's hand but I quickly shake that thought away. "You look amazing." He says smiling over at me and giving me a quick once over.

"Thank you. You clean up nicely." I respond and he grins at me. I can't help but smile even though something seems amiss. Our hands swing between us and I am grateful for the bit of space. "So, what do you have planned for this evening?" I ask, trying to seem excited.

"You'll have to wait and see." I groan, tilting my head back.

"Please?" I whine a bit, hating surprises. This only makes him laugh and he shakes his head. "Fine, but if it is a fancy place I will be so mad at you for not warning me. I'm not dressed for anything fancy."

"Don't worry, you look perfect." I blush a little, looking down at the concrete, and watching our shoes take different strides. His are long and slow, while my stride is quick and rushed, my short legs trying to keep up with his lengthy ones.

He lifts his arm, our hands still intertwined, and drapes it over my shoulder, pulling me close to him. The air is muggy and I don't need the extra heat but I know he is trying to be sweet so I lean into him, our hips bumping as we walk.

"I hope you don't mind walking. I thought it was a nice night for a walk. That way we can spend more time together and if you get really hungry, there are a bunch of restaurants around here so we can always stop if you see something you like." I smile, appreciating the thought but wondering if he doesn't have anything planned except for stopping whenever I get hungry. He seems to sense my hesitation. "And yes, I do have something planned but it's a few blocks away and I know you, you are always hungry. And I am just trying to show that I am flexible when it comes to things you want to do." He points out and I laugh.

"Alright, alright. Well, I am a bit hungry but I think I can wait."

We continue our walk, in silence, taking in the lights and the scenery around us. The sky gets darker and the lights of the city come to life. Bicycles pass us, their orange and yellow lights flashing, making their presence known. The headlights of cars light up the darkened alleys and expose their hidden secrets before moving on to their next target. The chatter of the people on the sidewalk around us blends into the humming of the street lamps and the chirp of the crickets. The moon comes into view as we round a corner and make our way down the block.

"It really is a beautiful night." I look up at the moon and then feel eyes watching me. I look over to Callum and smile. "What? Do I have something on my face?" He smiles at my usual line and laughs.

"No, no. Your face is perfect." I blush and look away. He stops walking and tucks his hand under my chin gently lifting my face to look up at him. He looks like he is about to kiss me and I panic. My body wants to accept his kiss but my heart and mind know I am not ready for it yet. He smiles at me before doing anything. "We're here." He releases my chin and opens the door of the restaurant for me.

"Thank you," I say, my cheeks still pink, a little embarrassed. Callum retrieves my hand when we enter the restuarant, pulling me through the crowded space. I let him lead me, trusting him while I take in the scene.

The restaurant isn't too fancy but it is very popular. The taco joint has high tables scattered around with a few lower seats thrown in the middle. I watch as couples of all ages, sizes, and ethnicities, munch on their delicious dishes and talk happily. The atmosphere is welcoming. The walls have murals painted onto the brick and concrete foundations. I take time to study them as Callum leads me to our table. We take a seat next to what I've decided is my favorite mural. The mural depicts a giant taco and a margarita with faces, having what seems to be a funny conversation. The speech bubbles have faded so I can't read what they have said to each other but their expressions are enough for me.

Once we are seated, I turn away from the mural and face Callum. He opens his mouth about to speak but a waitress appears at our table and places menus in front of us. "Hi, my name is Melissa and I will be your server for the evening. Have either of y'all eaten with us before?" We both shake our heads and it makes me a little excited to think about us sharing a new experience. The waitress goes on to explain a few items on the menu but I tune her out and start to look over the menu for myself.

"…and she'll have a Dr. Pepper." I hear and I look up from the menu. Callum looks over at me and smiles.

"Alright, I'll go get your drinks and give you some time to look over the menu." She leaves the table, leaving us to each other's company.

"I hope you didn't mind me ordering for you. She did ask you but you were very concentrated on your menu. You do still like Dr. Pepper, don't you?" He asks, starting confident and then wavering with his question.

I nod, assuring him. "Yes, I love Dr. Pepper. Thank you. I hope she didn't think I was being rude."

"To be honest, I don't think she even noticed. She wasn't really paying attention, just enough to hear the correct order." We both share a chuckle then I go back to looking at my menu. We spend a few minutes in silence then I figure out that I want the special burrito; beans, and cheese with rice, and their special sauce but I'll have to make sure to ask her to leave off the avocado. I put my menu down and look up. We choose our orders at the same time and he looks up from his menu too.

My stomach growls and I blush and laugh a little. "I am hungry. I probably should have eaten a snack before this. Don't judge me if I eat everything on my plate." He holds his hands up in surrender.

"Hey, I would never judge you for eating. I know you can take me." He adds at the last minute and I laugh then flex my muscles before poking them and shrugging. "Okay, maybe not."

"Hey!" I tease and whack him with my napkin. He laughs and easily dodges it. The waitress comes back to the table with our drinks then we place our orders, handing the menus back to her. When she leaves, the silence returns. I tuck my legs under me and unwrap my silverware, putting my napkin in my lap to busy myself.

"So, how is your band? Have y'all gotten any gigs recently?" I ask about the band only because I know it's something he can talk for hours about. As soon as I mention it, I cringe, thinking back to the party at Kurt's apartment and the way Callum used his music to hurt me. My posture shrinks a little but Callum doesn't seem to notice as he begins his long lengthy one-sided discussion about his band. I try to listen to be polite but my heart clenches and my eyes sting with tears threatening to spill over. I had almost forgotten about the terrible thing he had done to me in front of all of Kurt's co-workers and neighbors.

I lean back against the chair and try to erase that from my memory, deciding not to let it ruin the night that so far has been pretty nice. I nod along and make little comments here and there to keep the conversation flowing and am grateful when our food finally arrives. I dig into my food, my stomach thanking me immensely. I pause to take a sip of my drink and realize he is still going on about his band. Some of their gigs seem impressive and I tell him so, this boosts his confidence. Not like he needed it though.

I start slowing down after a few minutes, my stomach beginning to get full and I decide to stop and take the rest of the burrito home with me. It was really good and I don't want to waste it. I take a step back from the burrito but reach for a chip to dip in the salsa. I munch away on my chip, listening to Callum go on and on. I polish off half the bowl of chips and Callum hasn't said anything judgmental about my eating so I keep eating.

"So, how have you been? Trouble in paradise, I assume, if y'all aren't together anymore," Callum says, finally talking about something other than his band and himself. Unfortunately, this is another topic I don't want to discuss. I sigh and bite into another chip taking my time to chew and swallow then taking a sip of my drink before responding.

"Things were just moving a little too fast. For both of us." I say and leave it at that, he nods, seeming to understand.

We make small talk while we finish our drinks and then the check comes.

"Oh, I can pay for myself." I offer but he shakes his head and smiles at me.

"No, no. Then it wouldn't be a date." He pulls out his wallet putting some cash on the table then we stand up together and exit the restaurant. He wraps his arm around my waist, pulling me against him. I lean into him, the night air had grown cold while we were eating. I shiver slightly and rub at my goose bump-covered arms. "Are you cold?" He asks before releasing me and quickly shrugging off his jacket and draping it over my shoulders. "Better?"

"Yes, thank you. You didn't have to do that..." I say softly but I know he did. If he hadn't then Tatyana would have been right and I would have to walk away. He shrugs, kissing my forehead and pulling me back against him as I slip my arms into his jacket, the cuffs of the jacket dipping below my fingertips. I ball the extra material up and clench it in my fists, letting him hold me close.

We walk back to my apartment in silence and I can feel every breath he takes. It catches every so often and I know he wants to say something but I am enjoying the silence and am grateful when he doesn't say anything. When we reach my building, he lets go of me and opens the door. I thank him and then make my way inside. He follows behind me into the cramped lobby, I stop by the staircase.

"Thank you for walking me back," I say, trying to make it clear that this is as far as he goes. He takes a step back nodding, looking a tad disappointed. I smile at my new stance in this relationship. He isn't in charge of me anymore. "I had a nice time tonight."

"Me too," he says and grins at me. I smile back. "We should do this again sometime." I nod.

"I'd like that," I tell him honestly. "Oh, before I forget," I say as I take his jacket off. "Here you go. Thank you for letting me borrow it."

"Not a problem," Callum says a little reluctantly as he takes the jacket back. He leans in and kisses my cheek. "I'll call you tomorrow?" He looks at me for my permission and I smile and nod again. "Goodnight, Juli."

I wait for him to leave the building before I make my way up the stairs quickly. I burst into the apartment breathing heavily from the many flights up. Tatyana looks up from the couch surprised at my sudden entrance. She turns off the TV as I toss my keys and purse on the table by the door.

"Well? How'd it go?" She asks, tucking her legs under her and wrapping her arms around a pillow, watching me intently.

I take a second to catch my breath and smile at her sweetly before taking my time to take my shoes off. She throws a giant old t-shirt at me and I give her a look of gratitude before unbuttoning my pants and stripping down my stomach finally able to breathe after a night of tight pants. I put the shirt on and plop on the couch, pulling a blanket over my lap. "Okay, you've changed into something more comfortable, you can breathe. Now, tell me!" She throws the pillow she was holding at me and I laugh.

"Okay, okay," I say through my laughter and her protests before I calm down and begin to tell her all the details of the night.

# Chapter 54
## *Juliana*

"Wow, so he wasn't a complete…" Tatyana trails off when she sees the look I'm giving her. "Sorry, but he usually… is not the greatest?" I nod and we both laugh.

"You're right. On both points. Tonight, he was different."

"Did he kiss you?" She sits up on the couch, leaning forward. I roll my eyes and take my time responding, which of course, annoys her. "Juli! Answer me! He did, didn't he? You shouldn't have let him!"

"Jeez, girl, calm down. No, he did not kiss me. I don't think he even tried to really. He kissed my cheek though. Which was nice, I guess. Sweet." I sit back with a sigh. "I guess it's good. But after everything we've been through?" I pause and look up at Tatyana. "What do you think?"

Tatyana gives me an undefinable look before shooting up off the couch. "I think that we are going out! Just us girls. I'm calling Mike and telling him you and I need some girl time."

"Didn't we just have one of those when we sat in Kurt's apartment for, like, a day? And again the other night when we went dancing."

"So what?" She waves her hand dismissing the thought. "We are going out again. Get on your favorite outfit." She narrows her eyes at me. "Favorite outfit that does not include pants. At Kurt's apartment it was a sweatpants type of night, and then a jeans outing but tonight…baby, tonight is a no pants type of night!" She does a little hop and pumps her fist in the air. Her enthusiasm is contagious, and I get off the couch and let her drag me to her bedroom and into the closet.

"Now, what do we wear?" I jump out of the way just in time to dodge a big green fur coat.

"Where the hell did that thing come from?" Stooping down, I lift the monstrosity to examine it. "When did you get this? Is it real?"

"So many questions." Tatyana turns around and squints at the coat. "Oh, yeah, one of my friends brought us to this retro club. It was a theme night for some decade." She ends her story and goes off in search of two perfect outfits.

I go over to the corner of the closet, lean against the wall, and slide to the floor. Looking around at the piles on the floor, a gold sparkle catches my eye and I pull out a sequined dress.

"Yes! That's perfect. You're wearing it." Tatyana says, noticing the dress I found. "And your knee-high black, suede boots would go perfectly."

"You don't think it's too much?" I hold it up against my body and walk over to look in the mirror in the bedroom.

"Okay, fine. Maybe no knee-highs. Put the dress on," she instructs me and disappears into the closet again. I strip and wiggle into the dress. Tatyana comes out of the closet and helps zip me into the dress then hands me gorgeous black high heels with a touch of gold on them.

"How do you always have the perfect thing for me to wear?" I put on the heels and wobble a bit. She grins at me then holds up a cute golden clutch. A squeal comes out of my mouth before I can stop it and we both laugh.

"I'm amazing, I know. Okay, now my turn. Please sit back and relax and prepare to be amazed. Even more so than usual." I laugh and roll my eyes then fall back onto the bed, my dress riding up my thighs. "I'm wearing your boots, by the way!" She calls out to me.

"I'm not surprised that you had them in here," I respond then close my eyes for a few minutes.

A pillow hits my stomach and I sit up. "I'm awake."

"Are you?" Tatyana stands over me peering down at me. "I didn't take that long!" I just raise my eyebrow at her. "Right okay, sure. But look at the results! Worth the wait, right?" She holds her arms out then slowly spins around and strikes a pose when she comes back to face me. She found a similar sequined dress but in a pretty pink color. She paired the dress with my knee-high boots and a short black fur jacket. And pink hair.

"Whoa, where did the pink hair come from?"

"Oh, do you like it? It was just a quick chalk thing for my hair."

"Yeah, I like it. It looks good." I stand up and fill the golden clutch with all my necessities. "You ready to go?"

She stuffs her purse and tucks a flask in it. "Free vodka. Gotta be prepared." She pats her purse and then grabs the apartment keys.

I follow her out of the room and into the hallway. "Why do you have so many sequined dresses?" I ask as we make our way down the stairs and into the lobby.

"So many questions," Tatyana rolls her eyes smiling. "Should we walk? It's pretty nice out tonight." I nod, and we make our way down the street, the cool air blows my hair over my shoulders and I teeter in my heels. Maybe we shouldn't have walked.

# Chapter 55
## *Juliana*

I hear a squealing laugh and I know Tatyana is having fun. I look over at her and see she's trying out some ridiculous new dance moves. Everyone around her is loving it. She dances to the music but at the same time, dances to her own beat. She spins around and finds me in the crowd, she dances her way over to me and bounces around me. I laugh and let loose with her. Dancing off-beat, singing along to the songs we know, and making up lyrics to other songs. After a break in music, we step back and head to the bathroom together.

"It's getting late, should we start to head back to the apartment?" I ask while we wash our hands side by side. We've been here longer than the other night and I'm certainly getting tired but Tatyana seems to have gotten her second wind.

"It's only 1:20 in the morning," Tatyana says checking her watch. "Actually, there is a bar down the street that I want to check out." I throw away my towel after drying my hands and fix my hair in the mirror.

"Sure, I think I've still got a little energy left in me." I laugh and Tatyana gives a cheer. She's been such a great support, I can muster the energy for another adventure.

"One last song?"

"Of course!" I hear Waterfalls begin to play and I give her a look. "TLC? This is perfect." Tatyana laughs but nods, agreeing.

The door to the bathroom opens and a group of girls make their way in as we head out, they seem younger and make a comment about how "lame" this song is. Okay, the song might not be from my generation either but it's still an amazing song. We make our way back onto the dance floor and dance our hearts out.

After the song finishes we say goodbye to the people we were dancing with and then exit the club. "Which way is this bar?"

"I think it's that way," she points down the street, I give her a look. "What? I'm not good with directions." I gesture for her to lead the way. She loops her arm through mine and tugs me along.

"We better not get lost."

"Relax, it's on this street. I know that." She pauses and looks around, squinting in the dark. "Well, maybe. I think."

"T!" I give her arm a shake and she laughs.

"Look, it's right here."

"Oh, my gosh. I know this place," I tell her, a smile growing on my face. She raises her eyebrows and I nod, excitedly. "Kurt took me here once. I always wanted to go again. His buddy Benny owns the place!"

I must sound too excited because Tatyana laughs happily. We make our way to the front entrance and she holds the door open for me. "My dear," she says laughing.

"Thank you, kind sir," I giggle in return.

"Welcome in!" A voice calls from behind the bar. And when we walk further into place, I spot Benny pouring drinks. There aren't too many people in here, just like the night Kurt and I came but it's a pretty good crowd for how late it is.

"Hey! Juliana!" Benny greets me when he looks up, finishing the drinks in front of him. "How have you been?"

"Hi, Benny! Craving those delicious chicken strips and fries," I tell him, my mouth practically salivating thinking about them.

Benny chuckles. "Coming right up! Anything for your lovely friend?"

"Tatyana," I say as an introduction.

"Hiiii." Tatyana grins at him. "I heard about this place from some of my friends. I thought I was dragging Juli here when I told her about it but as soon as she saw the place she practically sprinted." Tatyana teases me and I roll my eyes.

"Well, I'm glad somebody loves the place," one of the patrons at the counter says gruffly. Benny chuckles.

"Just for that, I'm cutting you off," Benny teases.

"Hey, I was just joking," the man retorts with a humorous laugh. Benny shakes his head, chuckling.

"So, chicken strip basket for you and...?" Benny asks Tatyana.

"Two of those sounds good. And whatever you have on tap works for me."

"Alright, let me pour your drinks and I'll be right back with the food." Benny turns back to the bar, grabbing our drinks. He places an ale in front of Tatyana and a Dr. Pepper in front of me. I'm impressed that he remembered. We thank him before he disappears into the kitchen.

I look around the bar, falling silent. The last time I was here was after a very long, chaotic but also great day. The party at Kurt's place had been insane but it also brought us closer together.

"Hey, what's going on in your head?" Tatyana asks after a few minutes of silence. She sips on her drink, slowing down for the evening and staring at me over the rim.

"Yeah," I say but she narrows her eyes at me and I sigh. "It's just that the last time I was here, I was with Kurt. It was right after that disastrous party but then we had so much fun here and when we got back home… remember I texted you that night?" I ask with an embarrassed chuckle.

"OMG, yes! That was the night you two made out!" Tatyana practically cheers and I have to shush her even though I'm giggling a bit.

"Yes, yes it was. And it was amazing," I say, just for fun. "But it was also the night when he first admitted that he liked me, like really liked me."

I sigh and shake my head. Tatyana lets me remain silent for a few seconds before she reaches over and squeezes my hand.

"You okay?"

"I'm getting there, I guess," I say with a shrug.

Before we can say anything else, Benny comes back with two steaming baskets and slides them in front of us.

"Boom! Heaven in a basket." His antics cheer me up and I laugh. Tatyana's mouth hangs open as she stares at the deliciousness in front of her.

"This looks amazing," is all she says before her mouth is full with steaming hot chicken. She chews with her mouth open, blowing the steam out as she chews. My eyes widen, impressed and a little scared.

"Wow," Benny chuckles before turning his attention to me. "So how are you doing? How's Kurt? I had expected to see you again but I figured Kurt would be with you," Benny comments and I shove a fry into my mouth to give myself time to think of something to say.

When I swallow, Benny is still looking at me for a response. "I'm alright. We're alright. We've both been pretty busy." It's a lame excuse and even worse response but Benny just nods his head.

"I get it," he says. He stops and chuckles, looking around the bar. "Okay, well no, I can't say that I get it. But I understand. Man, Kurt was having the time of his life with you here last time. He was practically glowing with you by his side. I almost vomited every time he looked at you or snuck kisses." Benny pretends to gag and I blush but try to laugh to cover it up.

"Hey, it wasn't that bad," I protest, thinking back on that night. I don't remember anything too showy. Kurt did act more into me that night and I loved it but it wasn't overly affectionate.

Benny holds up his hands in surrender. "Not that there's anything wrong with a little PDA but damn, that man is in love with you. I've been around for a bit and he's had a couple of girlfriends, but you sweetie, you take the cake. I guess that's why he made you his fiancée, huh?" Benny chuckles, grabbing a rag to wipe down the counter.

I sit, stunned by his comments. "I-I guess so," I stutter, not wanting to leave the conversation with awkward silence.

"Good thing too, because it looks like you love him too," Benny says, giving me a soft smile, a happy smile. The man from earlier waves at Benny from down the bar so Benny excuses himself, walking away from.

"Well that was interesting," Tatyana comments and I jump a little, having completely forgotten that she was there.

"What are you talking about?" I ask, nonchalantly as I dig into my chicken basket.

"Oh nothing, just that everyone else can see that you two are in love with each other," Tatyana hums before shoving another fry into her mouth.

"Does it really matter at this point?" I ask with a sigh, swirling a chicken around in a little cup of ranch.

Tatyana narrows her eyes at me. I know she wants to point out that I didn't deny being in love but instead, she chomps down on some chicken.

"Tonight is about us girls," she says eventually and I nod.

"To us, and our chicken!" I cheers her, tapping my chicken against hers.

"Don't forget the fries," Tatyana holds up a fry so I grab one too and we 'cheers' again.

We chat aimlessly while we eat and once we are done, Benny comes back over to us, collecting our empty baskets.

"Refills?" Benny asks and I can see Tatyana considering it, I laugh and shake my head.

"No, thank you. And thank you for the delicious chicken strips but I think it's time we headed home." I smile at him and he nods, his lips quirked up at the edges.

"Do you two need a ride?" He asks, looking around the bar.

"We should be fine. I'll request a car." I pull up a ride-share app on my phone and put in the request. "Five minute away," I say, holding up the phone so Benny can see. He peers at my phone then nods his head approvingly.

"Here, drink some water while you wait." Benny puts two glasses of water on the counter in front of us. I thank him and chug half of the water and gesture for Tatyana to do the same.

While we wait, Benny goes off to help other customers. The bar only has a few other patrons but they still require his attention. I twist in my stool, facing Tatyana. She finishes her water and sets it on the counter.

"He's nice," she says and I agree. "He really went to Law School?" Tatyana sounds a bit shocked which makes me chuckle. I had a similar reaction when I found out.

"Right? And made millions creating video games," I tell her and her eyes widen.

"Man of many talents," Tatyana says appreciatively and I agree again.

"Oope, the car is here. Let's get going." Tatyana and I slide off of our seats and head toward the front door. "Bye

Benny! Thanks for everything!" I call out as we pull open the big front door.

"See ya!" Benny waves from behind the bar.

The ride back home isn't too long and before we know it, the car is stopped in front of our apartment. I thank the driver, leaving a 5-star review then drag myself and Tatyana out of the car.

It takes us a little while to get up the stairs but once we do, we both fall onto the couch.

"Coffee tomorrow? 9?" Tatyana looks over at me practically glaring at me. I laugh, "Yeah, you're right. Noon or one?" She gives me thumbs up then shushes me and pulls a blanket over herself. I curl up into a ball and fall asleep quickly.

# Chapter 56
## *Kurt*

My alarm blares too early in the morning and the sunlight streams into the room because I forgot to close the blinds. As soon as I open my eyes, the light jolts my system and I'm fully awake. Climbing out of bed, I switch on the TV in the living room before going to the kitchen and making a pot of coffee. A few files from work sit on the kitchen counter and I look over them while I drink my first cup of coffee, the news quietly on in the background. I finish my first cup of coffee and then take a quick shower. I hear my phone go off while I'm in the shower and wonder who else would be up this early. After my shower I sit down on the couch, spread the files out on the coffee table in front of me, and settle in on my second cup of coffee, forgetting to check my phone.

I wanted to get to work before 8 but I let the files distract me and only notice the time when the neighbor's dog starts barking. And he always starts barking at 7:30 in the morning. I check my watch just to make sure and it says 7:30 a.m. Shit, I'm going to be late. I quickly pack my briefcase and put a third cup of coffee into a travel mug before heading out the door a few minutes later to get to work. I get to work around 8:15 only a few of my co-workers have arrived before me.

"Good morning, Kelley." I go into my office and Kelley follows and leans against the doorframe of my office.

"Good morning, Kurt. Have you taken a look at the Penski file yet? I have a few ideas I'd like to run by you."

"Sure, let me get settled in first. Katy said we could use the conference room this week, can you bring all the paperwork in there to set up?"

"Sure, boss, sounds good." She says cheerily and makes fun of me for bossing her around. She laughs as she turns to get the papers.

"Thank you!" I call after her then unpack my briefcase and grab my phone remembering to check it. I see a text from an unknown number with an attached picture but I don't bother to open it so I grab the Penski files that I brought home and my cup of coffee then make my way to the conference room.

"Okay," I say as I set down the files and take a seat around the table, "Kelley, what ideas did you have?"

------------------

"You're going to join us tonight, right Kurt?"

I look up from my work and see Kelley standing at the reception desk, packing up to leave for the day. Looking at the clock on the wall, I can't believe how late it is. I start packing up my desk and shove some work into my back to bring back to my apartment to work on.

"I'm not sure. I have a lot to work on. I might just go back to my apartment…" I drift off hoping she'll drop it or continue asking, I'm not sure which I want right now. Maybe I should go out with them.

"Come on, you've bailed the last few nights." Another one of my co-worker's comments as he finishes putting his jacket on. He and Kelley head to the door and then look back at me. I wave them on.

"Sure," I say. "I'll be right behind you guys." I finish packing as they leave.

Making my way to my car, I take my time, knowing I should go out tonight but not really wanting to. I check my phone once I'm in the car. Still no messages from Juliana, but plenty of messages from Ashley. I sigh then put my phone away. Yeah, I need a night out.

Pulling into the parking lot, I stay in my car leaning my head back and squeezing my eyes shut tight before opening my eyes and making my way into the bar.

"Hey! You made it." I'm instantly surrounded by a couple of my co-workers and a drink is placed in my hand. I accept it willingly, needing to relax. "We've got a booth in the corner." Kelley points in a direction and I see some of our other co-workers gathered around a giant booth in the back. I nod and take a sip of my drink before we make our way back to the booth. I pull a chair up to the edge of the table while Kelley slides into the booth.

"Hey, you had some great points on that case today," I start to say but Kelley waves her hand, cutting me off.

"Please, no work talk. We are here to forget about work." She holds up her glass gesturing for me to do the same then looking to everyone else to follow suit. "To relaxing after work and the annoying coworkers we drink with!" She raises her glass higher and yells "Cheers!"

Kelley is the cheerleader of our office so we all indulge her and cheer with her then go back to our separate conversations.

I check my phone again and finally open the text from the unknown number. I click on the picture and it's a little blurry but it looks like a picture of Juliana and Callum out on a date. The text reads;

**Unknown: Do you know where your fiancé is?**

I look around the room a little confused, wondering if the text is a joke. I look at the picture and zoom in on it. I can't even tell when this picture was taken, it might have been a long time ago. I text the number back with a quick response,

**Kurt: Who is this?**

Then I slide my phone into my pocket and try to relax and enjoy the company of my co-workers.

# Chapter 57
## *Juliana*

I feel a sharp pain on my shin and I sit up quickly then groan when my head spins and lay back down. I reach over and whack Tatyana's side.

"Wake up, you kicked me." I yawn and roll over grabbing my phone to check the time. "Tatyana, wake up," I try again, nudging her. "It's after 1 p.m. Do you have work?"

I hear a groan and a pillow lands on my face. "No, day off today. Coffee at 2:30?"

"Sure, I'm going to take a shower." I let her know and she shushes me again so I smack her with the pillow she hit me with, returning it to her. She grabs it and covers her face.

Going to the bathroom I turn on the shower then return to my room to grab a wrinkled button-up shirt to hang in the bathroom to let the steam smooth the cloth. I step into the shower wanting to relax but all I can do is think about everything that has been happening recently. So much has been going on and I have had so little time to settle down and think about anything. My time with Kurt had gone by in a flash but I remember every little detail.

Living with Kurt was so easy. I thought it would be awkward and that one or both of us would be uncomfortable in different situations but we weren't. We worked. His apartment was a little small but I never felt crowded and I'd like to think he was comfortable too.

I turn off the shower and give a heavy sigh before exiting the small bathroom and finding Tatyana still sprawled on the couch. It's almost 2 in the afternoon now but the coffee shop we usually go to is just down the street so I don't bother to wake her. The light shines into my room when I open the door, I take the time to look around the room, the lack of anything Kurt makes me feel lonely. I know Tatyana lives in the room right next to me and Mike occasionally stays over but they usually stay in their own space and are private together.

I sit down on the bed and grab my phone; the screen lights up when I lift it and I see a text from Callum asking if I am free for dinner tonight. I text him back.

**Juliana: 8:30?**

I get a response back quickly.

**Callum: Great! I'll pick you up at 8:29**.

I smile, put my phone down, and get dressed to get coffee with Tatyana.

Once I am all dressed and ready, I almost forget to pick up my phone but at the last second, I remember to grab it before I exit my room. And I see that Tatyana has vacated the couch and the bathroom door is shut.

"T! You almost ready?" I call out to her, making my way to the kitchen and filling a glass full of ice and water then sucking on an ice cube. The bathroom door opens and a functioning Tatyana walks out of it, dressed for the day.

"Yeah, I'm ready. Oh, I have to run to the post office after coffee then have some errands I need to do after. Do you have time for that today?"

I down the rest of my water then toss the ice into the sink, feeling bad for wasting it. "Sure, I'm free until 8:30." I pause then change my mind. "Actually, make that 7:30," I say, wanting to leave time to get ready for my date with Callum tonight.

"Oh? Hot date tonight?" She asks then grabs her purse swinging it onto her shoulder and grabbing the keys to the apartment.

"Maybe..." I say vaguely and smile when she gives me a look.

"Be careful." She opens the door and gestures for me to exit. I put my cup in the dishwasher and walk out the door with Tatyana following behind me. I pause by the door to wait for her to lock it, leaning against the wall I watch her struggle with the lock. "This damn old building. I always complain to Hank about these stupid doors and their stupid locks but he has never done anything to fix it." I nod, Hank the Handyman does not live up to his name.

"Here, let me try." She huffs and moves out of the way for me and I yank the handle up and snap the lock shut. "There! I got it!" I cheer in triumph which makes Tatyana groan.

"Shh, I still haven't had my coffee yet."

"Okay okay, let's go. I want to stop in the bookstore afterward." I tell her as we head into the stairwell and down to the lobby.

"The post office is right next to that so I'll pop in there while you are in the bookstore."

"Sounds good." We make it to the coffee shop in under five minutes and only have to wait in a short line before we order. The line moves up and we step up to the counter, ordering together as always making it easier for the line behind us and the cashier. Clearing my throat, I tell the cashier my order. "Mocha Frappe, please. Blended." I add. I always forget what the blended drinks are called. I order breakfast as well and then step aside to let Tatyana order then hand her a couple of dollars to pay for my drink while I go and find us a seat.

When Tatyana makes her way over to the booth I've chosen, she sets our drinks down with a large piece of coffee cake and an iced lemon loaf. "So, this date is with Callum right?" I nod before taking a sip out of my straw. "What ever happened to Kurt? I liked him a lot more than Callum."

I laugh then sigh a little. "I don't know. I want to reach out. I have been thinking about him recently but I don't know if he's thinking about me." I lean back letting the foam of the roughed-up booth back pull me in. "It all went by so quickly. I know it was a bad situation to bond over but I don't know. I'm glad we had that chance to get to know each other a little bit. I think I really messed up telling him it wasn't real to me."

"You did," I agrees with me, much to my annoyance. "You guys were really great together." I sit forward and take one of the forks to try the coffee cake. I put the fork down and make a face. "Coffee cake not your thing?"

"No, I've never really liked it but I always try." I look across the table at her. "Do you think there's any way that we could be together for real? After everything that's happened?"

"Juli, I'm going to be honest with you, I don't know. It would be hard. You would probably have to tell both of your parents why you faked being engaged but maybe they would understand and be happy that you two are trying to be together for real?" She says like a question then shrugs. "I don't know if it would work but I do know that you should not go crawling back to Callum. Who knows what kind of scheming he's up to or what dirty trick he'll play next? But that option should be crossed out." She rubs her head, trying to get rid of her hangover.

"Hey, I'm not 'crawling back'. And he seems like he's changed. But maybe you're right. I feel like we've had this conversation a thousand times." I sigh and take another sip of my drink. "It's probably time to be done with Callum."

"Yes, definitely time." Tatyana pulls the coffee cake closer to her and continues eating it while washing it down with her coffee.

"I'll tell him tonight." I peek up at her to see if she agrees with my idea.

"You should. And do it before you go to dinner or whatever you two are going to do. You don't want to get his hopes up with the dinner and what might come after it. So yes, do it tonight but early on in the night."

I nod, agreeing with that plan. "But that's still in a few hours, let's take our drinks to go. You can head to the bookstore, and I'll stop in the post office," Tatyana says, stacking our plates to make it easier to bus.

"Okay." I finish my lemon loaf and then scoot out of the booth wrapping a napkin around my drink. We walk out the door and head down the street. A couple of doors down I stop at the bookstore. "I might take a while so come back for me. Or if I finish quickly I'll come find you."

"Sounds good. The line shouldn't be too long this time of day, so I'll probably be finished before you." We exchange "See you later" then I go into the bookstore searching for cheap, used books to read.

# Chapter 58
## *Juliana*

Sitting on the floor, in the middle of an aisle of books, I have 8 different choices spread out around me. I pick up each once again to read the inside of the cover flap or the back of the book. Then I flip through a couple of pages to see if the condition of the book is decent. I don't expect perfect conditions because it is a used bookstore, but I don't want a particularly gross or destroyed book.

While I am looking over the books, I get distracted by the books on the bottom shelf and start sifting through them to see if anything looks interesting. After a few moments of zero noise except the shuffling of books and the turning of pages, the bell above the door goes off but I don't bother to look up until a shadow falls over the pages of my book.

"Juliana?" A familiar voice questions, laughter at the edges of my name.

"Kurt!" I smile up at him then quickly tamper my happiness. "Hi, can I help you find anything? Well, I don't work here but I know this place pretty well, so I could probably help you find whatever it is you're looking for…" I trail off when a goofy smile appears on his face and I realize I am rambling. I blush and look back down at my books to hide my rosy cheeks.

"No, I'm okay, I just saw you in here, on the floor so, I thought I'd stop in to say hello," he laughs a little and I join in because it is silly to be on the floor. "Oh. Also, I got a text last night and I wanted to know if you knew anything about it?"

He hands his phone down to me and I look at the screen to see a picture and the text below.

**Unknown: Do you know where your fiancé is?**

I click on the picture and see that it's a photo of Callum and me on our date from the other night. I'm shocked.

"Who took this? That's so creepy. What the hell." I hand him his phone back before I hurl it in anger. Standing up off the floor, I look around to see if anyone is following or taking pictures of me today. "Who would do or send something like that?"

"I'm not sure. That's why I came to you. I was wondering if Callum would have done this, maybe he had someone take the picture for him?" He pockets his phone and crosses his arms over one another.

Realization dawns on me. "He asked me out, and he acted like he had changed. But he's always been one for revenge or petty schemes. God, I'm such an idiot." I huff, "I even said yes to a date tonight, who knows what he's got planned."

"You wanted to get back together with him?" Kurt asks and I can hear an emotion in his voice but I can't tell if it's surprise, jealousy, curiosity, or disappointment. I decide that it shouldn't matter to me but I feel the need to explain myself anyway.

"Yes, well, he came back and was really sweet and he seemed like he had changed. He was polite, took things slow… And after I saw you with Ashley, I couldn't face you again without that image in my head and I know I shouldn't have reacted that way because our engagement wasn't real, so it was totally fine and I guess I just… Well, I don't really know what happened. A moment of weakness?" I stop to breathe, and I look up at his face finally and I can clearly read the guilt and regret that resides on his face. And shock at my revelation that I had seen them together. "You don't have to feel guilty. You and I were never really a thing. Not a real couple. Right? Right. Ashley was your girlfriend, maybe still is. So, you did nothing wrong."

He clears his throat. "You're right. I did nothing wrong." I nod, looking down at the ground but he continues, "Because nothing happened. I did nothing wrong because I did nothing. We didn't do anything, Ashley and I."

"What do you mean?" I look up again, confused and a little surprised.

"I was drunk, yes, a bad excuse but the next morning, I told Ashley it had been a mistake and to leave the apartment and she told me that nothing had happened, but that you had thought something had. Why didn't you ask me about it? I would have told you the truth."

"Is that why you came to see me the next day?" I pause and then ask another question, my voice raising an octave, being defensive, "Why didn't you bring it up?" We both stand there, not responding to each other's questions. After a few seconds of silence, I smile and he smiles back. We're both sad, confused, and exhausted. "It doesn't matter anymore. You didn't do anything?" He nods still smiling at me and I immediately feel butterflies in my stomach and I think to myself, oh no, not this again.

I direct my attention back to the creepy photo. "Callum knew we weren't together anymore, I told him that. You and I weren't together when this picture was taken so I'm not sure why whoever it is texted you that." Again, I make a huffing noise, and Kurt looks equally as frustrated and confused. Then he sighs and takes a step back as if distancing himself from the problem, me.

"Well, it doesn't bother me as long as you're okay?" He poses it as a question.

I shrug, feeling a little shaken but not horribly so. "Yeah, I'm fine. It's just strange that someone would send that to you. Do you really think Callum sent it or had someone else do it?" I go back to the original suspect. "Besides revenge or pettiness, I just don't really understand what his motive would be." Letting myself drift back down to the floor, my eyes glaze over and I lightly drag my fingers over each book laid out before me. Kurt stands near me and I can practically hear him thinking. A few seconds later, he clears his throat.

"I never told anyone that we called off our engagement. So, it could be any number of people who think we are still together."

"I never told anyone either, besides Tatyana, who already knew it was fake." I look up at Kurt and catch him watching me, but he doesn't look away, he just smiles. He squats down in front of me, I keep my head tilted back a bit, so I can look him in the eyes. His eyes sparkle a little which makes me blush and I am about to turn away when he grabs my chin between his forefinger and thumb and leans in and barely brushes his lips over mine.

"I found myself wishing it wasn't fake...," He whispers softly against my lips and I find myself leaning into his warmth when the bell above the door chimes and I jolt back and away from him, my heart pounding wildly.

"Ooo, well, well, well, what do we have here? Did I interrupt something?" A smug voice says, and I can hear the smirk on Tatyana's face before I even look up. I quickly gather all my newly found books into my arms and stand up, Kurt wrapping his hand around my elbow to help me up. I nod my head as a thank you then scurry to stand by Tatyana.

Kurt clears his throat and I feel the butterflies in my stomach again and wonder why the butterflies seem to like him clearing his throat so much. "Hi, Tatyana." He says, in lieu of an answer. Then he turns to face me, "It was nice running into you today. Let me know if you ever need anything." He hesitates before leaving and watches my face, searching for a reaction. All I can do is nod and look back down at the floor. I hear him sigh quietly, "Bye, Tatyana." Then the bell goes off again and I know he's left.

I look up and see Tatyana staring out the door until he's out of sight then she whips around to face me. "Damn! What did I walk in the middle of??"

Blushing, I move to the counter and pay for all my books. I clear my throat before responding to her. "Someone texted him a picture of Callum and me when we went out to dinner."

"What the -? That's weird." Tatyana digs through the bins on the counter trying to see if there is anything interesting.

"That's what I thought too. They sent the picture along with a message asking if he knew where I was, like making the accusation that I was cheating? I don't know. It's so messed up." I thank the cashier and take the bag of my books. Tatyana tosses a few little goodies onto the counter and leans her hip against it, facing me while the cashier totals everything out. "It's just strange…" I let out a breath and wave my hand. "I don't want to talk about it." Tatyana picks up her bag of goodies and the bell on the door rings as we leave the shop.

# Chapter 59

## *Kurt*

Running into Juliana in the bookstore was a happy accident. I had been wanting to reach out to her but ever since our goodbyes at her apartment, I felt the need to wait for her to approach me. Everything had seemed so final, yet I found myself wishing she would reach out. When I saw her sitting there, on the floor of an old bookstore, my breath caught in my throat and I couldn't move for a second. I watched her shift through the books and watched as she tucked her hair behind her ear.

I shake my head trying to get rid of the images that my mind seems to have immediately stored away. There's no point in reliving every little moment. She and I are only friends now if we are even that. The thoughts subside as I head down the sidewalk towards my car, when I near it, I see someone leaning against it.

"Dave, how are you doing?" Dave grins at me and we shake hands as I unlock my car.

"I'm alright, man. How are you and Juliana doing? Nicole keeps bugging me about getting you two over for a dinner or barbeque or anything really. She doesn't really care what, she's just so excited to have another couple to hang out with…" He trails off when he notices my expression. "What? Trouble in paradise? Don't tell me that."

"You could say that," I hold off on telling him the truth. Honestly, I haven't told anybody the truth yet. Maybe I just don't want it to be true.

"Okay well get over whatever that issue is because Nicole wanted me to invite you over for dinner Thursday night. Don't ask me why Thursday, that's just what she decided. Okay? 7 o'clock sharp. You don't need to bring anything, she will have the whole meal planned out." I can't come up with an excuse without having to tell him what's happened, so I just nod.

"Sure, sounds good. Now, get off of my car."

Dave laughs as he pushes himself up. "See you then."

"See you at work tomorrow." I remind him and he waves, laughing.

"Right, right, work. See you tomorrow." He walks off and I get into my car.

After turning on my car, I reach for my cell phone to call Juliana. I scroll through my contacts finding her under W for Wifey. I smile, she must have changed that at some point. When I look up from my phone, I notice a car, with its turn signal on, waiting for my parking spot. I decide to call her later and put my phone down to head back to my apartment.

The light turns red and I ease to a stop. My eyes dart to my phone. "No, it can wait. I'll call her when I get home." I nod, trying to convince myself. I can't. Reaching for my phone, I swerve a little bit. "Okay, that convinced me." Hands at ten and two, I grip the wheel and concentrate on the road. The call can wait.

Finally, I pull into the parking lot of my apartment building. With a turn of the key, the car shuts off, letting out one last huff.

"It can wait," I repeat after sitting in my car for a few minutes. I grab my things and head into the building, stopping briefly to talk to Marvin, once again trying to distract myself and calm my thoughts. It only lasts for a minute before I excuse myself to make the call.

Once in my apartment, I drop everything and pull out my phone. Clicking on Wifey, the phone begins to ring.

"Hello?" I hear her voice answering her phone without checking who's calling, it makes me smile.

"Juliana? It's me, Kurt." I add for good measure.

"Oh, hi," she seems surprised or confused, I can't tell. "It's been a while." She chuckles.

"Hah, yeah. Sorry to call, I ran into Dave right after I saw you." I pause and I can hear her tapping her nails on a keyboard before they stop.

"Dave? Oh, Dave, you work with him, right? I met him at the house party..." She drifts off remembering that evening. "Sorry, what were you saying?"

"Dave and Nicole, his wife, have invited us over for dinner. This Thursday. He was very adamant, or well, his wife was very adamant on wanting us to come over. So, unfortunately, I was not able to say no." I stop talking and listen to her calm breathing and I hear the tapping on the keys continue.

"Oh yeah," more tapping, "sure. I wouldn't want to be rude and say no. But is that going to be too weird for us?"

"Possibly." I wait to see if she'll say anything but all I hear is more tapping, "I can just tell them we can't make it because we didn't make it… hah." I try for comedy.

She lets out a little laugh, more like a puff of air but it has some humor in it. "Well, that is the truth, I think."

"You think?" I clear my throat and try to bypass the questions forming in my mind. "Should I just tell them we can't? I should. Sorry, I called you." I'm about to hang up when I hear her speak again.

"Wait," more tapping and then a pause and I hear her more clearly. "No, no I'll do it. We should do it. Dave was a great help at the party. I want to go."

"Really? Okay, I'll let him know. Oh, he said 7 o'clock sharp. I'll pick you up at 6:30." I say automatically then backpedal. "If you want me to, I mean. I can just meet you there if you'd rather."

"Well, I don't know where to go so I think it'd be okay if you picked me up." I can hear her teasing me and again she makes me smile.

"Right, okay, that sounds good."

"Okay, I'll be ready by 6:30. I should go. I've got to finish this by tomorrow." I want to ask what she's working on but I don't want to pry.

"Alright, I'll see you Thursday at 6:30."

"Thursday, 6:30." She repeats back to me. "Bye." She says softly then I hear a click, indicating the line has gone dead.

I'm not entirely sure going through with Thursday evening is the best idea but Dave has been a great friend to me and he made it seem like his wife is very excited and already planning the entire meal. So, I am glad Juliana agreed to go with me. I find myself looking forward to Thursday evening at 6:30 p.m. But until then, I have to get back to my cases. I've been so distracted with everything going on I haven't been putting in my usual effort at work. Well, time to get back to it. I can't do anything else in regards to Juliana until Thursday so I might as well throw myself back into my work. Good thing it's only Monday.

Case files scatter my coffee table hidden in the dark apartment. I cross the living room and pull open the blinds letting in the bright light, enough to brighten the whole apartment. No better time than when it's a beautiful day outside, to sit down and work on my caseload. I crack my knuckles and get down to work.

# Chapter 60
## *Juliana*

Hanging up the phone with Kurt, I check the time. Only 5:30, I have time to finish before Callum shows up, I keep tapping at my keyboard. A few minutes later I hit print, officially finishing my letter of resignation. It's time to move on from my current retail job and move up in the world.

I sigh and sit back, rubbing at my eyes a little. It hits me just how exhausting these last few days have been, weeks really. Reluctantly, I push myself up to get to the printer. After triple-checking the final paper, I see no mistakes and mark my end date in my calendar. I remind myself to tell Tatyana and hope she'll plan a girls' night out to celebrate. I also have big news to tell her.

I check the time again, it's only 6, so I decide to call Tatyana.

"Hey, what's up?" She answers the phone almost immediately.

"Were you waiting for me to call?" I laugh, teasing.

"Of course, I'm already headed to my car, so if this call isn't to remind me to come home and help you get ready for your date with Callum…well that is too bad because I'm coming home anyway. I'll be there in ten minutes or less." She adds before hanging up the phone but not before I hear the start of her engine.

I plug my phone into my charger and then decide to pop into the shower, leaving the apartment door unlocked, knowing that she has probably left her key behind at Mike's house. I hear the door close while I'm in the shower and hear Tatyana yell out that she's here. All of a sudden, the bathroom door opens and a hand holding a glass filled with something appears thrust through the shower curtain.

"Uhm hi, can I help you?" The cup wiggles back in response to my question.

"Just take the cup." I roll my eyes, which I realize she can't see then take it and set it on the soap dish in the shower. I hear a dejected sigh and the clunk of the toilet seat being shut before a thud of someone sitting on the lid.

"What's wrong, T?" I peek my head around the curtain and eye her. She raises her glass to 'cheers' me before taking a drink and then responding.

"Men suck," she says after making a face from what must be hard liquor. She must not have minded it because she takes another sip, making the same face again.

"Tell me about it," I say before disappearing back into the shower to finish up.

"Oh, I will." She pauses and I assume she's taking another sip. "Dammit, I'm out."

"Here," I hand my glass out to her and she takes it but then I hear another dammit. "What?" I ask as I turn off the shower, squeezing the water out of my hair and then grabbing my towel and wrapping it around myself before pulling the shower curtain back.

Tatyana is sitting on the toilet lid glaring at the glass. "You don't drink, so I poured you a glass of tea."

We stare at the deceiving little glass and then we both burst out laughing. Once we have calmed down, I speak.

"Go give yourself a refill while I get dried off. Then you can tell me all about why men suck. I mean I have my own reasons, but I have a feeling you're about to add to the list."

"Oh, you know it. Hurry up."

"Get out," I shoot back at her and wait while she grumbles and exits the bathroom.

I get out of the shower, wrap my shower towel around myself, and use my towel to dry my hair a bit. I look at myself in the mirror and decide Callum can wait. I head into my bedroom and grab my phone sending a quick text telling Callum something came up and I'll have to cancel tonight. He responds almost immediately with a sad face emoji, I send back a text asking for a rain check and he quickly agrees. I let him know I'll call him later in the week and set up a time. I don't wait for a response, putting my phone down and quickly changing into an old t-shirt and pajama shorts.

Emerging from my bedroom, I find Tatyana sprawled on the couch staring at the TV. I turn to look at it and frown. I go and kneel in front of her.

"The TV isn't on, T." She sits up and blinks a little.

"What kind of liquor is this?" She holds up her newly refilled glass and eyes it.

"I don't know, babe, it's yours. You bought it." I laugh and go to the kitchen to make us both some water and a snack.

When I come back to the living room, I switch her drink for some water which she is reluctantly grateful for. I set all the snacks down and settle in beside her. "Okay, what did Mike do to make you feel this way? I thought everything was going well."

"Well, yeah, that's the issue. I thought everything was too. When we went on vacation, I knew he would be busy working but the fact that he invited me to go… Well, it made me think some things…" Tatyana trails off and I feel my eyes widening before her face shifts into a grimace. I fix my face quickly.

"Oooh," I say softly. "Oh, I mean, I can kind of see why you'd think that. And you guys have had that conversation before," I say and Tatyana nods eagerly. "So, what happened? You seemed fine when you came back from the trip."

"Well, I wasn't. It was a good trip but obviously, I had expected something more. So, the next weekend I asked him about it and he laughed. He actually laughed at me. I didn't handle that well," Tatyana tells me and I nod, understanding. "I lashed out at him and got upset at his reaction. He did not handle that well either. And now, all we do is argue. Not even in person! We're arguing over text because he's been too busy to see me." Tatyana has started crying now. I hand her tissues to wipe her face.

"So, what do you want to do?" I ask as she sniffles." You love Mike."

"I do, so much. But after our blowup in person he's just acting so different. He used to always want to spend time with me but now he's too busy and I have no idea what's going on because he won't even talk to me." Her cries break my heart and I pull her into a giant bear hug.

When our hug ends, I pull back and look her over. She still has tears on her cheeks but the amount is subsiding. I dab at her face with a tissue then hand her more water. While she drinks, I think up a game plan.

"Okay," I say when she finishes the water. "Do you want to formulate a plan to resolve this or do you want to wallow in self pity for a bit?"

"Self pity," Tatyana says pretty quickly. I laugh.

"Okay, fine. You let me wallow more than once so I am onboard as well. Wallow in self pity for a few hours and then we'll get our shit together, okay?" I clarify.

"Perfect," Tatyana says before grabbing the remote.

# Chapter 61
## *Juliana*

After many hours of crying, drinking, and more than a few chick flicks muted in the background, Tatyana has finally fallen asleep. She didn't make it to her bedroom though. About halfway through the evening, we decided to build a tent and sleep in the living room. Since Tatyana was a couple drinks deep, I took over the entire operation while she directed me from the couch. In the end, the setup was not bad.

We had a mattress topper on the floor with a couple of layers of blankets to make it even more comfortable. Lined up along the edge of the makeshift bed were the stools from our kitchen counter, giving us enough height that even if the sheets over the top caved in, we would still have room to sit up. A final sheet was placed over the top of the TV to keep it included in our fort/tent. And while Tatyana searched for another movie to watch, I brought in more pillows and blankets and lined the couch cushions against the chairs to completely shield us from the outside world. Then we settled in for the night.

Somewhere around 1:30 in the morning, I shut off the TV and crawl out from under all the blankets and sheets. I turn off all the lights and made sure our door is locked. Then I set about cleaning up the kitchen, as quietly as I can knowing that I will not get any sleep knowing how much food we had left out so I put everything away.

By 2 a.m., I begin to yawn. Every so often I hear a soft ping coming from Tatyana's phone. I know it's Mike. They love each other, I know they do. They'll get over this fight.

I sigh and walk back to the living and grab her phone, glancing over the messages. Most, if not all, are from Mike. I don't read through all of them and only briefly skim a few but I can tell he's just worried and hopes that she is safe. I go to plug her phone in then step into the bathroom to wash up and place a call on my own phone.

"Hey Juli, is Tatyana there with you, is she okay?" Mike asks nervously like he thinks I'd be mad at him.

"She's here. And she is okay, Tatyana just needed some companionship." I smile at myself in the mirror when I hear him let out a breath of relief.

"I'm sure she's already told you what happened.." he begins, timidly. He knows she tells me everything which is why he treads lightly with me.

"Mike, she's going to be okay. I think she's just worried." I sit on the edge of the bathtub, speaking quietly.

"Why would she worry? She has nothing to worry about, I love her so much." His voice begins to sound a bit anxious but I can't tell him what she shared with me. It's not my place. Instead, I offer some advice.

"Tomorrow, she'll be desperately hungover." He chuckles and I go on, "Even though I did make her drink water and eat something, I don't think that helped too much. So tomorrow, bring her coffee, flowers, and donuts. Anything you want. But make sure you have coffee and donuts. And come here. Don't show up before noon though or she might not forgive you."

"That's a great idea. I'll even drive out of town to that donut shop she loves!" He starts getting excited.

"Yes, do that. And when you get here, just talk to her. And let her talk to you. Listen to what she has to say."

"Of course, thank you, Juli," he sounds grateful and tired. It's almost three in the morning now and he probably has to work tomorrow.

"Oh and one more thing, I would like a caramel mocha Frappuccino and just a plain glazed donut would be amazing. Thanks. Then I'll get right out of y'all's way." I stand up getting ready to finish the conversation.

"Thanks. See you tomorrow," he laughs and I end the call.

I finish washing up then exit the bathroom, crawl back into our little fort and finally fall asleep next to a lightly snoring Tatyana.

------------------

"Wake up!" Tatyana shouts close to my face and I jolt awake.

"Oh my god, what?" I sit up and rub at my face, the fort is still dark and I glance around trying to figure out what time it is. It feels like I've only been asleep for a few minutes.

"It's only 7:30 in the morning," Tatyana says and I groan, laying back down and pulling a pillow over my head to cover my ears. "Nooooo, come on Juli, wake up, I've figured it out."

She grabs the pillow off my head and before I can protest she thrusts a small velvet box in my direction, I squint at it.

"What is that?" She grins at me and wiggles it in my face. I look at the box and then at her then back to the back. "Wait, is that what I think it is?" I sit up and grab the box then slowly open it. "T, I'm flattered but..."

"Shut up!" Tatyana squeals at my horrible joke. "I'm going to ask Mike to marry me!" She shrieks happily, and I stare at the ring in the box, clearly ready to be placed on a man's finger. "I was thinking about it all yesterday and I even had a dream where I proposed," she rambles on while I stare at the ring, "and this whole fight yesterday and all the emotions I've been feeling recently, I just know that he's the one I want to be with. Forever."

She finally sits back, her eyes still puffy from crying. And I realize, last night, the crying wasn't because she was sad or angry, well it was definitely a mixture including those emotions, but she was crying because she loves him so much and she finally realized this is the future she wants. I start to tear up.

"Oh, Juli, I am so sorry. I completely forgot, with everything you're going through, I shouldn't even be thinking about marriage and weddings." She slumps back, looking dejected. I throw my arms around her.

"This is amazing! I'm not crying because I'm upset, these are happy tears. I am so excited. OMG, Tatyana, this is incredible. Don't even think about me and my issues for a second. This is something you want to do and I am so happy that you've found the perfect guy." She hesitates at first, unsure if I'm really okay but then she's squeezing me back and crying again too.

"He really is great, isn't he?" She giggles and squeezes me happily, we pull back and just grin at each other. A knock on the door startles us but I hand her the ring and go to answer the door while she sits happily in the fort grinning at the ring.

When I open the door, Mike is standing in front of me, holding a bouquet of a variety of flowers, and he has a drink carrier with two coffees resting on top of a box of donuts. I'm a little shocked to see him this early.

"I know you said not to come before noon but I couldn't wait." He looks past me anxiously and notices our fort. Upon hearing his voice Tatyana pokes her head out.

"Mike?" Her voice squeaks and suddenly I can tell how nervous she is. I grab Mike's arm and direct him into the kitchen.

"Put the flowers in a vase and water while I go get her cleaned up." I wink at him and he smiles thinking I'm winking because of our talk last night, little does he know the real reason. I quickly rush back to Tatyana, pull her down the hallway to the bedrooms, and push her into the bathroom. "Get yourself cleaned up real fast, I'll go get you something sexy to put on."

She laughs and I see some of the nerves fall away as her excitement grows. She shuts me out and gets to work while I go into her room to find something sexy to wear yet something that isn't trying too hard, especially since it's early in the morning.

A few minutes later, Tatyana comes into the bedroom and her face looks fresh, her eyes are still a little red but she looks stunning. Her excitement has added to her beauty and I love it.

"Okay here are my thoughts, it's still very early in the morning and you just woke up so here," I hand her a cute silk slip dress, a beautiful light pink that would match my skin but compliments her skin tone perfectly. "That way you are sexy but in an 'I just woke up' look." I grin and hand her the outfit. After she dresses I give her a big hug.

"I love you, Juli." She smiles at me and I see fresh tears welling up. I hold onto her right then push back.

"I love you too, now give me two seconds to get out of your hair then go get your man!" We both squeak excitedly and I quickly exit the room grabbing a jacket and my purse then I enter the kitchen where Mike is still standing waiting patiently, I grab my coffee and a donut and wave before exiting the apartment and skipping happily down the stairs.

Once I leave the apartment building, I realize that I have no idea what I am going to do for the day. And of course, I forgot my phone, perfect.

I step out onto the sidewalk and head into the city looking for a place to drink my coffee and eat my donut. Today is going to be a great day, I smile at everyone passing by.

# Chapter 62
## *Juliana*

After walking a few blocks I realize how tired I am. I didn't get much sleep last night and I was woken up early this morning. I yawn and take a sip from my coffee hoping it'll help to wake me up. I finished the donut on the way down to the lobby and although it had only been fifteen or so minutes, my stomach was starting to growl.

Luckily for me, there are more than a few breakfast shops in our area, and all of them open at 6 a.m. or 6:30 a.m.

I find one I've been to before and liked so I stop in and wait in the surprisingly long line to order my food while I sip my coffee. The line moves along fairly quickly and I order a spinach quiche. I pay for my food then wait patiently while the cashier warms the quiche then hands it over and I head off to find a seat.

I sit down to eat, tucking my legs under me and pulling a book out of my purse. If everything works out, I'll have to give Tatyana and Mike a few hours alone. Which I'm assuming it will. The quiche is good and I eat every bite while I also devour my book.

------------------

With the exciting week celebrating Tatyana and Mike's engagement, Thursday rolls around quickly. I almost forget about it but Tatyana reminds me.

"No, T. This whole week is about you!" I gesture around to all the decorations and bags covering our apartment. "Your engagement party is three weeks this Saturday! We have so much to do."

"Juli! Goooo! You deserve the night off. Plus I know you want to see Kurt again." She wiggles her eyebrows at me and I immediately fling a piece of candy at her that I had been about to stuff into a little gift bag. Tatyana gives me a look and tosses a few candies back at me then laughs.

"I'm not saying it wouldn't be nice to see him," I say as I get back to work, finishing the bag in hand and moving on to another one. "I just think this is more important."

Tatyana groans then pushes herself off the floor and she disappears down the hallway to our bedrooms. I've filled four more gift bags by the time she gets back. I look up and my hand stops midair.

"Why do you have my clothes?" Eyeing her suspiciously, I resume filling the bag.

"This is your outfit for tonight." She holds up an older pair of my jeans, that hug all the right curves and have a few tasteful rips in them, and my favorite dark green sweater. She tosses them next to me. "Oh, I almost forgot something!" She shouts and turns back down the hallway calling over her shoulder, "Put those on while I grab this!"

Reluctantly, I strip down and wiggle myself into the jeans and pull the sweater over my head. Tatyana comes back into the living room with my dark green booties.

"You don't think that's too much?" I put them on then take the small gold clutch she shoves in my direction.

"No, it's perfect. Damn, you always have the best shoes." Tatyana sits down, admiring my shoes. "Too bad not all your shoes fit me. I would steal a different pair every day."

"Hmm, I guess I know what to get you for each part of your wedding that requires gifts."

"Yes, please! But don't spend too much money. I know weddings include so many opportunities to give gifts but honestly, you don't have to give me any. Especially because you've been such a big help planning everything and making everything basically."

"I've actually already ordered some items," I say mysteriously, and now it's my turn to wiggle my eyebrows at her. Although, I'm not very good at it so we both end up laughing. Tatyana pulls me into a hug. "I'm so happy for you, T"

"I know it's so weird, especially with all that's been happening to you lately." I start to interrupt her but she plows through. "But it's something that I've been thinking about a lot and going through it with you and seeing you and Kurt planning and getting ready, well it just made me realize that I want that."

"Want what? A wedding?"

"No, well yes that too." Tatyana chuckles. "I know you don't see it but everyone else does. You two were great together. And Juliana, he really liked you. He probably still does. The way he looked at you. And you looked at him. I debated breaking up with Mike because I didn't think he looked at me that way. But I took the time to really stop and I just noticed, well, he does. I know it's hard for us to see when someone truly loves us. But I know now he does. And I love him. And Juli dear, Kurt loves you."

Tatyana renders me speechless so I just pull her in for another hug. She's right. Mike does look at her a certain way. I can't believe she had doubts. But I guess that makes what she said even more accurate.

"Why do you have to bring this up now?" I groan and pull away from her, Tatyana looks surprised by my reaction. "Now, I'm going to have to spend a whole evening with a couple I hardly know, pretending I am in love with the man sitting beside me but also pretending that I'm not."

"Wow, that was a confusing sentence. But what I gathered is that you are in love with him. So you won't be pretending. Just be you. Let yourself be happy. Even if for now it's only for one night. You never know what might happen." Tatyana grabs one of my candies, unwrapping it and popping it into her mouth.

"I'm taking a bag with me because lord knows I need to stress eat some candy." I hurry off to the bathroom to freshen up and before I know it I hear Tatyana talking to a familiar voice.

"She'll be just a minute. Can I get you anything to drink while you wait?"

I tune out the pleasantries and make sure I've reapplied deodorant and put on a splash of perfume. Fluffing my hair, I step into the hallway and see Kurt with his back to me drinking a glass of water. Even from the back, my heart flutters when I see him. He looks handsome and elegant. When I reach them Kurt turns around and smiles at me. His eyes flick up and down my body quickly before returning to my eyes, his cheeks turning a shade of pink because it was clear that he was checking me out. I try to hide my smile.

"Kurt didn't know Mike and I got engaged. So I was just filling him in." Tatyana gives me a look and I laugh awkwardly.

"Yeah, sorry about that. Everything's been so busy and weird I didn't get around to letting you know."

"It's no worry," he says to me and I feel butterflies in my stomach, his voice as appealing as ever. I ignore them and try to push those feelings away. Kurt turns to Tatyana. "Well, anyway, congratulations to both of you. That's amazing." He leans in and offers her a warm embrace before turning to me. "Are you ready to go?"

"Yeah," I step back, letting him lead, then smile at Tatyana. "I'll text you if I'm going to be back later than expected." Her response is to wiggle her eyebrows at me, I roll my eyes but stifle a laugh and follow Kurt out the door.

# Chapter 63

## *Kurt*

When Juliana turns to say goodbye to Tatyana, I take the moment to admire her. She looks great. She probably dressed up to be polite for this dinner, but some part of me hopes she dressed up for me too.

We leave the apartment and head down to the curbside where I parked my car. Juliana is quiet for a few minutes so I pay attention to the directions to Dave's house.

"Dave and Nicole. That's their names right?" Juliana says after a few moments of silence. Her voice is soft. "I remember meeting Dave but I don't think I've met Nicole. That is what you said her name is, right?"

"Yes," I reassure her. "You met Dave at our housewarming party but his wife, Nicole, was unable to make it." I turn onto the highway, rolling the windows up.

"Okay," Juliana hesitates. "That's probably a good thing," she adds, chuckling lightly. I nod in agreement.

"We don't have to do this. I knew it was going to be awkward but... I should just tell them we aren't together." I start looking for an exit to get off and turn around to bring Juliana back to her apartment. "I don't know why I haven't been able to tell anyone we broke up. Or called off our engagement I guess."

"I haven't told anyone either," Juliana admits. "Well, besides Tatyana but she already knew we weren't really together."

"Right. Why haven't you told anyone? Don't you think you should mention that especially if you're back to dating Callum?" I can't keep the bitterness out of my voice. I shouldn't feel hurt by her decision to go back to him, but I do. I hope Juliana doesn't hear the tone of my voice. Especially because I did something similar the day we broke up.

"I'm sorry," Juliana says softly, I wait for her to say more, why is she sorry? But she doesn't elaborate. "I think we should go. I liked Dave, I would feel bad if they have a whole meal set up and we bail at the last minute. So I think we should go. If you're okay with that? I mean, we are already on the way there too."

I give it a few seconds before I respond but I keep the car steady on the highway.

"Okay." My phone announces our next turn, allowing me to keep my response short.

Once we pull into their neighborhood, I look over at Juliana. She's watching the houses pass us by, I clear my throat and she looks over at me.

"Sorry, did you say something?" Juliana asks, shifting in her seat to face me.

"No, but I just thought I should warn you. They do have two young children. They are wild. I think one of them is two years old and the other is maybe 5. I know she's a couple of years older than her brother."

"Terrible twos." Juliana chuckles. "I like children."

I give her a quick smile then turn back to the road. Of course, she likes children. Because she's amazing. Wow, I need to calm down.

"Oh wow, their house is gorgeous," Juliana says, breaking my train of thought, just in time so I don't miss their driveway. I pull into it and park the car. Juliana blows out a breath. "Whew, why am I so nervous?"

I look over at her again and she is watching me. I smile and she automatically smiles back. I'm nervous too but I don't want to admit that to her or myself.

"We should go in." Juliana nods in agreement and we both get out of the car. Juliana is holding a small bouquet of flowers. "Where did you get those?"

"I've had them the whole time." She laughs at me and I smile. "Hostess gift. Didn't your momma teach you to bring a gift for whoever is hosting?"

"She did. You're right. Wow, she would be so disappointed right now." The smiling and joking has calmed me down a little. When I knock on the door and it flies open to reveal a grinning Dave, I'm suddenly excited.

"Kurt! Juliana! You guys made it, right on time!" Dave grabs my hand, pulling me into the house and he slaps me on my back then pulls Juliana into a hug. "Nicole, they're here!"

"Yes dear, I heard them knocking!" Nicole calls back to him then she appears out of the kitchen, still wearing an apron. "Hi, Kurt. Nice to meet you, Juliana." She says, coming forward and hugging both of us separately.

"Nice to meet you too, Nicole." Juliana smiles at them both and I can see some of her nerves fading. "Here, these flowers are for you."

Nicole takes the flowers, giving Juliana a big grin. "Thank you so much. They are beautiful."

"Well, thank you for inviting us to dinner," Juliana responds, smiling politely, beginning to relax.

"Where are the two little ones?" I ask, looking around the house. Before I can react, streaking children come running and fling themselves at me. "Oof!"

"Maggie! You know better than that. And your behavior teaches your brother that it is okay for him to do that too." Nicole bends down and peels Maggie off of me. "Sorry, Kurt." I wave away the apology then grab the two-year-old in one arm, lifting him up to say hello.

"Kurt, you know these two but Juliana these are our kids. Maggie is five, turning six soon. and the little one there is Benjamin. He is two. And it feels like he's been two for ten years." Dave makes the introductions and laughs when his wife smacks him for complaining. Dave takes Benjamin back from me but before he can get him to settle, Benjamin reaches out for Juliana.

Juliana doesn't hesitate and takes Benjamin from Dave and settles him against her hip, bouncing him gently. She holds his tiny hand and makes cooing noises at him. I try not to stare at how incredible she looks with a baby on her hip. It's so natural to her and it makes me think about our future, our fake future.

"I think he likes you, Juliana," Nicole says to her as she sets Maggie back on the ground. "Well, I have just a few more things to finish up in the kitchen, please make yourselves at home. I have to put these in some water." Nicole holds up the flowers, smiling again at Juliana.

"I'll help you in the kitchen," Juliana offers and follows Nicole into the kitchen chatting with her, with Benjamin happily watching the two of them.

Dave and I go into the living room with Maggie trailing behind us. Dave takes a seat in the chair by the couch and I sit on the couch leaning back to relax after a long day of work and the mostly awkward car ride.

"Juli is so kind. Especially to Benjamin, and I know he is a handful." Dave and I both chuckle. We chat for a few minutes mostly talking about his kids before Nicole calls to us.

"Alright boys, dinner is ready. Dave, honey, can you please get Maggie settled at the table."

"Sure, you need help with Benjamin too?" Dave responds, getting up and picking up Maggie. I get up with him and Juliana appears from the kitchen.

"I can do it if you don't mind." Juliana offers, still holding Benjamin. And he seems to like her a lot.

"Not at all, thank you," Dave gets Maggie settled and I watch while Juliana carefully handles Benjamin putting him in his high chair, getting him up to the table, and putting his little bib on him.

Nicole appears next to me and bumps her shoulder against mine. She speaks quietly, "She is amazing. Benjamin loves her. Are y'all thinking of having kids soon?"

When I can't answer right away, Nicole laughs and pats my back before joining everyone at the table. I clear my throat and then sit in the remaining seat next to Juliana.

# Chapter 64
## Juliana

Dinner goes pretty smoothly and I am actually having a great time. Nicole and Dave haven't asked any questions about our relationship and instead, they ask me about my family and my job. I brace myself the whole night just in case they do ask. I honestly am not sure what I would say if they did ask.

I think Nicole said something to Kurt earlier but I couldn't hear and it wasn't repeated so I didn't bring it up.

By the end of the night, I've had an amazing evening. Nicole and Dave are a sweet couple and surprisingly things with Kurt were not awkward. At all. I've missed Kurt. It hasn't been that long since we were living together and I didn't realize how important he had become to me. Of course, he was important to me. Is still important.

My heart starts to flutter while we stand in the driveway chatting before hitting the road. I place my hand on my heart hoping to calm it down. Nicole catches my motion as the guys talk, and she pulls me aside gently.

"Is everything okay?" Nicole cradles her little boy in her arms as we speak. He was supposed to be asleep before dinner started but he wanted to join us. He lasted about half an hour in his seat before Nicole had to hold him and then he quickly fell asleep on Nicole's lap. He's been asleep for almost an hour but she hasn't put him down.

I nod and smile politely. Nicole looks at me for a moment then she smiles back, a softer smile.

"You know, I was skeptical at first," Nicole says and her voice brings me back to the present, to focus.

"What do you mean?"

"Well, when Dave told me Kurt was engaged, yet we had never heard of you before, I was skeptical. I thought maybe he was rushing into things. His last girlfriend was very manipulative and Dave and I both worried it was too soon or the wrong girl." Nicole pauses and I look over at Kurt and Dave. Kurt turns at that moment and catches me looking, he smiles at me and I automatically smile back. "Now, I see that I had no reason to be skeptical. You're in love with him. And he is very much in love with you."

With her words, my heart cries out again and it takes everything in me not to physically react.

"How can you tell?" I whisper softly, barely being able to get the words out, fearing what my emotions might release.

Nicole reaches out and rubs my arm reassuringly.

"The way that you two look at each other, the way you act with each other. You can just tell."

I want to ask her more questions. I want to know if it's true. If this could be real. But Kurt and Dave make their way over to us and Kurt looks at me.

"You ready to go?" I nod and look back at Nicole.

"Thank you so much for having us over for dinner. It was great. You have a lovely home and adorable children." I quickly clamp my mouth shut to keep from gushing further. Dave and Nicole laugh and the boy stirs in her arms but doesn't wake.

"We are so grateful you both were able to join us. And please feel free to take the kids off our hands anytime." Nicole teases and I smile.

Kurt laughs then unlocks the car and holds the door open for me. There are hugs all around before I slide into the seat and wait for Kurt to say goodbye before getting into the car. Nicole says something to him when she gives him a hug and I see him smile. I look away to give them privacy.

We both wave as we pull out of the driveway and head down the street to get back to the main road.

"You look really nice tonight," Kurt's voice draws my attention and I look over at him. He's focused on the road. "I wasn't sure if I had mentioned that earlier."

"Thank you, you clean up nicely as well." I sit back in my seat relaxing on the drive home. "I'm not sure if this would be too weird but Tatyana and Mike are having their engagement party in three weeks, Saturday. They would love it if you would come. I know Mike thinks highly of you. As does Tatyana."

"I would love to come," Kurt interrupts my rambling and I smile grateful for his response.

We drive in a comfortable silence for a while before Kurt clears his throat and says something that takes me by surprise.

"The apartment has been kind of empty without you. Lonely. Well, I guess the apartment can't be lonely but it feels lonely."

"For a lawyer, you're not too great with words," I interrupt to tease him. "I miss you."

My admission causes him to start. Kurt looks over at me and then back at the road.

"I'm sorry," I say when Kurt doesn't respond.

"No! No," Kurt protests, stopping me from apologizing further. "It just shocked me. Juliana, I miss you. My apartment felt like a home with you there. Now it just feels empty."

"Hmm, 'lonely'," I tease him, copying his words from earlier.

"Yes, lonely." Kurt chuckles and pulls into the parking lot of my building. He puts the car in park and turns the engine off but neither of us moves an inch. Kurt turns to face me.

Before he can say anything, a loud *rap* on the window startles us. I look out and see an angry face staring back at me. Callum.

"What the -," Kurt starts to say, while Callum gestures for us to leave the vehicle, saying something muffled that we can't hear. I quickly exit the vehicle, walking around to the driver's side where Callum still stands and Kurt is exiting his car.

"Callum, what are you doing here?"

"You canceled on me last minute earlier this week. I wanted to come by to leave something for you. I didn't know you were still going out with this guy." Callum gestures to Kurt who is now standing beside his car, staying silent but watching carefully. I appreciate that he hasn't stepped in. I can handle this on my own. I think.

I pull Callum aside to distance us from Kurt. When we get a safe distance away, I put my hands on my hips and look up at the angry man staring down at me.

"Callum, I don't have to explain myself to you. In fact, why don't you explain something to me? The other day when we were out on a date, someone took a picture of us and sent it to Kurt with a very presumptuous message. Do you have any comments on that?"

As soon as I mention the picture and the text, Callum's angry red face shifts and he has the decency to look embarrassed. Even if it's only a little bit.

"What are you talking about?" Callum tries to act innocent but his initial reaction shows me the truth.

"Callum, don't. If that was some stupid, petty way of trying to piss off Kurt or hurt me, it didn't work. Kurt is a grown man, he is mature and this immature crap you're pulling doesn't work on him." Callum looks a little taken back and I'm a bit shocked at my harsh words as well. Callum opens his mouth to speak but I cut him off. "No, I'm not finished. The reason I agreed to reschedule our date was because I needed to talk to you."

Callum crosses his arms and stands tall, looking down at me. I sneak a glance of Kurt over Callum's shoulder and see that Kurt is still by his car waiting patiently, watching.

"What do we need to talk about?" Callum grumbles.

"We broke up for a reason, Callum. Well, a lot of reasons actually but that's beside the point. We broke up. And I do wish you a happy life and happy relationship, it's just not with me. And please don't be angry at Kurt," I speak before he can say anything even though I see him getting angry. "He's not the reason. I've grown up, Callum. And we've grown apart. We want different things and I just don't see any chance of us ever being together again."

Callum's anger is still behind his eyes but they soften ever so slightly. I reach out and take his hands in mine. Squeezing them gently, I smile up at him.

"I hope you can understand." Callum lets me hold his hands for a few seconds before he squeezes mine back. The corner of his mouth tilts up and he leans down to hug me.

"I know I don't deserve you, but I don't think he does either," Callum says to me, a smirk returning to his face, this time it's playful, not malicious. I laugh and shake my head.

"Thanks," I reply, not needing to say anything further. Callum steps back.

"Well, I guess I'll see you around then," Callum turns to walk away then he remembers why he came. "Oh, I almost forgot, I was at the store yesterday and this reminded me of you." Callum hands me a small keychain shaped like the Louvre. "I know you've always wanted to go there."

"Thank you, Callum," I say, clutching the keychain. Callum smiles at me. He gives a slight wave and heads off to his car without looking back.

I stand in place for a few seconds then turn as I hear someone approaching me.

"Everything okay?" Kurt looks concerned but when I smile the concern eases.

"I'm alright." I let out a breath I realized I'd been holding. I pocket the keychain before speaking again. "Thank you for a lovely evening."

"Thank you for coming with me. Will I see you again?" Kurt watches me closely. After admitting we've missed one another, I realize it's true but I also realize I don't need to rush this. "At least for the engagement party."

"Yes, the engagement party." I don't know what else to say.

Kurt looks a bit hurt but he leans down and kisses my cheek.

"Goodnight, Juliana."

"Goodnight, Kurt."

With that, I turn to go inside the building and only look back once to see Kurt getting into his car and driving away. I can't help but feel my heart tugging me to go after him but I know I made the best decision.

# Chapter 65

## *Juliana*

A couple of days have gone by since that evening and Tatyana is finally home with me, after spending a couple of nights at Mike's place. I didn't want to ruin her excitement with Mike so I kept everything to myself to give them a few days of bliss before spilling everything to her.

"No more men, only focusing on yourself?" Tatyana eyes me skeptically as she throws herself on the couch and shovels popcorn in her mouth.

"Look, I love Kurt. I do. I'm admitting that now."

"What about Callum?" Tatyana interrupts.

"I can't keep going back to him. And honestly T, I don't want to. I think I am over him. No, you know what, I am over him. Completely."

Tatyana sits up and leans forward, getting serious. I turn to face her to show her I am serious too. She eyes me for a few seconds then sits back and nods.

"Good, I never liked him anyway, I was just too polite to say anything." Tatyana smiles and pops another piece of popcorn into her mouth. I reach into the bowl between us and grab a handful.

"Yeah, okay," is all I said before eating a few pieces myself. We sit in silence with only the background noise from the TV.

"You should probably throw away that keychain. Just saying." Tatyana remarks, referencing the keychain Callum had given me. I hold it up admiring it. I know it's a gift from someone I shouldn't hold on to, but the pretty Louvre charm makes me want to travel. Finally, go to all the museums I've been dying to see. "So," Tatyana interrupts my thoughts. "If you love Kurt, why 'no more men'?"

"It just all happened so fast. I don't think either of us planned to fall in love."

"Kurt's in love with you? Did he say that?" Tatyana jumps up, almost spilling the popcorn.

"Yes, yes, we both confessed the other night. When we had dinner with his co-worker. Okay, well, maybe there weren't "I love you's" exchanged but we admitted we missed one another and he said the apartment wasn't the same without me.." I trail off when I see Tatyana eyeing me again. "What?"

"So you still haven't told him??"

"I'm sure I have. I probably have. He should know, right?" Tatyana rolls her eyes at me. "Anyway, it doesn't matter right now. I had just gotten out of a long, mostly bad, relationship with Callum and I threw myself into this fake relationship with Kurt, then actually fell in love with him. It's all too much, too fast."

"Yeah, even listening to that was a lot to handle. I can't imagine living it. Well, I kind of did!" Tatyana laughs and I shoot her a look which makes her laugh harder and I can't help but laugh at the situation as well.

"So what now?" Tatyana says when our laughter dies down.

"Well, I have my new job on Monday. So for now, I think I just need to focus on that. Excel at work. Maybe do some self-care with my BFF."

"Ooo that sounds fun. I'm so glad you left that clothing store. Content Creator is such a lovely title for you." Tatyana sits back and grabs more popcorn. "Oops! The bowl is empty, I'll go make some more."

"Thank you," I say when she jumps up and goes to the kitchen. "I am very excited to get started! Now, I can actually put my degree to use." I chuckle and then frown when I feel my phone vibrating beside me.

I check my phone and see messages from both my parents and Kurt's mom. Kurt must have told them about our breakup a few days ago, probably the night of his coworker's dinner. He said that he hadn't told anyone when I last saw him but who knows, maybe something changed. Or maybe Callum told people again. I wouldn't put it past him. He was the one who shared our 'engagement' news in the first place. But now, messages of condolence have been slowly trickling in. Mrs. Michael is trying to maintain a relationship with me but I'm struggling to reply without my heart hurting for Kurt. My parents are also reaching out to me more often just to check in and I'm grateful for that but it does little to soothe my broken heart.

"You are going to do amazing! You had two great interviews, one with HR and then with your new boss, so you already know she loves you. Plus, they probably have some sort of basic training so you know what they're looking for," Tatyana reassures me from the kitchen and I look up from my phone. "Are you still getting messages from people?" Tatyana comes back right when I put my phone away.

"Yeah," I nod. "It's official."

"Your parents know too?" Tatyana asks, for clarification.

"Yeah, not that it was fake but that it's over."

"It may have started as fake but you guys meant it in the end. Well, maybe not the engagement part but the relationship itself." Tatyana looks over at me. "Wait, did you start to believe the engagement was real?"

"No, no!" I protest. "I did not. I know it wasn't real. I just... maybe could see it being real, in the future. Okay?"

"You're crazy." We both sit back and revel in my crazy. "Is it crazy that I can see that too?" Tatyana admits and I grin at her. "Hey, I told you I liked him better. But no no let's stop talking about boys."

"Wait! We have to talk about boys! Because we have to talk about you and Mike. Duh. Honestly, the best way to forget about my boy issues hahah."

Tatyana jumps around on the couch excitedly, some more popcorn spilling from the bowl.

"Yesss, so exciting! We only have like two weeks to plan the engagement party!"

"It's going to be so much fun! The wedding will be the most fun obviously, but we will also be going all out for the engagement party." We both giggle with excitement and Tatyana pulls out this huge notebook.

"I've already started planning for both but for now, the engagement party is the main focus." Tatyana flips open the notebook and finds the right page beautifully titled 'Engagement Party'.

"Wow, I see you've got some big ideas. Okay, where to start first? Well, where do you want to have the party? Ooo, that popular restaurant. The one that has those cute decorations on the walls. What's that place called?"

"Amelia's? The little Italian place? Off of Westheimer." Tatyana offers but I shake my head.

"No, no, the Mexican one that's.."

"Oh, yeah!" Tatyana interrupts. "The uhm the... Oh! El Mezcal. Right?"

"Yeah! You love that place, right? We can reserve a back room or even the whole restaurant. Hm yeah, we should reserve the whole restaurant."

"OMG! Yes, I do love that place. I think considering how many people I plan to invite, we definitely should reserve the whole restaurant."

"Okay, I will go call them right now to make sure we can reserve it before we start sending out invites." I get up off the couch to make the call in another room but pause before I go. "Wait, should we check in with Mike first to see if he's cool with it?"

Tatyana chuckles. "He's pretty much given me free rein for all party planning. Although, he did mention wanting to help with the wedding so that could be interesting." Tatyana grins up at me. She loves teasing Mike on his poor sense of style but I know she always appreciates his effort.

Once I've shut the door to my bedroom, I make the call to El Mezcal and am able to speak to the owner who happily allows us to reserve the entire restaurant. Especially when I mention how large a group will be joining us. We speak for a few minutes and he tells me he'll email Tatyana and me a menu for catered groups to make it easier on the house to have only a few items but items that are ready to serve many. I thank him profusely and let him know I will keep an eye out for his email.

"Okay, so the owner is going to be emailing both of us so we can decide what menu to set up for the party and he said we can bring our own decorations..." I trail off when I see that Tatyana has flipped to another page in her binder that has different decoration ideas for the engagement party. "Wow, you really do have everything planned."

"Well, for the most part, these are just ideas for decorations or seating arrangements or menus! Yes, even menus. But here are the decorations for the engagement party. I haven't bought anything yet so maybe we can go shopping later this week and pick up a few things?"

"Yes, sounds perfect. I don't know how much storage space we'll have to hold all your ideas so we should probably go shopping towards the end of the week so we only have to live like hoarders for a week. No more."

Tatyana nods in agreement, looking around the room to spot places to store decorations.

"Oh, and the owner said we can come two hours early to start setting up decorations for the party but the restaurant won't officially close for us until 5 p.m. and then we have it the rest of the night!"

"Oh, perfect!" Tatyana claps her hands together excitedly.

We spent the rest of the evening eating more popcorn and ordering pizza while we browsed different sites to see if we could find the right ideas. We ended up calling shops and ordering online to make sure we secure the perfect decorations for the engagement party. Most things will take a week to come in which fits our timeline perfectly. By the time everything is squared away, it's almost 3 a.m. We lay back on the couch and admire our handy work.

"This is going to be so much fun!" Tatyana yawns and wraps herself in a blanket. I can't help but agree and we both fall asleep with smiles on our faces.

# Chapter 66
## *Juliana*

Finally, the day of the engagement party arrives and a few minutes after 3, Tatyana and I walk into El Mezcal, our arms loaded with bags. The restaurant owner hurries over to us and I shift some bags around to shake his hand.

"So nice to meet you. I am Juliana and this is Tatyana. She and Mike are the ones who recently got engaged. Mike will be joining us a little later, he is still at work."

"But he is getting off early for tonight!" Tatyana pipes up, a big smile on her face as she reaches to shake the owner's hand as well.

"Lovely. My name is Don Lizarazo, I am the owner here. It's nice to meet you both and I look forward to meeting Mike as well. Please let me know if there is anything we can do to help set up."

"We should be able to handle it ourselves, I think. And we will try not to bother your other guests." I smile apologetically since I can tell people are already watching us. Don nods at me and then excuses himself to go assist one of his waiters.

"He seems nice," Tatyana comments, then goes to set up a large table at the back of the restaurant. She places all her bags on the floor by the table and I do the same.

"I'll run out and grab the rest of the items. I should be able to carry them by myself." I grab my keys and head back outside while Tatyana gets to work inside.

I am able to get the rest of everything but struggle to close the hatch of my car. When it's finally closed, I let out a breath and make my way back into the restaurant. Someone grabs a bag off my arm and hands it to another person.

"Here let us help with those," Sam, one of our friends, smiles at me while taking the rest of the bags to divide between the three women who have just shown up.

"Thank you. And thank you all for coming to help set up." I express my gratitude and look around at all the smiling faces surrounding me. Oh no, some have a hint of sadness or maybe pity in their eyes. I guess word did travel. Well, it has been three weeks. Everyone probably knows about Kurt and me at this point. Although we had never directly addressed anyone outside our parents about our breakup, everyone knew that I was back living with T and I hadn't spent much time with Kurt recently. I feel the need to remind them. "Tonight is about Tatyana and Mike."

They all nod in agreement and head off into the restaurant to help with the setup. Sam stays behind, loops her arm through mine, and tugs me along.

"This is going to be so much fun!" I chuckle at her enthusiasm but agree and let her drag me to the rest of the girls.

"Thank you all for coming to help!" Tatyana throws her arms around the women nearest her and everyone squeals excitedly. "The party doesn't start till 6 p.m. so we have an hour after the restaurant officially closes for our use at 5 p.m. but I figured we'd better set up now so we have time to get ready before the party and of course arrive fashionably late."

"Not too late," I scold her, teasingly. "I did book us all a quick spa appointment at 4:45 p.m. so we only have about an hour and a half to get all of this finished. Nothing too fancy, just a mani-pedi. Alright now, let's get to work ladies!" We all cheer then quiet down realizing there are still guests around us.

The other women start laying out tablecloths and setting up stands for cute placement of the food and carefully hanging things on the wall. Adding it to the decoration already there trying to make it look right for an engagement party without completely cluttering the wall.

By 4:30 p.m., only a few tables remained filled by customers while the others had been taken over by our party. Some of the customers even offered some ideas which we gladly accepted.

When the last table gets up to leave, they congratulate Tatyana and comment on the amazing decoration. We grin and thank them and of course, Tatyana invites them to come back and join us in a couple hours. They happily accept and we laugh with our new friends. Finishing the last table is quick since we've gotten it down to a simple process now and while the other ladies are still making a few adjustments I check my watch and see we have five minutes to make it to the nail appointment.

"Alright, we have to go! Tatyana get your stuff. Ladies, are you all right to finish up here and meet us over there?" Everyone agrees as there isn't much left to do.

"I'll hide all the empty bags in my car," Sam offers.

"We can store everything in the back room and we will roll the bins out to the trash. Don't worry about it. Go have fun. Everyone," Don tells us and shoos us out the door. Don came out around 4 to help us decorate. I think he really enjoyed the process. I throw my arms around him in a hug and thank him profusely before shuffling everyone out the door. We decided to take two cars to make it easier to go back to our own places to get dressed for the party.

When we arrive at the nail salon, we are ushered in and Tatyana takes the middle two of five empty seats, leaving room for the rest of the girls to sit beside us. After soaking our feet for a few minutes, the salon doors open and the chatter of friends enters growing louder as they make their way towards us. They spread out around us and take their seats.

"Sorry, it took us so long," Kamie apologizes, tossing her purse into the little cubby beside her chair. "Of course, we couldn't find any place to park. How did you guys find a spot so quickly?" Kamie groans and rolls her eyes but doesn't let the annoyance ruin her time.

"Luckily someone was leaving right as we pulled in. Pretty decent spot too," I add just to tease her. "Okay so are we all matching colors or did everyone have their own idea?"

"Ooo! I think we should all get matching themes. We can do different colors but they just have to match the theme of the party!" Sam suggests.

"Yes! That sounds cool. And then we can do a similar thing for the wedding, well depending on how this turns out. What do you think, T?" Kamie adds in then turns to see how Tatyana feels.

"Oh my gosh, I love that idea!" Tatyana looks excited and another cheer goes up with the group. The ladies around us laugh and enjoy our excitement. "Okay, so the theme colors are light purple and light gray. So hm, let me see the options."

After a few minutes of deciding while the manicurist and pedicurist began the prep work, Tatyana finally chose the two exact colors she wanted.

"Perfect! Okay, I like these two colors. Feel free to use them any way you choose." Tatyana points to the two colors she picked and her nail artist goes to grab the colors and confirm they're correct. We all approve and the girls start chatting amongst themselves about different designs they could add.

When we are all finished, we are highly relaxed yet still excited. We stand at the front counter ready to pay and while we take turns, we all show each other our designs and newly painted nails. Kamie and Sam both choose variations of the purple and gray combo. Melanie chose to simply use purple and added a hint of sparkle, pre-approved by Tatyana just to make sure. Tatyana herself got the light gray polish turning into purple. Almost an ombre effect. And I got the reverse of her nails. All in all, we matched each other quite nicely, all of us.

"Now time to go get ready!" Kamie claps her hands excitedly. "See you all at the party at 6 p.m. Well probably a little later but hey, beauty takes time." We all laugh but agree and carefully walk to our cars so we don't mess up our nails.

Once back at our apartment, Tatyana flops down on the couch.

"Hey, what are you doing? We don't have much time to get ready." I check my phone to see the time and notice a few messages. I skim through them quickly, respond to some more pressing texts, and then set my phone aside, seeing that Tatyana hasn't moved an inch.

"I'm suddenly very tired," Tatyana yawns and stretches out on the couch. Not laying down yet but laying back and sliding down further.

"No no, you're just too relaxed. Go take a cold shower and I'll make you a drink. Then we need to get ready. It's already 5:45. But I figured you wouldn't be arriving before 6:30 anyway." Tatyana chuckles and nods in agreement then reaches up to have me help her up. I haul her off the couch then pat her bum as she passes by, to hurry her along.

"Alright alright, I'm going. No need to get handsy."

While Tatyana is showering, I go pick out stellar outfits for both of us and change quickly into mine then just as I'm entering the kitchen I hear the shower turn off. Tatyana emerges with a towel wrapped around her. Her first stop is the kitchen, of course.

"Here you go," I say and hand her a drink that I whipped up pretty quickly so hopefully it isn't horrible. "And yes it has alcohol, I have learned a few drinks from living with you."

"I was going to say 'my hero' but I guess I am the hero in this story," Tatyana gratefully accepts the drink and takes a sip. "Not bad."

"You're the hero for teaching me how to make drinks?" I laugh and shake my head.

"Oh yes, it's a much-appreciated gift to have."

"Go get ready. Dry your hair first then while you're getting dressed, I will get the hot iron warmed up.

Half an hour and one small refill later with mostly coke, and we are ready to go. I chose a light purple pantsuit for the evening and grab my gray clutch to match the theme and my nails. For Tatyana, I picked out her slightly sparkly gray mini dress but at the last minute decided we'd better switch outfits. Purple looks amazing with her skin tone. Although I'm not too comfortable with how short the dress looks, I'm a couple of inches shorter than Tatyana, so the dress comes down a bit further on me.

"Are we forgetting anything?" I ask on our way down to the lobby of the building.

"Yes," a voice grabs our attention and we turn to see Mike striding towards us with a big grin on his face. "You're forgetting the groom-to-be."

Tatyana launches herself at him and he catches her easily with a tight hug and places her back on the ground giving her a kiss before coming to hug me.

"Hey! Glad you could make it," I tease. "But you're absolutely right we were definitely about to leave without you. Whoops. But now that you're here I'll drive myself separately so you guys can be the last to arrive. Fashionably late of course." I squeeze Tatyana's hand and make my exit while they talk on the way to Mike's car.

Arriving at El Mezcal, I see the restaurant is already pretty decently packed with all of Tatyana and Mike's friends and families. I see my parents are here as well but I don't make my way over to them. The family that was dining here earlier have come back and our friends are making them feel welcome. I wave to them and say a quick hello to as many people as I can.

After a few minutes of mingling, I see Don gesturing to me and I make my way to him.

"Tatyana and her fiancé have arrived. Is there anything we need to do to announce them?" Don asks and I nod.

"Thank you, I will get right on it!" I make my way over to where we have music set up and get the music quieted down then switch the song to one of the songs I know Mike and Tatyana say is one of "their songs". The room grows quiet and perfectly timed too because at that moment Mike and Tatyana burst through the front door.

"She said yes!!!" Mike yells and we all cheer and holler in excitement.

"He said yes first!!" Tatyana yells in return and more cheers and laughter erupt in the crowd. Even though Tatyana proposed to him a couple of weeks ago, Mike revealed he had been planning to propose too. So almost a week after Tatyana proposed, Mike popped the question as well. Tatyana was not expecting it obviously so she was surprised and very excited.

The newly engaged couple make their way through the throng of people congratulating them and all saying how much they were looking forward to the wedding. Especially seeing how amazing the engagement party is.

I watch the happy couple mingle among friends and family then turn my attention to Tatyana's dad who has just approached me asking how my new job is going. We converse for a few minutes as other guests trickle in. At one point I look up from the conversation I'm having with Tatyana's dad, and my heart starts fluttering as I see Kurt enter the restaurant.

# Chapter 67
## *Kurt*

It's been almost three weeks since I've seen or even heard from Juliana. I've thrown myself into my work and the results were great. One largely successful case and just a few days ago my boss handed me the files for one of our firm's most important cases yet.

I'm honored to take on such an important case but my nerves about Tatyana and Mike's engagement party have kept me from anything more than a few glances at the files. I'm not so much nervous for the party but I am nervous to see her again. I finally told my parents we broke up and of course, they were heartbroken. I was too. Even if it was a fake engagement, the heartbreak I felt was real.

"Kurt, are you sure you should be going tonight?" My mom stands at her kitchen island cutting up vegetables. I only dropped by to borrow one of my dad's ties. I walk over to her and kiss her cheek while tying the tie properly. She of course adjusts it just slightly then smiles.

"Yes, mom. I know both Tatyana and Mike. They even sent me an invitation after Juli and I broke up."

"I know that," my mom sighs and I can tell she is holding back something.

"What is it?" It doesn't take much pressure for her to speak.

"You're not over Juli. At all. Even a little bit. It's been three weeks. And you're still deeply madly in love."

"Wow," is all I can say. "That's dramatic."

"Well, am I wrong?" My mom puts the knife down and gives me a stern look.

"I mean, it's a bit dramatic but okay, fine. I'm not over her." I sit down on a stool across from where my mom continues to cut the veggies. "But that doesn't mean I can't handle this party. Maybe she won't be there. Okay, she definitely will, Tatyana is her best friend but I probably won't even run into her."

Mom gives me another look which makes me keep talking.

"Even if I do, I'll be fine." I try to reassure her and myself. Wow, I'm getting close to 30 and I still act a fool over a girl. "I'll be fine," I repeat, firmer this time.

"Sure, you'll be fine." My mom gives a small smile, a sly smile. "You look very handsome. Have a nice evening." My mom practically shoos me out the door.

"Thanks for the tie, Dad!" I shout on my way out and I see him wave goodbye.

On the drive over I can feel my heartbeat speeding up. When I pulled into the nearly full parking lot of El Mezcal, I sigh and grip the steering wheel, trying to mentally prepare myself for the evening.

I join a group gathered in front of the restaurant, introducing myself and recognizing some of them, and then I make my entrance with them. The room is crowded. Tatyana is quite popular and super friendly so I am not surprised by the number of people attending the engagement party. I can feel eyes on me but from the looks I've been getting recently from my parents, it's probably just someone who feels sad about my broken engagement. I've already had a couple of people approach me and tell me how brave I am for coming here tonight. Smiling and waving away their worries is the only thing I can think to do at the moment.

The room gets too crowded for me so I make my way to the back patio which is also decorated for the evening. I admire the decorations while I walk further away from the restaurant doors, the noise growing quieter. I can still hear the chatter from the inside since the doors are propped open but it's quieter out here. A beautiful evening really.

"Hi, Kurt," a voice says softly and I turn to find Juliana a couple feet from me. I take a step back automatically and my fingers begin to sweat around the glass I'm clutching a little too hard.

"Juliana," I begin, then clear my throat. "Hi, wow you look incredible." I regain my cool but can't help from looking her up and down in appreciation. A light blush appears on her cheeks and she looks down at the ground but I catch a smile on her face.

"Thank you, you look very handsome." She offers in return. I look down at my own attire and am grateful I dressed up for this evening. "How have you been?" Juliana asks and I realize we've been standing in silence for a few seconds.

"Good. Well. Work has been great lately. I was handed a big case last week, so I'll have my hands full in the coming months." I chuckle and Juliana looks up at me smiling. God, I've missed that smile.

"That's great! I was always so impressed by how great you were at your job. I'm glad your bosses recognize that too."

"How is your job?" I ask, thinking of her retail days but having heard through my parents that she put in her notice shortly after our "break up" and was already into something new.

"Good," Juliana pauses, her hands holding each other and twisting slightly. "Actually, it's amazing. I love it. I'm sure you've heard that I have moved on from the retail life." I nod and she continues talking. "Well, now I'm doing something that I enjoy. And no more mean customers. Okay, that's not entirely true but for the most part, everyone is nice, they're just passionate."

Juliana again graces me with her smile and I can't help but smile back. I'm happy for her, and I want to hear more about her job. It seems like she is enjoying it.

"I wanted to talk to you..." Juliana begins to say but is interrupted by a crowd of guests joining us out on the patio. Before I know it, Juliana gets swept away by some of her friends. I see her looking for me but I can't reach her and I don't want to be rude and keep them from taking her.

My nerves again get the better of me and I drain the rest of my drink wondering what Juliana wanted to talk about.

"Hey, Kurt! Glad you could make it." Mike gives me a smack on the back and then shakes my hand.

"Congratulations on the engagement. I heard you both proposed. That must have been fun."

"Oh, for sure. We spent almost a week and a half alone in my apartment celebrating. First, because she proposed and then with renewed energy after I proposed. Haha," Mike's laugh booms in the enclosed patio. "So how are you and Juliana doing? Any update there? Of course, I hear things from Tatyana but I assume you have a side to this story as well."

I want to ask him what Tatyana had told him or hell even what Juliana may have said but I don't ask.

"We haven't spoken in a while," I admit and Mike shakes his head disappointed but acknowledging the truth in it. "Tonight is the first time I've seen her since about three weeks ago. She said she wanted to talk but she got busy with other guests so honestly I don't know what she was going to say."

"It's bothering you, huh?" Mike asks, looking at me.

"That obvious?"

"Oh yeah," Mike takes a few seconds to scan the room then points to a corner where a table is set up with little games on it. "There she is. Go grab her. I have to admit, Tatyana and I are rooting for you two."

"Thanks, man." I chuckle and shake his hand before I head off in the direction of the table, watching the pretty girl in the gray dress hand out games to different guests. "Juliana," I say when I reach the table, stopping in front of her.

"Oh, hi. Sorry, I got pulled away earlier." She starts to say more but I lean in closer to her and she goes quiet. I breathe her in and try not to lose my train of thought by how amazing she smells.

"Can we go somewhere to talk privately?" I try to say quietly so only she can hear but with all the noise and loud music, I guess I'm not very quiet.

"You can use my office," I look over and a man with the name tag "Don" hands us his keys with a sly smile on his face. Juliana laughs and takes them from his outstretched hand.

"Thanks, Don. We won't be too long." As we make our way to Don's office Juliana explains. "Don is the owner of the restaurant. He's been very helpful and quite accommodating as well."

We remain silent the rest of the way to the office, getting stopped a couple of times by friends of the couple and Juliana. Out of the corner of my eye, I see Juliana's mother approaching us.

"Hello, Kurt, Juliana," Juliana's mother stops us before we can disappear into the room.

"Mother," Juliana greets her mother and allows for a quick hug. She opens her mouth to say something more but her mother quickly starts speaking.

"I was so sad to hear that the two of you ended your engagement. And, sad that I had to hear it from a third party. But then again, I learned about the engagement from someone else as well," her mother chuckles sarcastically, teasing us and Juliana blushes.

"Mom," Juliana says quietly and I honestly don't know what to say.

"Thank you," I say. "I think I can say for the both of us that we were quite excited then quite devastated. It was a whirlwind of an engagement and then as quickly as it began, unfortunately, it ended." Maybe, I think to myself. Hopefully, it won't be over for long. Juliana looks up at me and gives a small smile of gratitude.

"It's nice to see you two together and being civil towards each other," her mother continues and Juliana gives her mother another look.

"Of course, we can be civil. Just because we broke up does not require us to hate each other." Juliana rolls her eyes but she smiles over at me, blushing slightly. "Have you congratulated Tatyana and Mike on their engagement?"

"Seems insensitive for them to get engaged so soon after you two ended your engagement." Her mother looks at both of us, giving each of us a sympathetic/sad smile.

"No, actually, I was ecstatic to hear about their engagement," Juliana opposes and I nod my head in agreement with her. "I am very happy for them. Everyone is happy."

Her mother smiles and reaches out to squeeze her hand before she nods and steps back. "I think I will go find them now and congratulate them."

"That's very thoughtful of you. Now, if you'll excuse us." I step back and gesture for Juliana to go in front of me down the hall to the office. "We have some things to discuss," I say before following Juliana. "It was nice seeing you," I add to be polite, throwing the comment over my shoulder as I continue down the hallway.

When we reach the office, the room grows quiet as the door shuts behind us. We stand silently for a few seconds before she speaks.

# Chapter 68
## *Juliana*

Once I shut the door to the office, it gets significantly quieter and suddenly I feel nervous and shy. I look up at Kurt and can tell he feels similarly. With the slight confidence of knowing we're both nervous here, I press forward.

"So, earlier, I said I wanted to talk to you. I still do. But, uhm, now I've pretty much forgotten what I was going to say. I mean I remember the general idea but how to phrase it well is scrambled right now. Please feel free to stop me from rambling at any point, soon hopefully."

Kurt chuckles and leans his hip on the desk in the office. He watches me closely and I can't help but wonder how he can be so calm right now. I could tell that he was nervous when we stepped into the office, maybe my rambling calmed him down. No, that's strange.

"Juliana," Kurt begins then he looks down at his hands. "These three weeks without you..."

Kurt trails off still looking at his hands. I shift a little, from leg to leg. Jitters running through my body. I don't want to interrupt him but I'm also so nervous, he needs to hurry up before I start talking and more than likely continue my ramblings.

"Yes?" I ask, clearing my throat. Kurt looks up at me, his eyes holding mine as he takes a step forward. Toward me.

"These last three weeks," he starts again, "without you, just haven't felt right." He finishes his sentence and maintains eye contact. "I know it's crazy.."

When he gets quiet again I step in to speak.

"I don't think it's crazy," I speak softly and give him a small smile. "I understand."

"When you walked away from me that night, I wanted you to stay. And I know you had just broken up with Callum, officially, so I understand why you needed time to yourself. But, Juliana, throughout everything we've been through, everything we've done together during our "fake engagement", somewhere along the way, I fell in love with you." Kurt watches me as he speaks but I hold my tongue because he doesn't look quite finished. "I know that may sound crazy but hey, you understood what I meant earlier when I said these past few weeks haven't felt right, so I'm hoping you understand this too. And I get it if you don't feel the same way. I know it can take longer than three weeks to heal or find yourself or whatever it is you need to do. I don't care. I'll be here if it takes another three weeks. Or three months. Hell, I'd stick around for three years, if it meant ending up with you. Because I am in love with you, Juliana. I love you." He repeats and my heart flutters, excited but I tamper it down, wanting to remain calm and collected for this moment.

Kurt lets out a breath and rubs his hands against his sides. The room falls silent except for the sound of our breathing. I replay his words over and over again. My heart fills with joy and happiness. I've always wanted a man to make a romantic gesture with the whole "I love you" speech, but this is by far better than anything I could have ever imagined. And I think that's because it came from the man I truly adore. *I love you, Kurt.* I think to myself but can't seem to open my mouth yet.

"Say something," Kurt pleads after the silence becomes too much for him to bear. "Please."

"Kurt," I start, still not looking away from him. I can't help it. My face breaks out into a huge smile. Kurt starts to smile too but he's cautious, waiting for my response. "I just want to point out that you actually walked away from me that night."

"Juliana!" Kurt gives me an incredulous look.

"Right, not the time." I laugh and Kurt rolls his eyes but lets out a chuckle. We're both nervous. I haven't responded yet. I need to respond. "I don't know what to say," I admit and Kurt looks confused and a bit hurt.

"I'm sorry if I sprung this on you. I don't want to freak you out. I guess what I said was a little strong but I meant every word." Kurt tried to explain but I lift my hand to stop him.

"No, it's not that. I've just never felt this way before." My hand balls into a fist at my stomach and Kurt shuts his mouth, watching me. "You know, I thought that I'd been in love before but it is nowhere near how strongly I feel for you. I didn't want to admit it for a long time, even Tatyana called me out on it, but I'm in love with you. I realized that a while ago. And I'm sorry I never told you or said anything at all. And I am so sorry that I walked away from you. Part of me is glad I did, it gave me time to see what you truly mean to me. The other part of me is upset that I walked away because I wasted three weeks where I could have been insanely happy. I don't want to waste any more time."

"I don't want to waste any more time either," Kurt agrees, grinning at me. Grinning from the moment I admitted I was in love with him. He takes a step towards me. "I love you," he says as he takes another step.

"I love you," I grin up at him and close the remaining distance between us. He takes me in his arms and holds me against him. He doesn't kiss me yet, just holds me. He looks down at me and I look up at him.

"Please come back to my apartment." Kurt watches my face light up. "Our apartment," he corrects and I nod.

"Yes, please," I say softly, seeing him leaning his head down toward me. I barely get the words out before I feel his lips on mine. He is soft and gentle but firm enough to claim me as his. I slip one arm up around the back of his neck and kiss him deeper. Claiming him as mine.

We kiss for only a few minutes before there is a knock on the door. We break apart, grinning. Giggles escape my mouth. Kurt pulls me to him once more and gives me another kiss before we go to the door.

"There you guys are!" Tatyana stands at the door then takes a step back and eyes us. She stares for a second before her eyes go wide and she squeals with excitement. She grabs both of us in a hug. "I knew it! I always liked him!" She adds as a whisper in my ear.

Kurt and I look at each other over Tatyana's shoulders and we smile. When she releases us, she grabs my hand.

"Okay you can have her back in a minute but I need to steal her really quickly!" Tatyana at least gives me a second to receive another kiss from Kurt before she whisks me away. I can't help but look back at Kurt and see him smiling after me.

Tatyana drags me through the crowd in the restaurant, only stopping briefly to thank people for coming and for the congratulations.

"So," Tatyana nudges me as we make our way to the gift table. "Are you guys back together or what?"

"Well, we didn't exactly get a chance to discuss that." I give her a pointed look.

"Ugh, sorry. We were running out of food and gift bags and you were the person I figured could solve this." Tatyana gives an apologetic look. "Please?"

"There are more gift bags in my car. I made extras because I know how friendly you are, I figured you'd invite more guests than originally planned." Tatyana laughs and holds her hand out. I pop open my clutch and hand her the keys to my car. "I'll go talk to Don about whipping up some more food for us."

"Ooh! When they're done please make sure to invite the kitchen staff and Don to join us at the party." Tatyana gives me a tight hug. "Thank you!" She releases me and skips off to go get the gift bags from my car.

"Okay, where is Don?" I say to myself and look around the restaurant.

"I think I saw him make his way back into the kitchen," a voice says beside me and I feel a hand slide into mine. I look up and see Kurt standing beside me, smiling down at me. I close my hand around his, holding on.

# Chapter 69

## *Juliana*

"Hi," I say softly, smiling back at him.

"Hi," he repeats back to me. We stand smiling at each other a few seconds longer until I hear someone a bit away asking another guest if there would be more food. I snap back to my mission of finding Don.

"Come with me?" I ask and Kurt nods. We make our way to the kitchen. Hand in hand. "Don," I stop at the door to the kitchen and Don turns to face me.

"Ah Juli, enjoying the party?" Don asks and makes his way over to Kurt and me. I hand him the key to his office and thank him quietly, he smiles and nods.

"It's lovely. We were wondering if it's possible to get another round of food for the evening?" I answer.

Don nods his head and gestures to the kitchen staff hard at work. "I noticed you all were getting low so I've already got them started on it."

"Great! Thank you so much! Oh and please know that you all are invited to join us when you have the time. A personal invitation from the bride." Don turns to the kitchen staff and repeats the news of the invite and there are a couple of cheers and the noise of their workstations grows louder as they pick up the pace.

"We would be delighted to join you all. Now, if you'll excuse me, I think I will go help my team so we can get the food out quicker and get to the party quicker." Don excuses himself to go join the line of workers and Kurt tugs me back outside the kitchen. With the door shut behind us, he leans me against the wall next to it.

"So," Kurt starts, looking down at me

"So," I say back.

"We love each other," he begins again and I nod my head in agreement. "I asked you to move in with me." Again I nod. "And what was your response to that?" He asks me, smiling.

"Yes," I say, "of course."

"Of course," Kurt continues to hold my hand but his free hand trails lightly down my arm. "I think that means we are back together. What do you say?"

"Is that your way of asking me to be your girlfriend?" I tease him, looking up into his eyes. "Your official, real girlfriend?" My smile grows as Kurt looks at me with lots of love in his eyes, something I had been so blind to before.

"Yes, I believe it is. Or," he pauses and reaches into his pocket and brings out a small, familiar box. I gasp a little. "Or maybe it's me asking you to be my wife, again" he adds, referring to the fake engagement in front of our friends and family and the nonexistent engagement before that.

"We shouldn't do that here..." I whisper, looking around at Tatyana and Mike's engagement party with wide eyes. I don't want to take away from their evening.

"I don't care," Kurt tells me honestly.

"We don't care either," another voice says and I look over to see Tatyana and Mike have appeared beside us and they are both grinning. No one else notices the four of us back here by the kitchen. I smile at Tatyana. And then at Mike. Then I look back up at the handsome man standing right in front of me and my heart grows with love for him and my friends.

"So?" Kurt asks. "Will you be my fiancée, for real this time? Will you marry me, Juliana?" He pauses to wait for my answer. I look over at my best friend again and she nods excitedly. I can see her bouncing on her toes a bit. Mike tries to hold her down so as to not draw attention to the group.

"Yes," I breathe out in a whisper. "Yes." I try again, my voice stronger, confident. "Yes!"

"Yes?" Kurt repeats. I nod and grin at him. I hold out my left hand and with slightly shaking fingers, Kurt slides the ring back onto my finger. "This is where this ring belongs."

"I love you," I tell Kurt.

"I love you," Kurt grips my hand in his and slides one arm behind my back pulling me close to him. I tilt my head back looking up at him. I don't know what else to say, I'm too shocked and excited. Luckily I don't have a chance to speak before Kurt leans down and kisses me. The first kiss for the start of our future. Or I guess we did make out a little earlier in the evening but this is different. This is officially my fiancé.

Kurt pulls back and Tatyana takes the opportunity to grab me. Squealing, she pulls me into a tight hug. Even bigger than before. Mike congratulates Kurt then hugs me as well when Tatyana finally lets go.

"Oh my gosh, we have to tell everyone!" Tatyana looks so excited and I love my best friend for wanting to announce it during HER engagement party. But I don't want to tell anyone yet.

"Let's wait," I say, looking at all of them. "I want to enjoy this for a while before we have to tell anyone else." I look over at Kurt and he smiles at me then nods in agreement.

"Let's keep this between the four of us," Kurt says.

"Smart idea. You want time to be together before everyone else wants to be a part of your business too." Mike says. He wraps his arm around Tatyana, remembering their time spent together before anyone else found out. Tatyana smiles at Mike and leans into him. She kisses his cheek and then looks back at me.

"How did we both end up with such great men?" We both laugh and Mike pulls her away to go back to their party.

"I don't know, how did I end up with such a great man?" I look up to Kurt, asking him with a smile on my face.

"It all started with a fake fiancé." Kurt leans down and kisses me once more.

"And ended with a very, very real one," I finish for him, my cheeks hurting from grinning so wide.

**The End.**

# Other Titles by Mairi Louise
### (Online only)

Witches in Suburbia

My Summer Affair
My Royal Romance


## Coming Soon

Betting on You

**Birch Lake Series**
Give it a Month (Book 1)

# Author Bio

Mairi Louise has always had a love of reading and writing. From a young age, she would create adventurous little stories and devour every book she got her hands on. Now as an adult, she has found joy in turning her stories into novels that she is excited to share with everyone.

Mairi Louise invites you to visit her on Instagram @AuthorMairiLouise and X (Twitter) @MairiLouise2